The Price of Defiance

She was trapped now and she knew it, but would allow no whimper of fear to escape her throat. Instead she lifted her chin and defiantly stared back into the gleaming brown pools of his eyes.

"Damn you," she hissed at last. "You should be dead now."

He studied her for an endless moment, and she was suddenly aware of his bare torso lying across her body, still holding a wrist pinioned with each of his hands. Suddenly the furious blood-lust in his eyes died and was replaced with a sardonic gleam.

"Why, Lianne of Fairlight," he drawled, "you turn up in so many places, I should not be surprised to find you in my bed."

His eyes left her startled face to roam with great deliberation down her body, lingering at her heaving chest as she began to struggle anew.

"Ah, my love, the sight of so much beauty almost makes amends for the number of times you have threatened my life. But there is more you must do before your full penance is paid." His free hand reached to caress her breast, cupping its fullness as he lowered his mouth to hers.

Laurie Grant

DEFIANT HEART

LEISURE BOOKS ❧ NEW YORK CITY

To
Prudence Schofield and Karen Harper
for
their friendship and tireless encouragement

A LEISURE BOOK

Published by

Dorchester Publishing Co., Inc.
6 East 39th Street
New York, NY 10016

Copyright©1987 by Laurie Grant

Printed in the United States of America

NOTE

I have taken the liberty of using modern French, rather than the Old French, with the single exception of the Norman battle cry, *"Dex aie!"*

—Laurie Grant

PART I
SUSSEX

One

The mid-September sun shone benignly down on the little gray stone church on England's southern coast, as if to bless the wedding taking place on the steps in front of the thick carved oak doors. The large crowd fanned out behind the wedding party and onto the lawn around the church, for it was not every day that the wealthy Thegn Rolf Rolfsson of Fairlight married off a daughter, nor frequent that such an illustrious match was made as this to one of King Harold's own housecarles, Edwin Wulfsson of Pevensey.

Lianne of Fairlight smiled mischievously up at her tall groom as the priest droned the words of the Sacrament, her blue eyes daring Edwin to laugh at the fly buzzing around Father Anselm's tonsure. To prevent the chuckle from escaping him, Edwin instead gazed at his bride's slender curves and the river of blonde hair that cascaded down her back. He thought what a fortunate man he was to have such a lovely girl given to him. It was a great honor to be part of Harold's elite fighting force, but he had spent the long, hot summer guarding the southern coast against Harold's brother Tostig and watching for the expected invasion from Normandy. Edwin was relieved that the harvest time and the poor fall weather in the Channel had caused his king to disband the fyrd and relax his alert somewhat, giving Edwin time to go marry his betrothed.

By Saxon tradition, the groomsmen held up a veil behind the bride and groom, shielding them from the assembled guests. Edwin took the gold ring and said, as he held it over the tip of her thumb, "In the name of the Father—" he moved it to the index fingertip—"and the Son—" he advanced it to the middle finger—"and the Holy Spirit—" he slipped it on the third finger—"Amen." Then he bent to kiss her as the priest pronounced them man and wife, and Lianne was glad the veil shielded her blushes from the multitude in the lusty embrace that followed.

Later, at the wedding feast that was expected to go on for days, Lianne drank deeply from the golden cup and passed it to her husband as the guests cheered. They made a handsome sight, the two golden heads pressed close as Edwin whispered some newlywed nothing that made the Saxon girl giggle.

"May your lance tonight, Edwin," bellowed a drunken comrade-in-arms, "be as sharp as the one you will stick into the Normans!"

The crowd guffawed, but Edwin, becoming a little tipsy himself, capped the toast: "Not sharp, look you! It need not be, with such a welcoming place to thrust it!" Lianne blushed again, as was expected of a virgin bride. "But as effective, I doubt not!"

It was the sort of foolery which would get worse as the evening wore on, until finally the bride was borne off to her bridal bed.

Lianne, after the heat of her blush lessened somewhat, thought of the toast and prayed that her new husband need never test his weapons against the Normans, even though he was the fiercest of fighters. They would have come by now if they were coming, she reasoned. These days nearly everyone in the realm held that opinion. Autumn is coming on, and we shall have a cozy winter in which to love and grow to know each other even better, and by spring Harold and William may well have worked out some compromise, and I might even be with child! She smiled, thinking of a fuzzy-headed baby with the blue-eyed look of both his parents.

"You must be thinking of the delights of the marriage bed to be smiling so," teased Edwina, a village friend who had served as her chief bridesmaid. It had been Edwina's task to marshal the other bridesmaids in decorating the church with garlands of greenery and late fall flowers, and to make the floral crowns that bride and groom wore. One of the other bridesmaids had been Lianne's younger sister Elfgift, another, Edyth, a cousin from nearby Hastings, and the third her new sister-in-law Edgiva.

"Really, Edwina," returned Lianne, "that's all you think of!"

"At least I *know* what awaits me in *my* bridal bed," the freckled redhead taunted back.

"Oh, just Thorold . . ." Lianne affected a yawn about the thegn who was Edwina's betrothed, then smiled to show that her boredom was all in jest. "Actually," she went on archly, "in truth I never should have allowed you to be my maid of honor, you know. The bride's attendants are *supposed* to be virgins all."

Edwina knew the teasing was not needling, and though she was too honest to pretend a lack of experience in earthy matters, she was not promiscuous. She and Thorold expected to marry soon. Indeed they had better, she'd confided cheerfully to Lianne, as she had missed her usually regular flux last month!

The table was heaped high with all manner of dishes: roast ox, lamprey, herring, pheasant, capon, dishes made of corn and barley, great loaves of wheaten and rye bread, and horn cups of ale, mead, and, for those with more Continental taste, wines imported earlier from Normandy. Many of the foods were plainly cooked, boiled or baked as was the Saxon preference, but others were spiced with cloves, galingale, powder-douce, canelle and ginger—even sugar and pepper, hard to obtain now, but Thegn Rolf was no miser at his daughter's wedding feast.

Everyone made merry, caught up in the festive mood of the wedding, made gayer by the sense of relief they all felt at the approaching harsh weather that rendered England an island fortress.

"Oh, Edwin, this is not the place for talk of war!" Lianne pouted, returning from her guests to find that he and some of the other housecarles had lined up pieces of bread crusts on the table and were deploying the "fyrd" in mock battles, discussing how they'd "drive the Normans back into the sea, should they be foolish enough to come!"

Edwin grinned, throwing an affectionate arm about his bride's waist, but his sister pronounced pettishly, "He is your lord, Lianne! It is not for you to dictate his speech!"

He stroked Lianne's arm, as if to indicate that he would be no tyrannical husband whose wife dared not voice an opinion. She smiled back, reassured, and impishly stuck out her tongue at the sour Edgiva, who rolled her eyes heavenward and retreated.

"Your elder sister does not feel me worthy of you, 'my lord.' " She smiled ruefully.

"No one could be, for her baby brother," Edwin laughed. "Don't worry, Lianne. A lot of her tartness is sour grapes. She is growing old to be a bride herself, and feels that soon she will have to accept some fat old widower with five children!" The fears had evidently affected whatever fresh beauty she may have possessed once, for her features were sharp and anxiety-ridden.

"My lord and lady," interrupted the accented voice of Robert, Lianne's Norman tutor, "a party of soldiers has ridden up and waits outside the hall, desiring immediate speech with my lord Edwin."

"Oh, my lord, don't let them spoil the feast!" Lianne exclaimed, fearing the interruption would snatch away her husband for hours as he attended to some minor problem the soldiers could most likely solve without him.

One of the soldiers had grown impatient with waiting and had come into the hall, ill at ease in his beaten-leather armor shirt among the festively dressed crowd.

"What means this, Egfrith?" queried Edwin with some annoyance. "You are welcome to the wedding feast, but your clothing bespeaks another purpose. Can it not wait, while I enjoy being a bridegroom for a while?"

"You are needed, Edwin. Harold marches on York—Tostig and Harald Hardraada have landed at Riccall, and harry the land. Harold is summoning the fyrd and all housecarles on leave immediately!"

Edwin groaned, knowing the answer before he asked: "I cannot even stay for my wedding night?"

"King Harold's orders are that you join him on the march immediately," the other man grimly repeated. "You must make ready to leave within the hour. There is no time to be lost! I'm sorry, my lady," he added, as if seeing Lianne, trembling in her bridal gown of light blue silk, for the first time. "I regret to snatch your bridegroom at such an inconvenient time, but England is invaded . . ."

"Of course," Lianne said with a tremulous smile, her blue eyes huge and welling with unshed tears. "England's needs must come first at such a time." She turned to her husband, as others in the crowd began to take leave of their families, knowing they would be needed to fight, too. "Come, I'll help you pack."

She watched Edwin straighten and fasten his cloak with its amethyst clasp as he finished his preparations in the chamber where they were to have spent their bridal night.

"I wish there were time for me to prepare vials of salves for bruises and cuts," she sighed, still perilously close to tears. Most ladies of her class had at least a rudimentary knowledge of medicinal herbs.

Moments ago, she had given him his wedding gift, since they would not be together in the morning—a dagger whose hilt, encrusted with mussel pearls, enclosed the head of a stag beetle to keep him from all harm.

"My thanks, darling," Edwin said as he held her close, "but I will incur no bruises or hurts, for all that Norwegian giant and Harold's foolish brother are redoubtable fighters! I shall be back before you have time to miss me!"

"You are already too late," she whispered through her tears.

"Now, now, no tears," he said bracingly. "How can the bride ask for her morning gift if she sniffles?"

"I want none but your safe return," she sobbed.

"A proper answer for a new bride," he teased, pushing her chin up with two fingers to meet his gaze. Mock-sternly, he then admonished, "See that you still feel so dutiful when I return, wife!"

"I shall," she breathed. "Come home soon, my brave housecarle! Harold is indeed fortunate to have you by him, when I cannot."

He drank in her tear-bright azure gaze, the gold halo of hair, with the wilting garland still perched forlornly there, and crushed her to him. "Ah, Lianne! I shall miss you, beloved!" He could feel her rapid pulse accelerate with his slower, steadier one as he felt the softness of her breasts against him. He reached inside her bodice and touched one of the soft mounds, feeling her gasp as the nipple hardened between thumb and forefinger. His breath was warm in her ear as he raised her up to him nearly lifting her off her feet.

She felt fevered as she caught his excitement, felt the hardness of his warrior's body against her. Their lips met and they drowned in each other, the invasion forgotten for an endless moment, the only sound in the room the ragged rasp of Edwin's breathing.

A horse whinnied outside, and almost guiltily Edwin loosed her. She nearly fell at the sudden loss of support, her mind reeling at this first experience of passion. She had known she loved Edwin, yes, and wanted to marry him, bear his babes, care for his household, but this! This feeling of fire and ice melded together, this arching toward—what? She stumbled blindly outside with him, hardly conscious of the knowing, amused glances of some at their flushed faces, the pitying looks of others at the bereft bride.

"God keep you, Edwin," she said softly as he mounted his bay horse, held for him by one of Rolf's servants.

"And may He be with you, Lianne. Here, this will remind you to say a Paternoster for me." He handed down a necklace of jet beads with a silver crucifix at one end. Then, with a creaking of leather and a flurry of farewells, he was gone.

She turned, finding herself next to Robert, and buried her face against the old man's shoulder. She could not remember a time when the Norman had not lived with them, speaking his Norman-accented English and teaching them everything he knew. Rolf Rolfsson's children were well-educated, even among Saxons; from Robert they had learned mathematics, to read and write English and Latin, and to speak as well as write Norman French. He also taught them a smattering of astronomy and geography, and discoursed with them of other religions, much to the horror of Father Anselm.

"Will he return safe, think you, Robert?" she asked her tutor fearfully.

The Norman ran a hand through his gray hair, cut short in the Norman fashion. "Why, Lianne, it will take much more than a seven-foot giant" (for such was Harald Hardraada's height) "to stop your young man!" He chuckled and gave her a hug as if she were still a ten-year-old, not a new wife, and the gesture warmed her. He stood almost as an uncle to these children, whose mother had died when Lianne was five, and many times they would confide things to him they feared to confess to their father. He kept his own counsel as to why he had left his native Normandy, however; neither Lianne nor little Elfgift, nor yet their brother Orm had been able to pry the secret from him.

"Let me tell you what else the soldiers told me while you were with Edwin," Orm said to distract his sister from the dust cloud raised by the fast-receding party of housecarles. The tow-headed fifteen-year-old's face was flushed with excitement. "William the Bastard's ships *did* sail, and were met by the English navy somewhere off Beachy Head! They were beaten, turned back by our navy, with some help by heavy weather. In fact, King Harold was down at the London docks, receiving the report of the victory, when news of Tostig's coming reached him!"

"Where is William's force now?" his sister queried.

"Who knows?" he answered breezily, with a youth's unconcern. "They had heavy losses—they've probably scurried clear to Flanders in their disgrace!"

"Well, it certainly sounds as if the Norman dogs have slunk back to their kennels for good—oh, I'm sorry, Robert!" She colored with embarrassment. "I did not mean to offend you! I've long since forgotten to think of you as one of *them.*"

"No offense taken, my dear Lianne," the tutor replied with a smile. "I love England, or I never would have stayed so long. There is a freedom here, a love of beauty and art, a love of learning for its own sake . . ." He raised his shoulders in a very Gallic shrug.

"Yes, and the Church here is not merely a puppet of Rome," added Father Anselm with asperity as he puffed over to join them. "It follows the dictates of the English conscience, not of some scheming Italian—holy as the Pope is, of course!" he amended hastily. He glanced over the crowd, mostly women, children, and old men left after Edwin and the other men had ridden or marched to join King Harold. "Let us pray for the victory of King Harold, and the safety of our men," he commanded. Oblivious of their finery, the wedding guests knelt in the dusty yard as one.

"Our Father . . ."

Two

Lianne left Fairlight the next morning, accompanied by Elfgift and Edgiva, to move into Edwin's house in Pevensey, a few miles east down the Channel coast. She planned to make the hall truly a welcoming haven for his return. Her mood was light, despite the mizzling rain that soon dampened the rich stuff of their clothes.

"Mind your mare, Lianne! Pay attention!" snapped her sister-in-law as the little black palfrey strayed too close to Edgiva's brown cob, which shied and laid back his ears.

Lianne stole a look at her younger sister, to find the girl gazing downward to hide her grin. Their eyes met, and they knew they shared the thought: Edgiva's horse was exactly like her in temper!

A giggle escaped the fourteen-year-old, and Edgiva's wrath was fanned afresh. "By all the Saints, girl! Your laughter is ill-judged! I suppose you'd laugh to look out there and see William's ships!" Her arm swept to the side, indicating the mist-shrouded bay below the cliffs.

"No, sister Edgiva," came her conciliating reply. "I did not chuckle at the funny face your horse made." She bent her head, but Lianne knew the younger maid was far from feeling repentent. She was glad Elfgift was going to stay with them at least until Edwin's return; her presence would help to balance the older woman's sourness, and might even sweeten Edgiva's disposition. Who could resist Elfgift's bubbling, cheerful nature?

It was late that night when the small party reached Pevensey and the welcome shelter of Edwin Wulfsson's hall, which sat on a headland overlooking the bay and the town. It was built of wood, surrounded by a palisade of sharp-ended poles lashed together. From the great hall radiated several smaller, interconnected chambers where the family slept. It was a luxurious dwelling by Saxon standards.

Lianne had visited here before, but her eyes rested joyfully, as if for the first time, on the beautiful tapestries on the walls, which depicted scenes from the

Greek and Latin myths. In the center of the hall a roaring fire greeted the chilled travelers and they huddled close to its warmth, ignoring their smarting eyes. There was a hole in the roof to draw the smoke, but in such weather it didn't always draw well.

Lianne was grateful that a few of her father's theowes had made the journey with her. These were now bringing in the packs from the sumpter mules' backs, which held the women's clothing and possessions. More would have to be sent for later, but for now it was a start. She would have no need of great finery in her husband's absence, and his hall was well-equipped to supply her basic needs.

A plump, smiling woman came forth from the shadows, holding a rush light.

"Welcome, Lady Lianne, Lady Edgiva, and Lady Elfgift," said the servant. "Ye must be tired after your journey. Here, I've warmed some mead." She indicated horn cups sitting by the hearth. "That should chase the Channel's chill!"

"Thank you, Mold." Even Edgiva seemed too weary to be sharp-tongued tonight.

Lianne smiled gratefully at the homely woman, whose right eye looked cheerfully back at her while the left was gazing slightly off to the side. Mold's grin exposed widely separated, protruding teeth, but the woman's kindness enveloped her like a warm cloak. Here, at least, was one other ally in her strange new surroundings.

Lianne lay awake that night, staring up into the darkness in the largest bed-chamber. Outside, she could hear that the drizzling rain had become a down-pour. Elfgift snored softly beside her, and Lianne envied her young sister's slumber. *After this long day it is utterly ridiculous to be still awake,* she thought, yet her mind darted from topic to topic. For several minutes she tried to plan the changes she would make in the hall to reflect her taste as its new Lady, but it was useless. Her mind kept turning to Edwin, wondering what he was doing now, whether he was warm and safe. At last she decided to give up trying to banish consciousness so strenuously, and instead thought of her first meeting with Edwin, and the events of the past few months.

The class of 1065 had ended an era. The long reign of Edward was nearly over, and the time of change that England had dreaded for years was upon the country.

Once the powerful Earl Godwine of Wessex was dead, Edward had felt secure on his throne, and England had enjoyed a period of peace unparalleled since King Alfred's time. Raids by neigh-boring Vikings were rare, thanks to the excellent English navy. The Saxons of southern England had begun to look on the folk of the Danegeld more as fellow countrymen striving toward a common goal, where once the two groups had eyed each other with constant suspicion.

After Godwine's death, as Edward grew older, his celibate childlessness caused him to put increasing responsibility on Harold Godwinesson, the "Golden Warrior" of Wessex, who succeeded to his father's earldom. It became apparent to most, from the favor Edward showered upon Harold, that he looked on the capable, well-liked earl as his heir. The thought of Harold as king caused most to smile. Yet, those with more far-reaching memories murmured: Had the king not also promised the crown to William of Normandy, a distant relative? As a young king freshly returned from a youth spent in exile there, Edward had once shown a marked preference for all things Norman. Those who loved Harold scoffed that the upstart duke would not dare challenge the will of the Witangemot, for English kings were confirmed by this advisory council, and they would never choose a foreigner with harsh French ways over a native son. But, answered those who remembered Edward's promise to William, had not Harold confirmed that William was the heir when he visited Normandy in 1064? There were those who said the visit had been deliberate, although Harold had been on a pleasure cruise and his boat had reportedly been blown far off course to the shores of Ponthieu. He was "rescued" by the crafty duke, who then "persuaded" Harold to stay many months. During this time, an oath was extracted from Harold to recognize William as the heir of England upon Edward's death, a promise made twice-sacred by its unwittingly being made over holy relics. There was much difference of opinion as to whether Harold would damn his soul by violating the oath, but most held the belief that an oath made by force and deception was not valid. And, Harold protested, the English crown was not his to confer. Almost to a man, the English stated they would follow Harold Godwinesson, damned or not, over any Norman foreigner!

Edward's life had waned with the year 1065, after living to see his dream, Westminster Abbey, consecrated on Holy Innocents' Day in late December.

Present at his deathbed on the fifth of January were Harold Godwinesson; the controversial Stigand, cynical archbishop of Canterbury; and Edward's wife, Edyth, also of the Godwine clan. She had apparently loved him devotedly although he was too saintly and otherworldly to bring himself to sire an heir upon her.

He had moments of lucidity that day and claimed to have spoken to two dead Norman monks who predicted great doom to England. He then conferred the crown on Harold, and loosed his fragile hold on life.

Thegn Rolf of Fairlight had been in

London at this time, and as a prominent thegn was present outside the chamber where the king lay dying. His daughter Lianne accompanied him. During the general hubbub when it was announced that Edward had breathed his last, Lianne first saw Edwin.

The housecarle had been guarding the door until Harold grimly left the chamber. As Harold strode through the anteroom, he acknowledged the deep bows and curtseys, but he was intent on getting to the Witan, where the council would formalize the succession. After he had passed through the room, Lianne had glanced back and seen the guard gently assist the weeping Queen Edyth from the room until he had passed her into the care of one of her ladies-in-waiting. Returning to his post, the housecarle had looked up and noticed the beautiful girl watching him intently, and he had smiled. He had been amused to see her blush, he told her later, and self-consciously stare down at the hands she was warming at a brazier.

Her first observation had taken in his broad-shouldered sturdy build, his shaggy blond hair and mustache, and the eyes a grayer blue than her own. Like most of the king's household soldiers, he was of Danish descent.

I think I loved him even then, to see his kindness to Edward's widow, she thought, half-aware of the roar of the storm outside the hall now.

He had contrived to be formally introduced to Lianne the next day, at the coronation of Harold, which had hurriedly followed Edward's simple funeral at Westminster.

In March three events happened, two of which had national significance.

A fiery three-tailed comet was sighted. The gloomy wailed that this omen confirmed Edward's dire prophecy.

In York minster, Edwin and Lianne were among those who watched Harold take Aldyth, widow of Welsh King Gryffyd, in marriage. It was a union desired by neither. Aldyth still mourned her husband and held Harold responsible for his murder, although he was actually slain by his own countrymen. Harold had a handfast marriage that had lasted many years, and had several children by it. He knew this political marriage would break Lady Edythe's heart, she whom men called the "Swan-necked."

At the wedding banquet the third event took place: Edwin asked Lianne to be his wife, and she accepted joyously.

So blissfully happy were Edwin and Lianne that they were scarcely conscious of the ominous news that came from the court as the spring wore on. There were Norman embassies bringing provocative messages from an angry William, met with Harold's sarcastic replies. Norman envoys were being met with papal favor while English ones were turned away at French ports. And there was the rumor of a great fleet being assembled at the mouth of the Dives in Normandy.

In April the "hairy star" lit the night sky for a week, which inspired the monk Aethelmaer to foretell the tears of mothers and the overthrow of the king. The two lovers, though, were grateful for the light of the comet as they discussed their wedding to be held in May.

King Harold, however, was aware of the Norman threat building across the Channel, and a nationwide alert was sounded. As new ships were built and weapons were readied, Harold's house-carles were called into increased service. Lianne and Edwin reluctantly postponed their wedding. When to call up the fyrd, or national muster, was debated by the king and his advisors. Summer would be the most likely time, especially in terms of advantageous weather, for William to mount an invasion, but to call up the army too soon would be a drain on food and supplies. Men kept from their fields would result in a disastrous harvest in the fall.

In May, however, Harold's decision was made for him as reports reached the king of raids on Wight, Sussex, and Kent by the rebellious younger Godwinesson. When Tostig seized Sandwich and murder resulted, the king had to commit himself. The fyrd was summoned. Tostig was driven off to seek refuge in Norway.

Edwin spent June under Harold's command, arranging the coastal defenses. He had little time to spend with Lianne, who used this interval to stitch linens for her new home and to make lovely clothes in which to dazzle her betrothed.

It was now high summer, and Edwin confided in a message to Lianne how worried his commander was. The fyrd was restless, with no sign of William, and the crops were ripening in the fields unharvested, except what the women and children could do. He wished, if William were going to invade at all, he would come now, he wrote, so that English soldiers could drive him back into the sea and march off victorious to the harvest. It was known that Aldyth, the Lady of the English, was pregnant, and the land rejoiced that it would soon have an heir.

Harold reluctantly released the fyrd, and although the housecarles still kept their vigil on the coast, Edwin obtained leave and the wedding could at last take place.

Pray God my husband is safe, thought Lianne drowsily. Damn that scheming, jealous Tostig and his Norse ally, Hardraada!

An owl hooted outside in a tall oak tree whose branches bent near the hall. Lianne, sleeping now, did not hear it.

Three

"The wind has changed!" William roared exultantly. Activity ceased at the mouth of the Somme as the Norman soldiers looked up from their drilling and maintenance of equipment and care of the big war-horses.

Baron Guy de Bayeux smiled at his overlord's joy as he moistened a finger and elevated it to confirm the southerly wind. They had awaited such a wind at the mouth of the Dives and had finally gotten it after weeks of prayerful waiting, but it had played them false. Once out in the Channel, the wind had turned treacherous, and the storm and the formidable English navy had combined to turn them back. There had been many casualties, buried in secret by the duke to avoid further lowering of morale. They had regrouped at St. Valery and waited for another favorable wind. And prayed. And waited some more. William's moods reflected the weather, and as the wind had not come, the duke's temper had been at best uncertain.

Finally, in desperation, William had caused the holy bones of St. Waleric to be brought from the monastery on the hill overlooking the estuary, and paraded them through the Norman camp. The Normans, cynical except in religious matters, had knelt as one and prayed devoutly.

And now, on the afternoon of the twenty-seventh of September, William's prayers had been answered.

"To the ships!" he bellowed, beaming like a child, and the army began the awesome task of loading a thousand ships with their cargoes: some five thousand horses, twelve thousand men, their armor and weapons, and disassembled boards that would form William's first temporary fortresses. The wheeling gulls looked down in amazement as the shouts and curses of the men reached them even over the crash of the waves.

Guy de Bayeux ran a soothing hand along his destrier's tossing neck as he helped his squire, Gilbert, load the unwilling beast onto one of the many flat-bottomed transport boats.

"*Soyez tranquille,*" he told the dapple-gray stallion. "Hush, Nuage. It is but a matter of hours," he murmured persuasively into the horse's ear, "on a sea that lies between us and adventure. You wouldn't let a little pond like that stand between you and the conquering of England, would you?"

The horse snorted and stamped a mighty hoof, as if skeptical of his master's reassurance, but after nuzzling the baron's hand, he consented to be loaded.

Guy brushed a lock of black hair away from his sweating forehead. "I'd like to travel with you, *mon vieux*," he told the horse confidentially, "but His Grace expects me aboard the *Mora* and you understand I cannot refuse such an honor." His brown eyes narrowed against the sunlight as he glanced around to the ducal vessel, and decided he had better board without delay. He left Nuage after a last pat and made his way in the beehive of activity to where the flagship was anchored. Stephen of Airadri, the pilot, assisted him onto the Duke's ship with its single large triangular mast.

The ship had been the loving gift of Matilda, the duke's wife. It had a figurehead of a leopard, the Norman ducal emblem. At the stern was a gold figure of a boy holding a pennant and blowing a horn. Truly fit for a conqueror!

Guy was fully conscious of the significance of his being invited aboard the *Mora* and that others had remarked it too. True, he had been reared in William's household, in every manner as other youths were fostered in noble houses, but was in many ways treated like a son. This favor was all the more unexpected because his could have been the lot of a hostage, had William been a less kind, forgiving man. Guy had come to the ducal household as a page shortly after the abortive rebellion at Val-ès Dunes in 1047, when Guy's father had been captured, along with other nobles who felt that the young, newly knighted "Bastard Duke" would be an easy target. Such had not been the case. Guy's presence at the ducal court was to help ensure Baron de Bayeux's continued good behavior, but Guy had never been made to feel uncomfortable. Grateful for the duke's magnanimity, Guy strove always to make him proud.

He had more than succeeded. At the age of three-and-twenty, the young baron was one of the duke's closest friends, after his trusted seneschal William Fitz-Osborn. He was sure to be found in battle in the midst of the fray, right at his lord's side, his mighty sword wet with the enemy's blood, his stallion Nuage screaming defiance.

"Welcome aboard, Guy. We will soon sail—the ducal ship should lead the way, eh?" laughed William heartily. "Here, a goblet of wine will give you heart!"

"My thanks, my liege, but I need no encouragement. I can hardly wait to glimpse the shores of England. Think you they will be bristling with Saxon spears?"

"I know not," answered the duke truthfully. "If Harold has been able to keep his 'fyrd' mustered this late in the year, he is indeed quite a commander. We shall just have to wait and see." He studied the young man as Guy turned to greet Père Matthieu, a monk of William's household.

Guy de Bayeux was tall, even for the Normans whose Viking forebears had bequeathed them greater height than that of the average Frank, lean and lithe, possessed of a catlike grace unusual in a man of his size. His hair, still an unruly coal-black thatch, was combed forward in the fashion of Norman warriors, but unlike the rest he refused to shave it clear to the crown in the back, loathing the time spent keeping it bare and privately thinking it a silly fashion as well. His eyes were honey-brown, expressive, and usually dancing with good spirits. He had a sharply chiseled, aristocratic nose and a mobile, sensitive mouth with even white teeth. He was clean-shaven as was the Norman custom. His hand, as it shot out to clap the monk on the back in friendly fashion, was strong, with long, thin fingers. On one finger gleamed the baronial ring with the family emblem, the unicorn, with a garnet at the tip of its horn. The ring had been passed to Guy when Ralph de Bayeux had died two years ago.

"What, seasick already, my poor Matthieu?" he teased merrily. His voice had a rich, pleasingly masculine tone that many a wench ached to hear directed to her alone.

Not that many had heard that voice whispering intimately for very long, the duke ruefully mused. When, he, William, was still quite youthful, he had met Matilda, and all other women were as nuns to him thereafter, but Guy seemed to value one pretty wench quite as well as the next. It was gossiped that he gave well-favored serving girls quite a tumble in bed, but never more than once or twice. He was betrothed to Lady Mabile of Harfleur, but this was an arranged marriage between friendly baronies and had little to do with love. Lady Mabile is well enough, the duke thought. She'll bring him a fair *dot*, and bear him sons and daughters. In time these things will draw them together. Not all lords and ladies could know the passion the duchess and I share.

He thought backward to their tumultuous courting, when he had beaten her for calling him "bastard" and for declaring she would rather take the veil than wed him. His action had somehow been the catalyst to transform her feeling for him, and theirs had been a strong, sure love over the years. He sailed for England now, he knew, buoyed by her prayers. He gazed up the mast at the banner she had so lovingly stitched for him, and at that moment the sail billowed and the ship was launched.

"By the Splendor of God!" he roared, using his favorite oath. The trumpet was sounded. A beacon signal was flashed to the other ships. "We sail for England!"

Four

Lianne awoke the next morning with a delicious sense of purpose, a feeling that partially numbed the aching of her journey-sore limbs.

The thralls of the hall, of course, had long been up and about, and a hearty meal awaited her in the hall to break her fast. Her sister, already seated at the long oaken table, waved cheerily and indicated a seat near her.

"Ho, slugabed!" she teased. "You never stirred when I arose this morning."

Edgiva, also seated there, sniffed, "It's high time you were up. It's disgraceful—nigh onto Tierce! The lady of the hall should set an example, not lie abed like the bishop's mistress." Part of her fretful tone arose, Lianne guessed, from having to vacate the central seat at the high table for Lianne, so the new bride resisted the urge to inquire how her sister-by-marriage knew the sleeping habits of bishops' mistresses.

"Forgive me," she said with an apologetic smile. "It was never my custom to be slothful, but I lay awake long into the night. I suppose I was just too tired to sleep. I shall normally arise much earlier. As the lady of the hall, I know there is much to do. Perhaps you would show me where the linens and the plate are kept, Edgiva, as well as introduce me to the rest of the servants."

Edgiva sniffed again, partly mollified, but said pettishly, "I had planned to go to pray at the minster—for Edwin's safe return—but I *suppose* if we did not take *overlong* about it . . ."

But Lianne would not be hurried. "No, you go on, dear sister-in-marriage, it is an excellent idea, one I will take advantage of later. Mold, I am sure, can show me around."

Edgiva could not hide a small sigh of relief, and Lianne guessed there was some two-legged ulterior motive to her devotions—perhaps some well-favored thegn's house must be passed en route to the church. At least, she hoped it was that and not a secret passion for the priest that set such a blush on Edgiva's sallow cheek.

In any event, Mold proved much more a

help than Edgiva would have been, tirelessly opening chests and cupboards for Lianne's inventory, all the while describing the hall's daily routine and its inhabitants to her new mistress. The woman was good-spirited and knowledgeable in the running of the large hall, and Lianne soon surmised that Edgiva had largely turned her responsibilities over to Mold, while enjoying the benefits of being "the lady." Mold did not seem the least reluctant to pass the leadership role to Edwin's wife, and seemed so confident of Lianne's ability that Lianne felt her uncertainty and confusion slipping away, as she warmed even more to the cheerful Mold.

"And this is the still room, Lady, where I make my medicaments and potions for the ills of the hall folk," said the peasant woman proudly, showing Lianne into a small room where drying herbs hung in bunches from the beamed ceiling, and stoppered jars covered several shelves.

Lianne, like most women of her station, knew something of healing and natural remedies, but here was clearly an expert who could teach her much more. She indicated her interest and willingness to learn.

"Here is lady's smock, for digestion, stitchwort for boils, agrimony for wound healing, comfrey for poultices to put on swollen joints . . ." said Mold, pointing to the lavender, white, yellow, and dark pink-petaled drying plants. "There are also plants for making dyes: kingcups, larkspur, celandine . . ."

Lianne, taking a deep breath, resolved that she would master all these recipes and give Edwin even more reason to be proud of the girl he had chosen for his lady.

Five

Lianne did not rest well again the following night. Her sleep had been haunted with phantoms, and she had tossed and turned, moaning in her sleep. At dawn, Mold had awakened her, hearing her cries for Edwin.

Lianne looked hollow-eyed as she sat in the hall, playing listlessly with a hunk of rye bread.

"You must eat," urged Mold. "What if you already carry Edwin's son? A babe needs nourishment."

"I wish that could be true, Mold," the girl answered her with a rueful smile, blushing. "But I fear it would take a miracle . . . Edwin had to leave to join Harold's army before . . . you know . . ."

"Oh, I beg pardon, my lady, I didn't

know. Poor lamb," she clucked sympathetically.

Further concern for her mistress was interrupted as the sound of hooves was heard outside the hall, and a moment later Orm burst in, flushed with excitement.

"Greetings, sisters!" he shouted joyfully, embracing Lianne and Elfgift in turn, and smiling at Edgiva. "I have great tidings! I have ridden through the night to bring you such good news!"

Dread of disaster was banished by the youth's cheerful face and happy words. All three women began to talk at once, all asking different questions of Orm, who at last held a hand up to silence the chatter.

"Edwin sent a messenger to us—he is well, and sends you loving greetings, Lianne" (Lianne's sigh of relief was echoed by the others). "Tostig and Harald Hardraada are beaten—both killed at Stamford Bridge, their army slaughtered or scattered, fleeing for their ships!"

Lianne stopped his flow of words at this point, and it was not until he had been seated at the table and heartily broken his fast that she would permit him to tell the details.

Three days previously, at Stamford Bridge over the Derwent, Hardraada's and Tostig's troops had been awaiting the demanded submission of representatives from York. It had been a hot fall day and the invaders, overconfident after an easy victory at Gate Fulford, lounged by the water. Many took off their armor and splashed in the shallows.

Harold of England's forces had met the survivors of Gate Fulford along their march northward, who told them of the appointed meeting where five Roman roads converged on the Derwent.

The invaders had so relaxed their guard that the dust and noise of the approaching army was not noticed for a long time. When they did see them, however, there was a frantic struggling into armor and sounding of trumpets. One horseman thundered away to summon the rest of the enemy troops, left with the long Norse ships at Riccall. Many, trapped on the wrong side of the river, died without reaching their weapons.

As the Viking shield ring was assembled, Harald's horse stumbled, which the superstitious Norsemen accounted a bad omen.

Harold Godwinesson, stated Orm, had sent a messenger to Tostig offering forgiveness even now to his ever-rebellious brother if he would turn and side with England. Though Harold offered to restore Tostig to his earldom, all knew that Tostig could not with honor accept. He and Hardraada (the "hard-to-counsel") had half the forces his brother commanded.

"What do you offer my ally, Harald of Norway?" he had asked the ambassador.

"Seven feet of English ground!" came the reply—for Harald was a giant, even among the Vikings. Tostig sent the messenger back, and both the rebel brother and the "messenger" bore the look of unbearable sorrow. The latter had been, unbeknownst to Hardraada, Harold Godwinesson himself. The Norwegian king was angry to learn of the subterfuge, but Tostig had known his ally would not have been above treachery if he had recognized him. He had said nothing until his royal brother was safely back among his men.

To the Saxon's cries of "Holy Cross!" and "Out!" the battle was joined. Harold sent his mounted men across to feint and retreat, and the hot-headed invaders were lured into a trap as they chased the "fleeing" English. Soon the Derwent was damned with corpses and red with blood.

Harald Hardraada died fairly early in the battle, with arrows through cheek and throat, but managed before expiring to urge Tostig to repent and submit to his brother. Tostig, who had ever been jealous of his elder brother's charm and possessions, would not capitulate, even though he knew he was doomed. A well-aimed arrow not long after that killed him instantly.

Norse reserves arrived then and the invaders refused to surrender. The bridge over the Derwent was still held by one stalwart Viking who with his bloody broadsword kept the English from crossing, until one very wily Saxon took a small boat under the bridge unobserved.

With a sharp lance through a gap in the wooden planking he fatally impaled the bridge's defender. The bridge lost, the battle became a rout, and those Norse who could still flee scrambled for their ships on the coast while Harold's forces looted the Norse and rebel English corpses. The ravel banner of Harald Hardraada, the "Land Ravager," was dragged through the mud in derision.

Orm's eyes gleamed with pride as he recounted the tale of victory. Even now, he told the attentive women, the king, his housecarles, and the remaining army (for the battle *had* been costly to the English, even though they had won) celebrated with feasting and thanksgiving in York. "Soon, Lianne, Edwin will come marching home to you! Won't that be a joyous day!"

She reached across the table to tousle his blond hair affectionately. "Indeed it will," she responded, tears in her eyes. "The saints be praised who protected my lord through the battle. I hope he may come soon! Now, however, brother, to bed with you! A boy up riding all night must needs rest this morning!"

"Oh, Lianne, I can't sleep yet! I'm still too excited. It can wait awhile!" She smiled at his energy, wishing she had some of it after her restless sleep of the past night.

"Come, Orm, let's walk along the shore. It *is* all right, isn't it, Lianne?" Elfgift queried anxiously. "I haven't had

Orm to talk to the entire se'ennight we've been in Pevensey!" she proclaimed dramatically.

"You make it sound a year, Elfgift!" said Edgiva critically.

"It seems one!" returned the younger girl stoutly. Lianne gave her permission, knowing how her sister longed to escape from Elgiva's shrewish tongue, if only for an hour. Lianne thought how much her sibling resembled herself at that age— mischievous, full of spirit, tomboyish and fearless. In another year or so, though, Father would doubtless be nego- tiating for her diminutive sister's wedding.

"Your chores will wait, I'm sure." She smiled sweetly. "Don't keep Orm out too long, though—he's more tired than he is yet aware!"

Lianne set about her morning tasks, the first of which was to order a chamber made ready for her brother. She was in the midst of helping prepare the midday meal when brother and sister returned, their shouts of "Lianne! Lianne!" echoing ahead of them as they pounded into the hall, out of breath.

"What is it? Did you sight a sea monster?" joked Mold as they ran past the servant woman. But Lianne saw their eyes, wide and blue against their blanched faces.

"The Normans have come," Orm said, his voice shaking.

Lianne, incredulous, a cold, icy feeling

spreading through her belly, ran down the path that led to the cliff overlooking the bay, accompanied by Orm, while Elfgift remained behind with an hysterical Edgiva. With her sister-by-marriage's shriek, "They'll murder us all!" still echoing in her ears, she looked out over the bay.

The truth of Orm's announcement smote her like a physical blow. The bay was white with their sails. The gulls circled overhead in the morning sunlight as the first ships drew near to the shore. From one, evidently the flagship, a figure jumped into the surf, not waiting for the assistance of a nearby knight, and strode the remaining watery yards to the beach. In his haste, however, he tripped and measured his length on the sand. Lianne could hear even from a distance the collective murmur of dismay and could see the concerned looks of some of the men.

The tall figure hesitated a moment only and then righted himself, assisted by a mailed knight, and in spite of a bloody nose held the sand he had clutched in his fists and shouted something in Norman French, laughing. The cry echoed against the cliffs.

"What did he say?" asked Orm, whose attention in his lessons with Robert frequently wandered. Languages were not his talent.

" 'Behold, I have taken ahold of England with both hands and guaranteed it with my blood!' " Lianne grimly translated, as cheers rang out from the Normans. Then, as the thousands of invaders continued to pour onto the beach, she turned again to her brother. "You must ride for Harold's army," she told him. "I know you are weary, but he must be warned. At this moment we are the only ones in England who may know of William's coming," she continued, eyeing the leopard banners of Normandy. "He must know, so he can rally his men to drive them away!"

"Aye, sister," agreed Orm. "But what of you and the others? I cannot leave you here, with an invading army for neighbors! You would not be safe."

"Of course not. We shall leave as soon as possible for Netherfield Abbey, where our aunt will give us sanctuary." (Their late mother's sister was abbess there.) "But first we must go to Father at Fairlight, and have him join us."

"He won't," the boy argued. "He'll want to stay and fight."

"He must! He's too old to do battle with those monsters!" Desperation colored her voice, for she realized Orm's prediction was probably correct. "They'll head first for London, won't they? They'll want that port and the city's wealth captured first, don't you think?"

Orm nodded, though in truth he knew no more than his sister what the Normans were likely to do. "You had better go back and get away from here. I don't want you anywhere near when they decide to explore."

Six

They did not linger to watch as the thousands of foreign invaders beached their remaining ships and disembarked, later unloading horses, arms, and foodstuffs.

Once back at the hall, Lianne set in motion a whirlwind of activity. While Orm saddled a leggy bay garron in the barn, she lost little time in packing a loaf of wheaten bread and some cheese in a leathern bag, all the while explaining to Edgiva and Elfgift what must be done. Mold and the ceorls and thralls stood in the background, listening and chattering excitedly. Her younger sister was pale but calm. Edwin's sister's hysteria had subsided to whimpers, tears, and nail-chewing.

Lianne realized she was truly in charge —she had no older, stronger man to protect her and rely on for advice. The menservants hung on her every word. She was "the Lady." In Edwin's absence her word was law, and what she decided would affect their safety. With the knowledge of her responsibility came a new realization, but she said nothing of it until the sound of Orm's horse's hoofbeats faded in the distance.

"Elfgift, I cannot expose the entire household to danger in warning Father . . . . Fairlight lies west of here, the direction in which they will probably march," she began.

"But we cannot just leave him!" wailed Elfgift.

"I don't intend to. But I can go faster alone, and avoid Norman soldiers more easily. I want you and Mold to lead those of the household who wish to seek refuge at Netherfield. I trust *your* good sense and capability—" Edgiva sniffed indignantly—"to keep all in order there until Father, Robert, and I, and those of his household who wish to come, can reach the convent." She did not give voice to the chance that she would fail in her mission. Elfgift smiled tremulously, proud of the trust her sister had placed in her. "Each of you take only what you can wear and carry in a single pack. We must leave within the hour, for who knows when the Norman monsters will begin to forage?"

* * *

As Lianne spoke in Edwin Wulfsson's hall on the hill above Pevensey Bay, Guy de Bayeux knelt by the sea as Odo, bishop of Bayeux and half-brother of William, held a Mass on the shore. As the main force of the Normans knelt, sentries scanned the cliffs alertly, watching for any signs of Saxon resistance.

Even as his lips murmured the "Our Father" and his slender, elegant fingers moved in the sign of the cross, a part of Guy's mind worried over the question that concerned each of the invaders, from William to the lowest footsoldier—where was Harold? When would the two armies meet?

Beside Guy knelt Père Matthieu, and the rise and fall of the monk's responses brought Guy back to the solemnity of the Mass just as Odo elevated the Host. He smiled, glancing sidelong at the plump monk's devotion. Guy and Père Matthieu had become fast friends in the months since William had summoned the barons together and began building his fleet of ships, attracting mercenaries from Brittany, France, and elsewhere on the Continent. It was an unlikely friendship— the lean, adventurous, sensual young noble and the chubby, serious monk, yet over the summer months they had become as brothers.

The Mass now over, the Normans scattered to assigned tasks, some gathering driftwood for fires as the food was unpacked and prepared, others seeing to the care of the horses, while the majority set up crude defenses and watched for Harold.

It was worrisomely late before the small band was ready to depart the hall. They had been slowed by numerous requests to go fetch this relative or that for the journey to Netherfield, and by Edgiva's continually remembering just *one* more possession she could *not* leave without. They took the half-dozen horses in the barn, leaving Lianne her black mare, Storm, but the majority of the refugees went on foot. Children were mounted double and triple on the animals with reins held by their elders for the trek.

The sun was low in the west as the sisters tearfully embraced.

"Don't you be worryin', my lady Lianne," said Mold bracingly as the other girl held her sister close. "This little lady and I will win safely through and be awaitin' ye at Netherfield, never fear. You just go now, and Godspeed ye to yer father. No doubt ye're right, and William won't bother with the likes o' us here. He'll be after bigger game, like Lunnontown. Harold'll be down on him like a hawk on a hare, with your dear lord's help, I trow!"

The party of refugees, babes whimpering, a mule braying in protest, set their course north for the abbey's sanctuary; Lianne and Storm galloped eastward on the Channel road for Fairlight and the unknown.

She had been traveling for an hour in the growing darkness of evening, conscious of the increasing wind that heralded a storm. The trail was lightly wooded, gently rolling countryside; it lay about a mile from the sea and was not a direct, widely-traveled route, but Lianne had chosen it at the advice of one of the ceorls, who recommended it for its isolation and cover. The girl was not eager to meet any scouting parties of the Normans. There was a half moon, but its light was fitful as it was increasingly smothered by storm clouds.

The mare laid back her ears and nickered in protest as the first drops struck her. Lianne had only time to pull her cloak closer about her and draw her hood over her head before the rain began in earnest, slashing down in frigid sheets.

"Oh, Storm, what now?" sighed Lianne ruefully, and as if in answer the mare picked up her pace, splashing through the downpour as if she knew exactly where she was going.

A few minutes later, the exhausted girl found herself in a grove of trees in front of a peasant's thatched cottage. Sliding off her palfrey wearily, she knocked timidly at the door, which was opened by an elderly Saxon freeman and his wife.

She was immediately bid welcome, and while the old man led Storm off to the lean-to byre behind the rude dwelling,

Lianne was set before a smoking but wonderfully warming fire, her sodden gunna removed and a woolen garment, shapeless and old, given her. It was musty-smelling and rough, but dry, and Lianne pulled it gratefully around her.

"How come ye to be abroad alone in the dark, my lady?" quavered the old woman. "The spirits will be after ye!"

"I'm not nearly as worried about the 'spirits' as the Normans," Lianne told her, and the old man having returned, they listened, shaking their heads apprehensively as Lianne told them of the ships in the bay that morning. "I must leave as soon as the rain lets up, you understand. I must reach my father in Fairlight!"

"It won't be stopping tonight, my lady," the old man told her with certainty. "It looks fair set to rain the night through. Ye'd best bide the night here. At least we be safe and dry, while this French duke be getting wet, I vow!" he cackled.

Lianne smiled, bowing to the unavoidable delay. "I thank you for your hospitality."

The old wife gave her a bowl full of broth with chunks of fish in it from a kettle over the fire. Lianne nearly fell asleep while sipping its filling warmth. I will awake at dawn, she planned as she lay down on the straw pallet in the far corner of the hut, and was asleep nearly before she completed the thought.

* * *

The sun, however, was high in the sky before the Saxon maid awoke. She had been more fatigued than she knew by the frightening events of the previous day, the sudden responsibility descending on her shoulders when previously she had had nothing more weighty to choose than whether to wear her blue kirtle or the green. Her sleep had at first been haunted by nightmares of Norman soldiers with bloodstained horns on their heads, cloven-hoofed feet, and forked tails finding Mold and Elfgift, but then she had sunk deeply into a dreamless, heavy slumber that ended as she opened her eyes and met those of the old peasant woman bending over her.

"Oh aye, there she be, bonny blue eyes," the woman chuckled. "Slugabed! If ye be going to Fairlight today, ye'd best be up and about it! I have a loaf of fresh-baked rye—have some with some of my goat's milk to break your fast before the journey!"

Lianne sat up quickly, gingerly feeling her aching joints. She was upset to have slept so late, when the trip was so urgent, but wasting no time bewailing the hour, she hurriedly donned the now-dry linen kirtle and the forest-green gunna with its jeweled girdle, and rebraided the thick rope of hair, tying it at the bottom with a leather thong. A short time later, the warm goat's milk and bread having satisfied her morning hunger, she bid the old couple a thankful good-bye.

Seven

A lark rocketed into the air at the approach of the cantering palfrey, but seemed little disturbed by the intrusion, for it broke into a blithe warble. Lianne momentarily forgot the urgency of her errand and lifted her face to the sun's rays. It was clear as only a Wessex day in autumn can be. The downpour of the night before forgotten, the changing foliage gleamed in hues of green, orange, and yellow.

The little mare picked her way daintily through the tall grass, avoiding a spider's web stretched between two bushes, its orb still gleaming with dew drops. Storm flicked her ears back appreciatively as her mistress hummed a tune.

They came to the end of the meadow,

where several poplars formed a gateway to a wooded area. The ceorl had told her to expect it; it was the last stretch of ground where she would have an extensive cover.

Behind her she heard a shout. Lianne twisted in her saddle. A bare hundred and fifty yards to her rear, where she had first entered the field, rode a score of Norman knights, mail gleaming dully.

Guy de Bayeux had seen the girl before any of the rest of the duke's small reconnaissance party.

"May I, Your Gracē?" he grinned. "Mayhap the wench will know Harold's whereabouts."

"I doubt it," William returned wryly. "But remember, Guy, we are in enemy country, Harold or no. Be not overlong at your wenching!"

Lianne, pulse pounding in her throat, had not waited to see if any of the Normans pursued her, but drummed her heels into the palfrey's side. The mare galloped along the forest trail, careless of branches whipping into her mistress's face.

"Faster, Storm!" sobbed the girl, as she became aware of the sound of a pursuing horse. She'd had a few precious seconds' start, and the advantage of a smaller, fleeter mount not encumbered by a mailed rider, but no more. Lianne tried to watch the sun-dappled path ahead for dangerous holes and logs, but found she had instead to lean over her straining mount's neck to avoid the low-hanging branches. The harsh sound of her own breathing was loud in her ears. On the little mare plunged, as the thin saplings of poplar gave way to older, sturdier growth.

Storm was growing winded, but Lianne could still hear the pursuing Norman horse. Desperately she looked about her, and sighting a venerable oak suitable for her purpose, stopped her palfrey in front of it. She prayed silently that she still had the skill of her childhood when, barefoot, she had shinnied up trees with the thrall children as agilely as any cat. Shaking, hoping her soft, leather-shod feet would not slip on the leather saddle, she stood on her horse for a moment and reached up to a sturdy low branch.

A moment later, she had pulled herself up close to the trunk several branches up and, huddled with her knees pulled up next to her body, held onto the tree and hoped the changing leaves of the oak were still thick enough to hide her green-clad figure.

But Storm had been used to Lianne's girlhood habit of dropping her reins when she dismounted, and stood obediently beneath the tree, waiting for Lianne to descend. It seemed a strange time for a game.

"On, Storm! Go! Leave here!" hissed Lianne despairingly from her perch, but she dared not call too loudly. She wanted the horse to canter off and be far from her hiding place by the time the Norman caught up. A handful of thrown acorns fell all around the horse, one striking her rump, but the ebony hide just twitched imperturbably as the mare lowered her head to graze, then raised it as the Norman destrier drew near.

Lianne cowered into the tree, pressing her face into the rough bark as the heavier horse approached. Below, a rich deep voice called out in Norman French, *"Heu! Qu'est-ce que ca?* Where did your rider go, little horse?"

He stopped beneath the tree, looking all around through the undergrowth. Lianne, hazarding a look, could only see the top of his conical helmet and the broad mail-clad shoulders. Mary, Mother, don't let him look upward! she prayed, eyes shut tight.

A chuckle broke from the man's throat, and Lianne knew her prayer had been in vain.

"What's this? A little English squirrel? God's Blood! They grow them fair here," laughed Guy as his gaze drank in the sight of the terrified Saxon girl, her body pressed against the mighty trunk, her cornflower-blue eyes huge in her pale face. Clearly, she expected her last hour on earth had come.

"Come down *ma petite!* I won't hurt you!" invited the young baron, lifting his free arm to her. "Ah, *Jesu,* this lovely creature does not understand! *Hèlas!"* He smiled ruefully up at her. "Had I but a knowledge of English, you would not fear me!"

Blue eyes stared down into brown ones. The nasal piece of his helmet gave him an even more alien appearance than his speech with its slurred Norman consonants.

"I don't *fear* you, *nithing*," Lianne lied, finding her voice surprisingly strong as she snarled the French words and the Saxon epithet at him.

"This vision speaks French!" He grinned delightedly, ignoring her tone. His dark brown eyes were so merry, his smile so friendly, that Lianne had to remind herself for a moment not to smile back.

"I am Guy, Baron de Bayeux. What is your name, fair one?"

"Go away, Norman dog!" she spat at him, but found her command ignored as he agilely swung himself up into the tree and climbed up to her sturdy limb after her. "What are you doing? Be gone!"

"If you will not come down, *demoiselle*, then perforce I must come up," he explained simply, and seating himself carefully next to her after testing the thick bough, studied her more closely.

She looked back at him frankly as he shed his helmet, and without the strange nasal covering part of his face, was conscious that he, though an enemy, was an extraordinarily well-favored man. He was perhaps five years older than she, as dark-featured as her Edwin was fair. His black locks, freed from the confines of the helmet, were somewhat longer than the Norman fashion, but shorter than the average Saxon man's. She met his eyes, and drowned in the honey-brown of them. Lianne looked away, a fiery blush staining her cheeks.

"How enchanting you are, *demoiselle!* Are all the Saxon maids as lovely as you? No matter! I will have only you!" He watched appreciatively as she gasped at his audacity. She reached out a hand to slap his clean-shaven cheek, but he parried it easily.

"Fie, my fair fierce one! No Norman lady is so disrespectful of her lord—"

"You're not my lord!" she hissed, fear forgotten in her indignation. "I am the wife of Edwin Wulfsson of Pevensey, housecarle of King Harold—"

"Hèlas. I am truly devastated. My lovely English squirrel did not wait for me. Ah, well," he shrugged his shoulders, a smile playing about his full mouth, "after we meet Harold the Usurper, you will be a widow." He spoke with calm certainty. "And then, *ma dame? Qui sait?"*

He was prepared for the blow when it came, and caught both her wrists in a viselike grip.

"You're not fit to bloody *King* Harold's axe—but my lord will cleave your Norman skull properly when he comes!"

"Where is he?" the Norman asked, tauntingly, and Lianne, maddened by his words and his nearness, threw caution aside.

"He has just beaten Harald Hardraada and Tostig Godwinesson at Stanford Bridge—William will soon be as dead as they when Harold marches from the north. Oh, yes, our king will soon know the Bastard is here!"

"Indeed? We had not known *that*," answered Guy de Bayeux smoothly, still smiling at her, and Lianne knew with a sinking feeling that she had given the Norman army valuable information.

"Perhaps you would like to come back to our camp in Hastings to tell my liege lord that news? Although, of a certainty, you must not name him 'Bastard' to his face!" He reached a hand out to the thick blonde hair which had come loose from its thong during the wild ride.

"No ... *please* ..." moaned the girl with unconcealed terror, not ashamed now to beg.

The Norman considered the thought of such a comely girl in the camp full of rough Normans, Bretons, and French and shook his head.

"*Non, ma petite,* you are right. I must carry your news to William. I cannot expose my future lady to the dangers of hundreds of fighting men." He ignored her denial of the possessive pronoun. "So that I may find you afterward, what is your name, beautiful one, and where is your home?"

"Lianne of Fairlight," she ground out

between clenched teeth. "But I shall *never* be yours!"

"But yes," he assured her. "And since I am letting you go free, I will take a kiss to seal our betrothal." He tightened his grip on her wrists with his left hand, while with his right he cupped her chin with his long fingers and kissed her.

The kiss surprised her, not that it happened, because she had no choice, but that his lips were firm and warm. She half-expected the Norman's mouth to be icy and strange, but, shocked by his gentleness, did not attempt to draw away for a long moment. Her eyes fluttered open.

"You may be wed, Lianne of Fairlight," Guy told her, his brown eyes searching hers, "but I think I have been the first to truly taste the honey there."

She had a moment to look indignant, then his mouth closed on hers again, this time more demandingly, his tongue tasting hers as the pressure of his mouth forced hers open. Lianne swayed, a leaf in the wind of this driving force, and they drew apart.

"I must go," she insisted, looking away.

"As must I, *ma* Lianne."

She ignored the possessive French word again, and gazed at the ground in dismay. Getting down would be infinitely harder than her scramble up had been. Storm had strayed a few yards away, where she and the destrier browsed together in apparent amicability.

"Permit me," the Norman said, and climbed down to the last branch, from there jumping to the ground, grimacing slightly at the jolt to his ankles. She climbed carefully down to the lowest bough, where he held out his arms to her. His dark eyes dared her.

He caught her easily, but instead of lowering her to her feet, he allowed her body to slide teasingly for an endless moment along the long, hard length of him, watching her eyes the whole while.

She stood looking up at him in the dim forest light. He still held her, not roughly, at the wrists. Now she could see that he was about as tall as Edwin, but lean and lithe where her lord was stocky and solid.

"Where are you going, *m'amie?* I must know you are safe. *Non—soyez tranquille* —I will not tell His Grace—"

"I must reach my father, Thegn Rolf, and bring him and his household to safety at my aunt's abbey, out of William's path." She didn't know why she was telling him this, simply because he asked. "He *will* march on London . . . will he not?"

The Norman shrugged expressively. "We are moving on closer to Hastings today, but after that? In truth I know not, Lianne. My liege's plan hangs on what Harold does."

"I suppose I must thank you for not behaving as I feared," she said, striving for a courteous tone, as she mounted her palfrey. "But we must not meet again. I am a wife, and you must not dishonor my vows." She found she could not look at him.

"When two armies meet in battle, my lady, many things change."

Shaken, she cantered away, not looking back.

Eight

"Régardez, Your Grace, such a smug smile on de Bayeux's face! A very satisfied look, *hein?* Tell me, my lord—how do they taste, these English wenches?" called Humphrey of Tilleul as the Norman rejoined the scouting party. Guy noted with relief they were not headed in precisely the same direction as Lianne had taken.

"They taste of honey, *mon ami,*" he said, striving for a careless tone.

"Ah, but Guy does not say *where* they taste so!" roared Ivon Taillefer bawdily.

"Why, all over, of course," returned the baron, poking the knight lewdly in the ribs.

"Mais, attendez un moment," another said consideringly. "Bayeux has not a

scratch, not a mark on him to show for his . . . 'little adventure.' Surely you'd not have us believe, would you, Guy, that she spread her legs without a fight?"

The Norman baron resisted the urge to run Judhäel of Totnes through as he thought of the innocence of the Saxon girl's kiss. He had never liked the Breton, who had managed to insinuate himself into William's closest circle of nobles. "But, of course, Judhael, English girls have never been made love to in the Norman tongue before. Just a few words *et voilà!* She opened her arms . . . and other things . . ."

The invaders guffawed enviously as they rode off to join the main force, marching on to Hastings.

Lianne, traveling alone and with a knowledge of the terrain, was able to reach Hastings long before the invading army. She paused just long enough to water Storm while she warned those village people around her of the advancing Normans.

The people of Hastings, of course, had heard of the landing at Pevensey, and those who had not fled huddled, for the most part, in their halls and huts.

"Where can we go?" an old woman demanded of her. "Do you go to safety, my lady? Take us with you!"

"I don't know if it will be any safer where I go, good mother," Lianne spoke gently, disengaging the woman's clutching hands. "I only know I must get to my father's hall swiftly. I can take no one else on my mare." Taking one last regretful look at the terrified ceorls, she whipped Storm's head around from the trough and galloped from the town.

Passing north of Bulverhythe and the marshes, William's army arrived in late afternoon at Hastings.

The thegns of Hastings, forewarned by the Saxon girl's report, as well as tales from a bedraggled refugee from Pevensey who spoke of peasants slaughtered and cottages burned, surrendered promptly. This act saved, in large part, the town itself.

The duke lost no time in having a sort of prefabricated wooden castle, brought over in pieces from Normandy, assembled on a hastily piled-up *motte*. This first crude defensive castle he placed in the charge of Humphrey of Tilleul.

While it was well that they had had time to consolidate, he told his barons over the evening meal, William felt he needed to provoke an early attack, now that he had Guy's report of Harold's presence in the North. It would be to Harold's advantage, he mused, to stay up there, taunting him, while daily the Norman supplies grew more scarce. If he, William, were forced to march after him, he would be on unfamiliar ground with its obvious hazards, and he would have the added danger of being cut off from retreat by the excellent English navy in the south. Therefore, he ended, speaking from his personal knowledge of the Saxon he had knighted, the usurper Harold must be goaded to protect his people in the south from the Norman menace.

"How, my liege?" queried Guy, though he feared he knew the answer already.

"We will create a little hell, right here in Sussex."

They rode out, armed and mailed, and William showed his young baron just what the grim answer had meant.

In the little time remaining of the night, and again the next day, the area around Hastings became a scorched earth. Women were raped, thralls and freemen murdered, their homes burned, their animals scattered or stolen for the army's use. There arose around Hastings a thick pall of smoke. Anguished screams and cries filled the air.

Guy was not new to pillaging and the violence attendant to war, but always before it had been in the hot-blooded midst of battle, or as William's revenge on a select group that had defied him.

This people had attempted but a feeble resistance. Knowing that many of these simple folk knew nothing and cared little who sat on the throne in Winchester, or why, Guy concentrated grimly on protecting William from the occasional wild-eyed Saxon who waited in ambush or shot arrows from behind a hedgerow.

"What is it, *mon fils?*" William asked as they paused in front of a blackened hall. Nuage tossed and plunged, nostrils flared, eyes rolling. The stench of burned flesh filled their noses. Smoke stung their eyes and trailed around their horses' hindquarters. "You seem plagued by conscience, of all things!"

"Nothing, my lord."

"*Merde!* Don't turn womanish on me now, Guy!" snapped the duke, and wheeled Bayard.

"Of course not, my liege." Looking at the destruction all about him, he wondered where the Saxon girl was this night.

On their second day at Hastings, a messenger arrived from Robert FitzWymarc, an Anglophile noble who lived in England. The letter courteously warned William that he had taken on too much in trying to conquer England, retelling the story of Harold's victory at Stamford Bridge. It was suggested that further strife be prevented by William leaving now.

The "Bastard Duke" laughed and crumpled the missive. "By the Splendor of God!" he roared. "I have not come this far to be turned aside by a letter now!"

Girl and horse arrived at Fairlight at the same time the Norman army was eating its evening meal at Hastings. At the outskirts of the town, a sickening

73

foreboding took hold of Lianne. When she passed the first few cottages, no noisy children ran out to mark her passing with boisterous greetings, no old men sat at their cottages' doorsteps. A door was opened a crack at one place, and wary eyes peeped out, then vanished immediately. From within another building, a dog barked a warning, and was silenced.

Dear God, what was happening here?

As Storm clip-clopped further along the high road into town, there were signs of burning and damage here and there. Flies buzzed around a pool of blackened, viscous liquid.

Around a bend in the road, Lianne nearly rode over the body of a woman who lay awkwardly sprawled, her throat cut from ear to ear. With difficulty, Lianne recognized the pallid corpse as her friend Edwina. From a nearby house, the keening cry of a woman blended with Lianne's scream. Storm snorted and half-reared, her mistress's fear contagious. Lianne kicked her palfrey into a canter, too anxious about her father now to even stop and say a prayer for her slain friend. Later, when she knew her kin were all safe . . .

Thegn Rolf's hall lay at the end of a row of prosperous merchants' halls. As she approached, her pulse pounding in her temples, mouth dry, she could see the massive carved door hanging at a crazy angle. The roof was blackened. Wisps of smoke still rose from the windows.

With a little cry, Lianne vaulted from her horse and, careless of her own safety, ran in.

Inside the hall it appeared a demon had been loose. Hangings were ripped. Furniture lay half-burned in a pyre in one corner. Wooden drinking horns lay on their sides at a bench. In front of the fireplace, one of the women thralls lay sprawled on her back, sightless eyes viewing the wanton destruction, her kirtle pushed up around her scrawny breasts.

"Father!" screamed Lianne. "Father!" she prayed soundlessly as she ran to his chamber in the glowing darkness.

"Lianne . . ." croaked the old man from his pallet. His face was blackened. A blood-drenched linen bandage swathed his temples. The girl barely noticed Robert as the Norman rose with a grimace from the old man's bedside. Her eyes and ears took in the limp hand that fluttered above the skins that covered his body, the rasping sound of his breathing, the weakness of his voice, and then her widened eyes implored Robert to tell her all. She knew her father had not the strength.

"One of William's ships went astray and came ashore at Romney," he told her. "Many of them were slaughtered there, but a dozen made their way here, apparently trying to find William, but murdering and looting as they passed through. They came to this hall, as they did to others. Your father was hurt trying to protect his thralls. They burned him with a torch when he tried to stop them from throttling poor Eadsige out there after three had . . . forced her. I . . . I regret to say I happened to be with Father Anselm and not here to protect your father. Some of the thegns and ceorls were able to overpower the raiders in another hall, and they're all dead now, burning in a pyre. . . . I've sent for Father Anselm, Lianne. . . . Your Father has not long . . ."

Lianne, tears coursing down her face, sat carefully on the edge of the bed and held the old man's one unburned hand. The thegn did not speak again, but his eyes never left her face as she told him where Orm had gone, and that she had sent the others to safety. She didn't look up as the priest padded quietly in and administered the Sacrament, but held the hand long after the gnarled fingers had relaxed their grip.

"He is gone, Lianne," Robert spoke gently.

Lianne shook her head, as if to shake off sleep.

"We must go, and now. If Hastings is their destination, that's too close to Fairlight to linger," he continued insistently.

"But . . . Father . . ."

"I will see him buried," spoke up the priest. "Robert is right. Every moment you delay may be dangerous. No—" he raised a hand to silence her protest. "Thegn Rolf would want you safe. After we've beaten the Normans you can do honor to his grave, and his memory. Go to Netherfield. Elfgift and your people need you there."

Too exhausted and grief-stricken to argue, Lianne numbly allowed herself to be directed to change her dusty, stained garments. Then, as night crept softly into Fairlight, mercifully veiling the sights if not the smells of pillage, Robert and Lianne rode out toward Netherfield.

Nine

The weary dark hours of riding seemed endless—a night full of apprehension at each loud sound as they journeyed to the haven Netherfield Abbey represented. Lianne and Robert met others fleeing the Norman advance, some on horseback, leading mules laden with hastily gathered possessions, others on foot, similarly loaded down. They did not pause for speech, merely exchanged terse words in passing: "Where are the devils now, know ye?" "When last we heard, the Normans were ravaging about Hastings, God rot them!"

The old man and the girl never knew, however, when the sound of approaching horses might mean enemy scouts, and once or twice they drew aside into thickets until the horsemen passed.

The danger of the journey occupied Lianne's mind fully. It was not until the half-moon's light outlined Telham Hill before them that she realized they were nearly safe, and had time to think of her loss. Their horses made their way wearily past Telham and crossed the ridge named in the Saxon tongue for the sandy stream nearby: Senlac. The sister hill of Caldbec lay before them after that, and Lianne looked up to see an ancient apple tree spotlighted by the fitful moonlight shining on its summit.

At the entrance of the mighty Andreadsweald lay Netherfield Abbey, inhabited by nuns of the Benedictine order, of which Lianne's maternal aunt was the abbess.

They knocked loudly at the gate, awakening Sister Portress. A moment later, torchlight flared as a shutter banged open at the side of the great half-timbered building, and shortly afterward, Elfgift had joined the nun in welcoming them to the convent.

Sliding wearily from her mount, Lianne steeled herself for the telling of her grim tidings.

"Sister! Robert!" Elfgift's shriek was joyful as, clad only in her night rail and a blanket, she embraced Lianne. "But . . . where is Father?"

"He is . . ." She lost consciousness and crumpled at her sister's feet.

* * *

What a coward I was, Lianne blamed herself one morning a few days after their arrival as she sat beneath a venerable apple tree in the abbey's orchard, munching a windfall apple. To have shamefully fainted away and left Robert the task of telling Elfgift our father was dead! However dear our old tutor is, it should have come from me, the eldest of the family now. The days of fear, her grief which had not then had time to be expressed, her exhaustion seemed to her to be no excuse. How recently she had been a carefree maid, planning joyfully her wedding! Those days seemed another lifetime, when the threat of William seemed another bogeyman of children.

It had been nearly midday before Lianne had been awakened by Elfgift and Mold bringing in a restoring meal of stewed lamprey, a favorite of the older girl's. Over that meal, after they had been joined by Edgiva, Lianne recited the events that had taken place since they had parted at Pevensey, thankful in spite of her guilt that Robert had already shared the painful details of Thegn Rolf's death.

She found herself surprisingly compelled to mention briefly her meeting with Guy de Bayeux, the Norman baron (though she omitted the details of what happened in the tree!).

"He chased you into the wood, my lady?" Mold paused in clearing the serving bowls, hands on hips. "Saints have mercy! The whoreson could have raped you and left you for dead. He didn't try . . . I mean, he . . ."

"No, Mold, never fear." She felt obligated to defend him. "He could have forced me, indeed. But he did not. He was very gentle. We . . . just talked."

"Talked?" Edgiva put in suspiciously. "What could you and the devil's spawn have to *talk* of?"

Lianne felt a flush creep scaldingly up her neck, and sought refuge in annoyance. "Really, Edgiva! He was there for a moment only! When he found I could speak French, he told me his name and not to be afraid. I asked him where the Bastard's army was going and he said he didn't know. I think he told the truth. . . ."

She stared out over the October haze hanging over the great weald, as the Norman's handsome visage appeared before her mind's eye. God damn his impudence! she swore, remembering the dawn, when she had awakened, languorous and content, dreaming of strong arms around her and a warm, passionate mouth on hers. The last vestiges of sleep had vanished, however, when she realized the eyes that teased her in sleep were brown, not the blue of Edwin's, and the voice that caressed her name spoke in Norman French. . . .

She deliberately shifted her thoughts to worries nearer at hand. Elfgift had become much quieter. Lianne had awoken more than once in the night to hear her sister stifling her sobs. When it was light, however, the younger girl made little mention of their loss; instead she channeled her sorrow into a great tenderness for Lianne, as if suddenly their ages were reversed.

Robert, too, was a cause for concern. Always thin, he had been possessed of a usual haleness that made the chill he had caught the night of their flight difficult to credit. But what began as a thin hacking cough and congestion had worsened steadily, and he now lay in the infirmary, where the Sister Infirmaress clucked over his flushed cheeks.

Travelers passing the abbey in the first two weeks in October were welcomed to the hall and pumped for any news. Where was the King? Was William the Bastard still holed up at Hastings? Couriers were riding to all points south, west, and east, they said, attempting to gather up any remaining men fit to fight. A monk had been sent to the Normans by Harold Godwinesson. He had met a man who claimed to be William's seneschal, Fitz-Osborn, but when the monk refused to speak to any but Duke William, the man finally admitted he was the duke.

William became angry when the monk urged him to return to Normandy. Harold's message, he had snapped, was not that of a wise man. After repeating the justice of his claim, he reminded the monk that the Norman invaders were prevented by the weather from leaving anyway.

The duke had sent his ambassador-monk also. Huon Magrot had been none too diplomatic to Harold, not even referring to him as "king." Harold's younger brother, Gyrth, had had to forcibly restrain the king from doing violence to the insolent monk. This meeting had taken place in London, after Harold had force-marched the fyrd from York in a little over a week.

Harold, the passing refugees told the convent, had been urged by his family to stay in London to guard it while Gyrth led the fyrd; this would prevent the king from perjuring his oath by resisting the Bastard, and he could create a wasteland around the city, should his brother fail, which would give the Normans no sustenance. The Godwines were not able to dissuade Harold from the fight. The "Golden Warrior" was quoted as being in haste to travel south to Sussex "before William could flee." The famous Godwine spirit, the travelers said with grins!

On October the twelfth a lathered horse bearing Orm cantered wearily up to the convent.

Orm seemed to have matured years in the fortnight he'd been gone, but Lianne and Elfgift were given scant time to appreciate this fact as he gave them grim news: "Harold marches for Senlac this day, Lianne. He will have just left Waltham, where he has been seeking heavenly blessing at the Minster of Holy Cross, his own foundation, but the fyrd leaves Southwark today and he will rejoin it on the way. There will almost certainly be a battle near here."

By this time, the convent was packed full of English refugees, but the convent had received several generous gifts from Thegn Rolf over the years and so the nuns found a cell with an empty pallet for the exhausted boy.

As Lianne drifted off to sleep on the lumpy straw-filled pallet in her own cell, she recalled what Orm had told her of his arrival in York: "Harold, his brothers, and some of the fyrd were feasting in a hall at York when I arrived. Bishop Aldred was there. They had been celebrating a victory at Stamford Bridge for days. But when I told my lord the king of William's arrival, he looked so sad. He clenched his fist and struck the table, like this—" he demonstrated—"and spoke so that many heard him: 'It might have been better,' he said, 'to have lost all that Tostig commanded so that I could have been at Pevensey and drowned Normans as they came ashore.' But then he looked so resigned, Lianne. He seemed to age before us. 'But it pleased the Heavenly King, I could not be everywhere at once.'"

"And . . . Edwin? Did you see him?"

"Of course. He sends his love, sister.

He promises to soon be home, and make you his bride in truth!"

Lianne could not respond to his gentle teasing as she realized she had believed that promise just two weeks before, after Stamford Bridge, but now he faced another, more deadly army, one that was fresh and more than ready to face the depleted English forces that had marched some two hundred miles from the north and must march sixty more to reach Senlac. Suddenly she could not picture her husband's face. A disturbing thought.

When Lianne awoke the next day, a nun handed her a hastily scribbled message from Orm.

"To Lianne and Elfgift, Greetings: I have gone to rejoin the fyrd. Do not try to stop me, as Harold needs every man. Stay in sanctuary, as Edwin wishes. He and I will return there once the Normans are beaten. God is on our side. Sisters, I love you—Orm."

Ten

Elfgift was naturally upset at the news of Orm's action, but was too busy caring for the very ill tutor to do more than sigh when Lianne came to her with the news. Robert's fever was becoming more stubborn despite the best febrifuges Sister Infirmaress could brew, and Elfgift had been sponging his hot, dry limbs since Prime without the desired sweat that would signal improvement. She looked extremely tired and swayed when she arose. Lianne immediately shooed her off to seek her pallet, and sat down to assume the nursing of her erstwhile teacher.

Robert's mind wandered, and he seemed to think he was back in his native Rouen. But the thought appeared to give him little comfort. "Nay, Father! I swear I never touched the daughter of *mon seigneur!* I cannot stay . . . he will put out my eyes . . . cut off my hand . . ."

It was while she struggled to spoon a little broth past the Norman's cracked, dry lips that the idea came to her, but she had to wait until Edgiva grudgingly relieved her at eventide before she could put her plan into effect. Edwin's nearness, and the thought of the battle looming ahead, haunted her. She must see him, touch him. . . . Perhaps it would keep that other foreign image away.

She mentioned nothing to Elfgift and Edgiva, leaving them a parchment message as Orm had done.

Lianne saddled her horse in the quiet convent barn, listening to the night noises: a scurrying mouse, the squeak of an unlucky rodent caught by a silent-winged owl, the chomping of horses as they snatched wisps of hay from their mangers.

Lianne made her way through the scattered gorse and broom on Caldbec Hill and was challenged by sentries. She told them whom she wished to see, looking over their shoulders at the figures by the flaring campfires. The men were singing war songs that sounded more Danish than English as they sloshed horn mugs of ale.

It was Orm, not Edwin, who found her in the dark as she made her way past the tents, some lit from within by lanterns. "I told you not to come. But you're here, so I'll take you to Edwin."

"I would have forbade you to leave sanctuary too, if you had asked, Orm," she returned the reproof gently.

She found him lolling on some skins in his tent, a horn cup half-full of ale at his elbow. A fellow housecarle who had been drinking with him hastily arose and staggered out of the tent, excusing himself in a slurred Northumbrian accent. Edwin's face was flushed. His eyes looked bloodshot, wild.

"Whooosh this? Some t-t-trollop?" His speech was nigh-incomprehensible. A wave of stale alcohol struck her. Unconsciously she wrinkled her nose in distaste. He was drunk! Loud laughter in a nearby tent confirmed that he was not the only housecarle in that condition.

"Oh . . . it'sssssh no tr-trollop. Ish my wife, Lianne. You've come . . . t'be wif me on the eve of battle. How nishe." He got uncertainly to his feet and pulled her to him. An overwhelming reek of sweat, ale, and fear enveloped him.

"Edwin. . . my lord, my love . . ."

He kissed her sloppily, wetly. "Come t'make my last hours happy," he went on, in the lugubrious manner of some drunkards. "You want to make shhure there's somethin' left o' me—even if it's only a seed planted in your belly. . . . Well, I'll oblige you, wife . . ."

"Edwin—" she protested weakly.

"You're going to *beat* the Normans tomorrow! The English will drive them back into the Channel! There will be plenty of time for us!" She struggled as he reached crudely up under her kirtle. "I want you too, my dearest lord. But not like this—" He was laying her back against the pelts, heedless of her pleas. The ale cup spilled, its golden fluid wet and sticky against her shoulder.

He buried his face greedily against her straining, heaving breasts and experimentally bit one through the woolen stuff of her gown. She cried out in pain, but the housecarle seemed not to hear, only threw a heavy thigh across her diagonally to still her thrashing legs. Rape seemed a skill at which he was very adept—how many times had he stilled a maid's protests so? She made herself cease struggling; hoping he would be gentle with her lack of resistance, but her mind still cried out in agony. Would he have taken me thus after our wedding? Does it all come to force, with a man?

Suddenly she noticed he had stopped his pawing and grunting. His breathing came in regular stertorous waves. His weight lay fully on her, nearly stopping her breath. Edwin Wulfsson had passed out.

A tear slid down Lianne's cheek as she wiggled cautiously out from under the sleeping housecarle. She left him prone on his animal skins, snoring, after covering him with his cloak and kissing his flushed cheek. "Good-bye, Edwin."

Orm had been guarding Lianne's horse and had not expected her to return for some time, but as he saw her trudging dispiritedly over to him, he noted her stricken look, the wisps of golden hair pulled loose from her plait, the blood at the corner of her lips. He wisely said nothing of them.

At a campfire a few yards away, a couple of men-at-arms watched her passage curiously, then went back to their rousing drinking song. "Was Häel! Drink Häel!"

"Surely it is not good for all Harold's army to be in their cups!"

"You worry like a woman, Lianne. Many of these are little more than Danish Vikings, barely Christian. They would not pass this eve bewailing their sins!"

She tried again. "Orm, I wish you would come back with me. You're over-young to be in a man's battle."

"Edwin has found me a byrnie and a shield—he says 'twas worn at Stamford Bridge!" he told her proudly. "Don't worry, sister, there are lads in the fyrd of my years, even younger. I'm too old to go creeping back to sanctuary like a babe! But stay you there until we come." He tried to look stern and elder-brother.

"God's blessing on the morrow, Orm," she said, drinking in his boyish features.

"It *is* the morrow, Lianne, see?" To the east the first faint difference between dark and dawn appeared. An owl hooted sleepily from a nearby tree. "Get you gone."

On Telham Hill less than a mile away, the Norman camp was awake, though in a decidedly more sober fashion. Confessionals were set up in several tents, and all William's men went to be shriven. To die violently, suddenly, in battle with not so much as a moment to utter an *Ave* was a fearful thing.

"Bless me, Father, for I have sinned. It has been, ah, a month since my last confession," muttered Guy de Bayeux above his clasped hands, then pulled the makeshift curtain aside so that he could see Père Matthieu. "Ah, friend, I have no more to confess than any other soldier in William's army, possibly less than some. Killing, destruction, looting, Holy Mother, I hate what seems to be necessary to get William his throne. How can this be a blessed venture?" He saw in his mind the burning buildings, the blood, the terror-filled Saxon eyes, and the prospect of more such tomorrow.

"Pope Alexander has given his blessing," Matthieu pronounced, as if there need be no further debate. "Harold is forsworn, and therefore damned to hell. William was Edward's choice to be king. We will give the English the blessings of moral leadership, and a Church more disciplined and closer to Holy Rome—"

"Yes, yes, I know." Guy waved an

impatient hand. "But surely the English on Caldbec Hill are just as certain that God will give *them* the victory tomorrow. Ah, friend, I *do* have sins to confess after all." The baron's eyes were troubled in their brown depths. "I hate a Saxon I've never met, and wish his death tomorrow."

"Who? Harold Godwinesson? Surely all William's army wishes that," Père Matthieu's voice soothed. "His brothers —Gyrth, or Leofwine?"

"Nay, good brother. Just a faceless Englishman, one of Harold's household troops. I believe they are called 'house-carles.' I covet his wife."

"Be careful, Guy. Remember David and Bathsheba. Do not be caught up in such a net. You have a dutiful Norman *demoiselle* at home, praying daily for your safety."

Guy snorted, unable to imagine the em-minently practical Mabile wearing out her knees on his behalf. "What heaven dictates, will be," would more likely be her approach.

At dawn Bishop Odo sang a quick Mass for the invading army, then all dispersed to arm. No activity could be seen as the sun's first rays struck Caldbec Hill. It was Saturday, the fourteenth of October, 1066, the Feast of St. Calixtus.

Gilbert, Guy's squire, assisted him to don his armor in the silver-gray light. He first held up a bowl of icy water, and Guy dashed the last vestiges of sleep from his eyes. He had the numb feeling one has after sleeping very little. Each of his actions seemed unreal, dreamlike, the quilted undertunic and braies insubstantial. The muscles of his back rippled as he moved to accept the garments from his squire and bent his dark head to receive the metallic coldness of the mail shirt that reached to his knees. As he was shaving, he started gingerly as Pere Matthieu bustled into the tent, sandals flapping.

"The duke put on his armor backwards!" he announced dramatically.

"And what do you suppose that means?" queried Guy tolerantly, knowing the rotund cleric's respect for omens.

"There were those who felt it boded ill," the monk said portentously. "But I, and His Grace, thought them silly, and said so. After all, nothing will go ill. William has promised to build a monastery on the site where the Usurper now camps."

"Indeed. Very commendable." Guy put the iron helmet on his head, adjusting the nasal into place. He buckled on the mighty broadsword with its golden unicorn at the hilt.

"And Brother William Faber asked that it be dedicated to St. Martin, apostle to the Gauls."

"A fitting choice."

Père Matthieu followed as Guy strode

out of the tent and over to where Nuage pawed the ground. "Well, it sounds as if we'd better go win the duke his hill." Guy mounted while his squire steadied the restless charger. He handed up the shield and lance, and checked the strap that held the mace secure by the cantle, ready to his master's right hand. All his lord's weapons were shining after many hours of patient polishing. They would come back with encrusted dried blood, and with bits of gray-pink matter clinging tenaciously to the lethal spikes of the mace, Gilbert had no doubt.

"Pray for me, Father. And for our duke."

"You have my prayers always." The chubby little priest sketched the sign of the cross at horse and rider, at which Nuage snorted and flicked his tail skeptically.

Eleven

Lianne was greeted by a grim Edgiva, who had passed the night in Robert's cell—"Where *you* should have been, Lianne, rather than chasing my brother like some camp follower."

"Your brother is going into battle this morn, Edgiva. By dusk who knows what might have happened?" I will not let her see me weep, I will not! "What of Robert, then? Is he worse?"

"He is failing, Lianne," Elfgift said, joining the pair, pushing a lock of fair hair away from her eyes tiredly. "I just left the priest with him. He will not last till nightfall, the priest thinks."

As a battle was beginning a few miles away that was to change the destiny of

Europe, the three women sat around Robert's pallet, murmuring prayers for the dying. Robert's breath rattled moistly in his chest, his skin getting hotter and drier as the morning wore on. He could not be aroused now, although earlier he had stirred long enough to ask for Lianne and take a few sips of water. Seeing her there, he seemed content. Lianne was glad he did not ask about Orm.

Echoes of the nuns' plainsong reached them as the convent marked the day as any other by their chanted offices. The last sweet notes of Sext were being sung as Robert took a deep last breath and died.

Nuage danced impatiently in front of the ridge of Senlac as some eight thousand men were divided into three sections: right flank, the French and Flemish under FitzOsborn; left flank, the Bretons, Poitevins, and those of Maine, under Alan the Red; and in the center, the Normans. The blue and white papal banner fluttered defiantly in the breeze, as if it mocked the banners on the opposite hill, the red and white dragon of Wessex and Harold's personal ensign, the Fighting Man. Half of the invading army were men-at-arms, in mail shirts and helmets like the cavalry, and carried spears and swords. Another thousand were archers, standing in the forefront, wearing lighter jerkins and caps. They jeered at their English counterparts standing not too distantly. The high tenor voice of Ivon Taillefer, Norman bard-turned-knight, filled the air on Telham as he sang the *chansons de Roland* to inspire the men.

Guy could see the English, packed close around the "Fighting Man" standard.

"*Régardez*, Guy," Robert d'Eu called, pointing scornfully at the enemy formation. "They do not even use horses! Instead, they pack in like little fishes in a school and hope to turn aside mounted men!"

"They form the shield wall," the young baron answered, shielding his eyes from the bright October sun. "In such close formation, even little fish may have teeth to rend us. In fact, they have the advantage of us."

"You mean the lay of the land." The Normans would have an uphill battle to reach Harold.

"That, of course. Also, it is their land they fight for."

Duke William, sitting his curvetting white stallion (a gift of the king of Aragon), took this moment to speak to his men. "Make no mistake. This is a battle to the death. It is either Harold or I who shall still stand when this battle is over, but be certain also that it is either you, or—" he pointed up the ridge—"or these. They will not offer you captivity if you fail. Only dishonor—and death."

Across the valley, Guy could see a tall

figure speaking also among the oxhide kite-shaped shields.

A collective chuckle broke out among the Norman troops, and Guy looked around to see Ivon Taillefer doing tricks with his lance, throwing it into the air, catching it with his hand. Suddenly, though, he glanced back at William, who smiled and raised his hand in salute.

Ivon spurred his horse, alone, straight at the English ranks. There was a collective gasp from the Normans as they watched him spear several surprised Englishmen with his lance until finally, inevitably, he went down under the flashing, deadly axes.

The battle commenced then. The Norman archers shot their arrows up the hill, but with few casualties resulting. William then ordered his footmen to advance. Guy felt sick at heart as he watched, held back with the other mounted lords, the men-at-arms cut down like so much mown wheat. A cry undulated down the ridge from hundreds of English throats screaming their war cry: "Out! Out!"

Nuage needed no urging at all when the cavalry was at last allowed to charge up the deadly hill. Guy found himself in a nightmarish world of screams, flashing steel, and the stench of blood. His warhorse caught the scent too, and maddened, trampled a Saxon axeman who was looking to the side of the mighty beast. The luckless man glanced up just in time to see the wild eyes and flaring nostrils of the rearing stallion as his hooves descended onto his skull. A man running toward Duke William, spear raised, crying, "Holy Cross!" likewise perished under de Bayeux's lethal sword.

Guy found himself shouting the Norman war cry, *"Dex aie!"* ("God aid"), though he could hardly hear it in the tumult.

Out of the corner of his eye, Guy saw some Bretons on the left *disappearing* into the grass. Suddenly the whole Norman force was fleeing madly down the hill, pursued by rumors of William's death. As they swept past, Guy could see that the grass and reeds concealed a ravine and could hear screams as the luckless ones who had fallen into the trap were slaughtered. He found he was much too occupied with the headlong flight down the hill, expecting at any moment to receive an axe's deadly bite from the rear, to care long about the Bretons.

At the base of the hill, however, William and his half-brother, Odo the bishop, forced the retreating men back, the duke shouting, "Look at me, all of you, I still live, and with God's help will conquer! What folly has driven you to flight? Turn around!" And as they obeyed, they saw a sight to gladden Norman hearts: the less disciplined shire-levies had broken formation and chased them down Senlac ridge, despite the cries of their captains to maintain the shield wall. Guy and his fellow horsemen needed no encouragement to turn and butcher them.

It was noon. Both armies seemed to pause for a few moments and consider. William had been unhorsed twice, but was mounted again. Gyrth and Leofwine Godwinesson were rumored slain. But the advantage still lay with the English; the shield wall from which Harold commanded was still impenetrable. Guy found himself wondering if a certain housecarle still lived and waited on the hill to kill or be killed. He felt the stinging of a gash on his cheek, received from the grazing flight of an English arrow. He supposed he would carry the mark to his grave, assuming he survived the afternoon.

Mid-afternoon. The ground was sticky with viscous clots of blood. The Normans had feigned retreat again, and, incredibly, the English fyrd could still be lured to chase them, to their own destruction. Once they left the hill they did not regain it. The shield wall around the fluttering standard had gaps now; and when William commanded that his archers shoot straight into the air, their arrows landed among the housecarles like so many hissing serpents.

During this sibilant, murderous rain, Guy heard a wail of dismay at the summit and saw the tall figure pulling off his helmet with frenzied agonized movements. A cry of sheer joy burst from those Normans who could see the Usurper with an arrow through one eye! Harold, however, broke the shaft in half, and, scarlet streaming from his eye, fought unsteadily on.

A score of knights, some Normans, some mercenaries from Ponthieu and Boulogne, swore to capture the "Fighting Man" standard. Given an order to stay at his lord's side, Guy reluctantly remained with the duke and watched, frustrated, as the group made its difficult way up the ridge, maces swinging, shields ringing with deflected blows. In the deepening twilight, the Normans saw all but four die before they reached the wounded king. These four, however, gained the standard, and Harold died beneath their swords, hacked and pierced long after he was dead.

The light was failing. The fyrd was separated now into sections, but they fought on desperately as news of Harold's death spread. Guy, his mind drenched with the fiery rage of battle, was everywhere, his sword reaping a bloody harvest. He had ceased to think of the Saxons as having an individuality— they were an entity to be slaughtered entirely. He was merely a machine rendering death.

There was another ravine, Oakwood Gyll, just north of Caldbec Hill, and many of the Normans chased fleeing Englishmen there. Bishop Odo, hearing that his men were being murdered in this trap, angrily spurred there, and Guy with him. Both would have perished there, had not Nuage sensed the perilous ground and reared, refusing to advance. Odo's mount, however, could not stop so precipitous a flight and plunged headlong down, but Odo jumped off just in time. He refused Guy's offer to give up Nuage. Instead, the warrior-bishop jumped on behind.

"It is an evil ditch," Odo shouted in Guy's ear (and the place was indeed known later as "Mal Voisin"). "I owe you a favor, Baron Guy."

Darkness was fast advancing over the battlefield. As more Normans chased the fleeing fyrdman, those English who could still run melted into the sheltering fastness of the weald, where the Normans dared not follow.

An unholy stillness cloaked the ridge, broken here and there by the moans of the wounded, curses and prayers often ending suddenly as the fallen English were found and dispatched. Guy strode alongside Duke William up the hill where Harold's standard had flown so bravely.

"Where is he?" rasped the duke hoarsely, removing his helm. No one had to ask of whom he spoke.

"None has found him, sire," Guy answered. They reached the top and found the trampled banner.

"Here. I'll give thanks on this spot, where the Usurper stood." He knelt and thanked God briefly; then, rising, decided, "We will feast here this night."

Walter Giffard, standing at his other side, spoke cautiously. "Many of these, Your Grace—" indicating the dead English, who lay in various contorted poses of death among the yellow gorse— "may not be dead, just feigning in order to assassinate you. Let us celebrate in safety, on Telham Hill."

"God's Blood, Giffard! I have said we shall celebrate here!"

Guy de Bayeux, more weary and sore than he had ever been, fell asleep a short time later, over his trencher at the victory feast.

Twelve

O rm had waited for full darkness, then stumbled wearily to the abbey's entrance and rang the night bell. Then he collapsed.

"Another one, Sister Portress?"

"Yes," spoke a voice above the youth's head. "Sister Infirmaress, he will need bandages for his head. And there are many cuts and bruises—oh, yes, and a laceration on his leg, a deep one. It's a mercy he didn't bleed to death of that one."

It was dawn before he woke sufficiently to speak to his sister, each word punctuated by his pounding, pulsing headache. Through his feverish haze Lianne's pale visage swam blurrily before him, blue eyes too large for her face.

"Edwin . . . I don't know if he lives, Lianne . . . Just don't know. We . . . were separated in the afternoon. I chased after the Normans, with the fyrdmen. Foolish . . . they were only pretending . . . retreat. I hope Edwin stayed . . . may have lived then. I heard Harold . . . died." Some tears trickled down his cheeks, and suddenly the soldier was but a boy again. "Must find him, Lianne. P'raps . . . wounded . . . lying on the ridge . . . I'll go with you."

"And offer yourself again to the Norman butchers? Even if you were able, it would be death if they saw you," Lianne pronounced firmly. "I shall go." Word had reached the abbey that the enemy was allowing women to seek their dead.

Edgiva immediately demanded to go, and Elfgift rose also, uncertainly.

"Both of you, stay here. You must guard Orm should those demons come here—hide him if necessary. I must find my lord."

It was mid-morning, and the Normans, searching the field in twos and threes, had still not found Harold's body. Many of the corpses were so mauled and disfigured it was doubtful their own mothers would have known them.

Guy de Bayeux glanced downward. By his boot a bright object had caught the sun, and his attention. Reaching down to pick it up, his sore muscles screaming, he found himself in possession of a curious dagger. In the hilt, set in amber, was the head of a stag beetle. Between the hilt and the blade was a row of pearls. Absently he stuck it into his sword belt and walked on.

There were women in the field also—singly, in huddled pairs or groups—local women come to find their dead, if they could. The clear Sunday morning was punctuated occasionally with cries of grief as someone identified a son, a father, a brother, a spouse . . .

Guy's brain was full of rage, but here was nothing to vent it on. The slain would not fight back, or even groan if he kicked their faces, paralyzed in grim attitudes of surprise, pain, or fear. There was no satisfaction in that.

His squire had awakened him with the news that Père Matthieu, who had been out long after midnight administering the Sacrament to dying Norman and foe alike, had come upon one Saxon who beckoned to him to lean down and listen to his last confession. A Norman foot-soldier, looting English corpses nearby, saw it happen but was too far away to prevent the Saxon's treacherous thrust into the priest's chest with the hidden blade. Père Matthieu had died almost instantly. The soldier, of course, had slit the Englishman's throat for his trouble.

To kill a priest! Guy's thoughts were a rending, tearing combination of hatred, grief, and sorrow. He had some friends among William's nobles, but none with whom he had shared the same quality of relationship. With Matthieu he had not felt the need to strike a brave pose, to pretend anything. The priest wold have known the secrets of Guy's soul even had he not been his confessor. Many of the other lords confessed to Bishop Odo, preferring the negligible penances imposed by one who was more warrior than holy man. For such a one as Matthieu to die so, after the day was won! If he had had any thought before dying, Guy mused, he probably protested at leaving the field before all the English, the Devil take them, were shriven!

A few feet away from Guy, a woman knelt to examine a body, then rose with a relieved sigh. Apparently it was not whom she sought. She turned, and the hood fell back from her blonde head. Guy saw that it was Lianne.

For a moment, neither broke the silence. He eyed her, noting the faint purplish shadows under her eyes, which were reddened from tears. Under her cloak he could see she wore a bliaut of gray wool.

She gave him back stare for stare, daring him to question her presence there. He was dressed in mail shirt and coif, but carried his helmet. His eyes seemed implacable, opaque, his lips grimly set. A jagged cut ran the length of his right cheek.

"Have you . . . found whom you seek?"

he asked at last, unnecessarily.

The blue eyes welled up with tears. "No," she whispered. "He may live, for all I know." Then, idiotically, "Your face . . . it is cut . . ."

"I am alive." He shrugged. His eyes studied her. "I will help you search."

"No, you need not—"

"It will be safer if I do, you know." Indeed, she had been accosted with soldiers' lewd, suggestive remarks twice already, and she started to accept his offer, when her gaze chanced to light on the dagger stuck carelessly into the belt at his hip.

"Liar! Murderer!" She launched herself at him, fingers curved to claw him. He caught her and spun her around, pinioning her arms, so she could only struggle uselessly, her back against his chest.

"What ails you, wench?" he grunted, holding her with some difficulty. "In the blink of an eye you are a madwoman! My aid was offered in good faith."

"Yes, whoreson! *Knowing* my Edwin is dead! 'Tis his dagger you sport at your side! *You* murdered him, and took the weapon I gave him! Where is he, son of a misbegotten Norman bitch? Where did you leave his body?" Lianne could feel her rising hysteria but was powerless to stop it.

He spun her around and slapped her. All the pent-up rage and bloodlust at the priest's senseless death put more force into the blow than he intended, and he knocked her to the ground.

She lay back on her hands, eyes enormous, and he cursed himself and her to see the livid mark on her face. She got up and ran a few yards, and then stopped with a choked cry, kneeling beside a dead Englishman.

"Edwin!" the scream came rolling out of her throat. He had bled to death from a thigh wound that had nearly severed his leg at the hip. It had not been very mercifully quick. His glazed, vacant eyes accused her.

Guy stood rooted where she had run from him, then strode over to her. She rose up fighting again, tears blinding her eyes so that she could not strike accurately. He caught at her wrists and she fell to her knees, and he followed. His harsh eyes were inches from hers.

"Woman!" he shouted over her keening wail. "I killed no one lying wounded on this field, after the battle. During it, who knows? No one had a face—they were just the enemy, who would kill me were I not the quicker! I knew not your husband's visage—how could I know if I had killed him? But this dagger—I swear, Lianne de Fairlight, I found it on the ground this morning."

He did not know if she heard him. Her voice had not ceased to hurl imprecations at him. His eyes were full of her anguish, but she did not see.

"Where do you bide?" he asked her,

and when she did not speak, shook her till her teeth rattled. "Tell me!"

"The abbey at Netherfield! It is sanctuary—you cannot come there!"

"It is well you are in a safe place. Stay there. I will come for you when the land is safe. See that you do not take the veil. I remind you, you are mine."

She gasped at his effrontery. "Demon from hell! Devil's spawn! I would not become a nun, simply to be free to revenge Edwin! I'll kill you, Norman!" she spat, her blazing eyes flashing hatred.

"You will need a weapon," he said shortly, and handed her the dagger, daring her to try. Blue eyes locked with brown, then looked away, and Guy de Bayeux stalked away, leaving her alone with the dead.

She looked about her when the anger had cleared her head somewhat, and wondered how she would get Edwin's body to safety. She could not just leave it for the flies and buzzards! Ah, God, to be already thinking of his *body*, once so immense and strong, as an "it," something limp and cold, that would decay! That would be the fate of many, she knew, to have no grave to mark with flowers and tears, to have no known spot for bereaved kin to visit.

Lianne trudged back to the thicket at the edge of the field where she had left Storm. Perhaps the mare could carry the body, if Lianne could enlist the help of some of the women on the field to hoist the grievous burden onto the horse's back. Each step took a major effort of her will to accomplish, so leaden did her entire body feel.

Storm was gone.

Lianne looked around, expecting to find the horse, trailing a broken branch in its reins, grazing a few yards off. She called her, softly at first, not wanting to attract attention to herself, then louder, desperately, the hysteria threatening to seize her again.

"Are you looking for a black palfrey, Lady?" a priest called from a few yards away.

"Yes, Father!" She looked up eagerly, joyfully, relief flooding in.

"Your horse was taken. I saw a wounded Saxon steal out of the bushes a few minutes ago and mount the beast. He rode that way—" he indicated a westerly direction.

Stolen.

With a deep sigh, she pulled up her hood with shaking hands and began the trip back to the abbey on foot.

Orm greeted her when she returned to the abbey, and taking in her dusty, tear-stained face, wordlessly embraced her. He had not thought she would find Edwin living.

"He's dead, brother." Her voice was flat, hard. "All I have of him is this dagger. And I know which Norman devil murdered him."

"You know his slayer's name?"

"Aye. And I'll kill him." Her tone discouraged any questions. She told him also about the theft of the horse, the only one they had had left from home, since Orm's horse had been left at Caldbec Hill before the battle.

"Lianne, did you see Elfgift and Edgiva on the way? They came to join you, at Edgiva's insistence—she could not wait any longer to know, she said."

"How foolish, after I directed them to remain," she said in weary exasperation. "It will not bring him back." Then apprehension dawned. "Elfgift is out there with her? With no one else? Orm, it is dangerous there! The soldiers think the women are fair prey! I was left alone, but she and that fool Edgiva may not be! We must find them!"

Orm and Lianne, accompanied by Mold, searched until the light faded, then went back out armed with torches. Orm carried the sword he had brought from Senlac, Lianne the dagger in her girdle. The boy hobbled painfully, the leg wound a fiery pain, but would not hear of staying behind, even at the risk of reopening the wound.

They finally found them about a mile from the abbey, beside a little stream marked by several oak saplings. With the torches raised, Lianne could see her younger sister, sitting with toes dangling loosely in the water, hands limp in her lap, eyes unseeing, humming tunelessly. Orm spotted Edgiva in the same moment, lying spread-eagled, head resting at an unnatural angle on a rock. She was dead, but it was apparent from her position and the bloody, torn garments that she had been violated many times before death came as a friend.

Lianne, moaning her sister's name, rushed over to her. The younger girl allowed herself to be helped to her feet; as she moved to stand, Lianne saw the dried, streaked blood on the dirty kirtle, the leaves clinging to the back of her head. The experience had caused the younger girl to lose her reason rather than her life.

She seemed totally unaware of her shocked, grieving brother and sister, gazing straight ahead as if blind, although she blinked when Orm passed his hand close to her dilated pupils. She walked willingly enough with them, but as if in a dream, and stumbled if they did not lead her away from protruding rocks and branches. In spite of their anguished entreaties she seemed unable to talk.

"The bastards," groaned Orm. "They shall pay. I, Orm Rolfsson, swear it."

Thirteen

"What will you do with her, Aunt? Make her one of the community, a nun?" Lianne addressed her mother's sister in the abbess's office. She spoke of Elfgift, who sat on a bench in the room, a waxen doll, eyes still void of intelligence. In the two days that had followed the battle, Lianne and the nuns had bathed Elfgift's wounds—would that they could bathe the wounded soul!—had dressed her and fed her as they would a small child. Never had the girl responded to their gentle touch with the least indication that she knew of their presence. She stayed where they left her, usually in the same position in which they had left her. She did not leave her pallet in the morning until Lianne came to take her to the privy, and if left too long, would soil herself.

"Yes, if she comes to herself again, and wishes it. I cannot make a bride of Christ of a walking puppet, my child! But what of you? You cannot return home. This conqueror will reassign all land held by Englishmen to his own, I doubt not. Nor would it be safe for you, a woman alone. Why not seek a life in the convent yourself, my dear niece?" the woman offered, concern in her voice.

"You're very kind, Reverend Aunt, but I am not alone. There is Orm to think of. He cannot stay here forever, and I fear he would not make a good monk." She smiled ruefully, thinking of her brother's aversion to scholarship.

"But what will you do?" The abbess raised her large, work-worn hands.

"I don't know. But there are those— there *must* be—that will not accept foreign rule meekly. We will find them, and join them. The Normans will pay for Edwin. And Edgive, Elfgift, my father, Robert. . . . They have much to pay for. . . . And one Norman in particular . . ." The abbess crossed herself to see her niece's narrowed eyes, hear the naked hatred. "There is no *weregild* sufficient for him to pay. I shall require his life."

Orm and Lianne, accompanied by Mold, who also had no desire for a convent life, left the abbey the following day, despite continued protestations by the sisters that they were welcome to stay indefinitely and dire prophecies of what should befall them at Norman hands. They looked back only once, to see Mother Mary Edburga's hand lifted in farewell, the other arm draped protectively around Elfgift, who only stared at the ground.

Ahead lay the dark green fastness of the Andreadsweald, which lay like a protective blanket between the ravaged Sussex countryside and London. The two had planned to go to the great port city, to seek safety behind its walls and perhaps meet others there who hated the Norman invaders. Their future seemed vague and insubstantial; perhaps London would give them a sense of direction and a new purpose.

That the Normans were between Hastings and Senlac, they knew; they surmised correctly that the great forest with its potential for ambush would seem inimical to the invaders, so they felt relatively safe as they hiked down the sundappled paths and left the open, rolling countryside behind.

Each had packed as much clothing as they could carry easily in a leather bag which also held a horn cup for drinking. Lianne mourned the loss of Storm, both as a friend and for the additional possessions the palfrey could have carried.

"Mayhap it is better that we travel so lightly," Mold said practically, as they passed through a darkened glade. "You never know when we might have to hide from the cursed foreigners, and with a horse it would be harder. And there are many fleeing them also that would covet your horse, and being English does not necessarily make them saintly. There will probably be more outlawry than ever, while things are so uncertain, my lady."

"Aye, but the devil seize whoever stole her. . . ."

A great shape suddenly appeared to fall from the sky in front of Lianne, and she gasped, drawing back from the gleaming spear that was pointed at her. She gave a low cry, seeing that they were surrounded on all sides by armed men.

"What have we here?" queried the apparent leader, a tawny-haired man of medium height, his lance still trained on Lianne, but with a grin stealing over his stern features. To the trio's relief, he spoke in a broad Wessex accent, and they saw that all of them appeared likewise to be English, most dressed in worn leather jerkins and braies, many with bandaged wounds.

Lianne stiffened as the leader lowered his spear and advanced on her, cupping her chin with a roughened hand and eying her speculatively.

Orm leveled his own spear and growled, "Take your filthy hands off her, ceorl!" His voice was full of the assuredness of the thegn toward the lower classes, as if Senlac had never happened. Just as quickly, he found himself disarmed, with his fists held at his sides, by another Saxon who laughed, "Hark at the whelp! As royal as poor Harold, God rest 'im!"

"We're loyal English too," Mold piped up. "My lady lost her husband at Senlac. Her grief is still new. You dare not dishonor a widow of the battlefield. Edwin Wulfsson was one of King Harold's housecarles!"

"I meant no harm," spoke the man, releasing Lianne. "Your pardon, Lady." He smiled at Lianne, who continued to regard him warily, although the merry twinkle in his blue eyes invited response. "I am Tofig, late of King Harold's fyrd, as are all of these men. Where are ye bound?"

"As to that, we are not certain. We thought perhaps London . . . we would find others like ourselves, who want to fight the Normans." Lianne found her voice surprisingly strong, now that her heart had left her throat.

"Folk from the south are pouring into London, I hear," Tofig answered. "Soon the walls will not hold them all. They'll be like rats in a trap for these Norman butchers. Why, a bridge into the city broke, there were so many refugees crowding onto it, and some drowned, pour souls. You don't want to go to London! Why not stay with us? There are more of us, back at the camp—a few more women, too, 'Your Ladyship,' " he bowed mockingly to Lianne, while her brother scowled, "and we plan to slit some Norman throats, and make the soil of England red with their blood! Are ye with us?"

"Aye. We'll join you," Lianne spoke for all of them. "I am Lianne of Fairlight and this is Orm, my brother, and Mold, who has been a servant in my hall, but now we are alike bereft of home and its comforts. While the Normans rule, there are no more thegns and ceorls and thralls. We are all just—English."

"Well said, Lianne!" Tofig bowed and kissed her hand, as graceful as any earl. "Welcome. We can well use another pretty face—two pretty faces—" he generously included Mold, who dimpled and beamed—"and capable hands around the cookfires, as well as another strong arm to slay the Normans!" He indicated Orm lastly, and paused to assess the youth.

"I'll help with the womanly chores, naturally," interrupted Lianne. "But my desire to kill the Normans is as strong as any man's."

"Listen to 'er!" guffawed another of Tofig's band admiringly. "Ye'd better look to yer laurels, Tofig! This one sounds a bloodthirsty beserker!"

The Saxon leader just looked at her, a long, measuring, considering look. "We'll see, lass."

Fourteen

William's forces stayed near the battlesite for nearly a week, awaiting reinforcements from Normandy. Guy's time was taken up supervising the burial parties that interred the Norman dead in mass graves. The English bodies not claimed by relatives were, at William's command, left for the carrion birds and animals.

After his confrontation with Lianne, Guy, still seething with frustrated temper, had had to guard the Lady Edythe, Harold's handfast wife, while she searched for his body. No one else had been able to find it, but it was hoped that she of the "Swan Neck" with the intimate knowledge of the lover would know his corpse among so many mutilated ones. She was accompanied by two monks from Waltham, her lord's abbey.

After searching grimly for hours, she finally did find it, and accompanied it with tears streaming down her face as it was borne to William's tent. Gytha, Harold's mother, waited there and silently enfolded Edythe in her arms for a moment, then both women straightened with a pitiful attempt at dignity as William strode scowling from the tent.

"My lord, we would take the body for honorable burial," the elderly woman said. Guy admired her tone, neither servile nor insolent.

"Honorable burial?" The swarthy duke laughed mirthlessly. "Not for Harold Godwinesson, forsworn traitor!"

Guy watched, grim-mouthed, as this merciless pronouncement sent Edythe into a fresh paroxysm of hopeless weeping. Gytha watched, but if she hoped Edythe's tears would soften the Duke's implacable features, she was disappointed.

"I will give Harold's weight in gold," the old woman countered. It was a cunning offer. Conquerors with mercenary armies to pay were always in need of funds.

"Madame, I regret I must refuse your generous offer. Harold will be buried, but in a secret place. I'll not have his tomb a rallying point for rebels nor a source of 'miracles' for those who'd turn him into a martyr. He is a damned soul," he went on unrelentingly, "having denied his oath to support my claim, and it will not be sanctified ground he rests in."

He was not moved by any further pleas. It was an effort for Guy to disguise his feelings as he watched the women's shocked, despairing visages, and he at last had to look away. Could William not be generous now? He had won the battle! Giving them their lord's body would be little consolation, but by the Rood, it was better than nothing!

He was glad when later William selected him to be of the small party that took Harold's body for burial on a hill overlooking the sea at Fairlight. The duke had instructed William Malet, the noble in charge of the detail, "Set him in the ground so that the traitor lies facing the sea, where he should have been watching for me!"

Guy found his humor a bit grating and wondered how much it covered a sense of guilt, to have caused so much carnage.

In the end, they buried him in a stone cairn, like a Viking warrior, overlooking the Channel, an unmarked but respectable grave. The task finished, Malet and Guy stood silently a moment, looking out over the water, until Guy at last made the sign of the cross over Harold's resting place.

"Amen, my lord," Malet agreed. "He was an enemy, but he died in battle, defending his country and what he believed to be his right. It is not for us to judge him."

After erecting a stone "mountjoy" atop Caldbec Hill to mark their victory, William's army moved out Friday, October twentieth, traversing the Fairlight spur to the northwest.

While the Normans marched on Romney, laying waste the town to punish it for the slaughter of those Normans who had mistakenly come ashore there, Lianne was learning the fundamentals of archery under Tofig's tutelage. He insisted his small band become proficient with the longbow. "If we had used them more and with more skill at Senlac, perhaps it would have been William instead with an arrow in his eye!"

"You draw back the bow string—so—" he instructed, standing close behind her and using the lesson as an excuse to lay his face close to hers as he showed her how far back to pull.

She did not find his attentions distasteful, but neither did she respond to them, and he accepted that somewhat ruefully, but with a gentle good humor, hoping that when her grief wore off she would feel different toward him. At least, if she did not, Lianne's servant woman seemed to look on him with favor, and there was a more knowing look to Mold's eyes when she responded to his gallantries and teasing. For all that Lianne had been married, there was still such an innocence about the beautiful widow! Perhaps Mold had not that river of golden hair, and her face was not as comely, but there was an air about her that spoke she would know what to do with him, did Tofig come to her after the others slept!

"There! You have hit the target! You learn quickly, little one!"

"I used to play at archery with Orm," Lianne admitted. "But 'twas only a game. I never could bring myself to shoot down anything living, such as a bird or a hare."

"Yet now you would aim your shafts at living people."

"At Normans!" she said fiercely, as if they were a different species, less than human, her mind flying unwillingly to one hated Norman in particular.

Lianne's and Mold's acceptance by the camp's other three females had been somewhat slower. Though Lianne refused to allow any to address her as "Lady," there remained an indefinable barrier between the thegn's daughter and the others, who had been thralls in Earl Gyrth's household. Mag was handfast-wed to one of Tofig's most trusted lieutenants. Hilda was barely out of childhood, and Huldyth, a slatternly blonde, seemed to impartially share her charms with several of the men.

They thawed somewhat toward the newcomers when Mold and Lianne showed their willingness to share in the "women's work": hauling water, gathering firewood, and cooking the fowl, hares, and occasional venison the men brought in. There were always clothes to be sewn and mended, and here Lianne chiefly won her place, her bone needle and deergut stitching being so fine that the women begged her to teach them too.

Mold proved herself to be a valuable addition soon after their arrival, when one of the men's wounds had begun to fester. A lance-slashed arm had turned angry red, with a core of dirty yellow pus, but the man had concealed it as long as possible, fearing the loss of his right arm. When the swollen arm could no longer be hidden, however, and Tofig was preparing to chop off the limb to try to save the man, Mold had intervened, bringing a small pouch of herbs from her leather bag. These she made into a paste and applied in a poultice, and made the man drink an infusion of willow bark, which he admitted relieved the pain and broke his fever. By the next morning, the purulence was draining, the redness lessened, and the arm was definitely on the mend. Lianne was amused to note the admiring, grateful looks Tofig flashed at Mold.

From Romney the Norman army marched on Dover, where survivors of

Senlac were reported to be holed up in an "impregnable" fortress. Had there been a real leader remaining among the English, a second battle might have been fought there, but all the English leaders lay dead at Senlac, and the fortress surrendered to William, who promised them no harm. The town, bowing to the inevitable, had also submitted, but some Bretons on the edge of the town and away from the duke's control fired some houses anyway.

William was furious and ordered the instigators whipped. He promised to repay the burghers who had come to complain, but it did not stop him from evicting many more from houses that had escaped the torch so that he and his lords could sleep in comfort.

While at Dover a deadly enemy did inflict many casualties, however—that nemesis of an army, dysentery. Some said it was from drinking at an accursed spot called Harold's Well. Others claimed the Saxons were poisoning the water, for men were seized with a griping bloody flux and were dead in a day's time or left debilitated, weak as newborn kittens.

Guy, spared by the flux and bereft of the company of Père Matthieu, found himself spending more time with his squire, a freckled, lanky lad of seventeen.

Gilbert de Caen, son of a poor knight, felt himself to be the luckiest of Norman youths to be squire to such a lord as

Baron Guy de Bayeux. He had been promoted from page in the baron's château to being his squire only that summer before the invasion. His training had been intense, the lessons of many months by necessity telescoped into weeks of riding, swordsmanship, tilting at the quintain, and learning to care for my lord's weapons and his clothing. To Gilbert, Baron Guy was the epitome of the warrior—skillful at arms, seemingly without fear, handsome and courteous. He never cuffed the lad when he made a mistake, but was possessed of a calm patience that caused the young man to emulate Guy's every move, from the way he handled a sword to his bold stride. Guy was different from the other nobles in having had a priest as his closest comrade, but to Gilbert this had placed him the more obviously above those coarse knights who spent their time only dicing, drinking, and wenching—not that Guy was inexpert at any of these pastimes, either. Gilbert, though, with the idealism of his years, felt he was the only one who could see the nigh-saintly aura that surrounded Guy, and would have cheerfully died for him.

Fifteen

William had made Dover a second
fortified base. Now they marched
east toward Canterbury, seat of the
English Church, spiritual heart of
England.

They met with no resistance as they
rode. Guy, riding just behind the duke,
was vigilant as he pulled his cloak
closer about his mailed shoulders this
frosty October morning. Nuage snorted,
and Guy could see his mount's steamy
breath in the air.

He found Odo, William's half-brother
the bishop, riding next to him, and smiled
a greeting, although the vainglorious
churchman would not have been his
choice of traveling companions.

"Good morning, Your Grace. Like you

this crisp fall air?" Guy asked pleasantly.

"Oh, *oui*, it's well enough. Do you realize we've been here over a month?" Not pausing for a reply, Odo went on, "You know, I've never really expressed my thanks for your rescuing me at Senlac. It could have cost you your own life, I'm aware. I never forget such a favor. Should there be anything you need that I, as God's servant, can grant you—lightening some penance, an English heiress released from her marriage vows, times lessened in Purgatory, preferment for any of your issue in the Church . . ." he promised airily.

I would that you could restore to me the life of my friend Père Matthieu, the baron thought, and change things so *ma belle Lianne* does not look on me as a murderer, an enemy . . . but he murmured aloud, "I would crave only your prayers, your Grace. I am in need of them, being only a poor sinner"—to which humble reply the bishop laughed merrily, sensing it was somewhat tongue-in-cheek. Baron Guy was such a *drôle* fellow!

The Normans were surprised to be met on the road outside Canterbury by a deputation of citizens who, hearing of the destruction of Appledore, Romney, and Dover, had assembled to give the duke their formal submission.

William was well pleased. As October drew to a close, he settled into a fortress called the Broken Tower at Canterbury.

What he had planned to be a few days of rest turned into many days of severe illness. The strain of the months of planning and anxiety over the invasion finally caught up with William, and the conquering duke had to surrender impatiently to ill health. After a shaking ague left him, the duke found his knee afflicted by gout, a condition which did nothing to improve his temper. He chafed at the enforced rest, and his irascibility made it difficult for his barons to visit him. It was to take William a month to recover.

During this time, he sent Fitz Osborn to Winchester, the ancient seat of English government, to speak to the Confessor's widow, Edyth, who readily gave the requested submission of the city. Although she was Harold's sister, she had always favored things Norman.

Guy, kicking his heels in idleness, reflected that it was as often the deadly boredom of the occupation as the blood-lust of active war that lured soldiers into crimes against the innocent victims. The Normans patrolled the streets, keeping an eye out for incipient rebellion, which they felt gave them license to take what they wanted from merchant or woman, as long as it was done in a quietly threatening way. William had enjoined against theft and rape, since Canterbury had submitted peacefully, but against these frequent covert crimes the victims seldom dared complain.

Guy found, however, that there were plenty of women in the town who found it easy enough to forget he was a hated invader, faced with his easy charm, dark, handsome visage—and ready coin. A man should never have to *take* the love of a woman, he mused, the strong English mead having gone to his head as he lay in the arms of a buxom blonde wench, but then unbidden, an image of Lianne of Fairlight came to his mind. He saw her fierce, angry, lovely face, heard her spitting defiant words at him, and knew the only love he *really* wanted would have to be seized from her against her will.

Sixteen

"Quiet now!" Tofig hissed as his men crouched on a rocky outcropping watching a tree-lined path below on which a division of the Norman army was expected to pass, leaving Dartford. Orm, sent out earlier as a scout, had seen the invaders heading this way, and his advance information gave Tofig's band of English resisters time to select this ideal spot for an ambush.

William had divided his army upon leaving Canterbury, taking the main portion southwest toward Chilham, while he sent a smaller division northwest to Faversham, with Guy de Bayeux one of its commanders, thus spreading his agents of terror and destruction over a wider path. Wherever they went, manor houses were razed, whole villages put to the torch, wealthy citizens stripped of their valuables. William hoped the fear he caused would lead to an easy submission of London, for he had no longing to besiege that walled city. His reputation preceded him, and refugees fled to London and the North.

—Except for Tofig and his band, and others like them, who planned to stalk the divisions, making them pay dearly for each foot of English soil.

"Stay silent until the last ones pass," Tofig commanded. "We will pick off the stragglers, then retreat into the wood before the head of the line knows what's amiss. Remember now, no one moves before I signal or none of us will live to see the day England is free again."

He looked down the line to see Lianne crouched against a fallen log, shivering in the early morning mist. She was dressed as any of his men, in leather jerkin and braies, her glorious golden hair plaited and tucked up under a leather cap. She grinned, and flourished her bow. He returned her smile, but hoped that allowing her to be here was not signing her death warrant. She should be back at the camp with Mold. A woman did not belong here, dressed as a boy, preparing to kill. Lianne of Fairlight did not belong at all. She should be in her lord's hall, graciously receiving guests, standing in front of a warm fire. Ah, none of us are where we should be, the Devil take William the Bastard. Before this fateful autumn, Tofig had been a prosperous farmer, son of a half-pagan warrior from the northern Danegeld.

I have prepared her as well as I can, the Lord Christ—*and* Odin or whoever—protect her. She had proven an apt pupil with the longbow, her accuracy amazing in one so new to the skill. He had taught her to defend herself with a scramasax, a long sword-shaped knife, as well, after he had fashioned one with a lighter ash shaft. She ought to be able to give a good account of herself with that stag-beetle-hilted dagger, should the need arise, he thought, though his practical nature scoffed at any miraculous protection the insect could confer. It certainly had not saved her husband!

"They come!" hissed the lookout.

The score of rebels watched, crouched low and peering through the thick undergrowth as the mailed footsoldiers and knights approached. Lianne felt sure they could hear her pounding heart over the plodding horses' hooves, the jingling of metal, and the tramping feet. What am I doing here? Holy Mother of God, protect Orm.

She had seen *him* pass, near the head of the procession, riding with one of the two other knights. All the enemy looked similar in their knee-length mail and helmets with nasals, but Lianne had recognized the dapple-gray war-horse, and looked up to see his rider, face turned toward her as he spoke with the knight riding next to him. Her lovely mouth tightened as she knew those bold, dark features and a snatch of low laughter reached her ears. She wished she dared disobey Tofig and send an arrow now between those eyes! To give away their presence now, though, would be a disaster!

The last soldiers were passing now, eyes on their fellows straight ahead. Couldn't they see the danger of the over-hanging rocks? Couldn't they sense the menace lurking above their heads?

Tofig gave the raven's call, the signal to attack, and the rear guard went down under a deadly rain of arrows, the air rent by tardy shouts of warning and the screams of horses and men.

Guy was one of the first of the front line to realize what was happening, but by the time he was able to turn Nuage on the narrow path and spur back to the noise and confusion, the attackers had vanished and only the dead and dying were left.

Lianne, arriving back at the camp, shepherded by Tofig and Orm, was met by an anxious Mold, who cupped the girl's chin in her rough, chapped hands and forced Lianne to look up at her.

"Be ye all right, my lady? Ye aren't hurt? Oh, I knew I should not have let you go!"

"I am well, Mold, don't fret yourself.

It's just that I've . . . well, never killed a man before." Lianne gave a shaky laugh, and the older woman raised her eyes to Tofig.

"The lass will be all right. She did well. There is at least one Norman who'll not live to grow fat on English blood! She wounded one or two others as well. The next time will be easier," he assured them bracingly.

The girl felt a sinking sensation to know that there would be another occasion to loose her arrow and send a living being, though Norman, unshriven to hell.

They followed the army to the southern banks of the Thames, where the northern division was met in the second week of November by the main one, after the former had had a skirmish with some of the warriors from inside the walls. These English, Danish, and warriors of other nationalities had been waiting for the Normans appearance and sailed forth to do battle. The resistance was soon forced to retreat back across London Bridge, however, and the advance guard had retaliated by burning much of Southwark, including Godwine's famous feasting hall.

Tofig declared it too dangerous to try to attack the Norman camp on the sandy banks of Battersea, though he ground his teeth in rage at the sight of the siege engines being constructed there to emphasize William's threats to raze the city.

Instead, he struck south, where a contingent of the duke's army was wreaking havoc through the settled areas from Purley to Gomshall. Here they set up ambushes, never striking twice in exactly the same manner. The Normans often found trees cut down, blocking their path, or bridges hacked to pieces, and once Lianne had been the bait, dressed up to appear a harlot, and had lured several unwary, lustful soldiers to their deaths. She had hated that, and stubbornly averred that she would not play the siren again.

William had decided a direct attack on London would be futile: he dared not dissipate his army's strength in a long siege, where they were particularly vulnerable to attack by Harold's navy, which still hovered somewhere outside the Thames. It was more his style to take a city by fear, and he set out to spread terror, joining the southern division at Guildford. Here he was met with reports of the sabotage and sniping for which Tofig's band had been responsible. The English patriot would have been amused to hear how the size of his ambushing force had been magnified some five or ten times its actual number, depending on the teller.

Fortunately, the autumn had been mild, but as November advanced the rebels had to be more concerned with finding shelter and adequate clothing. They continued to take deer, boar, hares, and wildfowl for their food, but the fish that had been so plentiful lay torpid in the bottom of the streams, beyond reach of hook or spear. They found some Saxons along the way willing to risk their own safety by giving the little band lodging in their halls for a night, and occasionally they were given gifts of used clothing to help keep out the cold. Many times the garments given to the men had belonged to men of the fyrd, fallen at Stamford Bridge or Hastings, and Tofig declared these especially blessed. At one abbey, Lianne received a rough-spun gunna, kirtle, and mantle left behind by some traveler, made bluish-purple with a larkspur-alum dye, and smiled ruefully to think how grateful she was for such practical garments. Before William's coming such clothes would have been cast-offs for the thralls.

She was thinner now, her hands chapped from the cold like Mold's, less recognizable as a thegn's daughter until she opened her mouth, and then there was always something that set her apart from Mold and the other women of the camp. Many of the men shyly addressed her as "Lady" although she had tried to discourage it.

Even with all the hardship she suffered in her outdoor fugitive life, she had never been more beautiful. Actually, it was surprising that her presence had not caused a problem before it did. Once the men of Tofig's band could see that their leader had not claimed her, they began to try to attract her interest in ways both subtle and open. Her response was always the same, however—a polite smile, a courteous indication that she was not inclined to favor that particular man.

It was incomprehensible to the men that such a one would not have a mate. Once she had selected one of them, they would rest easy and none would try to cheat the lucky man, but until she did, she was the focus of a storm. One man in particular, Wulfnoth, a frydman from York, proved especially hard to discourage.

The little force had been stalking William's army outside Hungerford, and had camped for the night in a little glade well-hidden from the Normans.

Lianne woke during the night, conscious only of strong arms blotting out the glow of the dying embers, and a face bent down to hers. She panicked and began to struggle.

"Quiet, my good lady, my pretty one. I only want to take ye—" he lifted her bodily from her warm pallet—"and teach ye that I, Wulfnoth, am the man for ye!"

It had been foolish for Wulfnoth to suppose he could take an unwilling maid without waking men who had slept the light sleep of outlaws for weeks. All around the guttering fire men struggled awake, clutching for knives or other weapons.

"What goes on?"

"Who has come?"

"Wulfnoth, what are you doing?" rang out Tofig's voice authoritatively. At his leader's tone, the man's arms dropped away from Lianne, who shivered, clutching her worn mantle around her.

"Nothing, Tofig." His voice was sullen. "This little morsel needs a man, that's all. I'm just trying to show her who's got just the—ha, ha!—tool for her!" the man guffawed lewdly, defiantly. In a flash, Tofig crossed the campfire and had a knife at the other man's throat while nigh-lifting him off the ground.

"She's not for you. Get out of here! I don't care where you go, but leave! And listen well, all of you—" he indicated Lianne, miserably aware of her crimson face in the firelight. "Lianne of Fairlight is not to be compelled to take any of you. An Englishman should be ashamed to force himself on a good honest Englishwoman—there's enough rape being done by Norman devils!" No one dared look up at Tofig's furious glare.

Wulfnoth sullenly gathered his possessions and, as dawn's first fingers of light reached the forest glade, slunk out of the camp, muttering threats of vengeance under his breath.

Seventeen

"He desires *what?*" William asked irritably of Guy de Bayeux as the baron came to his liege's bed in the commandeered manor house at Shrivenham.

"He would betray a force of rebels who have been ambushing the rear and assassinating our soldiers, Your Grace."

"Huh! What's his price?" grunted the duke, disliking being disturbed at this hour. "Thirty pieces of silver?" He laughed mirthlessly at his own joke.

"He hasn't said, but I think—a few *livres* ought to do? They *have* been costing us valuable men, Your Grace. An example should be made."

"Very well, pay him off and see to it yourself. Take plenty of men with you. It might well be a trap, you know. Then tell him to be gone. Judases have their uses, but I want him not in our train."

Guy, informed of Tofig's location, planned the attack for dawn. He would take no prisoners.

Lianne's blue eyes flickered open in the dawn stillness to see Orm poking up the large central fire around which most of the band slept under rude shelters made of branches and animal skins. Good. At least there would be warm water there for a wash. She stretched, and stumbled drowsily to her feet, noting as she left the crude lean-to's shelter that Tofig's was also empty. Mold did not lie asleep in Lianne's hut, so . . . The girl smiled to think of her servant—nay, her *friend*—stealing off in the mist with Tofig. She was glad someone could be happy!

"Orm?" she whispered as she strode up to him, warming at the fire. "Help me carry some of this water—" indicating the water he'd set to simmering in a big iron kettle—"over to that thicket so I can have a proper wash. I feel so filthy."

"Aye, ye look it," he teased, but assisted her all the same. Since Wulfnoth had been banished a few days before, Lianne had had to be more reserved in her dealings with the men, more careful of her privacy, which Orm would go along to guard now.

A few minutes later Lianne, sheltered by the thicket, was using the hot water to quickly wash away some of the grime encountered in her nomad life. She shivered, for the hot water on the rag made the cold air about her feel that much more frigid. It certainly caused one to not dawdle about one's ablutions!

The four people away from camp—Tofig, Mold, Lianne and Orm—were all that escaped destruction in the few moments that followed.

The peace of the still-slumbering camp was shattered as a troop of Norman soldiers came seemingly out of nowhere, bringing death with their slashing swords, lances, and smashing maces. Where had they come from? Where was the sentry placed on duty to warn of such an approach? A screeching crow flew off over the body of that sentinel, who had been silenced by the traitor Wulfnoth, who'd crept up silently behind him with an unsheathed knife. The camp had not awakened in time to be warned of the troop, which approached on foot lest the horses' jingling harness warn the rebels of their coming. Instead the English patriots died, some struggling to their feet, groggy with sleep, others reaching belatedly for weapons, trying to throw off their dreams. It was over after a few brief cries, a few moans, a whimpered prayer of a dying man. The three women they found were gagged and trussed up, to be enjoyed back at camp as the spoils of war.

"That appears to be all of them, my

lord," the footsoldier reported respectfully to the baron, who stood staring, lost in thought, at the guttering embers of the campfire.

"Very good, Aimeri. Poor devils. Perhaps 'twill serve as an example to other would-be rebels. I've no desire to die in England, especially by the hand of a sniper."

"Heaven forfend!" agreed the soldier. "Shall we return to the horses now, my lord?"

"No. Gather some wood and make a pyre of the bodies."

There was much grumbling as the taciturn baron strode off, for the men would have preferred to leave the bodies as they fell—after looting them, of course —and go off and enjoy the women, dirty, half-wild creatures though they were. There was also a risk of attracting other rebels by the smoke, but none dared disobey the Baron de Bayeux, who was normally a very fair commander and left nothing to the common man that he couldn't—or wouldn't—do himself.

Actually the baron was just looking for a place to answer nature's call and fully intended to return to assist the men. Thus it was that he wandered straight into the thicket where Lianne hid, terrified, having heard the sounds of the massacre and wondering when they would find her—and Orm.

There she crouched, staring up at the

tall form of the baron, who after a startled half-second recognized her and started forward, saying incredulously, "Lianne? What do you here?"

He still carried his sword at the ready, and Lianne was mesmerized by the darkened blood that stained it.

"Come here, *demoiselle*, I don't know why you're here, but I've seen you in my dreams long enough. I would taste to see if you are real . . ." He reached to pull her to her feet.

When the Norman noble entered the coppice, his eyes and mind had been so full of the woman he had desired in his dreams, that he had not seen the hunched figure of the youth. Shedding the natural caution that had protected him, Guy was easy prey to Orm's attack from behind, while delighting in the feel of Lianne in his arms.

He went down as if poleaxed, struck by the flat of Orm's axe blade on the back of his head.

Lianne drew back in horror from the sprawled figure of the baron.

"Orm! Is he . . . ?"

"Dead? Nay, not yet." The youth knelt quickly, feeling for a pulse. "But how did he know you?" Realization dawned. "*He's* the Norman swine you told me of, that met you in the wood that day, that you think killed Edwin!" He started toward the prone figure, lifting the axe, while Lianne stared, paralyzed by the sight of her brother about to commit murder. She told herself that the reason she then intervened was that she could not bear to have him wear the stain of cold-blooded murder of a helpless man on his soul.

"Nay! I forbid it!"

"But, Lianne . . ." He was bewildered. We have been slaughtering them for weeks, what is one more, his look said.

"Uh . . . there is no time. His men will come looking for him, especially if there's a noise. We must get away."

"I suppose you're right. His soldiers would not be any more merciful to us than they were to Tofig's men." His tone was bitter.

Numb from the suddenness of the disaster and their narrow escape, the two stole as quickly and quietly as possible more deeply into the wood, seeking Tofig and Mold. They had not long to look. Tofig met them a moment or two later down the narrow path, and with a finger to his lips led them to a cave where Mold waited, trembling. She was overjoyed to see Lianne and Orm alive.

"We heard the screams," she said.

"Aye. I could guess what happened," Tofig added grimly. "Damned Norman murderers!"

"Now what?" asked Orm, watching his sister's pale face, not liking the look of her dilated, unseeing eyes. The children of Rolf the thegn, and Lianne in particular, had been through more grief and terror in a few weeks than most would face in a lifetime, and though his sister was a strong woman, he knew not how much more she could take. He himself, though he never wasted time on self-pity, had had to leave boyhood with no time for a backward glance, at an age when most youths were still playing at weaponry and trying on the responsibilities of manhood, a little at a time—except in England right now. His young shoulders were burdened with a weight he unconsciously longed to shed, if only for a moment.

"Perhaps the women should go back to the abbey at Netherfield, or some convent along the way," Tofig offered tentatively.

"Never!" Both women spoke at once, and all smiled at their vehemence.

"What about . . . London?" Lianne queried. All were silent for a moment, knowing that the way there would be hazardous, for the Norman army lay between them and the city on the Thames, but the city's size and the anonymity it offered beckoned.

"Aye. London it is," Tofig said decisively. "And the sooner the better. We'll not stay here to be found by those cutthroats!"

Guy's life had been saved by his iron helmet, which protected the back of his head sufficiently that his skull was not split from the force of the blow. Even so, when the men-at-arms finally missed him and went searching, finding him unconscious in the coppice, he was sure when they aroused him that his head had been cloven asunder. He had the Devil's own headache! Groaning, he swore colorfully at the anxious soldiers as he struggled to his feet, ruefully searching the back of his head for the gash that dripped blood warmly down his neck.

"God's Entrails! Where have you knaves been? I could have been slit from throat to cock and you'd have been none the wiser!"

"My lord! What has happened?" cried one, eager to diminish the baron's wrath as he helped him to his feet. "We were doing as you bid—the corpses are burning . . ."

Guy wrinkled his nostrils as the breeze brought the acrid smell of burning flesh.

"Yes, Armand. Don't worry, I know you followed orders. I found a pair who had escaped the ambush, but I didn't see one of them in time before he brained me. Damn! It feels like a hundred little demons fighting to get out of my skull!"

"Let us go after them, my lord! They must not escape!"

"*Non*. They're long gone by now. 'Twould be a futile game that might lead us into a trap. We've annihilated their strength. They'll not rise again against Duke William." He knew not who had struck him, but he had no desire to inflict

the army's wrath on the English girl, the
fate of the other captured women. Oh, no
—he had a much more private and
personal revenge planned for that Saxon
bitch! His brown eyes narrowed,
becoming agate-hard, and his lips tightened as he walked back to the ruined
camp. He did not know where he would
find her, since she obviously did not
intend to make the game easy by staying
at the nunnery as he had bid. But someday when England lay subject, she would
cross his path again—flashing those
huge, stormy blue eyes, swinging that
river of golden hair in which he longed to
bury his face, and moving that trim
figure, alluring even in the ragged
garments of a peasant—and the wench
would know her own conqueror! His
brain wrathfully reviewed their
meetings, from the time he had chased
her, intent on some uncomplicated
wenching, and instead had wooed her as
gallantly as any lover, to their bitter
confrontation on the battlefield, where
she had called him "murderer"; to the
last, when he was sure she had lain in
wait specifically to lure him to his doom.
He knew now she had been running with
the pack of English outlaws who had
slaughtered so many Norman soldiers
over the past few weeks. No delicate
Saxon lady as he'd thought! Lianne of
Fairlight was as deadly as any woman
could be. When he had her, his would not

be loving, gentle arms that held her. She would be the spoils of war, shown no mercy. He'd break her heart, and perhaps her lovely body too!

PART II
LONDON

One

"Saints, the boy is a sullen brat this day," Lianne straightened from her task to whisper irritably to Mold as the two struggled to put Edgar Aethling's hall to rights after he'd departed. A deputation sent by the Witan had arrived at his door as prearranged to take him to the council meeting at Westminster that would probably doom his future as the next Saxon monarch.

"Aye, poor little king-who-never-was," the sturdy older woman answered. "Who can blame him? The talk is that Ansgar wants the Witan—and therefore London itself—to submit to William. And then where will our fine cockerel be? Neither fish nor fowl!"

Lianne was grateful for the roof over

her head, when so many English were homeless as the Normans cut their terrifying, destructive swath through the areas west of London—Surrey, Hampshire, Berkshire. Having failed to break the defenses at the southern entrance, William was determined that his reputation should precede him before he arrived at the city via his northeastern route. Lianne, Orm, Mold, and Tofig had arrived in London at a time when the narrow streets were packed with panicked refugees, but were fortunate to have overheard the disgruntled mumblings of two serving maids, whose conversation revealed that the Aethling Edgar had accused them of petty thievery and dismissed them.

"And who wouldn't take a little extra joint of mutton or swipe a horn cup to sell? Uncertain times be here!" one was saying, and the other agreed.

Mold, with the cleverness of the low-born whose position in life depended on snatched opportunities, had inquired the way to the Aethling's hall, which was near the western gate of the city, and boldly asked for the positions vacated by the two dismissed ceorls. "Honest women we be, Lianne an' me, not asking great wages, just the privilege of serving Yer Grace honestly!" She smiled her open smile, and Lianne smiled also, though the prospect of serving the pimply fifteen-year-old filled her with dismay.

He stood scowling at them, arms akimbo, and she felt at that moment much in sympathy with the two women they'd overheard. Edgar Aethling, the last of the line of Alfred, certainly did not have a very royal mien. His expression was pettish and grumpy as he inquired rudely, "And who might these fellows be? I can't be taking in every beggar off the streets!" He stared pointedly at Orm and Tofig.

Lianne was sure he would not accept them also, but Mold had been waiting for just such an opening and spoke up confidently, introducing them—"These be Orm, La—" (she had been about to say *Lady* Lianne's brother) "Lianne's brother, and Tofig—a finer master of your stable and his assistant you couldn't wish for!"

And Edgar had agreed to take them all into his service.

"Though, mind you, I'll accept no shirking," he said arrogantly, a trace of his Hungarian accent seeping into his English (for his father and the family had been brought out of exile in Hungary only very recently and Edgar Aethling, his father, had died of a mysterious stomach ailment before he could meet King Edward).

It was now the first week in December, and the spoiled youth had proved no more pleasant a master than they had expected. He was sly, cruel, and inordinately selfish; and Lianne could only be glad that he stood little chance of ever securing the English throne. He had once been supported by the ambitious Archbishop Stigand as the only successor to Harold, but now rumors circulated of Stigand's meeting with Duke William himself for the purpose of submission. Stigand planned, it was said, to persuade all the chief men of the country to do likewise. Then what would be the position of Edgar Aethling?

No mention had been made of Lianne's former status as thegn's daughter and widow of a housecarle, and Edgar was too self-absorbed to see the inherent difference between Lianne and the peasant, Mold, so he treated each with the arrogant assumption that they were as the dirt beneath his feet and should be grateful indeed that he deigned to walk on them. Lianne did not mind his arrogance nearly so much as the occasional lascivious pinch he gave her when no one else was near, from which she could only retreat in grim-lipped silence as the boy prince jeered cruelly.

Dear Lord and Saints! she thought wearily, seasoning the beef joint as she prepared it for the spit. To think that I had planned to spend this winter secure in my lord's arms! She had a fierce longing for the shores of Fairlight and a stalwart man standing beside her.

She dared not tell Orm or Tofig of the stripling's advances, for their reaction might cause them all to lose their places, but prayed they could endure and find a better situation before Edgar's approaching manhood made her own position in the household too miserable to continue.

And what of Elfgift, Lianne wondered, whose mind lay locked in terror in her habit-clad body at Netherfield? Would she be mad forever, ruined the rest of her life by her terrible experience? Lianne longed to have her younger sister by her, certain she could summon back that lovely cheerful spirit, given enough time and security; but Edgar Aethling's hall in the midst of uncertain London was no place for her troubled sister!

The meeting with the Witan had gone as Edgar feared. Some of the nobility, the churchman Aldred, William, Wulfstan, and Walter, had agreed with Ansgar and Stigand that capitulation was the only solution that would save London from the annihilation William promised, though Edgar Aethling fumed and sputtered, trying to remind them of his presence.

The Witan was most apologetic, but stood firm: they would submit and return for the coronation, so that London would be safe and their churches intact.

Lianne had no clue that Tofig's dissatisfaction lay as deep as hers, though she knew that Edgar had been as rude to him and Orm as to herself and Mold. She was surprised, therefore, when he told her, after having accompanied his youthful master to the assembly at Westminster, that he had decided to leave the Aethling's service and become the man of Earl Edwin of Mercia. Orm was to follow in a little while, if all went well.

"It's for Edgar's own good, actually," Orm told her, humor glinting in his eyes, the first smile Lianne had seen in months lighting his features. "If Tofig has to endure one more sneer from that silly popinjay, I'm sure he'll throttle him."

Lianne's laugh rang out gaily in the stable, knowing they could talk freely with only the horses and mules as witnesses. Her resolve not to tell her brother of the Aethling's pawing was strengthened, for he would be loathe to take advantage of this opportunity to better his position if he knew of it. And Orm Rolfsson had not been born to be a lackey to a puling foreigner!

"I'm glad to see that you are not sad, Lianne, for I've not told you the best part. Tofig and I were thinking that when we are both settled in the earl's household in Mercia, and see how things are there, we will send for you and Mold. You could serve in the household there."

"It'd be a good deal better than serving 'Foreign Edgar'!" Mold averred, rolling her eyes. "That little sprout has too many hands by half!" Tofig bristled, but she laughed reassuringly. "Don't fret yourself, love. He's learned I'll brook no liberties!"

"Perhaps there'll be a thegn in Edwin's service that will wed you, Lianne."

"Aye, that would be nice," she murmured, wondering if Mercia would be far enough away from William's direct control that anything approaching their former way of life would be possible. She cynically doubted it, but she longed for a more settled, pleasant existence. All of them would have to await the changes that would arise in the wake of William's inevitable crowning before their rosy dreams came true.

Two

A fortnight before Christmas, London was ablaze with the news that the Witan was to meet William at Little Berkhampstead to surrender the city.

Edgar Aethling had departed at dawn with his retinue for the meeting, pale-faced and trembling. What would his status be when he returned—*if* he returned?

Both divisions of the allied invaders had joined from their separate raiding paths at Little Berkhampstead to converge on London. The tidings that a deputation from the great city was en route, led by Stigand, caused them to remain encamped, waiting.

William was jubilant, even gloating, as

he spied the mounted party approaching the camp. Guy grinned, catching his lord's excitement as the nobles and prelates dismounted, handing their reins to soldiers, looking about them apprehensively, surrounded by the Norman host.

"You are welcome, Your Grace, my lords, and—oh, yes, Edgar Aethling!" The young prince flushed with rage at being the last that William mentioned. "Your pardon, my lord, I know not how to address an 'Aethling.' But fear not—you are honored here, my boy, for who you are—a member of the *former* royal house!"

The boy's fists clenched at his sides as William's casual dismissal of his hopes, a movement missed by none, but he was powerless to do more.

William caused the men of the English council, as well as his chief nobles (including Guy) to be seated in a great tent he had erected for this meeting. He stood before them, facing the Witan, and asked in a voice dripping with humility, "My lords, what would you have me do?"

Guy, seated toward the entrance, almost laughed aloud, and straightened his long frame in an effort to control himself. Glancing about, he met the eyes of other barons—Mortain, FitzOsborn, Montford—whose barely suppressed merriment said: To come so far, and have gone through hell, and then to *ask* such a question!

"You know, it's not such a foolish question," Robert of Beaumont, seated beside him, whispered. "Have you considered what this will mean to the governing of Normandy? It will needs always be under a regent, when William is across the Channel."

"And Henry sits like a vulture in France, waiting to exploit any weakness."

"Just so. I for one think he ought to appoint a regent *here* and return to the duchy."

Guy looked sardonically at him. "Would one remain a duke, when he could be a king as well?"

"Have you thought about your own lands, Bayeux? What of them?"

"I left my younger brother Gervais in charge. He would have inherited, of course, had I fallen at Senlac. But I think my destiny is here, in England—I cannot be lord of two baronies divided by a Channel! I believe Gervais should be made my seneschal permanently."

"A lucky man, to have a brother he can trust! What of your betrothed? When shall you send for her? What of the lands she brings you?"

"It's too uncertain a peace as yet to expose Mabile to the dangers of a rebellious land." With a start, Guy realized he had not spared the Norman lady a thought for days, with the exception of a brief message he sent from Dover. No, his dreams were haunted by a lovely she-witch who spoke French with an English accent, whose lips dared him to kiss and possess while her words wished him dead. . . .

William, a consumate actor, pretended to refuse the crown proffered with well-acted sincerity by the men of the Witan, much to the secret delight of some jealous barons, until at last one Aimeri made the persuasive speech that "caused" the duke to "accept."

He then appointed various of the barons to accompany the Englishmen, who had "given" themselves as hostages, back into London and see to preparations for the coronation.

"Guy," the stocky duke spoke quietly, taking him aside, "you are to guard that stripling Edgar. I know he looks a weakling but he has a treacherous eye, and he can't like this demotion. Stay in his hall. I'm sending two score men-at-arms with you, as I am with these others. I shall stay outside London, but do you send word if the brat is plotting, though I don't think he will."

"Nor I, Your Grace; he knows well you hold his life in your hands."

Late that evening, as Lianne and Mold helped the other women prepare the meal while the male ceorls set up the trestle tables, a large contingent of horse-men arrived with the Aethling. One of Edgar's men, sent inside, summoned additional help to see to the stabling of so many unexpected beasts, while inside word spread among the women:

"It's the Normans! Edgar is a hostage! They'll all be staying here!"

"Saints! They'll slit our throats!"

"Huh! Not bloody likely, when they're hungry and the meal not half on the table!" scoffed Mold bracingly, clapping an arm around Lianne's shoulders.

Lianne couldn't suppress a shudder at the thought, however. Normans, demons incarnate, right here in this hall, in numbers that assured they were the inevitable masters of any situation, with or without arms. There were none but a few male ceorls to protect them, and how dared a lowborn Saxon raise his hand against the conquering foreigners?

Lianne's mind was just turning over the possibilities of this new reality as she came through the dark entranceway from the kitchens to the hall when her attention was riveted by a commanding figure entering the hall behind the sullen-faced Aethling. Everyone else looked up too, and the rumor-laden chatter ceased. In the silence, Guy de Bayeux glanced around him, brown eyes studying the English faces that gazed back with fear, uncertainty, resentment.

Lianne stepped backward into the shadows, grateful for their concealment. That murderer here! Mold, coming up behind her, started to urge her forward, but as she saw the tall Norman a few yards away, and noted her mistress's furtive attitude, she waited, looking back at the baron and then at Lianne.

"Men and women of Edgar Aethling's hall, I am Guy de Bayeux, here to protect your lord" (the irony of "protect" was not lost on the residents) "as William, Duke of Normandy, would assure Edgar's safety. Make no mistake—any resistance shown my men will be dealt with— severely. I am a just man, as is my lord. Speak me fair, and you will be well-treated. And those of you women who are virgin, and desire to remain so—" he smiled wolfishly—"need only to retire to your sleeping rooms after the meal and *stay there.* Anyone wandering about after *coeuvre-feu* is fair game for my men."

There was a buzzing between the ceorls after this information was translated into English by the trembling seneschal. Lianne, not daring to look toward the baron, whispered urgently to Mold, "It is he—my lord Edwin's murderer. He mustn't see me, Mold. You must get me into his room tonight, before he enters it. Find out which it shall be. And make my excuses—if any miss me, say I am ill, lying down on my pallet."

"Lianne, what are ye thinking of? What mad scheme are you hatching?" Mold took in the stubbornly lifted chin, the tightening of Lianne's mouth; she had not seen her former charge give a command since Senlac had swept away the distinction between lady and ceorl; but she was being given one now.

"He has never paid the weregild, Mold, as if such a price could be set! *He must pay!*" The girl's voice was firm, her blue eyes gleamed in the half-light. "And he will pay. Mold, if you love me, there is else I would have you do. . . ."

Three

The meal was finally over, the soldiers somewhat less testy now that their empty stomachs had been filled by the hastily assembled meal, their thirst quenched by English ale (though most would have preferred a good French wine).

Mold had not seen Lianne since she had given her the desired information while the Normans feasted. She had watched her slip unobtrusively off in the indicated direction, the stag-beetle dagger tucked into her girdle. She turned her attention back to directing the others in the clean-up of the scraps and the removal of trestles, while others set out pallets for the night hours ahead. She murmured a prayer for Lianne's safekeeping under her breath.

* * *

Lianne did not know how long she had lain in wait, prone beneath the bed. The room was cold, but she had left her cloak in her quarters for greater ease of movement.

At last the dark was abated by a flickering candle-flame, and Lianne peered out across the rushes as a pair of legs paused at the brazier and lit it. Cautiously she peered upward and saw the owner of those legs, a freckled lad with auburn hair whose demeanor reminded her of Orm. This was obviously the squire. She smiled as he rubbed his hands back and forth over the fire he'd kindled, blowing to warm them, and Lianne wished she could do likewise. Her fingers were numb with the chill.

A knock at the door, and Mold's voice came softly to her ears: "Some mulled wine for my lord and for you," and the squire's surprised "*Merci*," though he probably did not understand the English words. There was a twin clank as the youth set the goblets down by the brazier, then she heard him take a long draft of his. Jesu-Mary! The poppy must not work too soon! It would not do to have the Norman find his squire snoring, unarousable!

De Bayeux's footsteps sounded immediately after that, however, and she heard the hated voice saying, "Gilbert, the Aethling sleeps in the chamber opposite. Make your pallet up outside my door where you may keep a watch. He has retired for the night. Let me know instantly if he leaves, or if any come to him. Disarm me now, lad, then you may leave."

They stood near the brazier as Gilbert helped remove the chain mail hauberk and padded gambeson beneath. It could not have been comfortable to leave those on during the meal, an indication of his feeling for the need of vigilance. Lianne, hardly daring to breathe, was treated to the sight of the Norman's powerful shoulders, narrow waist, and flat abdomen, and involuntarily the girl drew in her breath. The squire helped remove Guy's chainse and chausses as the man stood, his back to Lianne's hiding place, then handed him a warm woolen robe of blue, with long sleeves and an embroidered neck. Then there was the sound of footsteps receding, and the door closed.

Gilbert had assumed his master would sit by the fire and drink the wine awhile, otherwise he would not have bothered with the robe, as his lord, like most, slept as Nature made him, using the animal skins on the bed for cover. Lianne heard him take a sip, then mutter something unintelligible as if he were not pleased, then set the goblet emphatically down. Then, his footsteps; the door opened, and—"Gilbert—who brought this wine?"

"One of the women, my lord. She was kind enough to bring me some also."

"Terrible stuff. It could not be French.

Ah, well, see that it doesn't make you muzzy-headed!''

Then his muscular, long legs were standing by her place of concealment, and the garment was shrugged off on the side of the bed, and his weight settled down onto the bed, over Lianne. She was sure he could hear her heart. She heard him sigh.

If he's not going to take the draught I shall have to wait until he's well asleep, she thought, and her grip tightened around the dagger.

The hour candle had burned low. Lianne awoke with a start, realizing she had dozed off for a few moments. How could she have slept when she was about to take a life? Above, she could hear his regular, even breathing. Stealthily she slipped from her place of concealment, inch by painful inch, careful not to rustle the rushes on the floor, which were old enough to be dry and brittle.

What would happen afterward she dare not dwell upon—just the need to exact retribution. She didn't know if the act would go undiscovered long enough, or if it would even be possible to slip out of the hall with its Norman guards. And what then? Would she be able to reach Mercia, and Edwin's household, and bring Orm with her? And what of Mold— she certainly didn't want to leave without her! Perhaps it would be best to just slip back into the hall, for if she were to flee that would point to her as the murderess, and the Normans would be hot to pursue her. A woman of her distinctive looks would find it hard to merely melt into the crowd. What if the Normans sought to punish a certain percentage, or everyone in the hall, for the act? And what of the mortal sin she would be committing? Wouldn't even the English Church regard this cold-blooded assassination as such? It was too much to ponder, and she resolved to set it aside until she had avenged her husband's death.

In the dim glow furnished by the glowing brazier and the candle-flame, she studied the sleeping man.

Guy de Bayeux lay supine, one arm flung behind his head, the other at his side, black hair tousled. A livid line, the scar he would bear from Senlac, crossed one cheekbone. His jawline was dark with the day's growth of beard. A well-favored man, Lianne admitted to herself. *A pity he is who he is.*

He sighed again, shifting slightly. She froze; her heart threatened to leap from her chest. The moment was forever.

In his movement, the fur coverlet had fallen away, revealing his finely muscled chest, moderately covered with dark, curling hair.

I shall aim for the heart, then, she decided. It would be easier and quicker to plunge Edwin's dagger into his chest than to try to slit vital veins in his neck before the baron could awaken and struggle. The candlelight reflected off the gleaming silver blade as she transferred it to her right hand, drew in a quiet deep breath, and lunged at the sleeping form.

Guy had not become a powerful fighter in the duke's battles without also learning to be a very light sleeper with catlike-quick reflexes. In a heartbeat's time as Lianne's hand was plunging downward with the dagger, his arm shot out, imprisoning the dangerous wrist as she found her body grasped and tossed opposite his onto her back on the bed.

Guy had sensed the threat looming, seen the weapon, and reacted, assuming it was an Englishman trying to slaughter him in his bed, perhaps even the sullen Edgar. Thus he was amazed to see that the struggling form beside him was Lianne.

He wasted no energy on words for a few moments; her right hand still held the lethal weapon, and her dilated pupils in their wild blue irises told him she would use it if she could free her arm. Holding the other wrist fast by her side, he increased the strength of his grip, and though she winced and a tear ran down her cheek, she would not cry out. His teeth were clenched tightly with the effort. The ragged sound of their breathing filled the chamber. At last, the inexorable strength of his grip caused her nerveless hand to drop the dagger to the floor, the clang of the metal muffled by the rushes.

She was trapped now and she knew it, but would allow no whimper of fear to escape her throat though he could feel her trembling. Instead she lifted her chin and defiantly stared back into the gleaming brown pools of his eyes.

"God damn you," she hissed at last. "You should be dead now." Next he would raise those powerful hands and strangle her.

He studied her for an endless moment as she tried to think a final prayer, and she was suddenly aware of his bare torso lying across her body, still holding a wrist pinioned with each of his hands. Suddenly the furious blood-lust in his eyes died and was replaced with a sardonic gleam.

"Why, Lianne of Fairlight," his voice drawled, "you turn up in so many places, I should not be surprised to find you in my bed."

His eyes left her startled face to roam with great deliberation down her body, lingering at the heaving chest as she began to struggle anew.

"No . . ." she breathed. "No!" He looked back at her, grinning, but was surprised by the terror dawning anew in her eyes. It seemed to be more than when he had caught her with the knife, and for a second he wondered why. Then:

"Wench, I am obliged by your . . . ah, eagerness . . . to give you a real Norman welcome to my bed." He let go of her hands for a moment, and as her small fists drummed ineffectually at him and her legs pitched and bucked, he grasped the gray linen gunna and ripped it from neckline to hem. The kirtle easily met the same fate, then he caught her wrists together in his left hand and held them tightly over her head. Her thrashing limbs were subdued by a powerful leg thrown tauntingly over. Her captured body lay naked, open to his gaze, and he took full advantage of the view, returning at last to her fiery cheeks. She shivered, despite the heat that radiated between them.

"Ah, my love, the sight of so much beauty *almost* makes amends for the number of times you have threatened my life. But there is more you must do before your full penance is paid." His free hand reached to caress her breast, cupping its fullness as he lowered his mouth to hers.

There was nothing of the gentle knight of the wood in his kiss—it was the kiss of a conqueror, dominating, rough, demanding—but for a fateful instant she was brought back in touch with the memory that she most feared—that when he had kissed her before, she had desired him, and would have done anything he asked in that instant. And did so now—despite the fact that he was not asking. He was taking.

She tried to turn her mouth away, though it required summoning a will that was dying within her, but he held her chin firmly with his hand as his tongue demanded possession. His fingers roamed down her abdomen, touching at will, stroking, caressing, at last finding that secret place and making it known.

She *must not* reveal a response, she must not! Her honor and that of the slain demanded it! Her body she was powerless to refuse him, but those she had pledged to avenge would never rest if she gave way to the fever that was beginning to rise within her. He must not guess how near she was to returning his kiss, how her arms, if not held away, might of their own accord steal around those powerfully muscled shoulders . . . shoulders that now forced her smaller, trembling body deeper into the mattress.

"No, my lord—no! Why are you doing this? I don't wish to lie with you! Slay me if you will! I prefer it!"

He chuckled. "Your wishes are of no import, wench. You are one of a beaten people, remember?" he jeered at her, then shifted suddenly so that his knee was insistently pushing her legs apart and lowered himself onto her.

She could feel his maleness throbbing, demanding entrance, next to the inside of her thigh as her head turned futilely from side to side, and she whimpered now in earnest, "No . . . no . . . *please!*"

He turned her face to look into his eyes as his manhood found the passage and thrust in. A part of him reacted with surprise to see her grimace in pain as the sensation of resistance within suddenly gave way, then he was totally lost in the throes of his passion.

Before her wedding, Lianne had pictured Edwin taking her tenderly, with consideration for her virgin state, determined that her first experience with love should contain more pleasure than pain. But this was not Edwin she lay beneath, nor were there whispered love-words that were meant at least while the act of love lasted. His eyes locked with hers as her virginity was ravished, but he gave no indication that he was aware of the flame he was fanning within her with his rhythmic thrusts. Her hips began to move with his, as if they were no longer hers to direct. . . . She was about to fall into a fiery abyss. . . .

And then his breathing became more and more convulsive as the lids closed over those smoldering eyes and he loosed his seed within her, leaving her confused, still taut with unspent tension.

He withdrew and lay propped on one elbow, staring angrily at her in the half-darkness.

He had felt ashamed when he had discovered her innocence, and perversely, that renewed his ire. He raised up for a moment and stretched across her, bringing the candle in its stand to illumine her lower body, where the inside of her thighs were still sticky with blood.

"You lied to me," he accused. "Why?"

Bewilderment crossed the tear-streaked features. What was he talking about? He had just violated her, and now he spoke in riddles!

"I . . . lied?"

"You told me you were wed, before. That this . . . Edwin . . . was your lord. Yet you've never lain with a man! You were a maiden still until I—" he looked away uncomfortably and finished—"just took your maidenhead."

She began to weep then, not loudly, but with great gulping, despairing sobs.

Guy had always thought he would despise a woman's tears and the woman for weeping them, and sedulously avoided virgins, however willing they had been for him. Now he felt the more shamed and, to be doing something, strode from the bed and returned with a cloth moistened with water. Gently, silently, he sponged away the telltale stain from her skin. While he did so her voice reached him from the head of the bed, between sobs she was obviously having difficulty trying to control.

"I *was* wed to my Edwin. I told you . . . no lie. He was summoned from the wedding feast to attend King Harold . . . on the march t-to the battle—at Stamford Bridge." She watched him ministering to her curiously, unable to believe he was the same man who had just taken her.

"Before the bedding?" he asked quietly, as he stretched out again beside her.

"Y-y-yes."

"And after the battle in the north? He did not rush back to claim his so-lovely bride?" She could not understand why his voice flattened, became almost morose.

"There was no time. Your . . . duke had landed and King Harold was forced to march south again to meet him." She found that suddenly and inexplicably he was cradling her against him soothingly, and that she was involuntarily telling the rest.

"I went to see him on Caldbec Hill, the night before the battle. He was in his cups, sodden drunk, and he tried to . . . love me then." He could feel her convulsive shudder. "It was horrible. But he fell asleep, and I never saw him again, *alive*," she finished accusingly, remembrance of their confrontation over his corpse flooding back.

"Lianne," he murmured, glad to have the subject changed for a moment. "I didn't kill Edwin, you know." He arose from the bed again, powerful muscles gleaming as his fingers found the dagger among the rushes, and he walked to the shuttered window. Opening it, he threw the weapon as far as he could through the darkness outside the hall. "I don't trust my luck to hold giving that back to you *again*," he said wryly, leaning against the sill for a moment and taking a deep breath as he gazed out into the night. She watched him warily as he closed the shutters again and crossed the floor to her, asking disbelievingly, "And none of the band of cutthroats I found you among desired you? *Incroyable!*"

"None forced his attentions on me," she said evenly (not mentioning Wulfnoth's attempt). "My widowhood was respected by *them.*" It was a verbal slap, and he was challenged by it.

"So it was left for a Norman to make a woman of you," he taunted.

"All you did was ravish me, Norman. I don't feel any different," she lied.

"*Touché.* We must remedy that, *hein?* When this night is over I would have you know how it feels to be a woman."

She saw that she had inflamed him, but it was too late. He pulled her close and began to rain kisses on her as he loosed her golden hair from its plait, murmuring about its silky feel. His touch was fire, and it was everywhere at once. His warm breath caressed her ear, and she shivered. His hands found her nipples and he teased them into circles of fire, his touch instructing now, teaching all the new sensations she could feel. She tried to lie stiff and unyielding, but it was futile. He knew too many of her body's secrets. Lianne gasped as he left her shoulders, his tongue intimately seeking, incredulous that such an action could set in motion such waves of pleasure. In the haze of the sensations he had sent racing through her, she felt her arms tighten convulsively against his dark head pulling him close.

"Lianne, *ma douce, ma belle,*" he murmured hoarsely, responding to her response, and coming back to kiss her passionately. She could feel his hardness against her again. "Open to me, love me. . . ."

And her legs parted as if he were not her Norman enemy. She received his thrust with apprehension, but now it did not hurt. He moved slowly, gently within her at first, hands under her, lifting her to him, until she caught his pace and rose dazed, astonished, to the crest of the wave with him and cried out as it broke, leaving them spent on the shore, locked in each other's arms.

Her eyes opened and she looked at him, seeing who had wrung from her such a wanton passion—her Norman conqueror. She couldn't tell which time she had been the more violated.

Four

Her bridegroom had come to the flower-decked wedding chamber, accompanied by his laughing, merry friends. Her maids had made her ready for this hour, the one in which Edwin of Pevensey would make her truly his wife, a virgin no longer.

He reached a hand out to cup her cheek tenderly and, helped out of his festive garments, climbed into bed naked, a tall, solid, blond god, more Danish Viking than Englishman. Her eyes took in the compact muscles of his massive chest and shoulders as he gathered her into his embrace, her loins could feel the heat of his ready manhood. Lianne opened her mouth under the passionate pressure of his lips, and his questing tongue joined hers. . . .

"Oh, Edwin," she sighed rapturously.

"God damn Edwin!" a wrathful voice above her growled as the kiss suddenly ceased and all the warm sensations fled with the dream. Her lashes fluttered open to behold Guy de Bayeux's angry face. It had been he who had been holding her, kissing her, not poor slain Edwin. He had been trying to arouse her from sleep into passionate lovemaking before she completely awakened. She struggled in his arms but he held her still. "Edwin is *dead*," he said and went cruelly on, "a beaten, moldering corpse whose touch would be as cold as the grave, whereas I am *alive*. Edwin will never have you as his *ever* again—and *I will never let you go. I will* replace that dead Englishman in your heart, Lianne!"

Her blue eyes flashed defiance, but his head was lowering again, and she could only watch as his lips touched hers.

Just then, Edgar Aethling tramped petulantly into the chamber, sending the oaken door crashing into the wall, and the baron sprang up with a scowl.

"My lord, your captain, Sir Ralf, tells me I may not attend Mass without an armed Norman escort. . . ." His glance took in the glaring Norman, then Lianne, crimson-faced, clutching a coverlet of wolfskins to hide her nakedness.

"Ah, my lord, what's this!" he said, staring pointedly from one to the other and back again. "I see you did not heed your own rule—that all virtuous maids were safe from your . . . attentions unless they proved . . . willing? Which was the case here?" There was a nasty gleam in his eye, a peculiar smirk to his mouth as if he would strip Lianne even of that pelt.

"You forget yourself, stripling," the Norman's voice said with a steel edge. His eyes forbade the youth to gaze further as Guy stepped firmly between the embarrassed girl and Edgar, his whole attitutde one of menace as his powerful shoulders shrugged into the robe left at the bedside last night.

Edgar's face resumed its sullen attitude.

"*What did you want?*" was ground out between Guy's clenched teeth.

"I? Oh—merely the freedom to pursue my religious devotion," the boy answered sullenly. "When I prepared to leave for Mass before I broke my fast, I was told by those loutish fellows *you* call knights, that I, the Aethling of England, was not free to go anywhere without your permission and escort!"

"That is so."

"Even to Mass?" The youth's voice broke into a squeak at the end, which he tried to cover with increased vehemence.

"Even to Mass. If you had asked, I would have been ready to escort you."

"I looked for you," Edgar replied, haughtily rushing onto dangerous ground, "but you were not in the hall— you were still lying abed with your strumpet!"

Guy's sword had left its scabbard, which lay propped upright by the bed, before the Aethling could take a step backward, but now he began to back cautiously toward the door, Guy following him step for step, the thundercloud of his face darkening. The boy made a miscalculation as he retreated and finished somewhat to the left of the door, paralyzed against the wall by the shimmering silver blade trained on his throat.

"You braying ass," Guy ground out, furious brown eyes inches from Edgar's, "get out of here. And don't you ever enter again without my expressed invitation, lordling, or I'll forget who you *used* to be."

The vanquished boy tripped over the still-slumbering form of Gilbert, stretched across the door as he had been all night, snoring lustily.

"What's this?" Guy's attention was distracted by the sight, Lianne and the Aethling momentarily forgotten. "Where were *you* last night?" he roared, pulling the luckless squire up by the neck of his tunic. The boy tried to come alert promptly, but could not smother a yawn, even in the face of his lord's unusual temper. He looked so comical that Lianne still crouched on the bed in her pelt, could not repress a smile.

"My lord . . . you are awake betimes . . . it is early yet?"

"No, sluggard!" growled the baron

angrily. "Some protection you are during my sleep!"

"My lord," the boy protested, "I watched half the night, and slept with one eye open the rest—did aught arise?"

"I was nearly murdered in my bed! No, nothing *untoward* happened while you snored away!" yelled his master wrathfully, and cuffed him on the ear.

"*Murdered?* How? By whom?" Gilbert's eyes searched the room, as his hand went to his dagger's hilt, and found the girl. He looked away, blushing.

"You are not right to punish what he could not help."

"Ah, say you so, *demoiselle?*" Guy rounded on her. His ire was fully aroused now, after the morning had gotten off to such a friendly start! He had lost far too much sleep last night to be tolerant of womanly interference.

"Indeed. If you had drunk your wine as your squire drank his, you would have slept as soundly as he. And doubtless would have been in hell now, for your sins," she finished, grinning archly. "The wine was drugged."

Guy was taken aback. "You little Saxon bitch, your capacity for treachery never fails to amaze me!"

Gilbert was miserable, understanding little of what had happened but feeling the sparks that flew between the man and the woman. His idolized master was angry with him. That was all that mattered. He could see that the baron had apparently passed the night with this female, not an unusual occurrence with such a virile noble, but what had such a fair wench to do with talk of attempted murder and drugged wine? Splendor of God! He looked more closely as the blonde wench pulled the pelt more snugly about her. Surely even my lord had never taken such a beauty to his bed! There was such a freshness, an innocence that hovered around her, but there was a sensuous aura to her too. Her lips were swollen—from my lord's kisses?—and there were faint violet shadows under her eyes.

"Gilbert," the baron's voice broke dryly in on his thoughts. "If you have memorized the features of my would-be slayer, you may go. Do you go to the women's chambers and fetch Lianne a change of clothes. Then bring water for my shaving!"

The boy left, not daring to question further.

Again alone, Lianne and Guy measured each other.

"Now all will know what has befallen me," she spoke aloud her thoughts. "You have shamed Edgar Aethling in front of a woman and he will take out his anger in blackening my name."

"Ah—you would rather be known as a murderess than a harlot!" he jeered, eyes cold and hard. If Lianne had not spoken, he had been about to apologize for the youth's intrusiveness; now, he felt bound to disagree with anything she said.

"Surely killing a *Norman* can not be so great a sin!" she threw back in his face.

"You're not so angry that you failed to slit my throat—" he had crossed the room in a heartbeat and was perilously close to where she crouched on the bed— "you hate yourself because your heart proved traitor the second time and cried out for more of my pleasuring!" He held her face captive between his strong hands, dark eyes boring into hers.

"My body, never my heart, Norman dog!" she spat.

"I have a *name*, Lianne," he rasped, swarthy face pale with anger. "I am Guy. Or in company, 'my lord.' Say my name. Say it!" He shook her, and she felt a thrill of fear at the barely leashed power of those hands.

"Guy," she repeated woodenly. "Never will you be 'my lord.' "

"*Non?*" he breathed, leaning over her. "I am the lord of these . . ." he touched her lips with his index finger—"and this . . ." he touched one proud nipple and Lianne blushed with dismay to feel it respond—"and this . . ." He was reaching lower when the door again slammed open.

Edgar Aethling had spitefully wasted no time in informing Orm of his sister's shame.

The boy stood in the doorway, flushed with rage, clutching a pitchfork, the only weapon he could rapidly obtain. His eyes quickly took in Guy, who had been leaning dominantly over Lianne, his sister's nakedness concealed only partly by the pelt, the ripped remains of her garments lying on the rushes, the rumpled, bloodstained bed. His eyes dilated further. He charged the baron, pitchfork held on high.

Guy lured him easily away from the bedside and then effortlessly sidestepped the onrushing boy, wrenching the weapon from him as he charged past. Once disarmed, the struggling Orm was held with wrists twisted behind him.

"And who might this be?" Guy inquired coldly, becoming rather intolerant of the uninvited interruptions.

"My brother, Orm. Please, my lord, do not hurt him! He's but a boy! You can imagine what Edgar must have told him!" She sobbed wildly, terrified for Orm, forgetting entirely that she had vowed never to name him "lord" but a moment before. The Norman could easily have him hanged for turning a weapon on him.

"You . . . *nithing*," sputtered the youth, and miraculously found the Norman words learned at Robert's knee, "you have dishonored my sister? You must die for that!"

To Orm's and Lianne's astonishment, the baron began to laugh heartily. "I would say *that* is the very lightest thing that could have happened to your sister, you insolent pup! She tried to kill me last night—I'd say she got off rather easily!"

"Kill you? Lianne?" Orm looked at his sister in confusion, for he had known nothing of her plan.

"Aye. I tried, Orm. I believe he killed Edwin. But Satan whispered in the baron's ear and he awakened." Blushing, she tried to meet the her brother's incredulous eyes. "Orm," she continued firmly, "the Normans have the power of life and death over us now. Do not resist, even for my sake. There will come a time," she glanced at Guy who was watching her sardonically, "when England's true sons will rise and take back what is theirs. But you must live to see that day. Do not waste your life fighting over what cannot be restored now." She knew that Guy did not understand her English. His eyes darted repeatedly between brother and sister, ever alert.

But Orm was not so easily calmed. "I will fetch Tofig," he cried, speaking defiantly in French. "He will help avenge your honor!"

"Would that be Tofig, the rebel who ambushed and slew a number of Norman soldiers in defiance of Duke William?" inquired Guy with silky menace as he smoothly blocked the door. "It would seem, pup, if you are on familiar terms with him, you are very probably one of those outlaws as well—*you and your sister.*"

The full meaning of their danger was allowed to sink in. "I . . . I . . ." the boy stammered, all the fight gone now. They were at the Norman baron's mercy.

"Hear me, Orm, Lianne's loyal *frère.*" He turned the boy to face him. "I am in control here. You are beaten now. Let it remain so, and you will live. Raise your hand against me again—or any Norman —and you will not see another sunrise. And Lianne? I'm sure she would grace a certain brothel in Rouen rather well," he added cruelly, noting the boy tense and clench his fists again. "But unless you try this foolishness again, we shall not need to find if that is true.

"Lianne is *mine,*" he continued, speaking as much for her benefit as her brother's. "I shall not share her with my men, which might well have been her fate today. But neither is she free."

At that moment there was a timid knock. Guy called, *"Entrez."* Gilbert diffidently appeared, carrying a pitcher of hot water and a wine-colored gunna and a kirtle of a lighter shade. He set the clothing down on the bed near Lianne, flashing her an admiring glance. He then stepped back, looking uncertainly at Orm, who glowered back.

"This is Orm, brother of Lianne," Guy informed him with ironic courtesy. "From now on, he is in my service, as I must keep an eye on him. He is a serf now, but may find that hard to remember. He is your charge, Gilbert. Inform me instantly if he is less than loyal and industrious and I will . . . take appropriate measures. Help him perfect our language. His accent is execrable." He raised his hand in dismissal, and the two youths left, eying each other warily.

"You may dress now, Lianne," Guy told her as he shut the oaken door firmly, "unless you would pleasure my eyes further by the sight of your lovely body. I fear I have no time now to taste your delights further except with my eyes." Lianne gasped in indignation and turned around to pull the garments over her head. He did not turn to his shaving until she was covered, and she was fully conscious of his eyes appraising her even though her back was turned.

As they broke their fast in the hall, a summons came from Edgar and Guy to attend FitzOsborn and the Witan at Westminster Abbey to help plan the coronation ceremony and festivities, only a week away.

Lianne was left with her troubled thoughts, aware that the eyes of the ceorls followed her curiously. *Was it true*, she could almost hear them thinking, that she has *chosen the baron's bed, as lightly as any common trull?*

Mold wasted no time in seeking out Lianne. She came upon her in the kitchen, dicing vegetables for a venison stew, hacking at a stubborn carrot with an excess of ferocity.

"I have heard Edgar's slander, but of course I know it's not as he says, love.

What went wrong?"

"He wouldn't drink the wine," Lianne said disgustedly. "He came awake as I leapt at him and . . . then he . . . had me." She looked down at the vegetables, then collapsed in tears against Mold's buxom form.

"There. . . . Lord love ye. . . . Did he hurt ye bad? Was he a brute?" She held her away a moment, searching Lianne's tear-stained face. "O' course, any maid's apt to be a mite, uh, *sore* after, especially if she was not willing," she added, with good-humored frankness. A man having his way with a maid was nothing unusual to the lower class. Mold herself had been deflowered by Edwin's father at thirteen. She searched Lianne's arms and face for bruises.

"Nay, Mold, he did not beat me," Lianne said with a sigh.

"Then you're fairly lucky! You could've ended up with yer throat slit, just as poor Edgiva! A girl has to become a woman sometime, unless you're to become a holy nun! But come, tell Mold—what frets ye so?"

Lianne faced her then, blue eyes sparkling like wet diamonds. "He caused me—the second time—to act the wanton! He made me cry and scream and clutch at him and beg to be taken! And for a moment I forgot he was . . . *who* he was and I felt absolutely *wonderful*. . . ."

"Aye," answered Mold sympathetically. "That's a rare man who will trouble to give his woman pleasure. So does Tofig make me feel when we . . . love." She felt that Lianne, not a girl any longer, could endure her honesty.

"But I don't *love* that devil, nor he me! He did it to humiliate me!" Lianne answered fiercely, disturbed by Mold's comparison of Guy to Tofig. She stalked off angrily, reminding the woman of a cat lashing its tail.

"Yes, my lady, but sometimes hatred and love are but two faces of the same coin," Mold murmured thoughtfully to herself.

Five

Edgar Aethling and Guy de Bayeux returned just before the supper hour, tired and hungry. Guy, irritable from spending the day in the sullen company of his charge, found Lianne in the hall, overseeing dinner preparations, and pulled her to him, frowning as she stiffened.

"Ah, my loving friend, your warm welcome enchants me."

Ruffled and confused by his nearness, she sought refuge in a logical explanation and wrinkled her nose. "You, my lord, need a bath." She watched him carefully, but he was not offended.

"*Oui*, after last night and this trying day I doubt it not. You there," he called to a burly ceorl. "Bring a tub and hot water to my chamber." As the ceorl continued to stare blankly at him, he said with growing irritation, "Are they all simple? I said, I want a bath!" he shouted, as if raising his voice would aid comprehension.

"My lord, if you think to govern Saxons, you must needs learn our tongue. We may eventually learn some of yours, but being the *masters,*" she added with ironic emphasis, "you should become fluent in English. Else, how will you know if we are plotting against you or not?" she taunted daringly.

"I suppose you are right. Give me the words," he said grudgingly, and he repeated them, stumbling over the harsh, guttural pronunciation. The ceorl understood, however, and went to do his bidding.

"Now," he said with a wicked leer, bending close to her ear, "how do you say, *en Anglais,* 'I want to take you to bed and make love all night with you?' " She would have struck him, but he caught her wrist easily.

"Come with me, spitfire," he commanded, and she had no choice but to obey.

In his chamber, Lianne stood uneasily as the two ceorls emptied buckets of steaming water into the great oaken tub. When the tub was sufficiently full, the baron dismissed the servants with a wave of his hand and turned expectantly toward her.

"Alors . . ." Dear God, would he attack her now? Was this agreement to bathe merely a ploy to get her to his chamber— he who needed nothing but force to bend her to his will? But he stood there, impatience flashing across his dark features.

"Come, Lianne—are Saxon girls so ill-trained in courtesy? Did you never assist your father's guests to bathe?"

His remarks stung, for it was indeed part of the hospitality offered a male guest in the hall for the ladies to assist in disrobing and bathing.

"My father's guests never wore mail," she scowled.

"I see. *Eh bien,* I will teach you a squire's duties then . . ." and so he showed her how to help him remove the hauberk and the quilted gambeson beneath. She blushed when it came to untying the cross-gartered chainse. He could very well do this himself but he delights in subjecting me to his will, she fumed, and a glance at his dancing, amused eyes confirmed her opinion. Nevertheless she could not remove her gaze from the sight of his naked, magnificently masculine form climbing into the water. He settled with a grateful sigh into its warmth.

"No, you have no leave to go," he said a moment later as he caught her inching quietly toward the door. His arms and legs were covered with soapy lather.

"Scrub my back."

She channeled all her internal rage into the rough, soapy cloth, scrubbing roughly across the well-formed, powerful shoulders, trying not to take pleasure in the sleek feel of them.

He ducked his head forward, wetting his ebony locks, then leaned back with a pleasurable sigh as Lianne rubbed the soapy lather through his hair. Her fingers seemed to have a will of their own, savoring the thickness of his hair as they massaged his scalp. He cast a questioning glance up and back at her and it was as if she suddenly came out of a trance. She was furious with herself! Here she was, serving him like a serfgirl thirsty for a toss in the hay, hoping to attract her lord's lust for a night! Without further thought, she picked up the bucketful of rinse water standing by and dumped it on his head.

He sputtered, pushing his wet hair off his forehead and looking angrily from under water-drenched lashes. "You might have warned me to tilt my head back, wench!"

She was hard-pressed not to giggle at the sight of him. "I cry pardon, *mon seigneur*," she said with mock humility. "Will my lord get out and dry himself with this humble towel?" Her voice dripped honey.

"Nay, woman." He arose in the tub, moisture dripping from the hair on his chest and legs. "I think you need a scrubbing too." His next movement was too fast for the eye to follow. In the twinkling of an eye she found herself lifted off her feet and dropped with an unceremonious splash into the huge tub. He chuckled to hear her do some sputtering of her own.

"My lord! My clothes!"

"Ah, yes. We must remedy that, must we not?" he laughed huskily, and began pulling them off over her head, then laying the sodden garments aside to drip on the rushes.

Smiling with satisfaction, he began to rub the lathered cloth over her back and shoulders, ignoring her wrathful muttering. Then, as his attention turned to her upper body, the smile left his lips and he impaled her with his eyes. "We must not neglect *any* part, *hein?*"—as the cloth dipped underwater to wash between her legs. Then he abandoned all pretense of bathing her; he pulled her into the strong circle of his arms and his mouth closed on hers.

Lianne, bemused from the sudden dunking, did not resist for a moment while his tongue sweetly plundered her mouth, but as he arose, holding her in his arms, intending to carry her from the tub, she began to struggle.

"No! I will not be a vessel for your lust! Loose me!" She lashed out at his neck and shoulders futilely, and then her curved fingernails raked his cheek.

"Vixen!" He dropped her furiously on the rushes, but was upon her before she could move, holding her wrists, preventing her from doing any further damage. A thin line of blood welled up from the scratch mark, intersecting the scar. His glare was searing. "Why do you do this? You've already lost your virginity, so why this maidenly pretense of reluctance? You want me as much as I want you."

A lesser woman might have quailed before him, but Lianne responded to his scornful anger. "You lie! Is it so impossible for you to imagine a woman immune to your—" she looked meaningfully at his arms imprisoning her wrists —"winning ways and tender charms?"

"*Oui*—I don't doubt there are some, but you are not one of them. You're as hot for my pleasuring as I am to do it."

"Conceited wretch! Let me go! I desire you not!"

"Before I finish, sweet Lianne, you shall beg me to take you," he promised, brown eyes burning, his lips an inch from hers.

"When hell freezes, my lord!" she spat at him. Her struggling seemed to fan the flames of his ardor, so she forced herself to lie limp and passive under his hands. He gave her an amused glance which said that he knew what she was attempting, but it would not work.

His lips met hers again, gently at first, then as she clenched her teeth and refused him further admittance, the pressure of his powerful jaws forced her mouth open. His hand found her breast, caressing, teasing; she knew he could feel the racing pulse and rapid breathing that accompanied her unwilling arousal. His fingertips played over her flat abdomen, stroking, leaving a trail of fire. Guy's mouth left hers to close on her breast, his tongue teasing, circling the areola, making her gasp. Her fingers clutched at his back as his hand found that special center of her, between her legs.

Her breathing was as hoarse and ragged as his own. Dear God! The sensations that his touch sends rocketing through me! He came back to kiss her again, and her arms closed around his neck. She arched close to him now as he inserted a finger at the moist, warm entrance of her, rotating it gently, deeper and deeper. When she was sure she could stand no more and would have to cry out, he shifted, removing his fingers, so that he was over her now, manhood hard and ready.

"Well, vixen, do you want me?"

Blue eyes blazed at him. "Go to hell!"

He pushed teasingly forward, then withdrew, the tingling spreading in concentric rings as he repeatedly did this, meanwhile continuing to stroke her breasts. His tongue licked the outside of her lips, then his mouth spread the fire over her eyes, cheeks, forehead, and ears. His weight supported on his elbows, he rotated his hips slightly so that the thrusting was taunting, unbearable. She had to have him inside of her, all of him. She pushed against him and he backed away, raising his hips so that his manhood no longer lay against her, but was poised maddeningly just above.

"Guy!" Her fingers pushed convulsively at the small of his back, but the muscles were unyielding.

"Guy, what?" he chuckled.

"Take me!" His maleness touched her again, but again played teasingly around the outside.

"Beg me!"

"No!" Her head thrashed as she tried to deny him, but the feeling was a flood-tide that must break upon her.

"Beg, Lianne!"

"Please, Guy . . . I—*beg* you, take me!" And he plunged home and pressed her close to him as together they took their release.

A few minutes later, as she lay in the circle of his arms, listening to their breathing slowing to a normal rate, a knock sounded and a timid voice inquired, "My lord, supper is ready and served in the hall."

Guy looked down at her, then half-raised up to call, "Bring our supper and serve us here, Gilbert. We will not come down to the hall tonight." He looked down at Lianne and grinned infectiously, helping her to her feet.

"My lord, I . . ."

"It is 'Guy' when we are private," he reminded.

"Guy . . . my clothes are wet. I would not have your squire see me naked again."

"Your clothes are here." He went to a chest by the bed and opened it, revealing her garments. Her gaze flew to his face.

"I took the liberty of having them moved here today. You shall not sleep away from me while I am here, and I agree it would be a shame for Gilbert to see more of your lovely body. Clothe yourself!"—and he gave her bottom a playful slap.

"Tell me of yourself," he commanded later as he picked the meat from a capon and washed it down with a sip from the horn cup.

"What is there you do not know?" she returned bitterly. "You know all about Edwin and me."

"Yes, and you have an angry cub of a brother who would spit me and roast me for 'defiling' you," he said easily. "But where is your outraged father, who will want to do that or worse?"

"Dead," she replied dully.

He seemed surprised. "But you rode to Fairlight, you said that day, to fetch him."

"He died of wounds just after I arrived. There were some murdering Normans who had come there from Romney."

"Ah, yes. Aimeri's ship, that went astray. We wondered what became of them."

"Well, they're all dead now," she said with satisfaction and a flash of defiant spirit.

"Is there no one else?" he asked, ignoring her last jibe.

"My younger sister, Elfgift, is still at Netherfield Abbey."

"Did she desire to take the veil, then?"

"Hardly. She and my sister-in-marriage came out to look for me that day I came to Senlac field after the battle. Orm and I later found them, both raped. Edgiva was dead; they slashed her throat after they tired of her. Elfgift . . . her mind has left her. She's as a wooden doll, that says nothing and whose eyes are blank. The nuns care for her until she gets better, if ever that should be." Her voice was bitter.

He looked thoughtfully at her for a moment. "I'm sorry to hear of those things." His heavy-lidded brown eyes were limpid, sincere. She looked away, uncertain of what to say. "You are a beautiful woman, Lianne, in spite of all the tragedy that has befallen you."

Her eyes flew to his face, a blush staining her cheeks. Gone for a moment was the war-hardened fighter before her, and she decided to press forward in this atmosphere intimate with the afterglow of pleasure.

"My lord—Guy, what of me?"

"What of you, my lovely one?"

"What is to become of me?"

"I will never let you go again." A curtain seemed to fall down in those honey-brown eyes; they were again wary, watchful.

"Am I to be your . . . leman?" Once, in a tree, he had spoken of her as his intended lady—to be known now as his mistress was a very different state.

"If that is what you choose to call it. You are *mine*, Lianne. I will not share you."

"And what . . . what if I am got with child by you, my lord? What then?"

It was a long moment, during which she could not bear to look at him. He studied the woman before him, who stared at the glow from the brazier and chewed on her lip.

"Bastards of the nobility are always cared for in Normandy." His words fell like drops of icewater. "I see no reason why it should be different here. You shall never see want, Lianne, I promise you."

"My lord is most generous." The irony was lost on him. And what of her own people—how would she be treated by them? The English would see her as a traitor (however unwilling), a harlot who could forget her slain husband and go off with one of his murderers for the sake of a secure home.

"Will I not be out of place when you return to Normandy?" Her question was a test of many things.

"I shall be staying in England, for the most part. My future is here, as is Duke William's."

"But what of Bayeux?"

He was surprised—she seemed interested in the welfare of the barony itself. "I have a younger brother who will act as seneschal," he said, dipping a crust of wheaten bread into the sauce. "I shall perhaps go back to . . . take care of things once His Grace is secure on his throne, but after that it will be largely up to Gervais. I make no doubt that William will be conferring lands in England on those who helped him achieve his crown."

"Lands belonging to Englishmen," Lianne flashed. "They are not his to give!"

"They are, by right of conquest," he said evenly, "if not by the right given him by Edward, who meant him to be king. Besides, many of those lands are ownerless now, Lianne—their lords died at Stamford Bridge, or Senlac. It is not good for them to remain so."

"And what of Orm?" she asked, leaning forward. "You told your squire he was a serf. That means he is attached to the land, land that you do not, as yet, have. He was a thegn's son! Had William not come and changed all, he probably would have become a warrior, a housecarle, like Edwin—a proud man, not a slave!" Her tone was pleading, tears welling up in her eyes as she reached across and clutched his hand. "Please say my brother is not to be a serf!"

He was again surprised. Lianne had not tried to wheedle anything for herself, as his previous mistresses had in exchange for the gift of their bodies, after he had taken her innocence. His eyes gave no indication that, as a warrior, he understood the anguish caused by the thought that one not born to that state was doomed to menial servitude.

"What your brother becomes shall be somewhat up to him," he answered at last. "If he is trustworthy and serves me well—who knows? *But I shall break him if he thinks to play me false—as I shall do to anyone who thinks I am a fool.*"

She could only return his gaze, knowing he was warning her as well.

Six

I t was but two days before Christmas, when the anniversary of Christ's birth would be celebrated by a coronation. William the Bastard would be crowned on that day, ironically just a few days less than a year since his ill-fated predecessor had assumed the throne.

A year ago I was a maiden in love with my handsome warrior, mused Lianne as she supervised the bringing in of the Yule log, which would burn for many nights. She was determined that the presence of their foreign conquerors would not dim their traditional observances. So many were dead now whose faces were lit with joy at this time last year. . . .

"It's a beautiful log. You did well to find it," Lianne complimented the men who dragged it inside, among whom were Orm and Gilbert. Mold, coming into the hall just then, concurred. Gilbert beamed at the praise, understanding the tone if not all of the English words. Any word from Lady Lianne was a gift from a goddess, to him.

"Oh, do you think it will please Baron Guy?" inquired Orm with wounding sarcasm.

Lianne recoiled as if slapped. Mold was even quicker, leaping forward and boxing his ears. "You little wretch! You have no idea what your sister has endured!"

"I see that she is not homeless and begging in the streets, as are many honest English who would not tamely submit to the foreign devils—!"

"No, and neither are *you*," Mold said with asperity, glancing meaningfully at his warm clothing, the fire, and the comfortable hall. "Now look what you've done!" She boxed his ears again, bringing forth a howl of pain, after seeing Lianne bolt the hall, hand to her mouth, eyes suspiciously bright.

Guy had been gone when she awakened that morning, the chamber empty then as now, as she went there, biting her fingers to keep back the tears until she was safe behind the heavy oaken door.

It was as she had feared: her brother—and how many others?—saw her as a turncoat, a vile, weak woman. She recognized that Arm was undergoing the difficult period of maturing youth during a time of national unheaval; still, his words cut like a knife. He had always looked up to her. Anything his sister had done was obviously right and worthwhile. He had worshiped Edwin Wulfsson first because he had Lianne's heart. To be knocked from her pedestal so unfairly was a painful thing. Oh, *damn* Guy de Bayeux, with his dark, handsome features, his catlike grace, his lazy, caressing voice while he made love!

"Ah, there you are, Lianne. Waiting for me?" The owner of that voice broke cheerfully into her revery.

"You are happy, my lord?" she inquired flatly.

He was apparently oblivious to her mood. "Yes, I have learned that His Grace will soon rid us of that obnoxious youth, Edgar Aethling! He plans to deed him lands of his own on Coronation Day. I shall soon be free of that little wretch!"

Lianne could not help but smile as his hands mimicked throttling the sullen young man. His gaiety was infectious.

"Dinner is ready in the hall, Lianne. Shall we dine with the others tonight?"

She felt comfortable sitting with him on the dais, instead of at her previous position below the salt, as befitted a serving wench in Edgar's hall. It seemed that every eye was on her. That Edgar Aethling was seated on her left, in the center of the dais, made matters worse;

he lost no opportunity to make sniping comments when Guy's attention was diverted elsewhere.

"My Lady of the Bedchamber, we are honored with your presence. I am shamed I did not recognize your . . . uh, *potential* before."

Lianne paled with anger, fighting down the urge to slap the youth.

"Lianne, some mortrews?" Guy interposed smoothly, more aware than he gave evidence of Edgar's spite at finding a "ceorl" as a supper companion. "By the way, I was noticing the horses in the stable tonight, after I saw to Nuage's rubdown. What happened to the little black palfrey you used to have?"

"She was stolen, my lord, at Senlac. I returned from finding Edwin's body to discover her missing." Whatever had made him notice that?

"Oh, I see. Too bad—you should have kept her with you, you know."

She reacted defensively. "Doubtless. And if I had, my dear husband would have received honorable burial! Without Storm, I had no way to carry his . . . body . . . away." The last was uttered upon a sob, drawing the attention of those nearby.

"Indeed, I am sorry to hear of it," he replied, his buoyant mood having vanished with her outburst. He was the cold, remote lord again. Edgar smirked as the atmosphere between the two sharing a trencher became chilly and guarded.

Guy addressed no further remarks to anyone at the table, and his silence cast a pall over the rest who supped. No one lingered at their trencher, scattering quickly to their duties.

He took her quickly and efficiently that night, wasting little effort at arousing her, though by now his touch and his eyes on her alone were sufficient to start her treacherous pulse racing. After Guy rolled away from her and almost immediately slept, Lianne lay awake for a long time, staring up at the ceiling, listening to his breathing.

Seven

"Here, Lianne, this is for you to wear to the coronation," Guy said early on Christmas morning as he undid the package in the privacy of their chamber. His tone was casual, noncommital. "You have not other suitable garments."

"This is for me?" she asked, eyes enormous as the gown unfolded on her lap, a bliaut of the softest wool dyed a light blue that would match her eyes. It was floor length, with fitted long sleeves, and laced up the sides to tightly emphasize her narrow waist and full, ripe breasts.

"It . . . is beautiful," she stammered, pleased in spite of herself. But she could not help but add, "Where did you get it?"

"That need not concern you, wench." Instantly she knew she should not have asked. There would have been no time to have ordered it made; she wondered from which English lady it had been seized.

"I meant no offense," she murmured, pulling it over her head. "Merely, I did not expect to be going to the coronation."

"Certainly you shall go."

As she prepared her hair, she asked, "Will William want the conquered English seeing him crowned?" She could not avoid the defensive sarcasm that crept into her voice.

"*Bien sûr.* What better way for them to be convinced that the era of the Usurper, Godwinesson, is truly over?" he said archly, eyes unwittingly glowing as he beheld her, comely beyond words in the simple but elegant gown that hugged her luscious figure. It was belted at the waist with a garnet-studded girdle. Her golden hair gleamed, falling below her waist under a sarcenet veil of gleaming white.

"What a beautiful woman you are," he breathed, bad temper vanquished by the vision before him.

"*Merci,* my lord." She would not have been female if she did not appreciate his admiration.

Guy was himself a rather elegant figure in a calf-length overtunic of gray wool, with embroidery at the neck and tight-fitted sleeves. Over it he wore a mantle of rich blue, fastened with a gold brooch set with colored enamel. His dark hair gleamed. He fastened on the jeweled girdle that kept his sword ready at his side, and bid her go out before him. "It is time we left for Westminster."

Guy de Bayeux's mounted knights awaited him in front of the halls, as did Edgar Aethling, his prancing, curvetting mount betraying the impatience of his master to get this humiliating day finished. The servants of the hall, among them Mold and Orm, stood watching the preparations. Guy's great destrier, Nuage, pawed the ground, splendidly groomed, his dappled coat gleaming in the sunlight of the early morning.

Lianne looked around for some indication of whether she was to ride pillion with someone or if a cob or mule had been borrowed for the day for her. The baron, she knew, would farther on join a walking procession of the Norman nobility going into Westminster Abbey.

"Gilbert," Guy called his squire forward and the young man came, grinning, leading a beautiful mare of the purest white, her trappings and size proclaiming her to be a lady's mount.

Lianne felt her heart skip a beat, then settle into a rapid, excited rhythm as her mouth dropped open in astonished joy.

"For you, Lianne. An early *Hanguevelle*, a New Year's gift, shall we say? I only wish she could have been black."

The mare stamped her foot, as if in derision, and nickered at Nuage, who pricked up his ears and shook his mighty head as if to agree.

"She in indeed beautiful, my lord. I shall call her Noelle, in honor of the day."

Lianne's mind was racing as the procession set forth, headed toward the western gate of the city of Thorney, the marshy island on which Westminster Hall and Abbey were built. To have given such gifts—even with the justification that he did not want to be ashamed of her in public—argued a very different feeling for her than the selfish, dominating lust which was all he allowed her to see of him when they were together. He had not been able to disguise for a moment the admiration shining in those warm brown eyes, and when her careless, hasty tongue had not yet turned him defensive and cool, he had actually smiled. She stared down at the alabaster withers of her mount, and over at the baron, who rode silently ahead and to her left. He, meanwhile, had been regarding the way she beamed with pleasure at the mare, and his lips were set in a curious half-smile. Suddenly her mood was influenced by the fact that it was Christmas, and her mouth curved upward.

The crowd, mumbling and sullen, almost entirely English, had seen the smiles also, and seized upon them.

"Look at the slut! Grinning at a Norman murderer, and she's obviously English! What does he have, I wonder, that our good English lads have not?"

"Life and lands, I trow!" bawled a fat old fishwife, her face the color of a blood pudding.

Various ribald comments as to the Norman's sexual characteristics followed, the remarks passing down the line as Guy and Lianne rode past.

Lianne looked down at the reins gripped in her hands, a blush of shame staining her cheeks. She felt at that moment a harlot, however unwillingly; she was guilty, for she rode gorgeously appareled on a mount fit for a queen while many, cold and hungry, looked on.

Guy had correctly interpreted the tone of the remarks, and reined in Nuage so that Lianne's mount caught up. Hand tensing on his sword hilt, he directed a murderous, quelling glance at the hecklers. "What do the whoresons say?" he asked her fiercely.

"Naught, my lord." She would not look at him, but her radiance was dimmed.

"Damn their eyes! The English are a stiff-necked, stubborn people!" Nuage trotted ahead again, and all she could see was his ramrod-straight back. He leaned over and murmured to Sir Ralf, and suddenly the contingent bristled with lances, casually held before, now gripped at the ready.

The abbey was ablaze with candles and color. Lianne, seated only with Gilbert until the procession was done, gazed about her at the great rounded arches and massive supporting columns and thought of the simple, otherworldly Saxon king whose lasting memorial this building was. Had he been a more lusty warrior and less a celibate saint, she doubted she would be sitting here, one of several dozen Saxons among their Norman conquerors.

William strode in confidently between Bishops Aldred and Stigand, his eyes fixed upon the high altar. Behind Odo, bishop of Bayeux, paced several rows of priests dressed in ceremonial white and carrying the Host, a great golden crucifix, and saints' relics. They chanted the "Te Deum," the sound echoing off the walls in the hushed, expectant atmosphere. Behind them walked the English nobles who had survived and submitted, such as Earl Waltheof, followed by the Norman barons who had helped bring the Bastard Duke to this day.

Guy walked between Robert of Beaumont and William of Warenne, behind William FitzOsborn and Robert of Mortain, William's other half-brother. The Norman barons were sumptuously arrayed, but all looked about them with wary eyes, noting the sullen Saxon faces in the abbey, and kept their right hands near their weapons' hilts. The guard outside, also, was formidable, for who knew if the conquered city, with its former fyrdmen and discontent Danes, would attempt to rise against their masters while they were bottled up inside the abbey?

They should be realistic, Guy hoped as he stepped into the place beside Lianne, and accept the benefits of the just government William will ensure, and the blessings of a stable clergy, he added wryly to himself as he noted Stigand standing sullenly back as Bishop Aldred stepped foward to lead the ceremony. William was taking no chances on the sanctity of his coronation. He would not allow Stigand's fawning submission to blind him to the controversy clouding this churchman's position.

As the rest of the procession found their places, Guy stole a look at the Englishwoman whose body he had known so intimately over the last few nights, but whose spirit eluded his grasp. I have brought her to the point of tearful physical submission, he thought, and made her tremble with unwilling passion, but still she is not mine. I would not have her servile or cringing, but would to God that I did not feel I was wrenching the response from those full, lovely lips. He thought of the way her hair, respectably bound under its veil now, spread out like a golden river on the bed as she lay writhing under him, and his pulse quickened, even as he stood in the brightly lit abbey with the heat of so many close-packed bodies surrounding him.

Lianne also was not concentrating wholly on the pageantry before her but was thinking of Guy, not handsomely dressed as he was today but naked before her in their chamber, his magnificent male body close to hers as he pulled her against the hard planes of his chest, lowering his dark head to seize her lips with his own half-open, hot mouth, his honey-brown eyes darkened with desire. She remembered the sensation of his hardness pressing against her thighs. . . .

She gasped to herself at the reality of the daydream, then looked up to see if the sound had been audible. He met her glance, but his enigmatic hooded eyes would not answer her question. Perhaps he could read her mind, she wildly imagined, and a fierce heat suffused her cheeks. She looked away.

While at the high altar there were chants from Norman liturgy, and salutations to William in the name of the Virgin, St. Michael, and St. Raphael, Lianne wondered, Dear God, why did I never feel this raging desire for Edwin? We were betrothed, we kissed, he touched me, she puzzled confusedly, as if a friendly warm relationship legalized by a betrothal ceremony automatically conferred that magical alchemy between a man and a woman! I loved Edwin. I cared about him, but while I was glad to see him my heart never skipped a beat when he entered a room, my blood never felt like liquid fire where his hand touched my skin. . . . I thought of bearing his children with delight, but never longed to do that with him which would get me with his seed. . . . How can I feel that way for a despised enemy—a conqueror of my land, who has made me and mine like chattels, to dispose of at his will?

Just then the voice of the Bishop of York, Aldred, called in English for all present to acknowledge William their rightful king, followed by the Bishop of Coutances requesting the same in French, and the abbey echoed with the acclamation of the witnesses to the sacred ceremony. William looked pleased, even from a distance, especially at the heartiness of the native response.

Guy de Bayeux, after having joined his voice to the second assent, shot a triumphant glance down at Lianne as if to say: See how your countrymen grasp reality, *ma belle.* Should you not accept defeat, and submit to me with as good a will?

Her cool blue eyes flashed back the message: Never, Norman, you will have to take it, just as always. He looked away, lips compressed to a firm, tight line.

Then the uproar from the outside began to penetrate to the interior of the abbey—noises of shouting men, screaming horses, and slowly at first, an insidious crackle which built to a roar: fire!

"What is happening, my lord?" Lianne, alarmed, queried. Was this some planned destruction—burn London once it lay helpless?

"I could as well ask you, Lianne. Tell

me," he demanded as his grasp painfully tightened on her wrist, "was there some rebellion planned for this hour? Tell me, or, *par Dieu,* I'll break your arm!"

"I know not, my lord!" she gasped as his hold became more painful, his eyes blazing down at her. Her eyes were uncertain, innocent, and yet, damn them, defiant!

All around them men were nudging their neighbors, making whispered inquiries to which the answer was an inevitable shrug of the shoulders and a bewildered expression. And the uproar outside grew.

The ceremony attempted to continue, with chants from a Norman choir, but the attention of those present was clearly focused outside, where the roar of the flames and shouting grew louder.

"Gilbert, go out and see what is happening—quickly! Report back to me!" directed the baron urgently.

Gilbert returned after a few minutes, during which many got up and left, obviously afraid of being trapped in the church.

"Our soldiers thought the shouting of acclamation was rebellion in the church," gasped Gilbert, out of breath from fighting his way through the fleeing coronation guests. "They thought to set up a diversion by burning houses nearby. There are some English resisting the burning!"

"Fools!" growled Guy. "Are my men

firing houses with the rest? I'd not have thought them so jumpy!"

"Nay, my lord, our men tried to dissuade the others, but no one listened. I think they had been spoiling to do something, after listening to the English taunting them for hours."

"Well, I'd better leave too to help quell the disturbance," decided Guy, "and help put out the fire. Burning London is no way to celebrate a coronation. Lianne, remain here. You are far safer in the church than out in the streets, where it sounds like Norman and English alike have run mad."

She nodded, but the sounds of the growing tumult outside made her wonder if the church would be attacked next. As Guy departed, she turned her attention back to the coronation. William had paled, and obviously wondered whether to proceed with his hallowing or leave and fight. Shakily, hesitating at times and listening to the uproar outside, the archbishop continued, and William responded, his voice firm, "I, William of Normandy, swear to protect God's churches and their rules; I will govern all the people subjected to me with justice and will decree and keep right law, and will quite forbid all violence and unjust judgments."

Eight

An uneasy peace descended on London in the aftermath of the tragic mistake which had culminated in burning, looting, and unnecessary deaths.

De Bayeux and Lianne were at the Christmas court at Barking, which lay northeast of London. Here William had withdrawn until his fortress on the Thames could be built. Now officially the king of England, the "Bastard Duke" spent his time merrily, hawking for hours every day, dining in state with the nobles present each night, enjoying himself for the first time in three months. One would think that all England lay in peace at his feet, rather than the way it was: in the west and the ever-rebellious north, resistance still smoldered.

"I'll take them on in the new year," William promised aloud. Meanwhile, it was very satisfying to receive at last the submissions of English nobles such as Earls Edwin and Morkere, and Cospatric, who had waited until the coronation to accept reality. He returned to such their titles and lands, providing they could pay assessment per hide of land, which would be much more strictly enforced now under William's administration.

He conferred titles to other English lands to the nobles who had served him faithfully and who planned to stay on this side of the Channel. FitzOsborn was directed to raise a castle at Norwich and was given Hereford. Robert of Beaumont became Earl of Leicester; William of Warenne Earl of Surrey. Mere knights were not passed over, receiving cities and lands. One such "worthy" knight of which Lianne heard, Sir Engenulf, received Pevensey—Aye, and probably will squat in Edwin's hall as if he had the right, thought Lianne bitterly.

He gave Edgar Aethling estates, for which the once heir-apparent departed with all speed.

"And good riddance," laughed Guy, feeling as if he had dropped a clawing, clinging burden from his shoulders.

Guy was now a landed noble himself, having been created Earl of Hawkingham, in Hampshire, and he held also the honors of Chawton, Winslade, and Lingfield. These lands and those given to others had been confirmed at a large banquet given in the great hall, and each noble and knight had gone up to the dais, where William sat on his throne, and done homage for the honors.

Lianne watched, trying to ignore the feelings of admiration and pride as the tall figure of her Norman captor knelt in front of the sword held so that its hilt formed a cross, and took his seigneur's hands, repeating the traditional formula:

"Sire, I enter into your homage and faith and become your man, by mouth and lands, and I swear and promise to keep faith and loyalty to you against all others, and I swear to guard your rights with all my strength."

And William replied in the customary fashion: "We do promise to you, vassal Guy de Bayeux, that we and our heirs will guarantee to you the lands held of us, to you and your heirs against every creature with all our power, to hold these lands in peace and quiet."

Then William bent and kissed Guy, after which the new earl rose and swore on a golden reliquary of St. Peter, "In the name of the Holy Trinity and in reverence of these sacred relics, I, Guy, Baron de Bayeux, swear that I will truly keep the promise which I have taken, and will always remain faithful to King William, my seigneur."

Then William FitzOsborn, as seneschal, stepped forward and gave Guy a symbolic gilded lance and a rolled-up parchment that was the deed of conveyance.

William had sought out Guy afterward, coming upon him and Lianne at their table, saying, "Well, my lord Guy, Earl of Hawkingham, do your new title and lands suit you?"

"Very well, Your Grace. I thank you with all my heart."

The stocky Norman monarch's eyes took in Lianne, curtseying low before him, eyes lowered to the rushes.

"Rise, beautiful lady," he murmured, offering her his hand, and his interest was sparked as she raised her startling blue eyes to his, a hectic flush lining her cheeks. "Who is this, Guy? God's blood, she's a beauty!"

"Your Grace, I would present Lianne of Fairlight."

"Enchanting. You grace my Christmas court." Indeed she was an enchanting sight, gowned in a soft dove-gray bliaut, a white underdress showing at the neck and sleeves. Laced in and under the arms, it showed to advantage her high, proud breasts and narrow waist.

"I thank Your Grace," she murmured politely, so overwhelmed by this man that the insolence she planned deserted her lips.

"It is good to see Normans and English on warm terms, dining as friends," William went on, failing to notice the tension that stretched like a palpable thing between these two.

Lianne's head shot up at this remark, and after shooting a defiant look at Guy, she said impulsively, "I am not here with Baron de Bayeux of my free choice, rather by force of compulsion. He has made—certain threats—should I refuse to submit to his lust!"

Guy's face was a thundercloud. "Your Grace, I apologize for this woman's forwardness," he ground out, an iron grip on her shoulder.

"No need, my lord." William was unruffled. If Lianne had expected to appeal to the King's outraged morality, she was to be disappointed. "I took my own Matilda first by force," William said, musing on his wife's behavior before the marriage, when she vowed she'd rather be a veiled nun than submit to him, and he'd beaten her. "And we've been happily wedded ever since. But, my lord, before you proceed, there is another matter to which you must attend." The remark meant nothing to Lianne; she assumed he referred to the new lands.

Guy, however, knew he meant Mabile, to whom he was bethrothed, and he nodded uncomfortably. Betrothal was almost as binding as a marriage. William, a very continent man once he captured Matilda, had assumed he meant to marry Lianne. He—*marry* that wild spitfire who disgraced him before his king and whose tongue constantly spat caustic words! A wife should be dutiful, submissive, adoring! A small inner voice told him that he had never surprised an expression which could be called "adoration" on Mabile's face, either, but certainly there was respect between them. To Lianne he was merely the arrogant foreigner who had forced himself upon her, even if she *had* been behaving as a woman of loose virtue, chasing around the country with outlaws and behaving as one herself!

He bowed as William, with an amused twinkle in his royal eyes, passed on.

"Could you not resist showing the best of your Saxon manners to the king?" he inquired acidly.

"Are you afraid he could not bear the truth, my lord?" she asked sweetly. "I fancy he rather respected my frank speaking." Lianne realized she had felt a sort of *liking* for the Norman king, which irritated her, so she was determined to goad Guy still further.

"He would not have been *amused,*" he responded, "had he known of the pack of rebel dogs you traveled with since Senlac. His Matilda is now a model of obedience you would do well to copy, woman."

"What need have *I* to ape the actions of a *wife,* my lord?" she asked bitterly. "I am but your leman, to cast off at your pleasure. Perhaps if I act unruly I will the more quickly be free of your . . . 'attentions'?" She saw that the remark had thrust home.

"Ah, *oui,* to be thrown out starving on

the streets to ply your trade," he returned with rancor. By now they had strolled unconsciously away from the crowd into a passageway leading from the great hall to the sleeping chambers.

"What of your threat to send me to a Rouen brothel?" she reminded him.

"They wouldn't want you," he jeered. "You're not nearly accomplished enough for them, you know." He saw her eyes widen in offense, the taunt striking at her femininity in spite of herself. He went on, his anger too hot to give caution to his words, "A man could catch an ague just sitting next to you."

"It is said a cold woman will only warm with the right man," she taunted back, conscious of the rising storm of violence in him. He stopped his long stride, and with his weight forced her roughly against the wall, a hand leaning on either side of her. His eyes were nearly black in the dim light of a nearby flickering torch.

"You're with the right man," he told her, lips inches from her own. "I'll make you hot for me again," he promised, just before he ground his lips down on her. Her slender form could feel the roughness of the stone wall against her back as he leaned into her trembling body.

She was determined to remain stiff, unresponsive to him, but he slid his hands down her back to her buttocks, molding her even more tightly to his hard form. Unwillingly she began to catch fire from him, as his caresses became more and more demanding. She began to think he would take her then and there, and in her fevered state she half-wished he would! The flame was rising from her belly, spreading over every inch of her wherever his hands or mouth touched. . . .

Dimly she was aware of laughing, drunken voices coming down the passageway.

"Guy . . ."

Then he heard them too, and with a grin lifted her legs and carried her a few yards father to where their chamber door opened off the passageway.

Nine

They returned to London the next day, as Guy desired to close up the hall as quickly as possible and go to his new lands. He would retain it for his London residence, of course, and leave a few servants there to keep it ready at all times. He knew that Hawkingham boasted a manor house, but of its interior condition no one knew. Of the other honors, he knew nothing, and would have to survey each one's strengths and weaknesses.

His mood was buoyant, his mind full of the improvements he would make, the keeps he would erect, the first to be at his principal seat at Hawkingham, naturally. William would favor as many fortified castles as possible, built quickly by his barons to further aid in quelling Saxon rebelliousness. As more of England was pacified, William would distribute more lands, giving his lords scattered patches of land so that no one baron would become too strong on his own.

Lianne was quiet as she rode beside his great destrier on her petite mare, lost in a morass of self-hatred that rose higher and higher over her each time she caught herself stealing a glance at his handsome profile or starting to smile as he hummed a snatch of some French tune.

It's not as if I really had a choice, she mused. From her conversations with Orm, she knew that he was kept under as close surveillance as she was and that it was highly unlikely one of them could get away without the other. She could hope for no daring rescue by a band led by Tofig; now was not a time for Saxons to attempt foolish acts of rebeillion against Norman masters. It was a time of breath-holding, as the English watied to see how benevolent or harsh the new masters of the island would be, as the Britons had done before them when the Anglos and Saxons had been the conquerors.

The most troubling thought was, however, that even if she could leave Guy de Bayeux—if there were an honorable position open to her in, say, Edwin of Mercia's household—would she go? Barely used to being a woman, and as yet largely unaware of her own powers, she was disturbed by the magnetism of the virile creature riding beside her. Go? Far away from those warm brown eyes, those sensitive hands that could evoke such a trembling response, that demanding mouth on whose lips the name "Lianne" was transformed into a caress?

"Lianne!" With a start she realized he had called her name several times. She looked up to find him grinning maddeningly at her. He had laid his mailed glove upon her sleeve to gain her attention, and now he reined his mount closer in order to whisper into her ear.

"Thinking of last night, *ma mia?*" he teased. "I don't blame you. Here I am, dreaming of castles, while you remember the pleasures of our bed. Shame on me!"

She colored from her cheeks to the neckline of her mantle and wrenched angrily away from him. "You conceited French popinjay!" she hissed. "No woman daydreams of coercion!"

Guy turned his face away, and again she could see only his hard, chiseled profile. "Only an Englishwoman would lie to herself about her body's passionate responses and call it coercion."

"What would a Norman woman call it, my lord? *Droit du seigneur?*"

She had struck deeper than she knew. Though neither of them could honestly call last night's impassioned coupling an act of force, Guy's first taking of her could not have been mistaken for anything else, though her body had unmistakably responded.

Before Lianne, he had never had to use anything but the persuasion of his charm with a woman. He took pride in the fact that the dark good looks of which he was indifferently aware—in the same way one is aware of the weather, and uses his knowledge—and generous good nature were usually sufficient to cause any desirable woman to make herself available to him. What had resulted was usually a pleasurable interlude for both, as well as mere physical release for himself, for Guy was a skilled, generous lover who was careful to give as much or more joy than he received.

Until Lianne of Fairlight. With her, he thought, all his charm and handsomeness were as naught, and his person was as repulsive to her as any Norman man-at-arms with garlic and sour wine on his breath. The shuddering cries wrung from her as he brought her to climax were merely manifestations of her passionate nature, he believed, and capped this mistaken train of thought thus: Me she despises completely. It piqued his irritation, for the more she demonstrated her distaste for him—the only woman who had ever done so—the more he—all unaware—lost his heart to her.

Nor was it the kind of feeling that would lose fire if she should ever return his feeling. When Guy de Bayeux truly fell in love, his heart was irretrievable.

Ten

Mold had a warm, welcoming fire awaiting them, and a haunch of venison turning on the spit.

"My lord, my lady, you are welcome," she said as she poked up the fire in the center of the hall. Tacitly she had begun again acknowledging Lianne as mistress, their brief period of equality as fugitives and then servants over, but she did not seem to mind in the least. Lianne wondered whether Guy minded the equality with which Mold addressed them—"My Lord, my lady."

Gilbert strode up to them, leaving Orm, she noted, standing uncertainly by the fire. "My lord," he murmured as he bowed, and then, with a grin from one freckled cheek to another, he said in careful English: "Welcome back . . . to the hall, Lady Lianne. I . . . hope you had a g-good journey. Orm has taught me some English," he finished in a rush of familiar French.

She complimented him for his effort. It was then she noticed the bruise under his right eye, a discolored blue-green that indicated it was several days old.

"What happened, Gilbert?" she asked him, then looked over the boy's shoulders into Orm's guilty face.

"We fought, Orm *et moi*," Gilbert confessed uncomfortably, avoiding their eyes. "I regret, *ma dame*, I bloodied his nose for him." He looked up through his lashes at her, but finding her not angry at him, just surprised, turned his gaze to his master.

"What did the fight concern, Gilbert?" queried Guy, but the youth merely shifted his weight in the rushes and would not speak.

Lianne was staring at Orm, who returned her regard with some defiance.

"Ask your brother. God's Blood, I'll have an answer!" Guy growled. Lianne unwillingly complied, though when she had Orm's reply, she was as loath to tell Guy as Gilbert had been.

"It was nothing, my lord," she dissembled, "a mere quarrel between youths. Now, about the meal . . ." Her very casualness at passing on to other matters convinced him otherwise.

His grip tightened on her wrist and she

flinched, but held her peace until Orm at last defiantly spoke. "We fought, my lord, when I said my sister would wed no one but an honest Englishman, and Gilbert said his lord would wed my sister and she would be his lady, instead of just his whore as I said."

Lianne rushed to insert herself between Guy and her brother, sighing inwardly to hear that nothing had changed. Orm had grown no closer to accepting the reality of the situation so that it could go easier for him. Guy pushed her impatiently aside, as if she were a leaf, but he did not strike Orm as she had feared.

"Get you gone from the hall until your youthful arrogance is cooled," he ground out, his voice steel. "You will miss your supper this night, and may sleep with the horses, who have better manners than you. I should give you the lash, and I *will* whip anyone who gives you a morsel before breakfast," he said, raising his voice that all in the hall might hear. "By the morrow I would hear your apology to *votre soeur*—in your new tongue," he added crushingly. "See if you cannot improve that accent. You sound like a Breton peasant."

Orm, startled but relieved that he would not be lashed, or worse, quietly left the hall for the stable.

"Thank you, my lord," Lianne spoke up at his side, as he unclenched his fists, his eyes narrowed to follow the retreating figure.

"I just hope the puppy does not mistake my mercy for softness. I will not stand for any more insolence and disrespect."

"He offered *you* none," Lianne pointed out, "though I am sorry for his words."

That reminded him of Gilbert's speech, of his expectation that Guy would make her his wife, and he scowled afresh. "I wish everyone in the hall would mind his own business," he grumbled. "It is nothing to them what you and I do in our bed."

"Ah, but it is! You have scarce made it possible for your taking of me to be secret, my lord, with my brother finding me in your bed, with my garments moved to your chamber. Those people who know *care* about me—Orm and Mold."

"My squire also seems to be your willing thrall," Guy commented wryly, still morose at the feeling he was being pressed to "make an honest woman" of Lianne, against his will.

"You would do well to match Gilbert's ability to speak English," Lianne said tartly, leading the subject away from marriage and mistresses. "I shall speak to you at table only in English, my lord. If you want anything passed, you must ask for it in that tongue."

Guy grudgingly complied throughout the meal, and Lianne admitted that at least he knew enough English now that he would not starve—"if he can retain the

238

words in his scheming, devious Norman skull," she added pertly (but under her breath). He looked at her suspiciously, realizing she was probably being insolent, but refused to rise to the bait and demand a translation.

He excused himself then to go and speak to his men-at-arms. Lianne assumed correctly that it concerned the move to Hawkingham. Tomorrow would be spent, she knew, in packing up the clothing, food, and furniture that would have to be moved to the manor, for they knew not how well it was furnished, if at all.

She decided to take advantage of his absence to speak to Mold.

She found her at last coming in from the stables, and Mold met her look of concern with reassurance.

"Don't fret yourself, Lianne, I'm not contradicting Baron de Bayeux's orders. He said naught about clothing, so I merely took the lad a warm blanket. A night in the stables won't hurt him a bit— he has far too wounding a tongue, and that needs taming if he's to survive among the Normans."

Lianne agreed. "My thanks, Mold. I wished to speak to you." They sat on a bench not far from the fire. "My lord is an earl now and holds the honors of Hawkingham, Chawton, Winslade, and Lingfield, conferred on him by King William at court."

"The new king rewards his followers

well."

"Yes, and may the swine who received our hall have no joy of it," she answered with bitterness, then made a motion as if to brush away the futile thought. "In any case, we shall be leaving London soon." At Mold's inquiring look, she continued, "My lord apparently will not let me out of his sight. But you are free to go if you wish—you are not bound to the land, Mold, you know that. What of Tofig? Don't you miss him? Why not go to him in Mercia?"

"Bless you, Lady Lianne, for your concern for me. I know I could go. I would have done so had my place not been with you. Certainly I miss Tofig, that rascal. My bed is very cold and lonely of a night." She was frank and blunt, as always. "But it is not safe that he should come to me, and the time is not right for me to leave you and go to him. When the time *is* right, we shall be together. Perhaps we will even wed," she finished simply, and patted Lianne's shoulder. "You know, I wouldn't worry overmuch about Orm and Gilbert, either. They had that fracas the day you and my lord left, and had been getting along famously since then. Why, even now the squire is out keeping your brother company in the stables," she said, gesturing in that direction. "They're rehearsing the speech Orm must give on the morrow."

With a lighter heart, Lianne left the older woman to her tasks.

PART III
HAWKINGHAM

One

Several days later, they drew rein in front of Hawkingham's timbered hall, which was considerably larger than Thegn Rolf's residence at Fairlight had been. Radiating from the back, several outbuildings were visible. From the exterior at least, all the structures appeared to be in fairly good repair.

Such had not been the case at Chawton, which lay between London and Hawkingham. They had camped for the night in the blackened shell of the hall, over which a little thatch still covered the eastern third.

"Your countrymen have left their mark," Lianne murmured as they surveyed the ruins. Guy made no reply. He was naturally distressed to find one of his holdings in such a state.

Of the manor's former Saxon owner they had heard nothing, nor had any ceorls appeared at first, frightened off, possibly, by the sight of mailed men on horseback.

After they had retired for the night all huddled together under the roofed portion, they had been awakened by Sir Ralf who dragged an iron-haired thin Saxon man into the circle of light cast by the campfire.

"I caught him checking through our packs, my lord," the veteran knight told Guy, who was sitting up on his pallet. "I cannot understand a word he says," he added, looking hopefully at Lianne, who still blinked sleepily next to him.

Lianne quickly asked the old man what he sought and who he was. He seemed reassured by her calm English voice, and explained that he was Gudbrand, a ceorl of Chawton. He was merely hungry and meant no harm.

With some urging from Lianne, they gave him some food, and while he wolfed it down with great gulps of wine, she explained that the man stretched out on the pallet next to her was the new lord of the manor and would be erecting a keep here as soon as it was practical.

"There will be places for many loyal servants," she told him at Guy's direction, "and food and clothing as is the custom. Lord Guy promises to be a fair lord, just to those who treat him as is his due. Where are the other ceorls? Are you the only one left?"

"Nay, Lady. The others are in hiding. When the hall was burned, and our lord killed, many of the women were raped and the young lads beaten. They will not lightly trust the Normans again. But I will tell them of your words," he added, noting the dismay on her face at his story. "If *you* trust this Norman, perhaps it is true. Chawton will have a good master again."

Lianne had not dared admit that she was with the Normans by no choice of her own, and flashed a warning look at Orm to keep silent.

Now, however, sitting Noelle in front of Hawkingham, she breathed a sigh of relief that this manor seemed at least more habitable. It was set in a plain near the River Meon, and situated around it were several venerable oaks. A small village lay nearby with some dozen or so cottages of varying size, as well as a tiny stone church.

"They'll have to come out when the keep is built," said Guy, referring to the oaks. "All that cover will have to be removed as well." He gestured toward the clumps of gorse that dotted the countryside. "But the river will water the moat," he noted with a satisfied chuckle.

Just then a woman appeared at the door. Her most notable feature was her flaming hair, which, braided, reached below her waist. Loose tendrils hung around a pleasing oval face with slanted green eyes (cat's eyes, thought Lianne, bristling involuntarily), dark lashes, narrow little nose, and full, pouting lips.

"I am Wulfrune, Lady of Hawkingham, and I bid you welcome," she said in Norman French, speaking to Guy as if he were the only person there, her pose that of a temptress. Lianne had seen her eyes dilate and then flick with contemptuous dismissal over the blonde beauty at his side, and Lianne stiffened. Inside her somewhere, alarm bells rang. "And you are—?"

"This is Lianne of Fairlight, and I," said the earl coolly, not dismounting courteously because of the words he must say next, "am Guy de Bayeux, now Earl of Hawkingham."

She gasped and paled, as if cold water had been dashed at her. "But Hawkingham is mine, now that my lord is gone . . . died at Senlac . . ." There were tears in the green eyes now gazing beseechingly at Guy.

"Perhaps you heard the English lost that battle," murmured the earl, his voice still cool. "All land is Norman now, unless you possess a fortune to redeem it. In which case, I will be the loser . . ." He smiled wolfishly down at the flustered widow.

"You have family elsewhere, to whom you can go?" inquired Guy.

"No one, my lord," she sobbed, all the while gauging the handsome Norman's reaction. "I am quite alone and . . . in need of protection," she emphasized deliberately, "from marauding bands of homeless English. Perhaps your . . . wife needs a tiring woman?" she asked with touching humility.

Lianne wrinkled her nose as the woman courtseyed low, as Guy raised an inquiring eyebrow. Could he not see through her false pose? In her place, the only position the woman would likely have given Lianne was feeding the swine!

"I have a servant, thank you," replied Lianne, her voice icy as she indicated Mold on her mule. "And my lord is *not* my husband," she added bluntly, watching Wulfrune closely.

The woman struggled to keep the relief from her face. "I beg your pardon, Lady, I meant no presumption. My lord, will you then cast me out, in the midst of winter?" She shivered and pulled her mantle closer about her.

"Perhaps we can find a place for you," said Guy vaguely, more than a little aware of the woman's tendency toward histrionics. Such a one has never lacked for shelter, and never would, he mused, while her body was so ripe with promise and her hair, so boldly red and gleaming, kissed those swinging hips as she led the way into the hall. He was aware of the young widow's interest in him, both as a virile young male and as a powerful lord who could keep her in the comfort to which she was obviously accustomed.

Before Lianne had come into his life, he

would have been mentally plotting the red-haired beauty's seduction—no doubt an easy task in this case—but now he found himself strangely unattracted, and wondered instead if there was a suitable chamber for Lianne and himself for the night. . . .

He would have been amused if he had been able to identify the cause of Lianne's instant dislike of Wulfrune as jealousy, but Lianne herself had not recognized it as such. She only knew a feeling of immediate antipathy, which was echoed by Mold, who uttered darkly, "Keep your eye on *that* one," as they followed the Normans into the hall.

The hall was very large, with a huge stone fireplace in the center. Torches lit the great room dimly, but Lianne could see several tapestries on the walls made of bright colors and depicting dragons and other fanciful beasts, biblical scenes, and Saxon royalty. At one end lay a long dais on which the lord and his lady dined with their guests of like station while the ceorls and thralls dined at an intersecting trestle table below the salt.

During the evening meal Wulfrune, seated on Guy's left while Lianne sat on his right, made continual apology for the "meager fare," which was actually quite adequate, while at the same time calling attention to her cleverness at making do on short notice with the "little" she had.

"It has been long ere I served this number of knights, my lord," she sighed, casting her eyes down the table at Guy's retainers and fluttering her lashes. "But I am good with cooking in spite of the fact I am gently born—I could perhaps cook for my lord? I am also good with herbs, of healing as well as cooking." Her eyes promised much more.

Mold caught Lianne's eye in the torchlight. Her look said, Beware what that one serves you!

"We shall see," the earl replied noncommittally, and turned back to Lianne.

Wulfrune, however, was not content to be dismissed so easily and made frequent excuses throughout the meal to demand the earl's attention, often laying a hand entreatingly on his wrist. When the meal was over, she was quick to offer to show Guy the way to the "best" chamber.

"It was where my lord and I took *our* rest," she sniffed reminiscently as she took up a rush light and led the way from the hall. She had missed the beckoning look Guy gave Lianne.

Lianne, through some perverse whim, pretended not to notice and remained in the great hall.

"What are you doing?" hissed Mold, who had left her place to begin clearing the table. "Go with him! Don't leave him in the clutches of that slut!"

Lianne raised an amused eyebrow at Mold. "He's out of swaddling bands! Why should I care what he does with her? She's welcome to him!" she declared pettishly.

"Sister, she's right!" Orm said unexpectedly. "That woman wishes you ill, and covets the earl. Nay," he continued, putting up a hand to forestall her repeated denial. "He may be a Norman, but he has kept you fed and clothed, and none of us has fared as ill as we might have. Don't give her an opportunity to ensnare my lord."

"Why, Orm," she teased, nonetheless surprised, "Can Lord Guy have a champion in *you?*"

Mold's and Orm's fears of Wulfrune's intentions were quite correct. She was delighted to find the dark Norman striding at her side alone, and took advantage of his nearness while between the hall and the chamber, tripping over nothing and nearly falling against him. She recovered easily with the aid of his instantly proffered hand, but the rush light sputtered out on the stone passageway, dousing them in darkness.

"Ah, my lord, pardon!" she giggled throatily, clutching his arm closer than was necessary so that it brushed her voluptuous bosom. "I cannot think what has made me so clumsy!"

"Perhaps the mead you drank?" the earl inquired dryly.

She ignored that, for they were then at the entrance to the chamber. She opened the door, and they stepped inside.

From the glow of the brazier, Guy could see that it was a luxuriously furnished room, with dark velvet hangings on the large wide bed which was raised off the floor so high it had to be gotten onto by steps at the side, unless one were as tall as he. There were several thick pelts sewn together to make a warm, furry bedspread. The room boasted two backless chairs and a deep chest at the foot of the bed for clothes storage.

"My lord, I bid you welcome to Hawkingham . . . and my bed," murmured Wulfrune in the dim light, and thrust herself against his chest, pulling his head down to hers by insistent arms locked around his neck.

Guy knew he didn't want this woman, when there was Lianne; still, he was a man and it was impossible not to find his body responding to the hot little armful pressed against every inch of him, her wet mouth persuasively moving on his, her ripe breasts burning against him. She smelled of some rich, musky perfume.

"Oh, my lord Guy, you are such a man, and I have been so long without a man," she sighed. "I can tell you want me too. Together we shall rule Hawkingham." She snuggled more closely, a satisfied smile curving her lips.

Wulfrune's previous experience with men had been with those who, once their senses were inflamed, saw and heard nothing but what her body told them. Her words, betraying her true motive in seducing him, acted as cold water to his mindless lust, and he put her firmly from him.

"Ah, Wulfrune, I believed you desired me for myself alone, not what I could give you. I praise your honesty in reminding me. Fetch my lady Lianne, and this time I'm certain you'll manage to keep hold of the light," he said with heavy irony, ignoring her dismayed scowl.

They looked up to find that Lianne stood in the doorway, clutching a light of her own, and had apparently seen the redhead in Guy's arms. At what point had she entered? Guy wondered. Does she think I was going to couple with the slut had she not come? Suddenly he was disgusted with the way his body had automatically responded, though his conscious mind had taken Wulfrune's measure immediately.

"Nay, don't interrupt what you are doing," Lianne said scornfully, having seen the embrace but not having heard Guy's low words of dismissal. "I'm sure she'll suit admirably in bed, my lord, as I do not. She's a vixen, as her hair attests, perfect for the lusting animal that you are." Her eyes, twin blazing sapphires, raked the pair.

Wulfrune, understanding what Lianne had seen but not heard, nestled closer to the "protective" arm of the earl. He, however, had had enough of this little contretemps and pushed the red-haired woman roughly away.

"Go to the hall, where you belong

henceforth, wench," he growled. "And speak no more of 'ruling' to me. Mold will have need of you in the kitchen and clearing away the trestles." He spoke as to any serf.

Wulfrune's face was a thundercloud, even in the dim light, as she searched the Norman's face for any sign of weakening. There was none. She directed a murderous glance at Lianne as she stomped sullenly out, with none of the sinuous grace that had marked her entry. Lianne involuntarily stepped back, as one stays out of striking range of a poisonous serpent.

Once the door had slammed behind Wulfrune, however, she turned her attention back to Guy. "I meant it, my lord. Why not take one who lusts for you? You would have, had I not interrupted! You could leave me in peace."

Anger at himself having transformed into anger at her, Guy said maddeningly, "It might not be a bad idea at that. I'll keep her in mind for when you are cold to me."

"I'll never be anything else," she spat out as he crossed the room to her.

"Liar." He caught her to him, bending her nearly backward in a passionate embrace. "She had me quite skillfully aroused, beauty. We may as well not waste the feeling. I'm certain you can stir me at least as well as she, if you try."

Two

The following days were busy with learning about the running of the manor of Hawkingham.

Guy was up and about at dawn each day, riding out to inspect the land when the January winds did not blow too bitterly. He was usually accompanied by his squire and several men-at-arms. Sometimes he would take Orm also, but even then he left men-at-arms at all possible exits to the hall and its complex of buildings, evidently not trusting the English boy and his sister not to attempt escape.

One day the earl rode as far as Winslade and stayed several days, finding this fief also to be in a good state of repair. While there he investigated the availability of stone for beginning his keeps, and sought out masons to direct the building. England as yet knew few stone buildings, but with the Normans' coming this would change as the conquerors erected proof of their mastery. The master mason would probably have to be brought from Normandy, but with the rights that Guy had as lord to command his serfs' labor, the *motte* could be readied and a deep channel dug around it.

Lianne was far from idle in her lord's absence. On those days when he returned at eventide cold, tired, and famished, she was sure to have a hearty hot meal ready for him and his men, a meal soon devoured with great gusto and smacking of lips by the common soldiers. Guy seldom spared many laudatory words for the culinary efforts she had directed, but after he had eaten, his face lost its tense, stern look and his voice became less curt.

Wulfrune proved of little assistance to Lianne in her new position as chatelaine of the manor, giving vague or evasive replies about the number of pots or plate available, or the amount of stores left to see them through the winter. Sometimes her replies were outright misinformation, as when she denied the existence of any cloth to make new kirtles, only to have Lianne later happen upon several bolts of good woolen cloth in a well-hidden chest. Often Lianne would set her to some task and then find her louging indolently about the fire, stating baldly that the task was too hard or did not suit her.

"You work me as a slave," she whined to Lianne and all who would listen. "Remember, I have been a lady, not a serf, all my life. You will work me to death."

"I ask nothing of you that I do not demand of myself," Lianne said evenly, for in truth she had often worked long after the rest of the hall was deep in slumber, sewing much-needed garments for the serving-men and women, clothing to which they were entitled but which Wulfrune had been careless in providing. "Besides, I note a miraculous recovery every time food is placed on your trencher."

"You—you're just jealous becuase you know Lord Guy desires me," taunted the other.

"I have told him he is welcome to your overripe charms," said Lianne in a careless tone. "However, I have yet to see him forsake our bed. He is there *every night.*" She strolled away, tossing the words, "Get back to the kitchens, Wulfrune. As the priest tells us from the Holy Scriptures, 'They that do not work shall not eat!'"

The female ceorls of Hawkingham, far from aping their former mistress's attitude, were an agreeable lot who seemed relieved that they need no longer obey

Wulfrune as "the Lady." Lianne suspected that the other woman had been a difficult, unpleasant taskmistress. They did as Lianne asked, going out of their way to make helpful suggestions.

"We be glad it is an Englishwoman who is our lady," one woman, the laundress Hyrtha, explained one day as Lianne and several of the women were dyeing cloth. "Plenty of other manors be overrun by them foreign devils."

"But my lord Guy *is* Norman," Lianne pointed out.

"Yes, and you're not precisely his 'lady,' are you, Lianne?" taunted Wulfrune from the doorway. "Just what *is* your designation?"

There were hisses and shushes from the rest, but Lianne ignored her. To Wulfrune, *that* was intolerable.

"It is a shame to honest Englishwomen to see such a one giving ease to the enemy," she continued spitefully.

"My 'giving' was not by choice," said Lianne, weary of the same old defense. "*You*, however, could not wait to thrust yourself at him."

"Nor was that the first time she'd have spread her legs for a Norman," spoke up Hyrtha with glee. "When FitzOsborn marched here from the sea, she lay with half the men-at-arms!"

"Nay—only with FitzOsborn himself!" screeched Wulfrune, flushed with fury. She would have launched herself at the laundress but others barred her way. "I heard none of you complain when it kept the roof of Hawkingham over your spiteful heads. Why, think you, wasn't Hawkingham burned, as so many in their path were?"

"Yes, but by Our Lady, did you have to *enjoy* it so? Your shrieks of bliss kept us up half the night!" chortled Fat Mab, who helped tend the kitchen garden. Everyone laughed except Wulfrune, who stalked off.

"Ye can practically see her tail switching back and forth," observed Mold, reading Lianne's mind.

Lianne had naturally made the acquaintance of the hamlet's priest, a thin, gangling man with a tonsure of blond so pale it was nearly white, shy, pale blue eyes, a bony, long nose, and quick nervous hands that only seemed at ease when clutching his beads. Father Thomas was his name.

She had heard that he kept a wife, a plump, complacent dove of a woman, but since the coming of the Normans to Hawkingham the woman kept to their cottage as much as possible, obviously fearing the new lord would send her away. Wives of priests were unofficially tolerated by the English Church, but this ecclesiastical depravity scandalized the Norman prelates.

Father Thomas seemed pathetically eager to please, and Lianne realized after a few meetings that he was merely hungry for someone of his intellectual level to talk to. His spouse kept him well fed, mended his cassocks, and warmed his bed at night, but she was still only a serf elevated from her rude dwelling to the honor of being the "priest's woman" and of course was not literate.

Lianne made no secret of her situation, hoping, unconsciously perhaps, for severe enough penance that she could cleanse herself of her feeling of shame. It was soon clear, however, that the most harsh penance he would exact from her was a few Aves and Hail Marys. He was far too afraid of offending the only person since Wulfrune's old lord had died who could play a decent game of chess and discuss the Latin classics and who had even read *Beowulf!* She soon came to enjoy his nonthreatening company and gentle, unassuming ways.

The priest seemed frightened of Lord Guy, however. On the first occasion that Guy attended Mass with Lianne, Father Thomas darted frequent nervous glances at the dark, elegant Norman, apparently expecting him to rise from his kneeling position and slay him should a Latin word be mispronounced or the Mass be overlong.

He need not have worried so, for Lord Guy was at least as devout as the average Norman and took his religion seriously although he was apt to be cynical in other matters. Had their "Bastard Duke," now king, not been divinely protected throughout his perilous life, and hadn't their conquering invasion had papal blessing?

The priest visibly trembled when Lord Guy approached him after the service. "My lord, I bid you welcome to our humble church. We are honored by your presence."

"The honor is mine, good Father," replied Guy with no discernible mockery in his voice. "I thank you for your good offices toward Lady Lianne," he gestured toward the beautiful blonde woman at his side, "while I was away. I will be erecting a keep here, and would have you know, Father, there will be a chapel in it. I will rely heavily on your guidance for its decoration."

When the surprised priest raised his gratified eyes from his lord's feet, he met his solemn brown eyes for a moment and grasped his proffered hand firmly. Perhaps a Norman lord would not be so bad after all! When Wulfrune's husband had been alive, little heed was paid to religion, and the little church had suffered from the lack of its lord's benevolence. Wulfrune's faith was herself, and she had demanded that all others worship at that shrine.

Here, for all that was living in a state of sin with his lovely—and by her account unwilling—parner, was at least a noble who knew what was due to Our Lord and the Saints! He beamed at the coins Guy had pressed into his palm.

Three

Winter was passing, and everyone in the hall was restless and irritable from the enforced idleness.

Southern England had offered King William no resistance requiring aid from Guy's meinie, so he had spent the winter drilling his men and seeing that their arms were kept in battle-ready condition, so that the Saxons would know here was no weak, easy prey. Those who lived on Guy's lands learned to recognize their new lord on sight, and came to know him as a fair, though stern, ruler. It was said among his serfs that one need not fear evil from the Norman if one was doing what one ought. If not, the Norman's justice was swift and severe (though no more so than anywhere else in that time).

There had been one hanging, after Guy had presided over the hundred court: a serf named Oswald had killed his dicing partner in a drunken quarrel, and though the weregild specified by the court was one the man could have paid eventually in labor, Guy did not offer him the option. There was silence as Guy's captain, Sir Ralf, had whipped up the horse and left the serf kicking and thrashing in the air.

Guy privately felt sorry for the man, for on him had fallen the weight of the new lord's justice, to set an example that hopefully would not have to be repeated throughout Guy's holdings.

Lianne had said nothing, just retired in tight-lipped silence to the hall while the sentence was carried out. She knew why this judgment must be so harsh, but it could not make her happy to see any of her countrymen put to death.

There were no major crimes after that.

The men of Hawkingham had a tendency, when the Normans were seen outside of the halls, to yank all maidens out of sight. The women, though, even while fleeing, were apt to look back for a sight of those gleaming brown eyes, the sensual mouth, and the raven's wing-black hair of Earl Guy. Several of Guy's men also drew appreciative, though apprehensive, looks as well.

Guy made it clear, however, that maidenly virtue need have nothing to fear unless, again, one was not where one ought to be. None of Hawkingham's maids, while at work or in their humble wattle-and-daub huts, need fear the loss of her maidenhead. Those found wandering out after *coeuvre-feu*, though, or who behaved seductively toward the men-at-arms, were taken for what they appeared to be—and usually were.

Guy himself, although his eyes shone as appreciatively as any man's at the sight of a buxom wench's sweetly curved limb showing under coarse woolen skirts, did not exercise his right as the lord to command any of Hawkingham's females to his bed (to the infinite disappointment of some).

The golden-haired woman from Sussex seemed to keep him well-satisfied in that regard. The speculation about her grew as more tidbits of information were gleaned: she was a thegn's daughter and a housecarle's widow whom Guy kept as an unwilling prisoner, along with her brother. She never looked as if he beat her, however, and she seemed to grow in beauty as the winter ebbed. She had proven kind and generous and was well-beloved by the village folk, whose children pictured the Holy Virgin with Lianne's face and long rope of golden hair. The herbs she had brought with her from the hall in London were proving useful in treating Hawkingham's illnesses and injuries, and Lianne, dispensing them, gained confidence in their uses and in herself.

She assisted Guy to write a letter (for Guy, like many noble Norman warriors, could neither read nor write) to his brother Gervais in Normandy, directing him to hire a master mason to come over and direct the erection of his keeps at Hawkingham, Chawton, Lingfield, and Winslade.

"Who shall your castellans be, my lord?" she inquired, looking up from the parchment.

He glanced up in surprise that she should ask. "For one of them, perhaps Sir Ralf. The others? Gilbert is too young and not yet knighted. We shall see. Why, did you have a candidate?" he mocked sardonically.

"You would do well to find a Saxon to entrust to at least one of them, my lord," she returned with honest directness. "Your fiefs would be stronger if the people in them felt they had a representative, that they were not merely governed by foreign conquerors."

He raised an eyebrow at her. "You certainly don't sound conquered, *ma douce*. You find your way around me, and do what you will, for the most part."

"Aye. In all areas but the two most important. I may not leave. And I do not sleep alone."

Four

On a particularly mild day in March, the earl, Lianne, and several of the men-at-arms went hunting. The supply of salted meat had gotten dangerously low, but it had not taken much urging on Lianne's part to interest the men in the hunt in any case. They were becoming moody and irascible with boredom, and she too welcomed the exercise and fresh air.

Wulfrune's lord had kept a pack of hounds for hunting wild boar and stags, and now they barked their joy to be starting out, not having had the chance to do what they loved best for many months. Only one, a bitch heavy with her unborn litter, was left to sulk unhappily in the kennel. She must not be endangered;

good hunting bitches, which could give birth to many more like her, were valuable possessions.

The hall's inhabitants had arisen at prime; several ceorls assigned as beaters had gone out even earlier to the wood to search out the wild boar's lair.

Warmly dressed against the chill, Lianne yawned as she mounted her white palfrey. Beside her, Guy rode a black stallion, the former lord's, of lighter and swifter build, more suitable to the chase than the destrier Nuage. The dabble-gray war-horse had shown his displeasure, stamping and snorting in his stall.

"Ah, *mon vieux*, you are sure you would carry me better, that this English horse I have named Roland is not used to me as you are. Perhaps you are right, but when we meet the boar, *you* would want to run him down and allow me no sport!" But the stallion would not be comforted, even though Lianne had brought him an apple from the stores of the hall. He continued to stamp and roll his eyes at Guy even while crunching the fruit.

"He is jealous, my lord," said Lianne, amused.

"As am I. You do not feed *me* by hand."

"I would not have thought you *wanted* me to have you eating from my hand." The girl's meaning was clear to both, and had nothing to do with the white bread and wine on which they had breakfasted!

Guy ignored the jibe at his need for absolute control over her. " 'Tis all right," he leaned over from his horse and whispered, "I'll drink of your wine later."

The hunt continued all day, the swine proving to be elusive game, but none complained, thankful to be out in the freshening breeze under an azure, cloudless sky as the earth began its annual rebirth. Birds sang from the trees, where pale green buds were beginning to swell on the branches. The River Meon, which they passed at one point, was swollen with melted snow and spring rain.

Lianne found her heart bursting with an unreasonable joy, just listening to the distant calls of the pack as they attempted to track their quarry. She and Guy had become inadvertently separated from the rest of the party, but that was common when the hounds were not hot on the scent and the day was long. If the hounds gave tongue, indicating they'd found the boar's spoor, Guy would raise the horn and blow several blasts to call the other riders, who were also riding aimlessly about, waiting, and the hunt would re-form.

They were deep in a shaded glen when the earl stopped his mount close to Lianne's.

"The spring becomes you, beauty," he said, his voice deep and husky. "It has brought a becoming flush to your cheeks." His eyes were honey brown until the long lashes came down over them and he pulled Lianne against him, his lips parted to kiss her deeply.

Lianne's will was his. "Perhaps if we go deeper into the copse and dismount?" she whispered, and was answered by a low chuckle.

A grunting and rustling among the bushes interrupted them, however, just after Guy dismounted and was about to lift Lianne down from her mare.

It was the boar. Angry at being disturbed from his browsing and forced to flee the noisy dogs all day, the beast was extremely irritable. Finding two of the two-legged creatures that had sent the bothersome pack forth, the boar was determined that they should be destroyed.

"Guy!" shrieked Lianne from her horse, face ashen. On foot, unarmed, he was in mortal danger. She gathered her reins, hoping Noelle would conquer her natural fear if she had to head her straight at those fearsome tusks to save the Norman.

Guy called, "My spear, Lianne—do not fear!" and his voice sounded quite gay and carefree—as if this dreadful creature could not render him into a bloody pulp, given the chance! Quickly she complied, tossing it from where it was secured to Roland's saddle. He caught it easily. Was there no movement the man made that was not assured, a picture of catlike grace? Lianne began to relax slightly, knowing that now he was armed, Guy would like nothing better than to play the beast alone.

He laughed as the boar pawed the earth, its little eyes reddened with rage. He was balanced on the balls of his feet, waiting for the pig to charge.

It did, squealing angrily, but its wild rush took it somewhat to the left so that Guy's spear merely poked it in the ribs as it galloped past.

It wheeled, standing uncertainly, watching as the seemingly insane human began to run toward it, jeering at him.

Guy did not see the protruding root that caught his boot, tripping him head-long into the boar's path. The spear, flung from his grasp by his unexpected fall, lay agonizing inches away, too far to grasp and raise in time to save him from the charging maddened beast.

It all took place in a second. Even as Lianne was spurring Noelle forward in a vain attempt to head off the enraged boar, and Guy rolled in an effort to reach his weapon, a shaft sped past them. The boar, pierced neatly through the heart, tottered and fell, his foam-covered tusks scant inches from where Guy had lain.

Guy turned, expecting to thank one of the huntsmen of the party for his intervention.

Instead, it was Tofig who stood in the glen, just lowering his longbow.

"You are an excellent shot, and come most timely!" shouted Guy, struggling to his feet and going to examine the boar, which still convulsed in its death throes.

In that moment, the Englishman warned Lianne with his eyes, before a glad greeting to an old friend escaped her lips, not to betray knowing him. Tofig, to the Norman earl, was still a fugitive, an outlaw who had tried to kill him and his men months ago.

So Lianne contented herself with a simple "Thank you" to which the man bowed, hiding his grin of pleasure at seeing her again.

"Who are you?" said Guy slowly in his new English. "I am Earl Guy of Hawkingham, lord of this fief. Your aid was most appreciated. Are you traveling through my lands? I do not recognize you. You are most welcome to come to the hall and sup on this fresh meat with us—you have certainly earned it!" He blew several blasts on the horn to call in the rest.

Improvising quickly and avoiding Lianne's eyes, Tofig answered respectfully, pulling on a tawny forelock, "Aye, sir, I am Wat, late of Mercia in my lord Edwin's household, but my lord is releasing many in his service before he journeys to Normandy as one of William's hostages. I had a fancy to join another lord's service, having no lands to return to, and all the new lords being Norman," he grinned engagingly (Lianne had to admire the rascal's ready tongue), "but they were reluctant to believe me sincere in wanting to serve them. And so you find me traveling across your fief, my lord. My bow is at your service, if you will have me."

Lianne was torn between astonishment that he had submitted so readily to his Norman enemy and joy at his familiar presence.

"Welcome to Hawkingham, Wat of Mercia," Guy said heartily, raising him to his feet. "Lady Lianne, here, has been telling me I need loyal English about me. It seems I have found one, and I thank St. Martin you came when you did!"

As they rode back to the hall, the boar trussed and loaded onto a stout pole borne by two ceorls, Tofig (*Wat!* Lianne reminded herself) told them that King William had recently left England in Bishop Odo's care and traveled back to Normandy in a triumphant homecoming, the sails white to proclaim their victory. He had taken with him many prominent English as hostages; besides Edwin, Edgar Aethling, Stigand, Edwin's brother Morcar, and Earl Waltheof.

"Many Norman nobles are returning with him, my lord," Tofig went on. "Some, taking a monetary reward for their services, others just going temporarily to fetch wives and sweethearts. It is said the Norman women grow restive at home, lacking their men these six months!" He laughed merrily.

At these words, Guy's face suddenly wore a withdrawn, preoccupied look, but Lianne, thinking of how happy Mold would be to meet "Wat," did not see.

Five

M old and Tofig did, indeed, have a joyous reunion later that night, meeting as if by accident in the stable after the rest of the hall had retired.

Eyes straining in the dark, with only the quiet sounds of the horses' movements or the occasional hoot of an owl breaking the stillness, Mold found Tofig waiting for her, his cloak spread over a pile of clean straw.

"Ah, Tofig, I've missed ye so, ye rascal," laughed Mold.

"And I you. Come here, darlin' . . ."

Without further words they came together in the dark stall, and Tofig followed the peasant woman down onto the straw.

Their lovemaking reached its climax

swiftly, both of them reaching a fiery orgasm together, Mold moaning her joy, digging her nails into the Englishman's jerkin, which in his haste he had not bothered to remove.

"Sweetheart, I'd missed that," whispered Tofig, nuzzling her ear as he held her close.

"Go on, love! Would ye have me believe there are no wenches in Mercia?"

"Not to compare with ye," he answered gallantly.

"And my bed has been cold since ye left, also. But Tofig, did you find us by accident?"

"Of course not. I went first to the hall in London, and they told me where you and Lianne had gone. And with whom." He sat up, more serious now. "Mold, what is Lianne doing with that *Norman?* She vowed to hate them all, and Guy de Bayeux in particular, isn't it so? I returned to find Lianne, and Edgar's hall, in the hands of her enemy!"

"Aye." Briefly she outlined the events which had bound Lianne and her brother to Guy de Bayeux, bringing Mold with them out of loyalty.

"Does she wish to escape? Does she hate the whoreson? Does he ill-treat her?" Mold smiled in the darkness, hearing Tofig's fierceness. She saw that he was still a little in love with the winsome Lianne, though it was the worshipful love of a servitor for the lady of the manor, as personally unreachable as the moon. I prefer the more earthy worship he gives me, she thought . . .

"She . . . says she does . . . and would try something rash, I believe, but that the earl always has Orm close by her if he himself is not with her. But I see something in them that neither has wit, as yet, to recognize: they are made for each other, as the fire is made to consume dry kindling. If the fire is allowed to grow from embers, they will learn they care for each other—if Lianne doesn't flee my lord, or if he doesn't do anything equally silly."

"You think this Norman invader *cares* for her? More than just as a plaything, a bedmate?"

"I didn't say he knows it! But why else would she remain such an obsession to him? He chased her all over southeast England before he caught her, and she's shared his bed long enough by now that he would tire of her if that's all he wanted, especially with every slut in the hamlet thrusting her tits at him!"

Tofig chuckled. "And she could care for him, think you?"

"Aye. She can't mourn Edwin forever. If there had been no Edwin, no Senlac, if Guy had just been a visiting Norman noble, they would have fallen in love quite naturally, I think."

"But Mold, my love," Tofig pointed out in a cynical, suspicious voice, "how do we know that he's free to wed Lianne, if he

274

ever would? How do we know there is no lady awaiting him in Normandy?"

"We don't know," Mold admitted freely. "I do know this—there is none other who may lay claim to the Norman's heart. But he has made no move to bring over a wife, and there was no mention of such when he dictated a message to his brother in Normandy—Lianne acted as his scribe, and I was in the room! And another thing I know, of which Lianne must soon be aware—she carries the Norman's child."

She heard Tofig gasp. "But how can you know—if Lianne does not? Are you sure?"

"As sure as you're beside me, the girl has conceived. I don't know, mayhap it's the bloom in her cheeks. And there are other signs . . . I washed no cloths from her monthly flux last month. She's been so busy learning to be the chatelaine, she didn't mark it, poor lamb."

Mold was not embarrassed by the frank discussion, nor was Tofig. Both of them had lived closer to the earth than had Lianne, and discussed human sexuality with as little reticence as they would cattle breeding.

"My Mold . . . you are so wise," Tofig murmured, stroking her breast.

She reached out and touched his hardening shaft. "Wise in what *you* like, cockerel."

Six

Not much time passed between Mold and Tofig's conversation about Lianne's "condition" and the symptoms that made that condition manifest to Lianne herself. One morning she opened her eyes to see Guy, having nearly completed his toilet, sitting patiently in their chamber while his squire shaved him. She sat up in bed, holding the skins around her. He tossed her a smile, which she started to return, until the room began to spin crazily around. His look turned to one of concern as her color faded and beads of sweat popped out on her forehead.

"My lord, I . . ."

Gilbert thought more quickly than Guy and put the basin of soapy water under her as she weakly leaned over into the rushes, retching. Only a little liquid came up, sour-smelling and pale yellow.

"Are you ill? What's amiss, Lianne?" Guy bent over her, smoothing the hair clinging damply to her forehead.

"I know not. Perhaps the salted beef . . . was tainted? It's late to be using the last of the stored meat. Perhaps it was spoiled . . ."

"*Oui*, possibly. I will have Mold look into it, and bring you some bread and wine here, until you feel like coming to the hall."

It was all she could do not to vomit again at the thought of the sour common wine with which Hawkingham normally broke its fast. "Nay, don't bother. I'll be all right in a moment. Don't let me keep you, my lord." She just wanted to be alone, to lie back on the bed until the queasiness passed.

She felt nearly recoverred by Nones, so much so that she was able to eat, albeit lightly, when Guy returned from the fields at dinner. She went about her regular routine after the midday meal, on this day supervising the salting of some freshly caught fish.

By eventide her color and spirits were back to normal, though she found she was more fatigued than usual, and retired from the hall as soon as supper was cleared.

Guy followed her, relieved that her illness had been transitory, for he desired her fiercely. Never had she been so beautiful, her hair glowing with gold fire, breasts thrusting so full and enticing against the wool of her gunna. . . .

The retching reappeared the next day, though Lianne managed to force it down until she could go, unobserved, to the garderobe, where the contents of her stomach came up in a boiling greenish stream. She leaned against the walls, feeling the room tilting and turning. The sound of footsteps caused her to open her eyes.

Wulfrune stood in the narrow doorway, a speculative gleam in her eye.

"So it's caught up with you at last, your wicked ways."

"What?" the girl muttered, wishing Wulfrune would at least make sense if she wouldn't go away. Hadn't she, Lianne, enough to do, keeping the dim closet from revolving too rapidly?

"You're 'in pod,' my lady!" Wulfrune ground out in spiteful glee. Then, as Lianne's blue eyes continued to look blank in her pallid face, she went on, "With child! You have a little Norman bun in your oven, idiot!"

She whirled in surprise, falling to her knees with the force of Lianne's stinging slap.

"Hush! It's not true! It can't be!" Her tone was meant to quell, to remind Wulfrune of her place, but so much dawning uncertainty lit her face that the attempt failed miserably.

"When was your last flux?" the woman pressed slyly.

"After Christmas. Nay, there must have been one more recently than that . . . Holy Mary!" She began to retch again, remembering the unaccustomed fullness of her breasts, the frequency of her visits here to pass water, her hearty appetite, until this new *morning* queasiness had canceled the latter symptom.

"Mother Mary!" she whispered again, hardly noting Wulfrune's departure. "What will I do?"

She dared not tell Guy, not yet. Many men became sexually disinterested when a woman became *enceinte*, and though she told herself that would be desirable, what if he cast her out—and Orm? In her distress, the conversation she'd had with him in London, when he had assured her he would see that any issue of their relationship was cared for, seemed unreal and unreliable. Perhaps he would not have her leave, but how could she bear to look on, bloated with child, swollen and unattractive, as Wulfrune showed off her board-flat abdomen and vuluptuous breasts and flaunted the fact that with Lianne unavailable, Guy had sought her out? This dreary fantasy so filled Lianne with despair that she found herself weeping at intervals throughout the day, avoiding Guy and even Mold.

By the evening she had so worn herself

out with anxiety that she replied to Guy's conversation with monosyllables, if at all. He took note of her abstracted air by saying, "Lianne, you have been too long bound indoors! I have not seen it, so busy have I been with Maître Raymond" (the master mason from Rouen had arrived, robed in importance, to supervise the building of the keep) "and the hiring of masons to work under him. There have also been the meetings with the serfs, so that they understand the obligations of *corvée* and my duties to them. But that is no excuse! I have been out on Roland, enjoying your English spring, while you have been in this dark hall and cooped up within the palisade, growing more pale and wan by the day. Tomorrow you shall ride Noelle, and we will get the roses to bloom in your cheeks, *m'amie!*" He laid the long, sensitive fingers of one hand caressingly against the side of her face, and in spite of herself, she smiled into his dark, charming eyes.

Another, serving a dish of capon spiced with sage and rosemary, smiled also to hear the conversation. So my lady would ride on the morrow. . . . That should be enough time. . . .

Tofig, walking out to the stables after vespers to check the horses before retiring to his pallet, was surprised to see Wulfrune strolling out of the barn door, heading back toward the hall. In the darkness his lip curled, even as he gave her greeting, for there was that about the woman that made his hackles rise.

"Good even, Wulfrune, what do ye out here—at such an hour?"

Clearly she was startled and had not seen him coming, for a long moment passed during which he could practically see the wheels turning in her head.

"I . . . uh . . . oh! It's Wat of Mercia! Actually, I . . . was waiting for you!" she concluded with a rush, having quickly decided to use her usual, never-fail ploy. "I knew you had charge of my lord Guy's horses, and I thought perhaps you might come here, even as you have. . . ." She breathed up at him, and seized his arm in an intimate fashion. She shrugged her shoulders, as if leaving the rest for him to fill in.

But he refused to be played like a fish on a hook. "You wanted to talk to *me*, Wulfrune? What about?"

She looked around her, at the palfreys and, farther down, the great war-horse Nuage as if she had not heard. "My lord, Sir Thomas, kept his horses here, and my palfrey. I come here when I have been thinking how it was when Hawkingham was *English*, before the cursed Normans . . . Oh, I have been so *lonely*, Wat . . ."

Perhaps if he had not known the honest, down-to-earth Mold, Wulfrune's play for him might have held some appeal. But Mold was waiting, and if he did not get rid of this clinging woman, how could they steal back here later themselves? He was certain that Wulfrune had *not* been waiting for him, as she claimed, for her stride had been that of one whose purpose was completed, and her surprise at his appearance was obvious.

"I'm sorry to hear of your loneliness, Wulfrune, but wandering around Hawkingham after *coeuvre-feu*, you may find it relieved by some Norman men-at-arms, rather forcibly!" he advised stiffly, taking her arm and escorting her firmly back to the hall.

She did not, of course, tell him that she had tried out the rough-and-ready charms of several of Guy's men already, and found they made up in endurance what they lacked in subtlety.

Seven

The day was perfect for the proposed outing, as only a spring day in England can be. The chill that had been present at their boar hunt the month before was banished by April's warm, caressing breeze. Everywhere the trees were laden with bursting buds and the ground with the first-blooming wild flowers. A heron's call sounded as they passed by the rushing Meon, and then the bird burst from cover into flight, causing Guy to remark appreciatively, "God's Wounds! Would that my falcon were further along in training, to bring down that one!"

Guy had ordered the long-vacant mews at Hawkingham swept out and cleaned, and now had an eyas being trained to accept his jesses and eat meat from the earl's hand. Soon he would be allowed to fly loose, conditioned to return to the bait swung at the end of a lure. "Perhaps I could get you a small merlin, if you like hawking, Lianne?"

Hawking was an enjoyable sport which provided one with fresh air and meat for the table, but the girl was far more occupied at the moment with controlling her mount.

"She seems to be full of spring," she commented as Guy eyed the skittish mare who shied at every shadow, skipped and bucked.

"Perhaps she has a burr under her saddle," he suggested. "She is normally of such—what is the word?—*agreeable* temperament. It is time we stopped anyway, to sample the repast Mold has packed."

Lianne followed as he led the way to a glade of oaks sheltering a grassy oval area. The only sound was the trickle of a brook that fed into the nearby Meon.

"No, there is nothing here to account for her mood," said Guy after inspecting the saddle and its pad. *Peut-être* she is going into her season, though she had not appeared particularly interested in Nuage as she passed his stall. "*Eh bien,* a time without her saddle may improve her mood," he decided, loosening the girth and removing the saddle altogether from the mare's back. "As you say, an excess of spring," he murmured, coming up behind

Lianne as she unpacked the crusty loaf of white bread, the cold chicken, the skin of wine, and other tempting morsels from Roland's saddlebag, "and I can understand that feeling, for it stirs my blood as well." He grabbed her around the waist, turning her to face him.

In a moment, all her anxiety about her pregnancy and his reaction to it was swept away by the fiery warmth of his hands and mouth as he held her molded to him, drawing her soul from her to meet his.

But wait—he drew away from her. Why? Golden lashes fluttered open over blue eyes cloudy with desire as she protested with a low animal moan the interruption of the sensations he had loosed within her.

But he had only released her momentarily in order to spread his mantle on the crisp, springy grass. Then he was touching her again, mouth moving persuasively on hers as he lowered her to the ground, broad, powerfully muscled shoulders following hers, blotting out the dappled sunlight that found its way through the canopy of leaves.

Afterward she must have slept, for she opened her eyes to find Guy lying on his side propped on an elbow, twirling a violet teasingly at her nose.

God's Blood, he thought, if she knew how lovely she looked, her blonde hair spread out over his mantle, her eyes gleaming like sapphires in a brook as she awakened and focused them on his dark brown ones, a blush spreading up her cheeks as she realized her skirt was still hiked up over her hips where it had been pushed in the exigency of their passion. He smiled a slow, sweet smile, reaching down to pull the skirt over her legs, making the movement a caress, for there had been no same in the love they had made under God's blue sky and green canopy.

For it *had* been love, not just the lustful coupling of a lord and a woman subject to his will, for each had wanted equally to give and receive pleasure of each other.

And Guy had heard the cry she uttered as his skill and desire to please her had brought her to the blissful peak: "Ah, Guy! I love you! Ah, my love, give me more!" He was not sure she was aware of what she had sighed, but her gaze now was open and trusting, not the defiant hatred that had gleamed forth on occasion or the untrusting watchfulness with which she had followed his every act, or the shamed look she had worn every time he had brought her treacherous, betraying body to climax with his, the enemy's.

Shall I tell him that there has been a child conceived of our union, that my womb cherishes his seed within me even now? What will he say? She was afraid to shatter the perfection of the moment with a third presence, the unborn soul of their child. For now his lips were lowering toward hers . . .

Guy, in fact, was also loath to possibly spoil this wondrous interlude with the thoughts that had raced through his mind as he beheld her sleeping, thoughts that had darted hither and yon as through a maze, always coming to the same conclusion: I love her. I want her by me always. I would wed her, but I am pledged to Mabile of Harfleur. A betrothal was as binding as a marriage, and he was not free. A shadow had crossed his face at the thought of Mabile —so calmly beautiful, so sensible and practical—he had judged, before coming to England, that she would be the perfect lady for him, to manage his hall, give him sons and daughters, receive him into her bed, and not notice overmuch when his eye was caught by another lovely face. . . .

He could not picture, however, needing to tumble the serving wenches while away from Lianne, letting himself be entranced by the roving eye of a bored noblewoman whose husband was absent or complaisant—not if this woman of golden fire and ice were his lady. But how?

An indignant squeal from Roland interrupted his leisurely kiss, and he looked up, seeing that the mare was nipping the stallion's neck in an irritable, bullying fashion. The black horse kicked out at Lianne's palfrey, a hoof landing punishingly hard against her flank. The mare sidled away, but continued to fidget and paw the ground, rather than returning to peacefully graze as the other had done.

Still leaning on an elbow, he pushed a dark lock of hair from his eye and noted that the April morning had become cloudy and was no longer so warm. Always unpredictable, the weather of England was especially capricious in the spring. Looking at Lianne, who had sat up and was endeavoring to brush the grass from her clothes, he grinned again, thinking as a lover does that it would not be so terrible a thing to be caught in the rain with one's beloved. If only Lianne's mount would settle down . . .

"Guy, a leg of chicken?"

They were just finishing the delicious meal that Mold had prepared for their picnic when the sky became very overcast. Suddenly both realized that the birdsongs had long ago been stilled.

"Perhaps we should return to the hall, or I fear we shall get a soaking," Lianne whispered, though her eyes said, I don't care if I am wet to the skin if I am with you.

Her mount was not so sanguine about the weather, however, and from the moment of remounting she absorbed all of Lianne's attention. Her earlier curvetting and pitching were intensified now, and she was not apparently mollified by Lianne's soothing murmurs or the stroking of her hand down the lathered neck.

"I think perhaps you should ride pillion with me, and we will lead Noelle?" Guy suggested. "I hope Wat will be able to detect what ails her."

The thought of riding with Guy, holding tight to his waist—touching him anywhere—her nose breathing in the fresh male scent of him, was tempting to Lianne, but her desire to show her capable mastery of this beast he had given her was more pressing.

"No, my lord, I . . ."

" 'My lord'?" he mimicked teasingly. "Surely we are not close enough to the hall that you must take refuge in cold formality, *ma chère.*"

My dear. Her eyes shone. He had never said "I love you," but this was a start.

The clap of thunder took them both by surprise and plunged the jittery mare into terror. Whinnying, Noelle seized the bit in her teeth and charged into the sheets of rain that began to fall on them, galloping for home, heedless of Lianne's efforts to slow her headlong flight.

It may have been the fault of a fox streaking for his den in the downpour, for Guy, spurring the gelding to catch up with the runaway horse, caught a flash of dark russet nearly underneath the terrified mare's hooves as she reared, pawing the air and screaming.

The sudden movement threw Lianne up from her seat and hard onto the ground.

Guy was beside her in a moment, jumping from his stirrups in his haste, but the stallion stood steadily by, watching the mare, riderless, still racing for the stable at Hawkingham as if a demon were upon her.

Lianne had received a solid blow to her head as she fell, and was unconscious, though her chest still rose and fell regularly, Guy observed, his face ashen with alarm, oblivious to the rain.

Lianne's first sight as she returned to consciousness was of Guy's anxious eyes, pupils dilated with concern, enormous against the pallor of his face. At first she could not remember what had happened, or even decipher the thickly accented Norman French he was murmuring, a mixture of prayers and endearments as his fingers probed gently for any broken bones.

Then the pain struck her like a wave, not from his exploring hands, but arising from her lower back and radiating around her flanks to meet in her lower abdomen in dizzying, wrenching spasms.

She moaned then, and he looked up, startled, thinking his fingers had found an injury, and then saw that her knees were drawn up against her belly and all color had drained from her face.

"Ah, God!" she cried, her voice torn with agony and grief. "Guy, I am losing our child!"

But by the time he had comprehended her words, she had fainted again.

Eight

M old told her later how the riderless
mare had appeared at the hall, followed a few moments later by Guy,
riding Roland but with Lianne cradled as
gently as possible in his arms, bellowing
like a madman for aid from the hall.

Lianne's servingwoman had realized
instantly what had happened, seeing the
spreading dark stain on the back of
Lianne's gunna and observing the cramp
seize the unconscious girl in its grinding
hold, watching her tense and moan in the
earl's arms as he strode toward their
chamber.

Father Thomas was summoned, and
baptized the walnut-sized fetus solemnly,
moved by the sight of the powerful earl's
tear-streaked cheeks as Mold bore away

in a towel the little babe that would never be. The priest lingered in a corner of the chamber, for the sight of Lianne's waxy cheeks convinced him she would soon require the Sacrament too.

Once the miscarriage was completed, however, Mold reported that the bleeding had slackened. "Thank God!" whispered Guy, still clutching Lianne's limp hand. It was soon apparent that, while Lianne had suffered a concussion, the rest of her body bore only bruises and abrasions.

When it became obvious that Lianne would sleep awhile, Mold told her, Guy had stalked angrily down to the stables, after belting on his sword, intent on destroying the animal that had nearly killed his woman and had taken the life of their babe.

There he found Wat, who had stabled the skittish mare and rubbed her down, soothing her terrors, while the rest of the hall worried over Lianne.

Wat was running his fingers through what remained of Noelle's feed, examining it with the aid of a tallow candle. He looked up, seeing the earl's wild eyes as he tightened his grip on the hilt of his sword.

"Stand aside, Wat. I will execute that murderous beast." His voice was hoarse and ragged.

"My lord, stay your sword," Wat commanded, his hand calmly restraining the earl's.

Within him, a part of Guy marveled

that he permitted this—that a Saxon ceorl should presume to direct him and live to tell of it!

"It was not the wee mare's fault—she should not be punished. The palfrey was drugged." And he showed him the yellow, green-veined flower petals with purple centers that were mixed in with the mare's feed. "That's henbane, my lord. I have mixed a purgative draught for her, and she will soon be right as rain. The question is not whether to destroy the innocent beast, who never would have harmed my lady else, but what will you do to the person who sought to harm Lady Lianne?" He then told the earl of finding Wulfrune here late the night before, and of his suspicions about the woman.

They then went in search of the former Lady of Hawkingham, Tofig wondering what the earl meant to do when he found the scheming wretch, but knowing that this time he would not stay de Bayeux's hand, even if the Norman would strangle Wulfrune. It didn't seem too out of the question.

Wulfrune, however, had been hiding in the loft since she had seen the earl arrive with Lianne, had heard Wat's accusation and knew her plan had been discovered. While the two men were searching the hall and its outbuildings, she, clad in a ragged woolen shawl to conceal her flaming hair, scurried off toward the wood.

Guy and Wat were unable to find her.

"She is a witch, my lord. Most like, she turned herself into a crow or a bat and flew off to join her master, the Devil."

"Mayhap," growled Guy, his expression bleak. "If not, if I ever catch her, she will wish she possessed that ability, for she will beg for death after I have finished with her."

Nine

Lianne recovered consciousness later that day, returning from the shadowy gray place in which her soul had hovered after the fall, while the babe had been wrenched from within her.

It had now been weeks since the incident, and though she was physically healed, her spirit had not returned. Her face was wan and pale, her posture listless, her hair lying in lank, unkempt strands down her back. She put on the clothes Mold laid out without comment, and did what she bid her without a spark of resentment, no matter how bossy the woman's tone became in an effort to arouse her. Mold was forcibly reminded of her sister in Netherfield Abbey.

Lianne did not raise her eyes to Guy.

When he spoke she was polite; it was as if the hour of love in the oak glade just before the miscarriage had never happened. When they went to bed Lianne turned her face to the wall and appeared to sleep almost immediately. At first, because of her recent lying-in and the healing cuts and bruises, he respected what he felt was simply a reaction of disappointment and a need for rest, and he slept also.

It had become apparent, however, that her reaction was excessive, whether it was from grief, disappointment—or could it be rage? Could she hold him somehow responsible? Lianne's cornflower-blue eyes returned his dark gaze blankly one night in their chamber as he tilted her chin up to look at him.

"Lianne, *m'amie*, I have missed you," he murmured simply, and waited for some answering chord within her. She continued to regard him, unblinkingly, as if he were a stranger.

"By the Splendor of God, woman!" he almost shouted at her. "Don't you think that I, too, am full of regrets about the babe? You had not even told me, *shared* with me the knowledge that you were with child! But I also mourn for it!" His voice was low, hoarse, coaxing; he held her stiff body close and whispered, "Come to bed, *m'amie*. I will make love to you, and by Our Savior, fill your belly with my child again!"

In the illness of her mind, however, she

only recognized part of what he said: his anguish in not knowing she had conceived until the babe was lost.

What an unworthy, worthless creature I am, she thought (for no one had told her of Wulfrune's hand in "the accident," merely that she had disappeared, and Lianne, in her present state, had thought no more of the red-haired witch). How he must despise me for being unable to hold a skittish mare, for allowing myself to be thrown and endanger the babe! The fact that many a man could not have stayed astride the palfrey at that precise moment escaped her. She only knew that Guy—however unwittingly—had entrusted her with the most precious of possessions, a babe, and she, as foolish as a goosegirl, had lost it forever. I am not worth even his lust, she felt, for the memory of those moments when he had all but said "I love you" was buried away in some dark corner of her mind.

In desperation he made love to her, lifting her to the bed and falling on her fiercely, but she lay rigid and unresponsive, enduring it until he collapsed with a groan, spent.

Self-disgust rose thick within him, more strangling than that first time when he had taken her. When he had raised himself off of her, she again turned her face to the wall, causing him to pound his fist once, with an oath, into the mattress.

He did not try to bed her again. The following even, he sought out one of the village sluts (who had some days earlier rolled her eyes invitingly as he rode by) and went into the rude thatched cottage with the giggling girl, driving her gaping mother and slack-jawed simple brother outside to wait while he satisfied the rutting fury that filled him.

He found he could not even quench that primitive need with this dirty girl who stank of onions, garlic, and unwashed body, though she tried hard to please him, even taking him in her mouth, desperate to arouse his passion, for the earl was as beautiful as a god to her.

In the end, however, he pushed her away, leaving a handful of silver pennies which at least caused her to smile as her relatives filed back into the smoky, dark hut. She had not understood a word he had said—the earl unconsciously had spoken in Norman French the entire time, and the fact that he seemed unable to take his ease on her was a matter of extreme puzzlement, but Normans were strange, and perhaps he would return, with a shilling next time, and direct her with that dark moody gaze to spread her legs again for him. She'd please him then, by Our Lady! Until then, as far as her mother, brother, or anyone in the hamlet knew, my lord had swived her as well— nay, better!—than any Saxon—"For his tool was this long!"

Ten

Guy threw himself into his work around the fief with frightening intensity, ensuring that the serfs spent the requisite number of days tilling, planting, and weeding his fields of oats, barley, and wheat, as well as tending his beasts.

Every able-bodied man from his other fiefs, Chawton, Winslade, and Lingfield, also had been summoned to help erect the new keep, their women left to till the fields this year. Their feudal obligation—in bushels of crops, or the choice calf or piglet from the litter—would be lighter this year while their men worked to erect Hawkingham Keep. Later Hawkingham's serfs would come to work on keeps built on their lands.

Situated with the River Meon on one side, the *motte*, or mound, had been largely built up from earth dug up to form the moat on its other sides by the time Maître Raymond had arrived. The fortified stone tower would be on this raised area, in which the earl's men could survey the surrounding land and the entire household could retreat under siege if all other defenses failed. An inclined path leading up the tower opened out on its other end, to a large oval area or bailey in which the everyday living and working quarters of Hawkingham's people would be, the whole surrounded by a high wooden palisade. This motte-and-bailey castle was being replicated all over England by the Normans as the country became subdued.

A messenger came riding up to the hall one day bearing a letter from Normandy. It was from Bayeux, from the earl's brother, the travel-stained rider proclaimed.

Ordinarily Guy would have requested that Lianne read it to him, but the English girl had spent the day staring into the embers of the fire, unmoving, locked into her private thoughts. Guy felt reluctant to disturb her frozen silence. Instead, he strode into the village, stopping at the cottage beside the church, where Father Thomas nervously agreed to read it to him. It was as well that

Lianne had not seen the parchment, for Gervais wrote:

To Guy, Earl of Hawkingham, Lord of Chawton, Winslade, and Lingfield, Baron de Bayeux, Greeting:

It was with pleasure we received word from you of the honors awarded you by His Grace, the Duke of Normandy and King of England, William.

Our mother is well, although she suffered from a congestion of the lungs over the winter. She adds her greetings to mine.

Your fief here prospers. I was pleased to send Maître Raymond of Rouen to direct the building of your keeps, first at your principal seat at Hawkingham and later at the others, as I was to hear of your progress there.

However, I was surprised that you made no mention of when you intend to send for your betrothed Mabile, who waits for you at Bayeux, learning the duties of a Norman noble's wife, under our lady mother's expert tutelage. She has uttered no word of reproach, brother, but she has received no message from you since the short one of victory sent after the battle near Hastings. Her visage, though, appears very sad and worried to me and I write on her behalf, though I hasten to add that she does not know I intend to tell you of her malencholy.

Brother, I urge you to send for her that the marriage may be celebrated. Others in Normandy have done so, thus I know the land lies peaceful enough at the moment. Surely you have had adequate shelter in which to pass the winter; the finishing of your keep need not provide a reason for leaving her waiting here. Other ladies of Normandy have, I warn you, brother, lost patience in the return of their men and have married elsewhere. Mabile, being the virtuous, worthy maiden she is, honors the binding vow of betrothal and patiently awaits your word, which I trust will come soon, whether by letter or in your personally coming for her.

God protect you, brother.

—Gervais

Guy swore feelingly as the priest looked up, having finished reading the missive aloud.

"My lord?" he inquired, watching the lean form pace up and down his tiny cottage like a caged leopard, stopping at last to strike his fist on the trestle table, startling Father Thomas as he sat there.

"Father, I am in a most damnable tangle," he said at last.

"My son, do you wish to confess?" he offered kindly, motioning toward the church.

"No!—Yes!—I don't know. Perhaps . . . I just need advice. How . . . does one break a betrothal?"

That was the last thing the priest expected him to say. How does one do penance for keeping a mistress, perhaps, or how does one reconcile one's wife to one's leman! Or even, knowing the Norman capacity for ruthlessness as a race, where could he install Lianne in a convent close at hand?

"It is difficult, my son," he said at last. " 'Tis almost as binding as a marriage."

"I know that!" Guy sighed with explosive impatience. "But how is it done?"

"Through a bishop, I would think, my lord. I have never had need to know before. You . . ." he looked up apprehensively as he continued, " . . . do not wish to wed the maid to whom you were contracted before you came to England? It sounds as if she is a good woman, worthy of respect."

"So might Lianne of Fairlight have been described, prior to the Normans' and most particularly *my* coming. I took her, Father, in all her innocence, and before that, drove her, indirectly, to become an outlaw capable of murder—a far cry from the *lady* she had been! My original thought was to take her and enjoy her, selfishly, until I was tired of her enough to discard her, or at most keep her as my leman while Mabile of Harfleur was my wife, my honored *lady*. Now that she has been mine, though, I find that it does not suffice to keep her as a possession, nor do I find Mabile's virtue and honor enough to stir me any more, after knowing Lianne."

He looked up, locking the priest's pale eyes with his dark brown ones, the scar from Senlac a livid slash across one cheekbone. "I would wed Lianne, Father."

"It is well that you would do right by her, my lord. Yet do not let pity move you to make a greater prisoner of her than before. Perhaps Lianne would prefer the peace of a convent?" Father Thomas questioned, deliberately and skillfully baiting him.

"I don't *pity* her, priest! I love her! She is *mine!* She will be no walled-up Bride of Christ!"

"Yours—by right of conquest, Norman?" Father Thomas's heart raced with daring. Possibly the earl would slay him before he could utter a Paternoster. He looked furious enough.

"Nay! By the right of my love, and the love she bears for me!"

But his fury lost force as he remembered the wan wraith that had been his love the past month, and then the priest cleverly queried, "Does she know you love her, and would wed her if you could, my son?"

That day in the glade—he had come so close to telling her, but had not, being loath to intrude the complication of his betrothed status into the rich, uncomplicated pleasure of the moment.

"You know, it is by no means certain you will be able to be released from this contract, my lord," Father Thomas's voice interrupted his reverie, "unless you have a powerful friend in the Church. I would be willing to intercede for you, as I would see this Englishwoman honorably wed, but *I* am no one, just a humble village priest."

"It is all right, Father," muttered Guy, brightening. "Bishop Odo, William's brother, owes me a boon! I saved his life in battle!" He snatched the parchment almost gaily, thanked the bemused priest (who felt as if a storm had just passed through his home, leaving sunshine in its wake) and strode off, full of plans to ride to Dover, from which Odo was governing Kent in his brother's absence.

The English priest assisted his wife to crawl out from under the bed where she had been hiding since spying the earl's approach, terrified he would banish her from her man's side if he noticed her there. By the time Guy had left, however, there could have been a score of women there and it was doubtful he would have remarked it.

Eleven

Strolling through the hamlet, Guy devised a plan that he felt would gladden Lianne's heart and occupy her while he made the necessary trip to Dover and from thence to Normandy— for he would have to break the betrothal with Mabile face-to-face; he could not just coldly send her a message across the Channel with such news. In the main, he was a sensitive, thoughtful man, and would try to see Mabile content— whether in another match or in the convent, before taking up his own happiness.

He was eager to broach the plan to Lianne—her part of it, that is. He felt he could not in honor ask her to be his wife until he was free to wed, nor could he bear her disappointment (or his own, he admitted to himself) if Odo was unable or unwilling to break the tie to Mabile. The Norman girl was in fact a distant relative of the corpulent churchman; blood may prove thicker than a favor done during battle.

Here Guy de Bayeux made a large error, a natural mistake considering his upbringing. With a father accused of treason when Guy was but a child, he had been wrenched from his mother's side to a fostering with his father's lord, who in truth held him as a hostage for Ralph de Bayeux's continued good behavior, and he had been brought up in the intrigue-bound atmosphere of the ducal court, learning to keep his own counsel and bare his soul to no one.

Once back at the hall, however, thoughts of the plan were forgotten as he entered, for his arrival seemed to freeze the occupants of the room into a tableau.

Lianne had shrunk back against the hearth, an expression of fear and loathing etched across her beautiful features. Mold stood protectively at her side, her usually amiable face twisted in a snarl, both of them facing a man who stood near them in an intimidating posture, his back to the earl. "Wat" was entering the hall, coming from the sleeping quarters, his dagger drawn as he advanced. He, too, appeared distinctly hostile to the newcomer.

"What is the meaning of this? Who is this man?" Guy's voice was a thunderclap. "Wat's" arm slowly lowered and sheathed the dagger again. The women tried to assume the expressions of normal curiosity at a newcomer's arrival, but failed miserably. Lianne's figure was still shrinking as from a blow.

The transformation in the stranger was most striking, however, and he wheeled to face Guy, full of deference and amiability now as he bowed and murmured, "My lord, I give you greeting." His voice was the harshly accented English of the North. It was Wulfnoth, the man who had betrayed the band of outlaws with which Orm and Lianne had been traveling.

Wulfnoth raised his gaze at last in the heavy silence of the hall. Lianne, Mold, and Tofig hardly dared breathe as they stared at the Yorkshireman, who was dark like the Norman but who had none of the handsomeness of Guy's swarthy features. Wulfnoth's nose was bulbous and hooked while Guy's was well-shaped and patrician, his gray gaze cold as the windswept moors, his smile calculating and ingratiating. He shot a nasty grin at the others, guessing from their frozen postures that he possessed knowledge that could ruin them. Apparently Guy did not know that Tofig was the leader of the very pack of brigands he had sold to the Normans! Could it be he also didn't know that the rest were part of the same pack?

What a delicious opportunity!

Not being sure how much the Norman knew or how such knowledge could best be used to his own advantage, Wulfnoth decided to say nothing of them as yet. "My lord, it has been long ere we had the pleasure of meeting," Wulfnoth began in a careful, wheedling tone, testing the waters.

"Pleasure?" the earl shot back coldly, his eyes narrowed. "What do you want, Englishman?"

"Why, the honor of serving you again, my lord," the man answered fawningly.

"You served yourself, Englishman. Are the ten *livres* all spent, Judas?"

"My name is Wulfnoth of York, good my lord," he returned in an agonized tone. "I did you a good service, for did you not annihilate the English rebels?" His gaze flicked to the three "English rebels" who had survived. "I have been ill-treated since I did the Normans that service, good *seigneur*. William will not have me in his retinue, and of course I am seen as a turncloak by my fellow English —though I want only what is best for the land," he added obsequiously.

"I can well imagine," returned the earl dryly, though to what he referred was not clear.

"This winter I nearly starved and froze to death," he went on whiningly. "Will you not take me in, gracious lord? I would make a valuable addition to your meinie."

By now it was time for the midday meal, and the men-at-arms were filing into the hall. Guy, spying Orm coming in, did not miss how the youth stiffened at the sight of the Yorkshireman and warily watched to see what the earl was doing with him.

"I have no need for a self-serving Judas at Hawkingham," Guy said at last. "You'd betray your own mother if I gave you the price. Be gone."

"But, my lord . . ."

"Silence! Sir Ralf, escort him from the hall, and see him gone from Hawking-ham."

"How is it that you will employ one turncloak, Norman, but not another? Watch *he* does not murder you as you sleep!" Wulfnoth's tone was insolent now, and he pointed an accusing finger at "Wat" as he was hustled unceremon-iously out by Guy's captain-at-arms.

None spoke a word until Wulfnoth was gone. Then Guy directed his dark gaze at "Wat," who had paled and was watching him warily.

"What means this, Wat? Who are you, really?"

"Tofig of Wessex, my lord," he answered tonelessly, with the air of one who puts his neck in the noose. Mold made a little whimper at his side, and he gave her a reassuring pat on the shoulder before he returned his gaze to Guy.

"The same Tofig, I presume, who harried my troops and other Normans at great cost to their lives?"

"Aye, my lord."

Lianne raised her blue gaze to Guy then and spoke directly to him as she had not done in weeks. "My lord! Tofig has been a good and loyal man to you. He saved your life from the boar! Do not harm him, I beg you!"

Guy would have spared him for causing Lianne to leave her shell, for that act alone, but he allowed no hint of this to appear on his implacable features.

"And why did you come, Tofig-Wat?" he inquired with deceptive laziness. "Would you indeed murder me in my bed?" He watched with concealed surprise as a spirited light flickered in the Englishman's eyes.

"Nay, I'd have slain ye face to face an I saw ye mistreating Lady Lianne," he answered, defiant for a moment. Then his tone changed. "I find that not to be the case, though you do force her to live in a state of shame."

Mold gasped at his side as Guy's hand reflexly tightened on his sword hilt.

"Nay, I am your man, so long as ye deal truly with Lianne of Fairlight. I will guard your back, not stab it, my lord. I beg your continued trust and crave pardon for the deception I practiced on my arrival. You would not have allowed me to stay had you known my identity then, would you, my lord?"

"No, I suppose not. Nearly everyone else here—" he indicated, with a faint smile, Orm and Lianne—"has tried to take my life at one time or another. You might as well stay, if you will serve me loyally as you say. However," his voice became wry as Tofig visibly relaxed, "it ill becomes you to criticize my relationship with Lady Lianne while you are guilty of causing another lady to sin." His regard fell on Mold, who blushed, and back to Tofig, who was red as a cardinal's robe. "Is there any reason either of you cannot wed?" he asked, and both knew then that he was aware of their nocturnal meetings.

"Nay, my lord. I would be proud to wed Mold, with your consent," Tofig said with a grin.

"See that you do, as soon as the banns can be read."

Mold's face was transfigured with joy, and she beamed happily at Tofig, and then at Guy, who watched her with amusement and wished his own problem could be settled so simply.

"Thank you, my lord," whispered Lianne, smiling at him as they sat down to a dinner of mortrews, veal steamed in milk, young hares stewed in pepper sauce, a soup of fish spiced with marjoram, sage, and basil, great white trencher loaves, accompanied by dishes of beets, pears in a wine sauce, small beer, and wine.

"I have need of good men, *ma douce*, and your smiles." He took her hand and kissed the fingertips so that her pulse quickened. "*Mais*, Lianne, why were *you* so afraid of that man?"

For a moment, she turned away, twisting her hands, and he feared his question had undone all the good his acceptance of Tofig had accomplished, but then her blue orbs returned to him.

"You asked me once if no Englishman tried to claim me, after Senlac. I lied, for Wulfnoth almost raped me. I had never given him any sign of favor, but he tried to force me, one night, but Tofig intervened. Tofig banished him, and that is when he betrayed us to your duke."

"I see. It is lucky for this Wulfnoth that I did not know that when he stood before me. I wish you had told me—had I known he touched you, I would have killed him."

Lianne shivered at the fierceness in his eyes.

Guy broached the plan for the journey to Lianne as they strolled arm-in-arm to their chamber, and grinned as she gave an excited squeal of pleasure.

At the same time, the luckless Wulfnoth was stumbling through the dense Hawkingham woods on the outskirts of Guy's demesne, praying he would be well quit of them before the fast-approaching dark. Where he would lay his head that night and from whence his next meal would come were worrisome questions, questions he had thought to be done with once he found the earl's lands. Wulfnoth was more than weary of his wandering, comfortless life.

But the subject that twisted his gut with rage was the beautiful golden-haired woman (who at that moment was enjoying a very sensual reunion with the Norman earl). Wulfnoth had not known that the woman he desired to humble would be found with Guy de Bayeux. That was an unexpected bonus. He had foreseen, in those few moments before the earl returned, chances to catch Lianne alone—and, he had gloated, she could not tell. How would she dare tell her lord, with the threat of exposure hanging over her lovely head? He would threaten to tell Guy that she, as well as Orm and Tofig, were outlaws who had tried to kill him! But the plan had collapsed, and with it his plans for possessing the Saxon beauty.

What was this? A small hut in the midst of the woods—a charcoal burner's, perhaps? He knocked at the door.

It was to this deserted cottage that Wulfrune had fled. Rarely did folk pass by here, and few had cause to disturb the dwelling, which appeared to be abandoned. In fact, most who saw it crossed themselves, for the place was reputed to be haunted.

Wulfrune was not afraid, for she had spent many a pleasant hour here with her amours. Now she was merely bored to distraction. She dared not show her face in the village. The hut was well stocked with food and wine for several weeks, but there was a growing, nagging need in Wulfrune that she had seldom gone so long without satisfying. Then the knock sounded at the door, hesitant at first, then more sure.

She would have been glad to see a one-eyed cripple if he was willing to serve her purpose, but her pupils dilated with joy as she beheld the wiry, swarthy Wulfnoth, who gazed back with undisguised lust at the voluptuous red-haired woman who faced him, obviously alone and just as obviously delighted with his arrival for the same reason as he.

"Greetings, good sir," she breathed, studying him frankly. "What may I, a lonely widow, offer you, weary traveler?"

"Good widow, if I may make bold to say, I think you know the sustenance I crave." Just to prove it he reached out and backed her up against the wall, where she felt with a sigh his ready manhood.

"I thirst for the same, and from a good Englishman, too. These accursed Normans have no good weapons to please an Englishwoman." Her breath came in ragged gasps.

"Well, then, let me show you the most *English* part of Wulfnoth of Yorkshire!" he chuckled, and had her then and there.

Later, over a skin of wine, Wulfrune and Wolfnoth discovered the grudge which they held in common—a united hatred of Guy de Bayeux and Lianne of Fairlight. An unholy allience, bent on the destruction of those two, was born that night.

Twelve

O rm allowed his mount to drop back so that he rode next to Lianne.

"You are beautiful this summer morn, sister," he remarked. Indeed she was. Her cornflower-blue gunna had a low square neck; at the neckline and in deep slashes up the sides of the skirt an indigo-blue linen kirtle was revealed. A veil of gossamer-thin sendal partially covered the gilded gleam of her tresses which lay in a thick braid to her waist. But that which had occasioned Orm's observant remark had not been any of these things; rather, it was the flush of color that had returned to her cheeks after so long, and the joy that danced in her eyes once more.

She could not stop herself from glancing

ahead, where the Earl of Hawkingham rode his destrier Nuage, and this did not escape Orm. For most of the morning, the earl had ridden at Lianne's side, and it had been difficult to seize an opportunity for private conversation.

Now he was assured that the pleasant sound of Gilbert's singing would cover their voices.

"My thanks, brother." She looked with love at the lanky youth. So soon he would be a man, yet he had done so many things already that marked him as an adult.

"You are happy today, Lianne?"

"Of course, riding to fetch Elfgift! I just know that a stable atmosphere, where I can spend much time with her, will be healing, if indeed she is not already better. Though I think our aunt would have let us know if this were the case," she added.

Aye, so I thought. Doubtless she is just the same. Are you sure Hawkingham is such a good place for her, in truth, overrun as it is with Normans?" Orm inquired cynically.

"Ah, don't begin that chorus again, Orm," Lianne protested. "The day is too lovely." She was determined not to let him perturb her, for she had the same doubts: Hawkingham a *quiet, peaceful* atmosphere? Its master held Elfgift's brother and sister by the force of two rather ugly threats, and Lianne, was virtually owned, body and, she feared, soul, for hers was rapidly becoming his as well.

"I am also thinking of Tofig and Mold, and how happy they were to be wed." The wedding had taken place in front of the chapel, and Tofig and Mold had been given one of the vacant sleeping chambers in which to enjoy their honeymoon while Guy and Lianne were gone.

"Yes, they are well-suited," admitted Orm. Then, the grin gone from his face, he asked suspiciously, "Why is the Norman being so *good*, all of a sudden?"

"Orm, he is not a monster. He can be a hard man, true, but he knows that keeping loyal servants involves keeping loyal servants involves keeping them happy. He is basically a good man, I believe."

"Yet once you would have slain him, for the murder of your husband. . . ."

"Stop it, brother!" Her eyes flashed dangerously. "My lord *does* understand English now. I was but a green girl when the Normans won at Senlac. It was wrong and absurd of me to blame Guy for Edwin's death in battle. Even if he had wanted to slay him personally, they had never met—he didn't know his face!"

"You are quick to excuse the Norman *now*, sister. I marvel at the change. As I was about to say, what does the Norman *want*, in doing all these things for us? He's up to something."

"Nonsense, Orm. He's been very good to you—here you are, mounted, riding along as part of the earl's retinue! You could as easily have been out laboring in your lord's fields."

"It's kind of you to remind me that I am but a serf," Orm retorted caustically. "It explains why I am here, yet not bearing a sword! He fears I would impale his scheming foreign heart!"

But even Orm's adolescent sullenness could not spoil the day for Lianne. She nudged Noelle into a canter and soon caught up with Guy's mount.

Orm scowled as he saw the Norman earl's dark features break into a smile as Lianne laughed up at him, her even white teeth gleaming like pearls between her full red lips.

"Your brother seems rather unaffected by the beautiful weather," Guy remarked in a low voice, later. "All morning his eyes have cast daggers at me. I swear I can feel them with my back turned."

"Perhaps it is that he feels neither fish nor fowl." At his puzzled look, she went on. "You threatened to make him as the lowliest serf. *That* he could understand, though he would never be happy thus. He was raised always with the idea of becoming a warrior, a housecarle, and at the moment he is neither serf nor knight. He does not know what he *is*, or worse yet, what he can look forward to *becoming*."

His face was thoughtful. "I see. Lianne, I would like to make him more. I have need of good men, *tu sais*. But it is true that I do not place my trust lightly, or easily." She was silent, not knowing what to say, but feeling a flame of hope flicker to life for Orm's eventual advancement.

"*Ma chère* Lianne," he murmured, caressing the back of her neck briefly. "You are so good. Do you never ask anything for yourself?" Now it was her turn to look perplexed. His eyes were hooded and enigmatic, for he was thinking, Neither fish nor fowl; that describes you as well, beloved. Neither simple bedmate nor yet my lady wife. God grant I may remedy that ere long!

Thirteen

The journey lay behind them, and Guy
and Lianne sat in the common room
awaiting the reverend mother. The
plump Sister Portress had gone to fetch
Lianne's aunt, plainly agog at the rare
sight of the mailed retinue and the tall
Norman noble at Lianne's side.

In the relatively peaceful climate of
Hawkingham Guy had forgotten
somewhat the discontent and rebellion
that still smoldered in England. Before
arriving at the convent, they had seen
everywhere English faces filled with
sullen hatred and oblique gestures made
when they thought the foreign conquerors weren't looking. Naturally they
assumed the Normans were all still
ignorant of English, and some of the re-

marks overheard caused his hands to clench into fists momentarily. If there was this much rebelliousness still alight in the conquered portions of England, how much more must there be in the north and west, where William's armies had not yet marched?

"Ah, Lianne, dear niece!" The florid-faced old nun swept into the room, as regal as any queen, and gathered Lianne into her embrace before she could kneel.

"Reverend Mother," Guy murmured respectfully, kneeling himself.

"Rise, my lord earl." Mother Mary Edburga looked the Norman in the eye. She was tall for a woman, so much so that her gaze was nearly level with his. Her gray eyes were cool, assessing; she was not the least intimidated by the sword he wore at his side nor the men that waited for him without, men who could burn the convent to the ground and rape all her nuns if he but bade them to do so.

"My lord, you will doubtless wish to see to the stabling of your mounts and setting up camp for your men, for naturally they cannot stay within Netherfield's walls. I wish to speak to my niece alone and take her to see her sister."

And so the Earl of Hawkingham found himself summarily dismissed, and stifled a grin as he bowed. God's Blood, I like the woman!

Both women watched as the earl excused himself and went to do as the reverend mother suggested.

"What magic did you work, Reverend Aunt?" Lianne chuckled. "That haughty man was meek as a lamb!"

Mother Mary Edburga held up the wooden crucifix that dangled from the girdle about her substantial waist. "Magic, my dear? For shame! The Scriptures tell us to be 'wise as serpents and harmless as doves!' Now then, sit, my child." Lianne found herself responding just as obediently, taking a seat on a rough-hewn bench.

"This Norman . . . he is to you . . . as you said in your letter?"

"Yes, Mother." Lianne had painted as accurate a picture as possible of her position with Guy de Bayeux.

"Then why not claim sanctuary with us? Refuse to leave the convent—announce your intention to take the veil? On pain of excommunication, he dare not interfere with a vow like that." Her question was blunt and uncompromising.

"He would not let that threat stop him if he wanted me," Lianne answered truthfully. "He'd burn this abbey down first, in spite of the consequences to his soul. I believe, though, that he is a very devout person in his way, like most Normans."

"It is a 'very devout' people who invade another's land, kill its leader *and* the flower of its manhood, and seize others' homes for their own demesnes?" the nun questioned, baiting Lianne in order of gauge her reaction.

"In their own way, the Normans *are* very religious! Certainly they believe they had God's and the Pope's blessing on this venture! If nothing else, my lord was just doing his duty to his suzerain, Duke William!" Her impassioned reply suddenly seemed overloud in the quiet room. Somewhere overhead a fly's loud drone filled the silence.

"My, he has a passionate defender in you, my dear," Mother Mary Edburga said with a chuckle, and was amused to see the slow flush creep up her niece's neck.

"Nay, Aunt," the girl replied stubbornly, "I mean only to be fair. Enough of him! Where is my sister? Is she better, dear Aunt? May I see her now?" Lianne's face shone with eagerness tinged with apprehension.

The older woman arose with a rustling of black skirts. "Of course, my child. It is nigh onto the hour of Nones. I will have her fetched before my sisters and I retire to the chapel for the chanting of the Office."

"Is . . . is she more herself, Mother? I must know before I see her."

The abbess turned to face her. "No better and no worse. I have worn my knees out with prayers to St. Marthurin, whose intercession is for the insane, to no avail. She remains like a living, breathing puppet, and I must merely be thankful her physical health has been good. You plan to take her from here?"

"With your permission only, Mother."

Mother Mary Edburga raised her hand, cutting off Lianne's assurance. "Oh, I've no real objection. If she had improved under my care, and seemed eager to remain, perhaps I would oppose this move. But as it is . . ." she shrugged; " . . . perhaps the peace of the convent was good for her wounded soul at first, but now, with so many willing nurses, it is allowing her to stagnate in limbo. Perhaps the world—even a world where the Normans hold sway and all is changed from what she once knew—will challenge her spirit to rise again. She may find something out there for her. I pray it is so, child!" She rang a bell, and one of the nuns was sent to bring Elfgift to her sister.

"Ah, here she is!" Just then the abbey's two mighty bells began to toll, signaling the mid-afternoon Office to be sung, and Lianne found herself alone with a gaunt, vacant-eyed girl whom she had difficulty recognizing.

"Elfgift? It's your sister, Lianne! I have come for you, darling!" A cold feeling washed over her as she realized that the other did not even seem aware of her. She stood immobile, blank blue eyes staring at her feet, seemingly listening to some inaudible music of her own.

Lianne could not resist gathering her younger sibling to her breast and stroking the stringy, strawlike blonde hair. Even Lianne's touch brought no overt change; she was used to the gentle, loving handling of the Benedictines, but she did not distinguish that it was now her own flesh and blood that held her soothingly.

The evening meal was served to the earl's meinie at their encampment, for the abbess would not countenance so many armed men beneath the convent roof, but the earl and Orm ate in the refectory with Lianne, sitting across the trestle table from the abbess and Elfgift.

The nuns ate in a silence broken only by one sister reading from a work by St. Augustine, and Guy took advantage of the lack of conversation to study his beloved's sister.

The family resemblance was there; the same blonde hair, startling blue eyes, and tip-tilted nose that Lianne and Orm had, but Elfgift was a wilted, broken rose against Lianne's petal-fresh beauty. Those soulless eyes rested on him unseeingly for a moment. With no more emotion might she have viewed the Devil himself, Guy mused. She, too, had Lianne looked for weeks after their babe was lost. But she had recovered. . . . Guy prayed that when Elfgift began to remember, she would not be terrified of all things Norman. Perhaps it was well he would be away for a while. He needed to speak to Lianne of that.

After the evening meal, during the brief

period of recreation before the final service of Vespers, Lianne sat on a stone bench with Elfgift in the convent's enclosed garden area. Around them, nuns were strolling, conversing, admiring the garden, where a variety of herbs and late summer flowers scented the air. One nun picked up the convent's pet cat, a spoiled, enormously fat puss of inky black, and began to stroke it. Its purr was audible to Lianne several feet away.

"See the kitty, Elfgift? Kitty? Is he a friend of yours, too?" Nothing. The girl merely flicked an eyelash as Lianne's finger passed close to her face.

Lianne felt despair. How could she pierce this shell?

"My lady Lianne, my lord would talk with you," Gilbert said softly, bringing her joltingly from her reverie.

"But—Elfgift? I cannot leave her," Lianne protested, gesturing toward the girl. Gilbert studied Lianne's sister for the first time. He had heard of the girl's affliction, but he thought he was looking at one of heaven's angels. If her wandering spirit could only be restored to her, what a lovely girl she could be!

"Don't mind that, child," an elderly nun called. "She's used to our company. We'll take her in to Vespers soon. The music soothes her and helps her sleep."

"Lianne, I must speak to you, for tomorrow I will be going away for a fortnight, perhaps a little longer," Guy said as they strolled up a grassy rise some distance from the camp. The Vespers bell had tolled as they left the convent's walls, and now the sun's light was ebbing away quickly. Below them they could see men gathered around two fires, eating and drinking. Bursts of laughter occasionally drifted up to their ears.

"Going—away? Where, my lord?" she asked, though instinctively she already knew—he was going "home"—Bayeux. He would want to see his family again, share the triumph in the victory. "Do I go with you?" She hoped he could not hear the hopeful note in her voice.

"I think it best you do not. After all, there is Elfgift."

"Yes, of course. I could not leave her at this time." How foolish of me to forget that, to be filled for one joyous second with fantasies of traveling with Guy, seeing Bayeux, and meeting Guy's family . . .

"And the land is far from settled now— I have seen that especially since we have left Hawkingham. Perhaps my liege lord was not wise to have left so soon, with so much of England still rebellious . . ."

"Where do you go, Guy?" Lianne interrupted.

"To Dover first. I must meet with Bishop Odo."

"With William's half-brother? Why? You have always said you disliked him!"

He turned his face from her curious one, and his tone was abrupt. "He is in the position to do me a favor, and he owes me one." She nodded, remembering the story Guy had told of saving his life at Senlac at the treacherous ravine, but was still mystified. It was obvious the earl would shed no more light on this subject, however.

"From thence I go to Normandy," Guy was saying as they drew closer to a copse of scrubby oak and undergrowth, "where I must see my family and look over my demesne. Then I will return, Lianne. I do not plan to be away overlong."

"And I, my lord?" she asked, feeling ridiculously close to tears at the thought of his leaving.

"Return to Hawkingham, *ma chère*. I will send a number of men and my squire Gilbert with you for your protection. You will have an adequate garrison with the men still at the hall."

"But you are taking Orm, aren't you?" she accused flatly. "Is he a hostage for my good behavior?"

"Nay! Suspicious wench!" In the half-light she could not tell if he was angry.

In actuality, the thought of being parted from her, not being able to show her the lush beauty of Normandy, especially of his partrimony, and in turn showing off her golden loveliness to his mother and brother was greatly depressing and gave an edge to his voice. How could he take her on a journey where she would encounter his bethrothed? Perhaps he would not even be able to escape the bond and would perforce return wedded!

"Lianne, I'm taking him that I may get to know him better, mayhap even begin to train him as my *squire*, if I can overcome the hostility that all of your family seems to have toward me."

If he meant only to distract her, he succeeded admirably for a moment as she turned to him with shining eyes. "Oh Guy—I am so pleased! I . . ." Then, remembering she was being left behind, and he was not willing to tell her for how long, or why, her old defiance flashed. "You'll be lucky to have him. It's past time you recognized his worth." She whirled from him that he might not see the tears that threatened to spill over, and peered in the gathering darkness at the tiny fires below.

"I liked it better when you were pleased," his voice said caressingly into her ear, and then his hand was pushing the heavy plait off her shoulder and his lips were warm on her bare neck.

She could not bear his making love when she was so angry, and with a sullen gesture of her hand she moved away from him.

"God's Blood!" he swore hotly, and in a single stride he had caught her and turned her to face him, his mouth crushing down on hers.

"No! Would you take me in the open, under the bushes, like a trollop?"

"It was good enough for us once! Your

aunt certainly will not allow me to savor your charms on your narrow pallet, though I confess," he chuckled, holding her against him, "I would rather be with you the night long. I promise you, we'd not sleep much between the bells that toll the Offices. It's probably a better use than those bare cells were ever put to." As he noted her continued rigidity, a muscle worked in his jaw, and his mouth became a set, determined line. "I am leaving tomorrow before dawn, woman, and I want you now."

"Here, so near to where Edwin's blood still soaks the soil?" she threw up at him, her mouth a whisper away from his.

"Foolish woman!" he ground out. "I'll listen to no more of *that!*"

She tried to back up from him, afraid of her anger as much as his, and fell over his extended leg—as he'd intended.

She lay there dazed as the world receded for a moment and then returned with the air into her lungs. He had fallen upon her hungrily, taunting, "This is how you look best, *ma chère*, flat on your back." He paused, noticing at last that the fall had knocked the wind from her, and then kissed away the weak tears she despised from her eyes. His right hand went on a marauding path of its own, pushing the linen skirts away from her thighs.

His touch swept away the last of her resistance as with an angry sob she pulled him to her and sought to push his garments away as well. Once their clothes were shed and lying in abandoned heaps in the tall grass, they could not get close enough, could not taste enough, could not touch enough. The ache he had aroused within her demanded immediate easing, but he would not grant her that; instead, it became a delicious agony which he increased by his consummate skill with tongue and hands and voice. Lianne was far from being passive herself—she had risen up over him, and her teasing, half-biting kisses caused him to groan, "Damn it, woman, I can wait no more!"

He pushed her back against the cushioning grass and rammed his full length into her, stifling her moan of pleasure-pain with his mouth.

They reached a heaven neither had attained before. Guy was reluctant to withdraw from her, feeling that the separation would only underline the coming long, uncertain one. Still joined to his love, he began to kiss her eyes, her lips, everywhere he could reach, and felt himself becoming hard and ready again, so he took her back across the stars again and again.

PART IV

BAYEUX, HAWKINGHAM, EXETER

One

I t was well, thought Guy later, that we said our farewells in the wordless voice of passion so that Lianne was too exhausted afterward to do more than amble in a daze back to the convent's walls, for a question then would have brought me to tears.

Guy had managed to depart with his retinue before the tolling of Prime might waken her. He wanted to carry with him the image of Lianne, skin dewy with passion, golden hair spread on the green carpet of grass, blue eyes as they flew open during the shock of her climax, then closing as swiftly as she dug her nails into his lower back, sighing her pleasure —not a farewell of tears, possibly witnessed by others. For that reason he had forbidden Orm, selfishly perhaps, to wake his sisters to make his own farewells, and stubbornly refused to offer any explanation for his order, though he knew the lad was too proud to ask and turned away to hide his feelings. Guy felt too ill-tempered at leaving Lianne to deal with her brother's sullen resentment about their relationship just now.

"The bishop is not in Dover? Is he not still its governor?" Guy inquired of Dover Castle's captain of the guard. Frustration at an unexpected delay, as well as temper from exhaustion and being soaked through in a late August downpour, made his voice an icy blade, his eyes behind the helm's nasal flat, stony orbs of brown. In spite of himself, Captain Conan shivered in the chill rain —the Earl of Hawkingham, Baron de Bayeux, looked the very Devil.

"No, my lord, he has gone north of the Thames with most of the garrison in pursuit of English outlaws."

"How many days hence?"

"A week, my lord, so I expect him back any day now. By Saint Valery, you're a welcome sight, my lord earl, and your meinie—these English grow more and more openly restive daily. They know our strength is down and they taunt us with stones and jeers."

Guy assured the stocky captain, "I must needs wait for His Grace in any case—my men and I will assist yours as needed."

Dover Castle was not one of William's hastily built fortifications. Legend had it that it had stood guard over England's southern coast since the time of the Romans, who had built the original eighty-foot pharos out of the rubble of Briton dwellings and flint. The gray-walled castle had been the first major stop on William's victorious march after Hastings last autumn—a lifetime ago, Guy mused.

The English of Dover had more than wearied of the conquerors' presence in their coastal city in the months since they had invested the castle. Bishop Odo ruled with a greedy, heavy hand and allowed his men to make life miserable for the inhabitants of Dover, in contrast to his brother's stern but fair justice. Ruinous taxation, rape, and open theft from Dover's merchants by the Norman and Breton men-at-arms had made the citizens ripe for rebellion.

Seeing the coming of the earl and his men, and perhaps fearing to wait until Odo and the rest of his men returned to swell the garrison's strength, the English had attacked, just as a score of knights were returning from a routine patrol of the town at eventide. The gates had been opened for them, and the rebels rushed from hiding in the inn of a nearby side street, thinking to seize control of the castle by virtue of sheer surprise. Due to the increased drilling and tightened discipline of the garrison since Guy's arrival, they were easily repulsed and the gates closed against those who were left. The English foolishly did not press their advantage, and they reckoned without Guy de Bayeux, who swept only minutes later from the castle at the head of the mailed, mounted garrison, his sword flashing. Its blade was soon scarlet with the blood of the would-be insurrectionists, whom Guy and the other knights pursued through the town to the shore.

Guy later learned that a richly dressed man he spied from the docks being rowed out to a ship was none other than Eustace of Boulogne, who had fought for William at Hastings. That scheming fool had instigated the revolt, thinking to take revenge for what he felt was a lack of compensation for his service, but retreated when it became apparent the effort would fail, deserting those who had risked much for his sake and theirs.

Even William will not forgive this treachery, Guy thought as he wiped his blade clean. Most of those not run down by the charging destriers or cut down by Norman swords were taken prisoner and thrown into Dover Castle's roomy, dark dungeons to await Odo's pleasure.

After receiving Guy's message, the martial bishop soon recrossed the Thames and returned to Dover.

Guy was summoned into his presence in the great hall, where the king's half-brother awaited him, sprawled in a huge chair in front of the fire while a servant brought them mulled wine. He was already stockier than his baseborn brother, and his fleshy, florid face, small, calculating eyes and bulbous nose gave promise of obesity in years to come. His pose was deceptively indolent.

"It seems I am twice indebted to you, Guy," he said in a silky voice.

"I was glad to be of assistance, Your Grace. . . . Were you able to catch the brigands you sought?"

"Nay, worse luck—it was a futile chase. The Saxons can be slippery as larded swine, as you well know, and in the forests where they are at home—the animals—they can taunt mounted knights with impunity." He set his goblet down with elegant care. "But how did you happen to be at hand to save my garrison, Baron—nay, it's 'Earl' now, *n'est-ce pas?*" He made a tent of his fingers, the great ruby of his bishop's ring winking in the flickering firelight, and waited for Guy's reply.

"I came to seek *your* assistance, actually, Your Grace," Guy began, more coolly than he felt.

"And instead came to mine! Ha! Well, whatever it is, I'm grateful and it's granted. My dear brother the King would not have taken lightly my losing one of the key fortresses of England while I was out chasing will-o'-the-wisps! What may I do for you?" He strode over and clapped

Guy heartily on the back.

Guy had never liked Odo, and his forceful bonhomie did not make it any easier to ask this favor.

"You perhaps know of my betrothal to Mabile of Harfleur."

"A distant kinswoman of mine, in fact. Yes, I'd heard of it. A good match. You want leave to go and wed the lady? It's yours."

"No, Your Grace. I would know if there is any way the contract can be broken."

A log fell forward on the fire, sending up a shower of sparks. Odo looked up, startled. "You do not wish to marry the lady? Why? Has she been unfaithful to you? We could arrange to have her put away in a convent, and her dowry would still be yours. As I recall, Mabile is a rich prize!"

The cold, casual ease with which the man proposed to dispose of his relative's life and property was repellent to Guy. It was all he could do not to eye the carnal bishop with the distaste that he felt, so he turned his gaze to the crackling blaze.

"No, Your Grace. I do not need her wealth, and she is a most virtuous lady who deserves no punishment. I would wed another—an Englishwoman."

He looked up in time to see Odo clutch his side, laughing, and stiffened.

"*Wed* one of them? Man, they're ours for the taking! There is no need to marry them. Take the one you want and her lands too! Have two or three in your bed at once! We're the *masters* here, my lord!"

Guy's hand itched to clutch his sword hilt, but he dared not offend this powerful man. He looked away, feeling his face flush with anger. "I do not wish merely for a mistress, Bishop Odo. I have found the woman I want, whom I would make sons with, whom I can trust with my lands and my heart, but I must be free to wed her. I would not keep her any more in dishonor. Is it possible, Your Grace? Can my betrothal to Mabile be annulled? I would not want to shame Mabile, you see. She has done nothing for which to suffer disgrace . . ." Because the bishop was staring at him with such a bemused expression, Guy faltered. "You did say, after Senlac, that you would grant me anything in your power."

"Yes, yes, of course!" Odo waved a pudgy hand impatiently. "I could do far more than that, did you but ask! I do believe you're serious in your desire to marry what you may couple with for free. I don't agree with the wisdom of it, my boy, but if that's what you want, here's how we'll do it . . ."

Two

Thus it came to pass on a warm September morning that Guy, having left most of his meinie to return to Hawkingham, boarded a merchant vessel bound for Normandy, in the company of a Norman clerk who would travel on to Rome with a substantial gift to the Pope —"to pay for the annulment," as Odo carelessly put it. He assured Guy that it was generous enough to guarantee Alexander's automatic agreement. He stood on the deck watching the chalk cliffs of Dover recede behind him as Orm strode up.

"My lord, your goods are safely bestowed."

"Thank you, Orm." The youth started to leave, but Guy's hand on his forearm stopped him.

"I need to talk to you of the purpose for the journey, Orm, and why I could not take your sister, though I long to have her with me."

"It is not for a Saxon to know your whims, my lord." Although he had relaxed considerably around Guy after the earl had informed him he was to be his squire, the topic of his sister was still obviously a sore point.

"Loosen up, lad! I know you think I'm the Devil Incarnate, but I have a reason for this crossing other than homesickness, of which I was not at liberty to speak until I talked to the bishop." And he told him what it was.

"You would *wed* my sister? Put aside your betrothed wife in Normandy?" The blue eyes, so like Lianne's brightened under the unruly blond thatch. "Does Lianne know?"

"*Non*, I dared not promise that which was not in my power until I had spoken with Odo. I want to return to Lianne a free man. I know it seems to you that I have taken your sister's honor and treated her abominably, Orm. But I love her, and would be good to her now and always." His honey-brown eyes met Orm's unblinkingly.

The boy's mouth fell into a grin. "By the Rood, I think I believe you!"

Elfgift's presence on the journey back to Hawkingham was Lianne's salvation, for her sister's condition required

343

Lianne's almost constant attention. Unattended, she would drop her palfrey's reins and sit, staring woodenly at the cantle, until Lianne returned to her. At meal times she had to be fed. Lianne had to assist her when they stopped to answer nature's call—for Elfgift would give no indication of her need other than a certain restlessness and plucking at her skirt. This constant ministering left Lianne exhausted, with little time to think of Guy; many times it was more than one person could do, and increasingly Gilbert offered his help, holding onto a leading rein to Elfgift's mount, feeding the helpless girl while Lianne gratefully snatched a few uninterrupted mouthfuls.

When it grew too dark to ride, they would stop at an inn or monastery for lodging.

The most difficult time was the evening, before Elfgift fell asleep on her pallet, for the girl seemed to miss the structured, peaceful routine of the convent and would wander aimlessly about a room or rock restlessly back and forth on a chair.

"Perhaps it's the music she misses, my lady," suggested Gilbert. "The Vespers service was at this time."

"Yes, you're right, but I don't see . . ."

They were sheltering in a rude inn that night, not an abbey—no plainsong chant would be heard within these walls.

"Mayhap I could sing to her?" offered

the youth shyly, bringing a rebec from his pack.

"Aye, Gilbert, that would be very nice," Lianne answered absently, worn out from her charge.

Agreeably he sat down on a bench opposite their trestle table in the common room and began to strum the instrument, willing her to look up and listen.

It was not long before Elfgift did glance up under her pale lashes, an interested light in her hitherto lifeless blue eyes.

Gilbert possessed a pleasing though untrained clear tenor voice. He sang the chansons of Normandy and then turned to the epic sagas of the Danelaw, which made Lianne start with surprise that he knew them.

"It was a long winter, Lady Lianne," explained Gilbert after finishing a stirring song of Beowulf. "The servants in the hall taught me their English songs."

"You sing well," Lianne praised. "You could be a minstrel, were you not destined for knighthood."

The boy flushed with pleasure, but he insisted it was but part of being a good squire to keep his lord's ladies entertained. Then he switched to a love story about the ill-fated Tristan and Iseult, and at its tragic end Lianne was startled to see a tear glisten at the corner of her sister's eye and run unchecked down the alabaster cheek. Gilbert had noticed it, too.

"Did you like my singing, Lady Elfgift?" His hazel eyes challenging her, he wouldn't look away until the frail girl's head nodded affirmatively. She did not speak, but Lianne's heart burst with a paean of praise. Her eyes met the squire's and they beamed at each other. Elfgift was perhaps not hopelessly locked within the prison of her mind!

After the younger girl was asleep, however, the night was like all the others had been for Lianne since Guy had left. She tossed on her pallet, unable to drop into slumber, achingly conscious of the absence of his warm length stretched out next to her, his features haunting her thoughts, those dark, near-black eyes, slumbrous at times, the brows that would slant sardonically, the well-chiseled lips that murmured seductively to her in Norman French, *"Ma bien-aimèe*, your hair is a golden river, your lips like a rich wine . . ."* She ached to feel the thick, springy raven hair that fell carelessly across his brow, tousled after a bout of lovemaking. Her body burned to feel the touch of those long, sensitive fingers, stroking her slender legs, persuasively parting her thighs . . .

"Damn the scoundrel!" she swore, and pounded the brittle straw in her pallet. "How dare he create such a need in me and not be here to quench it?"

She was glad to reach Hawkingham, for she could immerse herself in the routine there and not have so much time to long for the return of the one who had irreparably changed her life.

Mold, with Tofig beside her, had been standing in front of the hall ready to greet them, and now gently helped the drowsy Elfgift from her palfrey and enfolded her in a warm embrace.

"My darling lady, welcome home."

Elfgift drew back from her slightly, a puzzled look stealing over her pale features. "H-home?" Clearly this was not a place she remembered.

"Nay, love, I didn't mean to confuse you. 'Tis not home to ye yet, but this is where we live now, Hawkingham, your sister, Orm, and me. And this is my husband, Tofig. We were but recent-wed."

Elfgift blinked at Tofig, then cast her eyes about, clearly searching for someone. She looked at Gilbert, then at Lianne. "Orm?"

"He is with his lord, Earl Guy de Bayeux," Gilbert answered her in an easy, natural tone in English, and although still appearing confused, she accepted this and allowed the squire to lead her into the hall, where the evening repast awaited the weary travelers.

"She depends on him more and more," Lianne confided as she walked in at Mold and Tofig's side, following her sister. "It is wonderful how he has made her respond to the world. She is speaking more, though but a word here and there. She was no different than when we left her, Mold, until Gilbert began to play and sing for her. The music seems both to soothe her and make her want to be alive again."

"He's a good lad," Mold answered approvingly. "You can see in his eyes, he thinks the world of her."

"Where is Earl Guy?" Tofig changed the subject.

"In Dover—he had business with Bishop Odo, or perhaps he has gone on to Normandy by now. He planned to be gone only a month, mayhap less. Isn't it wonderful," she chattered on, over-gay, "he is training *Orm* to be his squire?"

"Why didn't he take you with him? He's always insisted on dragging you along before," Tofig pointed out dourly, and she whirled on him, her brittle gaiety near to breaking, her eyes flashing.

"Of course I couldn't go—not with Elf-gift here, until she's better!" She did not admit how she had longed to be asked to go, how a rebellious demon had flashed through her mind—my sister is but a pitiful burden, holding me back when I would be free to be at his side. That she could have conceived such a selfish thought only pointed how low she had sunk since becoming the Norman's woman. She swore to wear out her knees with penance.

Mold and Tofig exchanged a look over

Lianne's bent head. Tofig had shared his thoughts earlier with Mold, that their mistress was drifting in a limbo-like relationship that held no promise of security should the Norman tire of her. He had grown to trust and even like his new foreign lord, but Guy's journeying to his Norman holdings without Lianne, yet with Orm surely along as hostage, was an ominous development. Would the Norman return with a wife? Once across the Channel, might he decide not to return at all?

Three

The gray donjon walls of Bayeux sat on a height above the town, solid and reassuring. Guy glanced at his new squire, smiling slightly, both at the youth's awed expression and the new haircut Orm sported this morn.

Orm had trimmed his towhead locks, disliking the suspicious stares and pointing of the Norman peasantry at his chin-length Saxon hair, but like his lord, he refused to go the full measure of shaving the back of his head. Even with his hair combed forward Norman-style, its blondness and his fairness marked him for an Englishman, but he felt less conspicuous.

"It's so big!" Orm exclaimed over the castle.

"*Oui*, though the ducal palace at Rouen

and the castle at Falaise are bigger. I hold it directly of Bishop Odo, but being the soldier he is, he's seldom here."

Minutes later, the two sat their horses on the other side of the moat as the creaky drawbridge was lowered. The guard at the gate tower, having seen that it was Baron Guy, returned from England, had given a glad shout and sent a man-at-arms to alert the castle's inhabitants.

A moment after they rode into the bailey, Lady Emma, a short woman with wisps of gray hair showing under her veil, glided out from the great hall, then, seeing them, ran forward with a glad cry: "Guy! *Mon fils!*"

Guy jumped from his destrier, whose reins were tossed to Orm, and enfolded the old woman in his arms. "It is good to be home, my lady Mother," he said with a grin as she kissed him soundly on both cheeks. She had to stand on tiptoe to do so, while he obligingly bent down. She released him then, looking behind her, and Orm's gaze was drawn with Guy's to the young woman standing a few feet behind Lady Emma, obviously hesitant to intrude on their reunion.

She was of medium height with glossy black tendrils stealing out from her *couvrechef*, her complexion of the ivory fairness of a rose petal. Her eyes were brown, shaded by sooty lashes, her lips pale and compressed now by whatever emotion she was feeling. Two hectic splashes of color on her cheeks belied her coolness as she stepped forward.

"My lord."

He took her hands in his and saluted her with a brief kiss on the cheek.

"My lady Mabile, you look well."

Orm stared at the woman, who was dressed in a gown of rich brown with a white linen undergown showing at the neck and hem, and a gossamer-thin headrail draped gracefully over her thick coiled tresses. *He calls her "my lady,"* and kisses her. Surely if she were his sister he would not be so formal.

"Gervais will be so glad you are here," the woman was saying in her clear, pure voice, which seemed somehow strained.

"Where is my brother?" *Ah, then she is perhaps his sister-by-marriage,* the boy thought.

"He is in the town, my lord, on business. I wonder that you did not chance to meet. He has been sent for."

"Bon. And you, Mabile? Are you glad I am here?" Guy had sensed a holding-back that had not characterized his betrothed last summer, and questioned it. His eyes searched her features, involuntarily comparing them with Lianne's. Mabile was a beautiful woman, but her beauty was like that of a cool marble figure of Our Lady set in front of flickering votive candles on an altar, compared to Lianne's more animated, sensual loveliness, and for a moment he longed to have this painful business

behind him and be back at Hawkingham, free to press Lianne's lithe, luscious figure to himself and demand that they wed.

Guy's betrothed was spared the necessity of making an answer by the arrival of a younger man, cantering his mount into the bailey and calling Guy's name. In a twinkling the two brothers were embracing, clapping each other on the back.

Orm judged Gervais of Bayeux to be younger by a year or two, perhaps by an inch shorter than Guy. He had a shorter, snubbed nose, full, smiling lips, and the characteristic swarthiness of the Normans. He was an attractive man, though lacking, perhaps, the degree of virile magnetism and aura of sensuality his brother possessed.

Their greetings exchanged, Guy at last recalled that he had left Orm standing shyly behind him, holding both horses.

"My new Saxon squire, Orm of Fairlight," Guy said, introducing the boy.

"Gilbert—?"

"—Is at Hawkingham, and well. I may knight him soon. Orm, take the horses and go with Herluin, there—" he indicated a stableboy standing nearby. "He will show you the stables. See that Nuage gets a good rubdown."

Over a sumptuous dinner of heron roasted whole and basted with a garlic sauce, rabbit cooked with onion and saffron flavoring the gravy, rose mortrews, and great loaves of white bread, all washed down with quantities of good French wine, Guy regaled his family with tales of the conquest of England. He was seemingly oblivious of his English squire, who served him dishes on bended knee which Guy shared with Lady Mabile, seated next to the earl.

Orm felt his hands tighten into fists as Gervais queried Guy about the suppression of the English "serfs" until Guy caught his gaze and winked. This action was reassuring, telling Orm: Relax, this is a pose I must assume, the debonair conqueror, until I can tell them all, particularly Mabile.

Orm was not blind, either, to the frequent glances exchanged between Gervais and Guy's betrothed, and pondered whether he should mention that to Guy.

"My son, come with me a few moments to my bower," Lady Emma requested as she arose, the meal finished. Guy murmured his assent, and the two strode out of the hall. Orm set himself to watch Gervais and Mabile, who had taken seats together at the crackling, smoky fire, as he helped clear the dishes above and below the salt.

Either they didn't think that he understood French, or he was being accorded the same thoughtless assumption that he was a nonentity, the way most of the nobility felt about their servants, for Orm was able to catch snatches of their speech as he passed near.

"What shall we do?"

"Be calm, my love, it will work out."

"I can't marry him, Gervais! I can't live in England, so far away!"

"You are betrothed . . . we knew he would return eventually."

Interesting. More and more interesting.

"You look fit, my son," Lady Emma pronounced with a smile as she studied the lean form of her son, seated on a bench near her, a goblet of hippocras held loosely in his long, slim fingers.

"And you, *ma mère.*"

"I am an old woman, Guy," she laughed. "The winter seemed to last like three, with you gone—though I would not call you back to Normandy permanently even if I could, away from the opportunities available in the ducal service," she amended hastily as Guy's dark eyes, so like his dead father's, leaped with concern. "Gervais holds your lands well. You are lucky to have such a trustworthy brother." Then, as if a contradictory thought had entered her mind, she cleared her throat. "I can see you are happy in England, and I rejoice in that. But I get no younger, and would see you settled. It is past time that I had a grandchild, a *legitimate* one, mind you," she added with a twinkle, "to dandle on my knee. How soon will you wed Mabile?"

Guy looked away, into the smoldering

embers in the brazier.

"It is about that I have come, mainly," he said uncomfortably. Betrothal-breaking was a scandalous thing and he hated to cause pain to this woman, or to Mabile. His father, through his rash rebellion so many years before, had created enough sorrow. Also, he knew she was genuinely fond of Mabile.

"You do not say 'I have come to wed Mabile,'" Lady Emma pointed out shrewdly.

"No." His dark brown eyes met her wise gray ones. He knew he could tell her all, and he did: his first meeting with Lianne in the Sussex wood, the death of her husband in battle, the occasions when she had tried to end his life, their first violent coming together, the blossoming of their love since then, though it was but barely acknowledged between them—everything. At the telling of the latter, Lady Emma's eyes had misted with tears.

"What will you do, *mon fils?* It would scarcely be fair of you to demand that Mabile enter a convent, that you would be free to wed. Yet you would live an eternity of pain, I can see, if you cannot be with this golden English girl, and you force a lifetime of shame on Lianne if you cannot make her your wife."

"I have a dispensation, *Maman*, from the Bishop of Bayeux, to break the contract," Guy told her, "but—"

It was as if the sun had broken through

the clouds. "But it is a miracle! Bishop Odo granted you that? Why? He is a distant cousin to Mabile, you know."

Guy told her of saving Odo's life at Senlac, and of helping put down the Dover rebellion.

"*Grâce à Dieu!* It will all resolve itself!" she cried joyously.

He thought for a moment that her relief on his behalf had perhaps addled her, for normally she was a tender-hearted woman, concerned for all. "But, *ma mère*, that still leaves Mabile, who will be looked upon as discarded goods by the world, however unfair that is. I hate to hurt her! I am quite fond of her, though it is merely a brotherly fondness now."

But this reminder did not seem to dampen her happiness. "Speak to her, Guy. You will see, all will be well."

Four

A private audience with Mabile of Harfleur proved impossible that day, for she had already retired for the night.

Guy slept restlessly, curious about his mother's words, not able to believe they would relieve his difficult task in the slightest. He dreaded the meeting with Mabile and wished it swiftly finished. He had left a message for his betrothed, a request to meet him in the orchard the next morning after Mass.

She was there before him and stood under a gnarled old apple tree, nervously twisting and untwisting the long hanging sleeve of her light blue wool overdress. Her black, slightly almond-shaped eyes were enormous in the pallor of her face.

Mabile watched him striding toward her, taking in at a glance his lanky, easy stride, the catlike grace that was his alone, and her heart began to beat so loudly she knew he must hear it.

"God's greeting, my lord," she said softly. "I am glad you wished to see me. . . ."

"My Lady Mabile, I . . ." He did not want her to continue. Any gladness she might feel at his presence might be changed to bitter tears in a few moments.

"No, let me speak, I pray you, or I may never have the courage." As always she felt threatened and overwhelmed by him, by the aura of sexuality he exuded so unconsciously and effortlessly. She longed for the kind, loving presence of Gervais, who adored her and, noting her great loneliness over the months that Guy had been gone, had gently wooed her until her heart was irretrievably his. Both of them had been conscience-stricken when they realized what had happened, for Gervais loved Guy and would never have willingly betrayed him. It was just that he could not bear to watch the beauteous Mabile waiting, pining for a word. . . . Yet somehow he knew she also dreaded the summons to the strange foreign land and to his larger-than-life brother. Mabile would not for the world have set brother against brother, and her meek soul quailed at the possible consequences. She could see but one honorable way out.

"I believe my decision to wed was

wrong," she said, unable to look at the narrowed, unreadable dark eyes, afraid to see the full, sensual lips turn hard and flattened. "I have decided to enter religion instead. I know you can honorably be released from your betrothal if I am a nun, so be easy, my lord, none would say ill of it."

He felt a strange desire to laugh hysterically. After all his worry about leaving her disgraced, she *wanted* to be a nun!

"You would make a lovely abbess someday, Mabile," he said, touching her cheek. "Is this what you truly want? You evidenced no vocation before—you seemed glad at our betrothal."

"Yes . . . no!" To his astonishment, a glistening tear slid down her alabaster cheek.

"No, she wants to become my wife," a third voice said behind them.

They whirled to see Gervais standing there, looking as guilty and miserable as Mabile.

"Your waiting woman told me where you were, my love," he addressed Mabile, "and I guessed your purpose. I could not let you face him alone. I am sorry, *mon frère* . . . we did not mean it to happen. But you were gone so long with scarcely a word. . . . I tried to comfort her, for your sake. She was worried for your safety, you know, afraid that a Saxon axe or arrow would find you. . . . And then it became more than that."

"And if I had returned and wed her?"

Guy asked wryly.

"I never would have betrayed your trust, Guy. I love both of you, nor would I stain your honor. She is everything good and pure to me. I would have left Normandy, gone on pilgrimage to the Holy Land, perhaps."

"There is no need, brother," Guy gently spoke as he saw tears shine in the other man's eyes too. "It so happens that what you both have told me makes me very relieved, and overjoyed for you. For I had come to break the betrothal myself, with Bishop Odo's blessing." And for the second time he found himself telling the story of his love for Lianne of Fairlight.

Guy was persuaded to wait three weeks, while the banns were read, so that he could be a happy observer of the wedding of Gervais and Mabile.

It was time not wasted, for he went through the necessary legal steps to sign Bayeux Castle and the barony over to its new lord, Baron Gervais.

The bestowal of Guy's birthright made Gervais speechless with astonishment. "You should not, you *cannot* do this, it is not right. I would still serve you loyally, Guy, as your seneschal, when you are absent."

"I know, younger brother. But it gives me joy to do it. I stand to gain more land in England as William campaigns northward. I would feel like a man with his feet in two rooms to have to worry about

Norman holdings too. Oh, I am doing myself a favor, never fear."

"You are a good man, Guy," whispered Mabile, her eyes bright.

"Not always, not like Gervais. Just be good to her, brother, that's all I want."

"With all my heart."

Lady Emma, watching the three from her seat on the battlement, felt as if her heart would burst with happiness.

Five

As the first anniversary of the Battle of Hastings came and went with October, Lianne began to look for Guy's return. News had reached her of the abortive rebellion at Dover, and she surmised correctly that Guy had been involved, and probably delayed there. But certainly by now he had crossed the Channel, visited his lands, and was on his way home!

She could not wait to show him the progress of Hawkingham Keep, which was rising steadily on the banks of the Meon.

Lianne and her women had kept busy night and day spinning and weaving, making warm, serviceable garments of wool and linen that all the folk at Hawkingham should be well insulated from the winter's chill. Mold and her mistress had also spent much time in the stillroom, distilling herbs and flowers that would be remedies: the poppy for pain, Lady's smock for digestion, stitchwort for boils, agrimony for wounds, and more; plus the plants that would furnish dyes for the fabrics they wove.

The harvest had been good, and serfs industrious, and none should go hungry on Guy's lands this winter. The cattle, sheep, and pigs had fattened well and meat should not be lacking. The woodsmen reported plenty of boar and deer in Hawkingham Wood, and Lianne longed to ride at Guy's side in the chase.

The biggest change had been in Elfgift. Through Lianne and Gilbert's assiduous therapy, the girl's spirit and mental faculties had largely returned to her, though she still seemed very fragile. She seemed to have no memory of the brutal rape near Senlac, for which Lianne was thankful since there were Norman men-at-arms whenever one looked. Elfgift seemed most secure in Gilbert's company; seemed to require it as a plant needs water, and Lianne was eager to hear Guy's wry comment on that friendship. Gilbert was obviously and unashamedly smitten.

Most importantly, Lianne wished for Guy's return to share a secret she had imparted to no one else, not even Mold. That first time the Norman earl had made love to her after her miscarriage had resulted in the conception of a new life. It seemed particularly miraculous that it should be so when she remembered her wooden lack of response on that occasion, when she still grieved for that other infant, lost to them. This time, she vowed, nothing shall take our son from me!

As she pondered the future joys of motherhood, she would have been surprised to know that she was the subject of discussion between a man and a woman deep in Hawkingham Wood.

"The village peasants tell me the Norman's whore has returned," Wulfrune said pettishly at dusk as she and Wulfnoth devoured the remains of a hare he had poached.

"Oh, has she now?" A coward, Wulfnoth had no desire to tangle with her Norman protector a second time. This time he'd not let him off so easily!

"*Without* the Norman," she said provocatively, knowing that his unsatisfied lust for Lianne of Fairlight still festered. *Now* she had his full attention! A peculiar light shone in his eyes, and a wolfish grin began to play about his lips.

"Wulfrune, my love, you know how I long to have that bitch just once—to humble her, of course," he added quickly, as she looked up with a possessive frown.

"I'd not mind humbling that high-and-mighty wench myself," she admitted, though she did not add that taking Lianne's magnificent Norman lover away would be the greatest triumph she could imagine in her fantasies.

"I'd love to stick it to her," mumbled Wulfnoth, picturing it vividly in his mind's eye, "and leave her bleeding and sticky with my seed—he'd not want her then!"

They came to a sudden understanding.

Lianne, in an effort to keep busy, had made for Guy a magnificent robe of deep blue, dyed with larkspur, of wool she had carded and spun herself. It had a slit neckline with silver embroidery edging there and at the ankle-length hem, and to go under it she had made a shirt of the finest bleached, close-woven linen, with tight-fitted sleeves whose edging matched that of the overgown.

On an impulse born of loneliness and need, while putting away the new garment she picked up an older one, the rabbit-fur lined cloak he had worn almost constantly last winter. She had intended only to press it to her cheek and breathe in the clean male scent of him, but when she raised the garment, a piece of parchment was revealed beneath.

Guy of Bayeux had the unlettered man's carelessness with the written word. After having received the communication from Gervais that had resulted in his journey to Normandy and having it read to him by the priest, Guy had without another thought stuck it in the chest in which he stored his clothes. Lianne read with a growing horror that the man she loved was betrothed, as good as married in the eyes of the Church.

An animal moan escaped her lips as she sank to her knees, clutching the cloak possessively to her as the room spun before her blinded eyes. The tears fell scalding on her ashen cheeks. There seemed to be a great tearing pain in her heart, a grief which, protectively, turned to rage.

The man she loved, who *knew* she loved him, had never been honest with her, had never told her he was trothplight with some Norman woman—in her mind's eye she already thought of her as "*that* woman," alternatively dark, stooped, and older than he, but rich, or dauntingly more beautiful than she, as well as wealthy. He had played with her feelings, dominating her until she was a willing slave to satisfy his body's cravings. Even now the stories he had told returned to taunt her, of past Norman dukes, half-pagan Vikings who had kept mistresses as well as wives, sometimes in the same hall. Many of those mistresses had been better-loved than the lawful spouse, he had averred. Had he been hinting at her fate? Did he think, the handsome, arrogant cockerel, that she would meekly stay in such a situation, with Orm and

Elfgift to view her shame? So that was why he had journeyed to Normandy and would not take her! That he would take his leman's brother with him did not seem too high-handed for such a man. He would return to her, all right, with a wife in tow, perhaps already with child—as she was, bitter fool! Did he plan to install her in one of the lesser keeps, Winslade perhaps, and ride over to pass the night with her when his pasty-faced French wife bored him with her fawning adoration? (Oh, she was already sure of that woman's weak qualities! Any woman but she, Lianne, would not fail to fall at the scoundrel's feet!)

She'd be damned first! She'd spent too much of the last year weeping because of the blackguard, but no more! The room was too hot, even with the wood shutters opened. She must have air!

Six

Lianne told Mold nothing of the letter, only that she wanted no supper and preferred to walk about the new keep instead. No, by the Saints, the *last* thing she wanted was company! She needed to think!

Maitre Raymond and his men had gone for the day. The half-finished tower rose above the sparkling Meon, the gray of its stone gilded by the rays of the setting sun. It would be a magnificent, strong fortress, worthy of its earl, but she would not be here to see it.

Hardly knowing where she put her feet, her thoughts darted hither and yon as she tried to decide her course of action. Flee for the north, with her brother, sister, and Mold? Her spirit quailed at the thought of uprooting them again, just for her own sake, particularly the fragile Elfgift, who was just beginning to bloom and grow toward Gilbert's sunny nature.

Looking around, she saw that her wandering had taken her to the edge of the wood, though she had no recollection of leaving the mound on which the keep grew.

It was an unexpected, golden (hellsent?) opportunity for Wulfrune and Wulfnoth. The latter had been setting snares to catch young rabbits in the dense undergrowth, while Wulfrune lightly pelted him with acorns, complaining of the necessity of eating rabbit again, when both heard the snapping of twigs that heralded the unhappy Lianne's coming. She clearly had not seen them, and after a hasty whispered consultation, Wulfnoth stole back a little way into the forest, handy if Wulfrune should need help in subduing Lianne, but invisible if guile should suffice until the trap was sprung. All hinged on whether the Norman had denounced Wulfrune's role in drugging the mare to his leman.

It appeared he had not.

"Why, my Lady Lianne," quoth the red-haired woman, arising from the thicket as if she had been dozing, "you startled me! Do you remember me, your humble servant, Wulfrune of Hawkingham?" There was no sign of anger, fear, or distrust in Lianne, just a vagueness that indicated she was absorbed in her own misery.

"Wulfrune? Is it you? I thought you had gone from these parts. No one has seen you . . ."

"The serfs know where I live. I have become their white witch, dispenser of love philters, charms, amulets, and brews that heal and strengthen."

Lianne fought the urge to cross herself.

"But you seem so unhappy, my lovely lady! Care sits heavily on your brow!" crooned Wulfrune soothingly. "Tell Wulfrune how she may help! A charm? A dose of pennyroyal, perhaps?"

Lianne put up her hands in a gesture of loathing at the last suggestion of an abortifacient. Rid herself of his child? Never! She would never be able to call him hers, but no one would deny her his child!

"Ah, I see you have no need of that. Well, then, let Wulfrune show you her humble cottage and give you a horn cup of her special Jerusalem sage tea, guaranteed to drive away sorrow and pensiveness of mind and to comfort and strengthen the heart."

Numbly Lianne allowed Wulfrune to take her by the hand and lead her down the forest path in the amethyst glow of the setting sun. She had no desire for the woman's company or sympathy, had no intention of unburdening herself to the sly former Lady of Hawkingham, but it seemed too much trouble to refuse.

A few minutes later they were there, and Lianne could easily see why she and Guy had never found it before, hidden as it was by a dense, high thicket that effectively concealed its entrance. Wulfrune picked up a particular section of bush that swung back to reveal the door of the tiny thatched building that was really little more than a hut.

"I am honored that you should visit my humble abode," Wulfrune was saying in her dulcet tones. "It's quite a different place from the hall, but I am content."

They entered, and Lianne saw the other woman immediately shoot the bolt on the door.

"But why—?"

"She merely wishes to make sure ye don't escape me again, my lady Lianne," explained a familiar, nasty voice from the pallet by the smoldering fire.

Lianne started, peering through the smoky haze until her eyes at last adjusted to the dim light and recognized the lust-hardened face of Wulfnoth of Yorkshire.

She drew herself up like the lady she was and attempted to summon forth the firm, disdainful tones Guy might use on a recalcitrant serf.

"Let me go from here instantly!" Her voice was chilling, haughty; a less obsessed man might well have been daunted by it. "I have no desire to converse with *you*. Wulfrune, it was not wise of you to trick me thus. I assure you, my lord the Earl will deal with you severely, no doubt banish you at the very least, unless you allow me to leave *now*."

"Fancy words, Lianne the outlaw. I might almost believe you were a Norman countess born, instead of a traitor to your own countrymen." Wulfnoth leered at her, rising from the pallet and advancing on her.

Wulfrune, taking heart from his lack of fear, added, "Aye, traitorous bitch! Ye'll see how we punish those who spread their legs for the Norman devils!"

Lianne felt the door at her back. She had nowhere to run. "You were glad enough to take the Normans' silver, you Judas!" Lianne screamed in defiance, "and would have served Guy, had he need of foul whoresons like you!"

"Close thy lying mouth, bitch!" he shouted, and struck her temple with his balled-up fist. Instantly her world went black and she collapsed bonelessly onto the dirt floor.

She was aware first of the coolness of the close-packed earth, then of a voice that sounded alternately overloud and fading somewhere over her head, saying in a peevish Northern-accented tone, "Damn the wench and her soft head! She looks to sleep all night!"

Through an effort of will Lianne managed not to convey by a single flicker of an eyelash or change in her breathing pattern that she was conscious. It was difficult not to leap up screaming in panic after she realized that her wrists were bound tightly behind her, her ankles lashed together also, leaving her helpless as a trussed fowl to resist anything the unscrupulous pair might advise.

"Well, go ahead and stick it to her, Wulfnoth," Wulfrune replied crossly. "It's getting late and I'm weary o' waiting. At least you'll have an easier time of the bitch with her tied up that way!"

"If it's too easy there's no revenge, woman!" he shouted exasperatedly, making Lianne's already painful head thump in an agony that threatened to cause telltale tears. "It's no sport to bed a corpse! I want her to *know* she's being ruined, too soiled for her fine Norman lord! I want her to *crawl* with the shame of it! I want her to fight me and know there's no interferin' Tofig to rescue her this time!"

She felt his leather-shod foot poking her side experimentally, and forced herself to groan as if still unconscious from his blow.

"Well, if it's fight you want, Wulfnoth me dear," the other woman began in a husky, wheedling tone, stepping closer to Lianne's prone form as Wulfnoth crouched beside her, "I could *pretend* I was that high and mighty 'lady' . . . kind of give you practice, like. You could sort of, ah, 'act out' raping me, as if I was her, don't you see?" she purred.

There was a rustling sound of clothing

being shoved aside and dropped onto the floor and harsh breathing quickening its pace.

"That *would* be different, Wulfrune—*ye* acting like ye don't want *this* . . . and *this* . . ."

Wulfrune giggled as he pulled her down so that she lay close enough to touch Lianne, then tried to assume her role in a haughty falsetto: "Oh, do not *dare* touch me, knave! Whoreson! You have not a *noble* enough instrument for me! I—"

There was a grunt as Wulfnoth turned the red-haired Saxon woman over, laughing coarsely.

"Not noble enough, is it? Too common a cock for ye? Then perhaps ye'd deem it more proper as yer hounds do it!"

Wulfrune squealed as she was forced onto her knees and the Yorkshireman entered her roughly from behind, grunting and moaning as he thrust repeatedly into the woman.

He was so close Lianne could smell his sweaty body, tinged with the sharp essence of lust. She wished she could shut her ears. . . .

He's hurt me . . . my baby—I'll lose Guy's child again, she thought, every bone screaming in agonized protest from the fall and her cramped, unnatural position. Surely her fear and the violence done to her would unseat the babe within. She waited for the wrenching cramps to start, uncertain she would be able to distinguish them from the aching she felt everywhere. . . . She expected the hot sticky feeling of blood flowing from between her legs.

The pair was done with their sexual acrobatics and had collapsed, still clutching one another, and drifted off to sleep.

Lianne, unable to budge her bonds, lay awake for a long time as each separate nerve communicated its misery, but her womb lay quiet. At last, exhausted, she too dozed.

Seven

She awoke in the gray half-light of dawn, cramped limbs tormenting her as if the woodsprites had draped her with nettles. Her mouth was dry and filled with the acrid taste of blood. A headache pounded dully between her temples.

The pair beside her slumbered blissfully on, both snoring lustily, the stale fumes of ale drifting nauseatingly over to Lianne.

Such a pair—they deserved one another! What would they do next to her? Kill her? Nay, there would be no gain for them there. Hold her to ransom? If only Guy . . . But she could no longer look to *him* for rescue. When he returned, he'd have a wife and would doubtless little wonder at her disappearance, let alone pay a ransom. . . .

From Wulfnoth's drunken words it was obvious he intended to use her body until she was ransomed. And if he found out the powerful Norman no longer cared . . . there would be little to stop him from strangling her in his anger.

She would not wait patiently and be his victim. She would be free, for the baby's sake, and her own, but she'd have to use guile against the Yorkshireman's brute strength and Wulfrune's jealous lust for revenge.

"Mornin', my lady, what would ye gie a hadsome jack to loose yer bonds? I'll warrant them lovely white limbs is stiff —as stiff as something I could gie ye!"

Lianne forced a wan smile to her lips. It was all she could do not to snarl and spit.

"Please untie me, Wulfnoth," she pleaded in an enticing voice as the crude ceorl yawned and stretched.

"Ah, a little nicer it is today! I see ye've learned thy lesson! You'll be kinder to Wulfnoth now!"

If he touches me, I must submit, she vowed silently, so the babe will be safe.

"Aye," she answered him. "What will you do with me?"

"After I've had my fill of ye? Send ye back to the Norman—perhaps with my babe swellin' yer belly!" He leered at her, and despair knocked at the door of her mind. She laughed crazily within, to think that getting her with child was the one danger to which she was *not* vulnerable! He was mad—he just wanted revenge, like Wulfrune. She could not appeal to his greed. If she had to be used by him she would soon be as lunatic as he. No, she must use his lust against him. . . .

"After what I saw last night, that does not sound so dreadful . . ." she said, forcing herself to sound shyly coquettish, and saw him start to grin as he reached for her wrists.

"Aw . . . ye wuz peekin' after all. Yes, quite a lover, ain't I?"

There! Her arms were loose, and she rubbed the circulation back into them as he set to work on her ankles.

"But Wulfnoth, I am a shy woman. It makes me . . . more seeming-cold to you, to have *her* there, looking on. I'm sure I could show you more . . . ardor . . . if we could . . . ah . . . be alone?" She looked at him with artful innocence, fluttering the dark lashes over her blue orbs, using her beauty for the first time in a cold, calculating way.

The grin became wide, besotted. "Now ye're talkin', wench! I know once you have a taste of a good Englishman's loving . . ."

Good! Wulfrune was starting to stir behind them, and Wulfnoth was so intent on Lianne's words he paid no heed. Perhaps the red-haired woman had already heard them.

Lianne kept on with her chatter, painting a ridiculous fantasy aloud of the bliss she and Wulfnoth would enjoy once Wulfrune was out of the way. They'd leave Hawkingham, flee to the west or the north, where it was said Englishmen were still free. . . . She managed to accept his stinking, pawing embrace as he helped her to her feet, tugging her toward the pallet. . . .

"But—Wulfrune—"

"Still sleeps. I was tired of the bitch's overused charms anyhow. You have a freshness, woman—ye haven't had half of England and Normandy 'atween yer thighs! I was just biding my time, wi' her . . ." He jerked his head back toward Wulfrune's sprawled form, and Lianne pretended not to see the Englishwoman's awake, glittering glare. She had heard at least Wulfnoth's last words.

He was fumbling with his hairy hands at her breasts, imagining in his crude way that Lianne was aroused from the sighs she manufactured, when Wulfrune launched herself at him, clutching the long-bladed hunting knife he usually wore at his belt.

She had stuck it in his side, nearly to the hilt, before the interruption had penetrated Wulfnoth's lust-clouded mind, screeching, "Whoreson! Traitor! Toss me aside for this slut, would ye? I'll carve both your hearts out!"

Lianne shrank as far away from the struggle as she could, not knowing whom she wanted to win. They were fighting by the door, making escape impossible.

The Yorkshireman had pulled the blade out, and the blood oozed darkly out of the wound between his left lower ribs as they thrashed about on the dirt floor in deadly parody of last night's coupling.

Wulfrune grabbed with both hands for the knife, but he clutched it firmly in one powerful hand while he struck her brutally with his clenched fist.

"Prick me, would ye? Sure, I was weary of ye, with yer demanding, whining ways, yer conceit that ye were still a 'lady'! Ye *never* wur a lady like Lianne, even when they called you so."

He might have let her off with a beating, even in his blood-mad fury, but she spat in his eye and hissed, "Bastard!"

It was the last word she ever spoke. He stabbed down repeatedly into her heaving breast, slashing and ripping, until at last her screams died and her body had stopped its spasmodic jerking.

"Well, now, I've killed for ye, *Lady* Lianne, I guess that makes me yer worthy knight." He grinned, Wulfrune's spattered blood making a grotesque mask of his coarse features. He stood up, away from the sprawled corpse, held his arms out toward her, then collapsed as the blood continued to flow from the gaping wound under his heart.

Hardly daring to breathe, she watched the spreading crimson pool on the earthen floor beneath him. Wulfrune's first slash had been as deadly as his jabs.

Lianne edged toward a chest in the

corner, praying it contained clothes, worrying that even now one of the bodies would reach out and grab her ankle. She had no wish to wear her own gunna and kirtle, soiled by the dead man's sweat and his seed which had oozed stickily out from between her legs as she lay tied. Her search was rewarded, for the chest held several of Wulfrune's gowns. Lianne wondered idly how she'd managed to carry off so many without being noticed, and guessed correctly that this hut had served as the dead woman's "lovenest" even before she'd left the manor house. She chose a serviceable gown of rough, thick serge, with a woolen cloak and hood, fastening the large enamelwork brooch over one shoulder. She forced herself to search the hut for provisions when all she really wanted to do was flee the charnel house. At last, armed with a skin of wine, some dried apples, half a loaf of bread, and—wonder of wonders! —a few silver pennies she'd found in a jar tied up in a cloth, she closed the door of her prison behind her.

Where to go? Never "home," back to Hawkingham, to be the object of her sister's and brother's pity. They would grow content with their lot over time, serving the Norman. They were not vulnerable to him as was she—he had never held their hearts in his hand, as he had hers, and carelessly tossed it aside.

Where was it she had promised Wulf-noth they'd go—Northumbria? Its chilly, wintry name, now that it was autumn, discouraged her, as well as its distance. In Devon, she had heard, the men of Exeter had made a pact with nearby towns to resist the Conqueror and live or die as free English. . . . To Exeter she would go.

Once, before she had left Hawkingham's boundaries, she had heard Tofig's strong voice calling her, and his beating the bushes for some trace of her, and she felt heartsick for the pain she must inflict on those who loved her, thinking her murdered, vanished without a trace. . . . She hid until the voice passed on and dimmed as he searched farther away. It was better this way.

She lay that night in the guest house at Waltham, the abbey Harold had endowed and which he had visited just before Senlac. She was footsore and exhausted and fell asleep, only to dream in agonizing detail of Guy joyously returning home, only to find her gone. Her unconscious mind did not accept the picture of him accompanied by a Norman wife, for in her dream he was alone, and distraught at her disappearance. Not likely! she thought bitterly, and cried herself back to sleep.

Eight

Many times she cursed the lack of a horse as she skirted the port of Southampton, thinking lovingly of her white palfrey at Hawkingham, or even one of the less attractive but serviceable garrons. But she knew it would have been impossible to obtain one of them without her family knowing she was there, and she could not have borne their entreaties.

She stopped the next night at a small inn just outside Southampton, but left when a troop of Norman men-at-arms arrived and one began eying her with obvious lustful intent. Assuming she knew no French, one of his fellow soldiers disputed with him as to who had seen her first and had first right to her body. While they quarreled she slipped out, leaving one of her precious coins on the trestle table for the innkeeper.

She walked through the night, just wanting to put plenty of distance between herself and them, sticking to the coastal road westward. At last, bleary-eyed and nauseated, she stopped on a grassy knoll under an ancient elm to eat some of the remaining bread in her pack. She lay down, resolving just to rest her eyes—she had never been so weary and footsore. . . .

When Lianne awoke, the sun was high in the sky, but its light was blocked overhead by the tall form standing over her.

Startled, she opened her eyes and screamed when she saw who it was.

"Nay, Lady Lianne—I'm no ghost! Damn Wulfrune's soul to Hell! And why did ye leave me for dead, slut? I still lived, no thanks to ye!"

"I thought you *were* dead," she said, still trembling. "There was so much blood."

"Aye, so did I. I thought the bitch had done for me. But I came to, later, and found ye gone. I started after ye, after I determined ye hadn't returned to His Lordship's hall."

She noted then the bay gelding cropping the grass, tied to a nearby bush. It was Orm's mount—that meant they were home!

"You . . . went to Hawkingham?"

"Aye. Where else did you think I got

this fine steed?" he asked sarcastically, for the bay, though sturdy, was no knight's palfrey. "Wulfnoth of Yorkshire is nothing if not a good thief. They never heard me in the excitement."

"Excitement?" she prodded.

"Aye—His Lordship's back. Everyone was in the hall, so it was easy to slip into the stable."

"Was there anyone with him. A lady?"

He saw the unsuppressible gleam in her blue eyes. "How would I know? Miss 'im, did ye? Why, then, are ye walking away from yer soft life as his whore?" His puzzled expression cleared. "Ah, he went to bring a *wife* back from Normandy, eh? And you won't be content as the second string to his bow!" He laughed hugely, chucking her under the chin as she flushed angrily.

Forcing down her longing to ask more about Hawkingham and its lord, she said, "How is your wound, Wulfnoth?"

He pulled up his greasy woolen tunic to reveal a dirty bandage, brown with old blood.

"It pains like fire, ye daft wench! But I'll live—if only to have you! It'll have to be some other day—perhaps tomorrow, when I'm feelin' better, but th' time *will come*. I've waited too long—you'll not escape me another time. Ye're Wulfnoth's woman now! And you can start actin' like it . . . from now on you're to serve my every whim. I'm your 'lord and master' now! You'll do whatever I tell ye, if ye want to live, no matter how low. Ye're no lady anymore. And when we settle somewhere, ye'll cook my meals, tend my clothes, even whore for me if I decide I want to share ye. . . ."

She thought, as she listened in horror to his ranting, that she had left a painful situation only to be subjected to one to which death would be preferable.

Nine

Wulfnoth was immediately in agreement with her planned journey to Exeter.

"They do say Harold Godwinesson's mother, Lady Gytha, be there, holding out against the Norman Bastard."

Lianne was held in front of him on the bay, where his roving hands tormented her, frequently pinching a nipple painfully.

They forded the Stour into Dorset, stopping at a crude inn at Wilbourne.

Wulfnoth was ill-humored from the painful wound being jostled all day and the strain of holding Lianne against his chest as they rode. Also, a new, mysterious soreness caused him to keep rubbing his stubbly jaw.

"P'raps it's the toothache," he sighed, as Lianne watched him warily through weary eyes. "Go to the innkeeper and see if he has any draughts to kill the pain, woman!"

She obeyed him, glad to get away, though she heard him call threateningly, "If ye ain't back inside a few minutes, wench, I'll come after ye and beat ye soundly!" She would not be running from him tonight. She was too exhausted to flee in the dark.

The innkeeper had nothing to give her but strong wine, for which he demanded one of her last precious pennies. She returned to find Wulfnoth snoring stertorously. Pulling her cloak over her for warmth, she lay as far from him on the lumpy pallet as she could. No doubt they both would be carrying live passengers from the inn tomorrow. The dirty rushes are alive, she thought drowsily.

When he awoke, Wulfnoth pronounced the pain and stiffness in his jaws worse. He had difficulty chewing the coarse fare the innkeeper served to break their fast.

He was intensely irritable as they traveled that day. At one point they had to turn aside and hide behind some trees while a contingent of Norman men-at-arms passed. He was so vexed at the delay that he boxed her ears, taking perverse delight in the fact that she dared not cry out, for the Normans were still near. The violence caused the bay to half-rear, nickering in alarm, but the noise apparently went unnoticed, covered by the creak of the enemy's saddle leather and the jingling of their harness.

After they were far away, he shoved her roughly off the horse, forcing her to walk loaded down with the contents of the saddlebags as if she were a sumpter mule herself. Laughing at her humiliation, he rode the horse in circles around her.

It was his last amusement. By evening, when they sought shelter in an abbey, his jaw was so painful and rigid he could not eat at all, only trickle sips of broth past his clenched teeth. His face had taken on a strange, fixed expression, somewhere between laughter and crying.

Seriously alarmed, Lianne sought the advice of the Benedictine infirmarian, Brother Edward, who after examining the pacing, morose ceorl's jaw, motioned for Lanne to follow him out of the austere guest room into a corridor.

"Has he a recent wound, daughter?" In her rough woolen clothes he took her for a ceorl as well.

She told him of the knife wound in his side.

"Ah, that explains it." Brother Edward's face was grave. "Then I must prepare you for bad news, I'm afraid. Your husband will die. I've seen it happen many times—days, even weeks after a deep wound, a burn, sometimes the merest scratch. He will die most painfully, I am sorry to tell you." His voice was gentle, comforting, for he thought this was heartbreaking news for the ceorl's wife. Lianne did not bother to inform him of her true status.

"Will he be . . . delirious . . . at the end?"

"Nay, if only he could be. This will be as the pangs of Hell to him, a sharing of Our Lord's agony on the cross. Surely it will shorten his time in Purgatory." The monk was a devout, good man, and Lianne could see he almost envied Wulfnoth his pain. He gave her a vial of some potent herbal painkiller, but warned her she soon would not be able to force it past his clenched teeth.

They did not leave the abbey the next morning. At cockcrow, Lianne had wakened to find the Yorkshireman lying bent like a bow, muscles rigid, eyes staring in terror. He could only utter hoarse, muffled sounds. His face and scalp were bathed in sweat. Lianne was startled when she touched his forehead, for he was burning with fever.

Her motion set off a new paroxysm of arching, spasmodic movements, and his eyes glared at her with frightened pain. His manhood was grotesquely swollen and rigid as the rest of him, standing out obscenely from his lean body.

It would have been easy to leave him to face his fate alone, to go out to the stable or some pretext and continue her journey without a backward glance. But Lianne, ashamed of her early thoughts that he deserved such a death and aware that she would be free of him soon enough, forced herself to stay by his side, praying for his release. One of the Benedictines accompanied her, his voice murmuring constant prayers after he had annointed the ill man.

Again, when nigh-constant convulsions racked his body, Lianne's resolve to stay weakened. Surely Hell must afford no worse torture than these spasms which were set off by anything—a movement, a flicker of light, a stirring of air in the tiny cell—and which deprived him of breath, turning his face a purplish blue for agonizing seconds.

No, a voice within hissed, you'll not leave till it's over. He'll be in the fires of Hell—or at least Purgatory if God is more merciful than Wulfnoth deserves— soon enough. He is a Saxon, and English, like yourself. He deserves that little that you can do for him, sitting by his death-bed. You've been the Norman's whore— hungered and thirsted for his caresses— when it would have been more honorable to plunge a dagger into your breast, rather than give yourself, body and soul, to the enemy.

Just as the abbey bells were calling the sleeping community to matins, Wulfnoth, eyes dilating as if in terror, had a final horrible convulsion and gave up the ghost.

The compassionate black-robed Benedictine bent to close the dead man's eyes as the ceorl's "wife" said in a flat, emotionless tone, "I have not a penny to give your order for his burial, good brother."

"It is of no importance, woman," the monk assured her in his broad Devon accent. "St. Jude's has buried many another of God's poor. If you would but remember us in your prayers—?" He noted the beautiful but haggard countenance, and pitied her for what he assumed was the overwhelming loss of her spouse. Ah, well, the tears would come later. These were perilous times for an Englishwoman—even *with* a man's protection!

Lianne watched, unblinking, as Wulfnoth's body was borne away to be prepared for burial.

When the monks came to summon her for the funeral Mass the next day, she was gone. A check with Brother Porter confirmed that she had left without breaking her fast, heading west down the coast, riding the bay gelding.

Ten

"I fail to understand, Tofig. What do you mean, disappeared? Lianne has just—vanished? When?"

Tofig had not wanted to bear this news, to see the joy of homecoming wiped from the handsome Norman's face. Before his gloomy message, Guy de Bayeux's countenance had radiated happiness; his dark eyes had glanced hither and yon in the yard for the woman's presence who would give his return meaning.

Now the dark eyes were twin storm-clouds lit by bolts of lightning within, and were narrowed, wary. He dismounted before speaking further, tossing Nuage's reins carelessly to Orm, not even seeing the youth's alarmed face.

"Gone? Do you mean she has . . . left

394

me?" It was difficult, Tofig could see, to admit to a Saxon such a possibility, but Tofig could glimpse more than male pride shattering in the deep brown eyes.

"Nay, my lord. We don't know. Perhaps, yet there is more that I have found, that suggests otherwise."

The earl's hand gripped his sword hilt till the knuckles stood out whitely. A muscle worked in his jaw.

"Go on, man."

"She has been gone since eventide, two days ago. We have searched all over Hawkingham, without a trace of her coming to light. We have sent messengers to the other manors. However, deep in the forest I found a hidden cot, a hovel really, where Wulfrune had apparently been staying since the slut left here some time ago." Tofig had never kept his distance for the manor's former chatelaine a secret.

"Did you ask the woman? Did she know aught of my Lianne?" It was heartbreaking to watch the flicker of hope smolder in those dark eyes, and painful to extinguish it.

"Nay, I could not, my lord. The woman was cold, dead with a dagger in her heart and drenched in her own life's blood. She had been stabbed many times."

"Then what has this to do with Lianne?" The Norman dismissed it with a wave of his elegant hand. "Someone had finally tired of the wench's bitchy tongue."

"In the cabin, my lord earl, was a ripped gunna and kirtle. It was the one we had last seen Lianne wear when she went to walk by the keep."

"You let her wander outside the palisade—*alone?*" the earl's temper was terrible to behold, and he struck Tofig with his mailed fist, knocking him to the ground.

Tofig stared up at him, dazed, as Guy stood over the Englishman, chest heaving, a murderous gleam in his eyes.

Mold could stand no more. Heedless of her safety, she rushed from the entrance of the hall, crying as she caught his hands with both of hers—"My lord, forgive us! She would allow no one with her. She was distraught—I know not what set her off, but she wanted to be alone! We thought there would be no harm. In this vill, the peasants respect you, and love your lady. They would not harm a hair on her golden head!"

"Then where is she, Mold?" His voice was bleak as winter, eyes like frozen stone.

Already tired by the journey from Southampton, Guy refused to rest and refresh himself but would wait only long enough for his lighter mount, Roland, to be saddled and led forth, along with a fresh horse for Orm, who, like his lord, appeared pale and strained.

Minutes after their homecoming, they were again in the saddle, accompanied by

Tofig, heading for the forest.

He beat the woods like a crazed man, crying, "Lianne! Lianne!" Only the sleepy hoot of an owl, startled from his perch by the crashing horses, met his searching ears. The wood was as empty as his arms. Tofig directed him to the hovel, where he searched in vain for some clue as to his love's whereabouts. Wulfrune, of course, had been taken away for burial, but the bloodstains remained on the earthen floor of the dwelling.

Sir Ralf had been rounding up the villagers in his absence, and when Guy de Bayeux returned, half a dozen men-at-arms with drawn swords guarded a score of homespun-clad, apprehensive serfs, who shrank back as one as the earl reined in and jumped off his horse, striding over to them.

"I am your lord," he cried in hoarse, thickly accented English. "I have dealt as fairly with you as ever an English noble would. No man has reason to fear me if he has behaved rightly. I have raped no man's wife or daughter, nor caused any man to labor unreasonably. Now I require your help. I would know if any has seen my lady Lianne, or knows aught of those who may have harmed her, for example, Wulfrune, former lady of this manor." He gestured with his bared blade to the timbered hall against which they huddled.

"If you help me regain her, you will prosper. If any would hide her from me, or would shelter her enemy—" he gave them a look which made their simple hearts turn to ice—"he will wish he had never been born."

The Norman paused, staring through each of them, from the oldest crone to the youngest child.

"My lord," spoke a quavering old farmer, "I wish ye well, truly. The lady was always good to me, bringing poultices for me sore knee this winter and all. But I have not seen her since two nights agone, when I saw her strolling out to the keep ye be a-building." He pointed to the half-finished gray shell, just visible in the fading light.

"My lord, that woman Wulfrune," added a plump wife with two children hanging onto her ragged skirts, "she be hanging around Hawkingham. She never left the area. My man Ednoth, here, seen her in the forest, plenty of times." Ednoth was one of Guy's foresters, one of the few permitted to roam the wood at will, for the purpose of catching poachers.

In the end, it was obvious the serfs knew nothing of great value not already known. Why had Wulfrune stayed? Surely, even if the conniving, jealous slut had been capable of murder, she could not have hidden Lianne's body without a trace?

The serfs were freed, and departed to their rude cots thankful and relieved. None had been sure they would escape punishment for this disaster, even if it was none of their making. Normans, it was known, were not incapable of meting out chastisement such as summarily hanging every third man until their end was accomplished.

Guy sought his chamber, banishing all who would help him to disarm, bathe, and eat, much like an animal that crawls off to lick mortal wounds alone. He half-consciously hoped for some comforting sense of her presence there, as she had sought his when, carrying the newly made garments, she had knelt before the oaken chest.

The room had not been disturbed since she had left it; the garments she had made with such love lay abandoned on the rushes beside the chest. He started to examine them, recognizing their newness, when his eye was caught by the crumpled, splotched parchment that lay beside it.

He did not have to be able to read to recognize it as Gervais's missive to him, the one that had told of "your betrothed, Mabile" 's great sadness and longing for him. Lianne had found the letter and read it. She had not known the purpose of the trip was to secure their happiness together, Guy's and Lianne's. She would have come to the only conclusion she could have reached: he would return from Normandy with a wife. For a moment he could feel her anguish, before the crushing weight of is own settled in; could feel the pain she must have felt, that she was to be the cast-off mistress. Thinking the worst of him, he mused bitterly, she probably thought he would have both women living in the same keep, there being no sin too black for the "Norman Devil."

Gilbert's knocking on the oaken door went unheard, drowned out by the sardonic laughter. The door was not barred, so he went in cautiously with the food he'd brought.

The Norman was hunched convulsively over the oak chest, clutching a parchment, with his face buried in his hand. A muffled sound startled the young squire; he realized with alarm that his lord was crying!

He tiptoed out, hoping Guy had not heard him, leaving the cold roast venison and wine on a low table by the bed.

Eleven

G uy arose at dawn after a night
spent restlessly tossing and turning,
found the food left last night and downed
it hungrily, then went to call for his
horse.

Orm and Gilbert exchanged looks as
they answered their lord's bellows and
assisted him back into his mail.

"I ride for Chawton this morning,"
Guy's voice broke the silence at last as
Gilbert shaved him, "and will go on to
Winslade and Lingfield from thence. I
will find your sister, Orm, if she is living,
if I do naught else till Hell freezes. You
are perhaps still fatigued? Do you wish to
remain at Hawkingham and see to
Elfgift? I can take Gilbert."

"No, my lord, I want to help you find

her. But why do you believe that she has left the manor?"

"If foul play was done, if she is *alive*—" Guy opened his eyes and met the blue ones of Lianne's brother squarely, "she feels she has no reason to stay. She found and read the letter from my brother, and learned of Mabile. She left here that evening, believing I would return a married man. She would want nothing to do with me then! I must find her, Gilbert, and tell her the truth!"

Orm swallowed nervously and glanced at Gilbert for support. "My lord, if she is running from you, I do not believe she would go to your manors . . ." He waited apprehensively, to see if Guy was angered at his words, for his mood was so uncertain.

"Say on."

"Well, my lord, I think she would go to our aunt at Netherfield, or London, perhaps." He let out a sigh of relief as Guy appeared to consider his words.

"Perhaps you have the right of it . . ."

"My lord . . ." Gilbert began, gaining courage from Orm's boldness, "messengers have already been sent to your other manors, and I could follow them up, making a round trip to all and checking to see if any have seen her, bearing the news that you are returned, and seek her—"

"And am free to do so," Guy put in dryly.

"And then I could return here, to see if

she has come back, and if there be any news, I would ride for you immediately." He did not point out that Elfgift would fare better if he were gone for a less protracted time. The Norman would not be able to spare any concern, just now, for Lianne's sister, but nonetheless the girl had been doing well, was well-nigh normal for a *demoiselle* of her age, though she had been worried about Lianne of late.

"No, my lord, my niece has not returned to Netherfield."

"Would you tell me if she had?"

Her pale blue eyes flew up to meet his. "Yes, my lord, unless I had reason to believe you meant harm to her."

"But you don't."

"No. But as the Lord is my judge, she has not come here, nor have I had word from her. What has befallen?"

Guy sketched a brief history of the events since both had left Netherfield, ending with an explanation of the misunderstanding.

"Yes, my niece would want to be gone from you if she thought you had played her false." She studied the warm brown eyes that, full of pain, returned her regard somberly.

"I love her, Reverend Mother. I would make her my wife."

"Yes, I believe you. But I think you can see you have erred greatly in not trusting your love with all the facts. An Lianne had known the purpose of your journey, she would have waited, loyal as a lioness, and loved you the more for the difficult road you had to travel to claim her. Instead, your vaunting pride bade her stay on your manor to await your pleasure, like a cloak you may or may not don again, as she thought."

Guy hung his head, knowing it was true, and looked like such a miserable little boy that the nun had to restrain herself from embracing and comforting the powerful earl.

"Nonetheless, I will pray that you find her, and will send you word if I hear aught of my niece. Now, before you travel on to London—" (for he had told her he would seek her there next)—"sup with me, and rest here the night, that you may be fresh for the journey."

He had eaten with the abbess, hardly tasting the plain but ample fare, listening as Orm informed his aunt of Elfgift's progress.

"I rejoice to hear of it," the nun answered. "And you say a Norman lad brought about this transformation?"

Orm told her how Gilbert would sing to her and talk gently to the fragile girl, until she had begun to respond, for Gilbert had told him all about it before they left her in Mold's care.

"God is good," the abbess replied simply. "He has used a Norman to undo the damage a Norman has done. He is reminding us that He knows the heart, not the nationality."

Twelve

They reached London on Christmas Eve, with a light snow falling in big wet flakes about the horses' rumps and necks. Guy was pensive, remembering that only a year ago tomorrow he and Lianne had ridden to William's coronation. She had looked so beautiful then, in her new gown that matched her eyes, riding her new mare, and the smoldering rebelliousness she felt at attending the Conqueror's coronation had just added to her loveliness.

Where was she now? Hungry and cold, perhaps, believing him faithless? In a torment of jealousy, he pictured her finding some lusty Englishman to take care of her, and he ground his teeth at the thought of her passionately embracing another as she had him. But he would rather have her thus than being abused and degraded by some brutish Norman or Breton mercenary in a Southwark stew. Was she even alive?

Once they had stopped briefly at the old castle that once was Edgar Aethling's and was now Guy's town seat, Guy rode on to Westminster, for he had heard that the king had returned from Normandy. While he reported to his suzerain, Orm and half a dozen men-at-arms fanned out through the city, asking at every *cumerhaus* (tavern), church, convent, and brothel—had any seen a blonde woman, surpassing fair, of medium height? The Earl of Hawkingham would pay well for any information!

Guy found King William in excellent spirits. He was still exuberant over his triumphant progress through Normandy, where ecstatic crowds had cheered his return. There had been services of thanksgiving in many cathedrals. Everywhere he paraded the noble hostages, Edgar Aethling, Edwin, Morcar, Archbishop Stigand, and Waltheof, curious crowds had formed to stare at the exotic foreigners with their long blond locks and pink-and-white fairness. English plunder was exhibited also, to the joy of the Norman populace. They cheered their wonderful duke, who had subjected the near-pagan English!

Leaving Matilda again as regent, he had returned to find them far from subjected. After leaving streets thronging with the cheering Normans, it was a rude awakening to see the sullen-faced Londoners, who either glared defiance or turned their backs as he rode through the streets.

Reports had reached him of the rebelliousness still thriving in the West and North. Gytha, Harold's mother, was at Exeter, he had heard, and the ever-unruly Northumbrians were united in their determination not to bow the knee to the Norman king. He would have to see them brought firmly to heel in the coming year.

He had also been informed of Guy's part in putting down the Dover revolt, and received him with warm thanks.

"Ah, my lord of Hawkingham, you are most well come! I missed you sorely while I toured my duchy, though upon my return, I was told you had put the time to good use!" He laughed heartily, embracing the tall young man, and in spite of his gloomy mood Guy felt the great leader's magnetism. Men would always flock to his banner while he possessed this winning charm.

"How does your earldom?" the king asked. "I promise you, this year will see your honors enlarged as we subdue the rest of this island," he pledged expansively.

"Merci, mon roi." He gave a brief account of the rising keep.

"Ah, yes, Maître Raymond, a genius,

even among master masons. I doubt not we could keep him busy across the Channel at his trade for the rest of his lifetime, for I will need dozens of castles to keep dominion over this conquered people.

"But where is the so-lovely English damsel you had with you at Barking last winter? At home in your hall, big with your babe, or already suckling him, more like? Ah, I seem to remember your trip to Normandy had somewhat to do with her," the king added, surprising Guy with his knowledge. "Odo told me of a certain conversation you had with him after the siege, of a favor repaid. . . . Was Mabile content to retire to a convent? If I know you, you charming dog, you had her convinced it was *her* idea!"

"My king is remarkably well-informed," Guy answered, smiling at his sovereign's chaffering. "But it was not necessary for Mabile to leave the secular world—she was glad to wed my brother Gervais, for whom I have abdicated my Norman barony."

"Very generous! And the Englishwoman?" the king was tenacious, sensing some reluctance in his former hostage to discuss the matter.

"It's why I am come to London, *mon seigneur,*" Guy admitted at last. "She has disappeared, and I must find her. She thought I had betrayed her, and left at about the time I was recrossing the Channel. But there are those who would harm her, and I . . ." the earl's voice was tense with worry, and he broke off, fearing the king would think him foolish to be so upset over a "mere woman," and an Englishwoman at that.

But William, that man who was astonishingly faithful to one wife in an age when men gave free rein to their passions, merely smiled encouragingly.

"You'll find her, my son. I pray that it shall be so." Privately, he thought: Oh ho! The young Cupid is shot with his own dart at last!

But Guy did not find her in London, though he spent the cold wintry days between Christmas and the New Year searching for her, rather than celebrating in the torchlit warmth of William's Christmas court at Westminster.

Thirteen

Lianne had had to sell the garron long before she reached Exeter, for the hoard of pennies had soon dwindled, even with the additional ones she had found among Wulfnoth's clothes.

At Axmouth, where she had patted the horse good-bye, she used some of his price to buy a warm woolen cloak and a filling meal at an inn near the river. By then, however, she was already sniffling miserably and coughing, a horrible racking cough that seemed to tear her apart inside.

Though the innkeeper urged her to stay —"Those winds zhure be howlin' fierce-loike," he pointed out in his broad South-western accent—she resolutely set forth again.

Indeed, the innkeeper had said sooth, for the gales howling on the colorful blue and yellow limestone cliffs cut right through the new cloak, chilling Lianne to the bone.

She sought shelter in a cave formed in the headland overlooking the sea, its twisting mouth giving it some shelter from the icy Channel winds. Crouching against the cold rock inside gave no warmth, of course, and she had nothing with which to build a fire.

It was here, wet and miserable, shivering, that she first felt the tiny, tentative, butterfly-light movements within her that betokened life. The baby. Guy's child and hers—nay, just hers, for he would never know of it. Would she ever tell her (for she *knew* it was a girl) of her Norman father? Ah, pray it be blonde and blue-eyed, not a dark-eyed charmer to torment her with her sire's looks. She smiled to herself, thinking of the babe, and, hearing that the wind had died down somewhat, set forth with new resolution.

A far-off babble of voices threatened to shred the velvety black warmth that surrounded her.

"Feel . . . she burns with fever."

"She's so thin, the poor gel!"

"But with child, look you. Some four-five months gone, I'd judge."

Her eyes flickered open against her will, but all she could see was a haze of black and white framing blurred features.

She didn't remember being found by the Devon farmer who had happened by on the way to Exeter's market day, or his bringing her here, the Benedictine convent near the eastern gate of the stone city wall. She only knew that at least here was an absence of the screaming cold winds and the continued need to walk, walk. Indeed, she was too hot. . . . In her delirium she kicked the covers off. Would she never be cool again? Was she in Hell? It was that hot!

A se'enight later, when the year of Our Lord 1068 was still newborn, she began to stay awake long enough to answer the nuns' gentle, persistent questions. At first her replies were nonsensical, for, weakened by her bout with lung fever, she was confused and disoriented. Seeing the black robes of the Benedictines all about her, she was sure she was at Netherfield and puzzled when her requests for the "Reverend Mother, my aunt," brought not that familiar face but a strange one.

Mother Mary Algifu was as short as her aunt was tall, and as diminutive as Mary Edburga was formidable, but she possessed a serene, warm temperment that was reassuring.

"Nay, child, this is not Netherfield, though I know it well—took my novitiate there, and your dear aunt sent me here to start this house the year before the sainted Edward died. Here, have some of this broth," she urged, holding the horn to Lianne's lips. "You and the babe need it." Noting Lianne's startled eyes, she laughed, a merry, tinkling sound that was unexpected, issuing from beneath the austere white coif that framed her wise blue eyes.

"Aye, you're starting to show, lass. Pretty soon your apron'll not cover it. But how did you come to be wandering around on the sea cliffs in December, with a babe on the way?"

The notion that Lianne was a runaway serf was dispelled by her careful, educated speech that proclaimed her in truth a thegn's daughter from Wessex, despite her rough garb.

Lianne told her she had no one, her father and spouse having died by Norman hands.

"Who's the father of thy babe, Lady Lianne?" the abbess asked gently, and her suspicions were confirmed by Lianne's truthful answer.

"Does he love you? Would he not care for you and the child?" She winced inwardly as the icy curtain fell over the beautiful girl's eyes.

"Aye—a good Norman takes care of all his possessions—be they cattle or bastard children. I'm sure I'd get a pallet in the hall where his Norman wife is lady, or perhaps even a private alcove or cottage near the keep where he may visit me and sire some more of them."

Such bitterness in one so young! But it

was a common enough story. Convents all over southern England were sheltering women fleeing the lustful foreign masters.

"He was married, then," she concluded aloud, and Lianne did not bother to correct her. "Well, what do you here? The Normans have not troubled Exeter thus far, though there is no guarantee our blessings will last." Her gaze shifted to Lianne's gently rounded abdomen.

"What you need, my girl, is a husband, someone who'll protect you and the babe." She gazed across the room, lost in thought, wondering who she could find for this young woman. "I'm afraid I know of no one of thegn rank in need of a wife, but though he is older, Ednoth, the farmer who brought you here, is a widower and has five children. I'm sure he'd grow to love you, and you could be such a help to his motherless little ones."

"Nay, Mother, I'd ask no man to be saddled with a new wife already carrying a half-Norman child," Lianne pronounced firmly.

It was likely she was right. Even the amiable Ednoth might be chary of such a burden, and with worldly practicality the abbess reasoned that Lianne's pregnancy was too far advanced to make a prospective bridegroom think the child was his. The nun could not know how the thought of any other man but Guy touching her, kissing her, making love to her made her shudder.

"Besides, Mother, a man may be no protection from the Normans. Being wed to Edwin protected me from *nothing* when the Normans came." Her eyes glitterd a wintry blue.

"Perhaps you are right. But then, what will you do?"

"Mother, may I stay here?"

The older woman was startled and studied anew the thin features of the convalescing girl. Even after her close encounter with death, she was fair, and Mother Mary Algifu could see that regular meals would soon bring back the lush golden beauty that had attracted the unknown Norman. Here was no nun!

"Hush, child," she temporized, seeing the pallor of fatigue on the girl's cheeks. "We need not settle all today. We will speak of this anon."

Fourteen

"Sister, have ye heard the news?"
Sister Osburga fairly flew into the
room in which Lianne, garbed in the
same black serge habit as the nun, sat by
the window using the bright March sun
to light her work.

Mother Mary Algifu had soon found
that, while Lianne was willing, her talent
lay not in cooking for the community,
and her rapidly increasing girth made
heavy toil in the convent's vegetable
garden impractical. After discovering the
wide range of the girl's education, the abbess had thanked the saints for the
treasure they had sent her and set Lianne
to the task of translating her corres-
pondence from France and Italy and
foreign books—lives of the saints and

such. Lianne also found she had a talent for illumination, so that when she wasn't translating French or Latin into her heat, flowing English, she was making the gorgeous gold-leaf illustrations at the chapter headings of what promised to be the most beautiful Book of Hours in England.

"What is it, Sister Osburga?" Lianne looked up, smoothing the black skirt unconsciously over her swollen belly and rubbing her hands wearily down her lower back.

"Ah, the babe tires ye—ye should rise and walk around more," the florid-faced nun counseled. "It must not be much longer ye must wait!"

Lianne smiled. Osburga was so distractible. She loved to discuss the other woman's pregnancy, perhaps experiencing vicariously what she had forsaken for herself.

"Ye put me in mind of me mam, holdin' yer back loike that. Me mam bore four after me, and she was always rubbin' her back, God rest her . . ."

"You had *news*, Sister?"

"Ah, yes. Sister Edwina, that went in to market today, heard that King William in London has demanded Exeter make its submission, and Lady Gytha has refused, and all the town council with her! They have offered money to any of the foreign traders in Exeter at present to stay and strengthen the outer defenses."

Lianne sighed heavily. King Harold's

mother, Earl Godwin's widow, had made Exeter her home since Senlac, and thereby the old walled city had become the western rallying point of English resistance. Harold's children by Edythe Swan-Neck were said to be with her, and Gytha's remaining daughters too, with the exception of Edward the Confessor's widow, Edyth. *She* had made her submission much earlier, naturally, having always been pro-Norman.

Defiance would bring William—as soon as the roads were passable. He would not allow such unified resistance to go unchallenged, Lianne thought wearily. He would win, too—the English these days could not seem to unite under any leader, and in any case Devon was too isolated from the North to hope for reinforcement.

Would that I had energy enough to care, Lianne thought, amazed at the lethargy that overwhelmed her these days. Her world was slowly narrowing, closing in on itself so that there was no universe beyond the kicking, shifting burden she carried below her heart. The whole Norman army could be outside the convent's gates this moment and I believe I would still take my nap after Sext.

Her days had assumed the rhythm of the convent bells. Prime, Tierce, Sext, Nones, Vespers, Matins . . . The food was plain but plentiful and nourishing, and Lianne could feel the baby growing strong and lusty within.

Though she wore the Benedictine habit for convenience, and chanted the Offices with the rest of the community, the question of Lianne's future was far from settled.

"Mother, let me join the community and be a true nun," Lianne still pleaded with the abbess. She was as eager now to escape the world as she had been to stay in it while at Netherfield.

"Daughter, I feel I am led by St. Benedict to refuse you entrance into the community at this time," the abbess replied firmly, as she had several times before. "Wait until the babe is born. The little one may change your mind, you know."

"Nay, Mother."

"But, Lianne, to have to give the child up after you have suckled it, held it! Ye can't understand what that would mean!"

"I can, Reverend Mother," the girl said impassively, but her mind whirled with pain. If she renounced the world, the child would be sent out for fostering at some farmhouse until he or she was of such an age to be entered in a convent or monastery, to become a monk or nun himself or herself. Did she have the right to condemn an innocent baby to such a narrow, austere life, albeit a more secure one in Norman England—from its cradle? Her daughter would never know the joy and pleasure of a man's caress . . . or the pain of its aftermath. Aye, perhaps that would be better!

Lianne had been persuaded to post-pone any decision until the baby's birth.

She stood up from the stool on which she had perched to do her work, while Osburga chattered on in alarm about the possible coming of the Normans. Suddenly the yawn about to escape Lianne's lips turned to a grimace as the first tentative fingers of pain stole around her flanks from her lower spine.

"Sister Lianne—you're pale of a sudden. Is it the babe, at last?"

Above them, the convent's mighty bell tolled the hour of Sext.

Sext was chiming again the next day before the babe was born, his lusty cry threatening to drown out the sonorous bell.

"A son, Lianne," announced Sister Infirmaress, beaming as if the healthy infant were her own grandson.

Lianne, her face bathed in sweat, grinned in spite of herself at the child she had been sure was female, and ruefully noted the thatch of unruly black hair that crowned his well-formed head. Here would be no easy forgetting of his sire!

"What will you call him?" one of the nuns questioned shyly from the doorway.

She had thought of Rolf, for her father, or Edwin, but the lad's Norman features would make those names a mockery.

"Ranulf . . ." she answered, nuzzling the baby as it was handed to her.

"A *Norman* name, Lady Lianne?" the

nun who had acted as her midwife questioned her in horror.

"Aye, Ranulf." A name conjuring up ruthless Viking-descended French raiders.

"Why not a good Saxon name—Osric, or Edward, or . . ."

But Lianne heard her not, and was thinking with pride, I doubt his prim, puling Norman wife could produce such a son as this!

Fifteen

It would have indeed startled her to know that Guy de Bayeux, now of Hawkingham, had been without the city gate on the very morning of his son's birth and had been refused entrance.

He had come at William's behest, as his envoy, to receive word of Exeter's capitulation, which Guy had realistically known would not be forthcoming.

He had been surprised to learn that, while he and his retinue would be denied entrance as William's preliminary vanguard, the citizens would be willing to pay tribute.

His lips compressed angrily, though, when the Exeter elder elected spokesman had added to the offer, "It's nothing to us, Norman. We've been paying off invaders since Roman times. We paid the Vikings to leave us alone. Come now, what sum of money shall we agree upon to pay William to let us be English freemen within our walls?"

He knew what the king's answer would be, so he gave it, eyes narrowed to dark glittering slits shaded by the nasal piece of his helm.

"It is not my lord the king's custom to receive his subjects upon their own conditions, Englishman. Have a care! William will be upon you before you know it, and will show no mercy for such foolhardy speech. Submit, and open your gates to me and my meinie!"

"Nay, you have had Exeter's answer, my lord."

Guy wheeled Nuage around and, surrounded by his men-at-arms, cantered back from whence he had come.

Ranulf was a month old, and Lianne had still neither left the shelter of the abbey nor taken the veil. Indeed, Mother Superior would not have countenanced her leaving with the newborn babe, with the Normans expected daily outside the gates.

The inhabitants of the city had not long to wait. One April morning the watch on the gates blew the horn, for he had seen the cloud of dust and faraway glints of sunlight off armor that betokened the Norman army.

Soon afterward came a scrambling of

nearby farmers to herd their beasts and their families within the gates, for none wanted to remain in the path of the marauding army.

The convent, which bordered on the stone city wall, then witnessed a curious procession of Exeter's prominent citizens—its well-to-do thegns, the bishop, and a priest—riding straight toward the oncoming army, now only a league or two away!

"What means this?" asked the abbess, troubled, standing where she could see over the wall. With her were several of the nuns and Lianne, holding the baby Ranulf, who seemed not at all troubled by the event. He smiled milkily up at his mother, whose eyes were scanning the horizon grimly.

"Sister Osburga, go speak to the watch. Discover why they have left," the abbess commanded. "Nay, hold—thou'lt be there all morning chattering and still not discuss the matter. Lianne, you go—and I will hold thy son."

The young woman was soon back.

"They mean to treat with the Normans," she announced indignantly. "They would open the city's gates to the tyrants without an arrow sped from its bow!"

Over the other nuns' murmuring, Mother Mary Algifu said pensively, "Mayhap it will be for the best, only God knows, daughters. It will be a blessing if we can avoid the horrors of siege, or worse yet, the sack of the city."

"Did I flee all this way in the winter only to see the very devils I fled be welcomed?" breathed Lianne rebelliously, taking the babe back and holding him close and safe. "Nay, that I did not!"

The abbess put an arm around her shoulders. "You are safer in your habit, Lianne, than in the habiliment of the world, you know. Is not King William reputed to be a religious, God-fearing son of the Church?"

"Aye, but his minions may be demons incarnate," she answered, thinking of one in particular in whose dark eyes the Devil danced. Unconsciously she held his infant son so tightly he squealed in protest.

"Let us retire to the chapel and pray," the abbess said as she returned to the shelter of the abbey.

The convent's inhabitants were not the only ones to observe the nobles' leaving. The humbler inhabitants were a roiling, angry mob which met those who returned—the latter fewer in number as they had left hostages with King William, the Bishop of Exeter explained. The Normans, because of the peaceful submission, had promised to allow no pillaging of the conquered city.

"Peaceful submission, my arse," roared a tall youth, on whom an aged woman leaned.

"That's Godwin, the eldest of Earl

Harold's sons," murmured Osburga, who even in the isolation of convent life seemed to know all that happened in the town. "And the woman be Lady Gytha."

"I say ye had no right to submit, shaveling coward," continued the angry young man, whose hair was the same tawny blond mane his father's had been. He ignored the gasps at his disrespect.

"What, would ye subject this city to rape, youngling? Ye are not even of Fxeter—what gives ye the right?" challenged His Grace the bishop.

"My father spilled his blood for England, and I would do the same before tamely submitting to these French devils!" he answered angrily, then turned to the crowd. "Do I speak amiss? Do ye want to surrender? I will be silent if that be so!"

"Nay! Nay!" yelled scores of voices, old and young, nearly everyone, in fact, except the nuns, who stood silently watching through the grille of the gate, and those who had negotiated with the Normans. The latter appeared uneasy to see their lack of popular support.

"Ye asked not *our* opinion before cravenly sneaking out to the enemy!" yelled an other youth. "We'll not open our gates, will we, gatekeeper?"

"Never!" roared back the wiry fellow who controlled the city's main entrance. "Not unless all Exeter wills it!"

"Come, sisters," said Sister Infirmaress, gathering her black skirts. "It looks as if we will have much work to do in the infirmary in days to come. There will be many who will fall ill if the siege be prolonged, and others in need of bandages if the Normans cannot patiently wait to starve us out."

But Lianne stamped her foot and remained watching the crowd, her eyes flashing blue fire as she spoke angrily to the abbess, "I cannot docilely just await my fate!"

Mother Mary Algifu turned her eyes upon Lianne placidly. "See thou why I have said ye were not meant to be a nun? Ye lack the gift of obedience."

Lianne's eyes were downcast, for she was ashamed. "Will you turn me out, Mother, if I help those who would resist?"

There was a long, considering silence as the abbess stared at the drowsy infant in Lianne's arms. "So long as you endanger not that little angel, no."

If any in Exeter had needed a spur to their resolve, it was provided before dusk when the Normans, learning of the town's decision to continue resistance, blinded one of their hostages in the full sight of scores of jeering townspeople hanging over the walls.

"That should turn their catcalls to meekness," Guy de Bayeux sighed, wincing involuntarily at the brutal sight as he sat his horse at the head of his men outside Exeter's walls.

He spoke to Gilbert, who was armed cap-à-pie like his lord, and mounted beside him.

Orm had remained at Hawkingham at Guy's bidding, though he had expressed a willingness to go.

"Would you slay fellow Englishmen, pup?" Guy had asked him, studying the lad intently.

Orm's gaze had not wavered. "I should not like to, of course, my lord, and I would not go out of my way to do so. But I would guard your side with my life, and if any offered you harm, they should not live to boast of it!"

Guy had smiled at his fierceness, and was warmed by his loyalty.

"Why do you honor me so, pup?" he asked sardonically.

"You have grieved for my sister, my lord, even as I have," he answered honestly. "I have come to know you as a just, good man."

"Thank you for those good words, lad. I'll not take you this time, though, for I need a loyal Englishman to care for my lands in my absence, for these rebels at Exeter may spark rebellious tinder elsewhere. Perhaps this is the only time English shall have to fight their own—" for he was taking a score of trained foot-soldiers and archers from his manors. "I don't believe we shall be so fortunate, however."

After he left, Orm had pondered the

earl's grim, sad visage. Since Lianne's disappearance, he had lost all joy in life. He continued to be fair and even-handed to his serfs, but nonexistent now was that flashing charm and vitality that had drawn women and disarmed men; his eyes now were cold and guarded, his smile rare, his laughter mirthless and mocking. He sought no lady as a wife or even a wench to share the cold winter nights in his bed. He was up at dawn and stayed late in the hall, moodily quaffing wine until he could fall into a restless sleep.

"The mutilation of an enemy turns you squeamish, my lord?" sneered an oily voice. Guy turned to see Judhäel of Totnes, a Breton noble on his other side. "They are dogs, they don't even feel the pain."

This obvious untruth caused Guy's mouth to tighten into a hard, angry line, and he did not give the mercenary the courtesy of a reply. He had never liked the Breton, even in the early summer months when he, like other greedy men, had flocked to William's banner in search of gold as much as the glory of a righteous cause. He had always seemed a little too anxious to please, to insinuate himself into the circle of nobles closest to William, in which Guy effortlessly belonged. Seeing he could not win the duke's favor by being Guy's friend, he became jealous of the trusted position that Guy held. Judhäel thus far had been rewarded for his services only with a few hides of less than prime land in Sussex, while Baron de Bayeux, a former *hostage*, had garnered three manors already and, it was said, could easily expect more!

"I shall inform His Grace the king you disapprove of his treatment of the enemy," murmured the Breton, and reined his horse toward the king. He was eager to drive a wedge between the monarch and his favorite earl.

"I have said nothing to make anyone think so," the earl replied curtly. "But you must do as you think best, my lord. But I would warn you, William does not make policy on his vassals' opinions. He knows well his own mind."

The remark was double-edged, meaning that William could not be influenced against his own better judgment, whether in the treatment of hostages or the selection of trusted associates.

Guy noted that while Judhäel rode over closer to the king, he made no move to speak to him. Such snakes are never satisfied with hissing, he thought. They will thirst until their fangs sink into living tissue.

Sixteen

Lianne was up betimes to volunteer
her service to the leaders of the
defense. At first, they were horrified to
hear a "holy nun" boasting that she could
shoot a bow as well as a man. But refusing to be daunted by their shocked
expressions, she explained her true
status at the convent and how a "mere
slip of a girl," as one stalwart rebel
disparagingly called her, came to have
such skills. At last they grudgingly
admitted they could use her help, if only
to keep the fighters on the walls supplied
with arrows, stones, and boiling oil
against the Normans.

"But stay off the walls as much as
possible, Sister, uh, Lady, for if the
Normans see a nun fighting, they may
offer violence to the convent."

Lianne could see the logic of that.

She was soon a familiar figure behind the walls, fetching armaments, lugging pots of oil for boiling, and carrying messages from one sector to another. Every few hours she would return to the abbey, for though Ranulf had settled himself to somewhat of a regular schedule, he was still far too young to be fobbed off with cow's milk.

Many times she could hear him wailing in his cradle as soon as she entered the convent's walls, and with a guilty sigh she would take him from the infirmaress, who watched her reproachfully as she settled to nurse the hungry baby. It felt like an island of serenity in the tumult of the city, for the shouts and screams of the fighting and the wounded men left her tense, her head aching, muscles screaming from carrying the heavy pots, her nerves frayed from dodging the arrows and missiles hurled by the Norman trenchbuts. It was a miracle that the stress did not affect her milk, and she was able to return after each such peaceful interlude, rested and refreshed, to the fray.

The jeering, resistant citizens of Exeter, more determined rather than less after the atrocity of blinding the hostage, must have reminded William gratingly of those reckless men of Alençon so long ago who had hung hides out on their walls and had called him "the tanner's grandson." He was grimly set on making Exeter capitulate, and was everywhere outside the city, urging on the archers who kept a steady, unnerving flight of arrows zinging over the walls, cheering the stout footsoldiers who hurled the battering ram against the gates, lending a hand to the sappers who sought to mine the walls and tunnel into the city.

Guy was, for a time, in charge of those who blockaded the city from those who would bring in supplies. Determinedly he and several of his men patrolled the perimeter, stopping those few who sought entrance. Nuage tossed and stamped, clearly preferring to be in the thick of the action.

It was eighteen endless days before the defenders of Exeter would admit to themselves that it was a hopeless fight. Arrows, missiles, and oil were now nearly nonexistent; food supplies were dwindling; illness, injuries, and fever from wounds were beginning to weaken those men who had not fallen victim to Norman arrows. When it was quiet the inhabitants could hear the unsettling sound of the miners beneath the city wall.

The older, more cautious of the magistrates at last convinced the hotheaded rebels that continued resistance was futile; indeed, the wisest thing they could do was throw themselves on William's mercy and hope he would spare Exeter.

* * *

While an unseen bird sang from a leafy branch in the convent garden that spring morning, Exeter made its submission, sending out its fairest maidens and youths, its prominent thegns, and its priests bearing what sacred relics were possessed by the minster there in an effort to placate the dread Conqueror.

Lianne stood on the walls that morning, unashamedly sobbing as she watched the hostages' procession march toward an unknown fate behind the waiting Norman lines. Of her own future she gave no thought; even the son she had left babbling contentedly in his cradle seemed an unreal being as she watched the drama below.

"I pardon thee, Exeter, in God's name," William announced in a tone that carried to those on the walls, then turned to disperse his nobles as needed.

"Robert, guard these hostages. Humphrey, see you to the guarding of the gates, and let none of the soldiers enter to pillage or rape. Hear, all of you—I forbid those crimes. And especially he who disturbs the religious, know that he will forfeit his life—that is no new law of mine, as those who followed me from Normandy know! My lords of Bayeux, Beaumont, Warenne, Mandeville, Totnes —come with me into the city, and we shall find the most suitable place for a keep by which to assure this city's loyalty to me."

Once, Guy would have grinned, conscious of the signal honor he was being paid, along with select others, but now he merely nodded assent, preoccupied by the unusual sight of what appeared to be a Benedictine nun on the wall with the rest of the city's defeated rebels. It was too far to see the features clearly, but what an odd place for a holy nun, by God's Wounds!

Lianne, preparing to descend and return to the abbey, had suddenly spotted the familiar dapple-gray charger, Nuage, and had watched, horror-struck, as its master had maneuvered him into the group of Normans heading for the now-open city gates.

Becoming more and more certain as the horse neared that it was indeed Guy's war-horse, she lingered at her perch longer than she should, perhaps unconsciously hungry for the sight of him whom she loved and hated. The streets were jammed with people fleeing to their homes and with incoming soldiers. Lianne was carried, willy-nilly, down the high street away from the abbey by the force of the crowd.

She was made conspicuous by her black robes and by being the only one of the English trying to make her way toward the soldiers, for she had to pass them to reach her goal. She held her head low, hoping that he would notice nothing beneath the nun's wimple and veil that hid her glorious hair.

"Sister, halt a moment please, I pray you."

His voice over the crowd's babble! He had spotted her! She raised her eyes, aghast, and met his. They were separated by half a dozen people. She ducked and ran, dashing into an empty passageway that led to an alley.

"Gilbert—see to my horse!"—and he was in hot pursuit, heart sinking at the sight of his beloved in the robes of a nun.

Judhael of Totnes, the Breton noble, had been riding just to Guy's rear and noted this odd action. He stopped Gilbert and questioned the young squire with sly curiosity. "What means this, the great Sieur de Hawkingham goes chasing after one of Our Lord's brides? Surely he heard King William declare them forbidden, ah, game, even to the king's favorites?" The jealous mercenary saw a chance to drive a wedge between the monarch and his young protégé.

"I believe he knew the woman, my lord," Gilbert said stiffly as he made to follow his master. "What she does in nun's robes, I know not, but she was dear to him."

"Ah, is that so?" the Breton chuckled. "The dog!"

Gilbert knew he should have prevaricated, said that the woman was his sister, or a dangerous rebel, anything; but after he had served such a straightforward, honest master for so long, lies did not come quickly enough to his lips.

Seventeen

Lianne was trapped, for it had been a blind alley she had entered, which led to a house. There was no space on either side to escape. Not pausing to knock, she tried the door, hoping the occupants would consent to hide her. It swung open, though, with a lonely creek.

The house seemed empty. From its appearance, it belonged to a freeman of the town. Had he been slain on the walls, perhaps? The hall was sparsely furnished, having only a long table and some benches in its main room. It was utterly deserted. No fire burned in the central fireplace, and the early afternoon light filtered down through the smoke hole in the hammered-beam ceiling, casting a dim, eerie light in the room as

Lianne turned at bay. Guy had shot the bolt on the door and stood between her and safety. There was nowhere left to go but through the door that led to the sleeping chambers, and that was the last place she wanted to lead him!

His sword, belted at his side, clinked in its scabbard against his mail as he strode purposefully to her until he was but inches from her. She could read no message in his eyes and her heart thudded in erratic joy-terror against her breast. She raised her hands as if to ward him off, her breath coming raggedly. Her nostrils flared as his scent came to her, compounded of horse, the smell of metal, plus that indefinable ingredient that was simply male.

"Lianne—I thought you dead. What do you here?"

"You must leave me alone, my lord, I have taken the veil and renounced the world. Go now, leave me in peace." She averted her head, unwilling to meet those measuring eyes.

"By the Splendor of God, woman! I have sought you everywhere. I will not give you up to God's Son, or to the Devil himself!" he thundered, striking the table at his side.

"Beware your soul, my lord! It is damnation to molest a professed nun!" She was lying desperately, praying he would not discover the hair concealed still beneath the black veil, long and thick in its braids, which would have been

438

shorn off had she taken her vows.

"You are mine, Lianne." His mouth was inches from hers, his strong hands reaching out to pull her to him. Her knees became utterly without strength, and she swayed toward him.

"Go back to your Norman wife, my lord," she whispered, tears threatening to spill, her voice lifeless.

The quiet words echoed like a thunderbolt in the vacant room.

A grin began to play about the sharply chiseled features she loved so well. "Wife? I have no wife. You fled for naught, sweetheart. I know now why you left, but you didn't know I went to Normandy to *annul my betrothal.* I am a *free* man, Lianne—free to wed you, and I will, for I have spent more than enough time chasing over England after you, foolish one."

"Lies . . . the Norman conqueror tires of force, and now he must use guile with the English maid from whom he has taken everything, whether by violence or by deceit. . . . You never told me you were betrothed—you let me believe you were a bachelor knight, my lord, and I began to love you, not knowing of the woman across the Channel who waited to acknowledge her prior claim on you—not that I ever expected you to honor me with your name! Not I, the humble, defeated Saxon!" She lashed bitterly out at him, angry tears welling up. She would not let him cozen her now, to while away his boredom in the vanquished town! She would not allow him to work the magic spell of his charm on her until she drowned in his warm brown eyes and melted in his arms. . . .

"It is not a lie, '*Soeur*' Lianne," he said, eyes narrowed, "but *this* is, is it not so?" He flicked a finger against the Benedictine habit. She could find no words to strengthen the falsehood, and he became impatient with her silence.

"*Isn't it?*" he hissed between clenched teeth, and his powerful arms shot out and grabbed her to him. His hands made short work of wrenching off the veil and confining wimple to reveal the golden glory of her hair, braided and coiled beneath.

His eyes transfixed hers. "Is the English convent so worldly and depraved that the Brides of Christ do not sacrifice their hair when they become nuns? Lianne, *tell me the truth.*"

"I am not . . . a nun," she gasped, feeling that his eyes could lay bare the way to her soul. "I sought shelter in the convent here when I . . . because I . . ." (was carrying your child, she almost said). "I became ill, and . . ."

He seemed not to notice her hesitation. "You fled," he finished for her, "thinking I was the worst of perfidious demons. But when I went to Dover, I obtained permission for the annulment from Bishop Odo himself, and then traveled to Normandy, to Bayeux, where I talked to

440

Mabile, whom I found, to the chagrin of my male pride—" he allowed a boyish grin to escape—"that she was as relieved as I to end it. She really preferred my brother, Gervais, you see, who is not nearly such a fierce, rough fellow as I—" he caught a quick glimpse of a smile then on his beloved's lips—"and I left after seeing them wed. I took ship for England and rode posthaste to Hawkingham only to find—"

"I had gone . . ." she finished for him, blue eyes shining clearly now. But by the shadows in his eyes she knew he had found Wulfrune's body.

"I thought you murdered, my love . . ." he said, unsmiling, taking her face firmly between gentle fingers before he lowered his lips to hers. It was a gentle, brief kiss, but she could feel his lips tremble at the contact. "Then I tore my fiefs apart, then London, trying to find any trace of you. Oh, my love, I'm so glad you are alive."

How she suffered, first at Wulfrune's and Wulfnoth's hands, then from the elements, and had nearly died of the lung fever, and how she had given birth to his son, there would be time to tell him later. Now there was only his lips, his hands, his lean hard body against hers, fanning the fire within, the flame she had thought dead forever.

He slipped the habit from her shoulders and lifted her in his arms, striding toward the simple bedchamber. The coldness of the chain mail against her skin was a sweet pain.

Sometime later, near dawn, as he slept, a bare arm flung possessively over her waist, Lianne wakened. Wriggling carefully out from under him so as not to awaken him, she gazed tenderly down the length of his hard warrior's body. He could wring such passion from her, could bring her to the height of ecstasy, yet now his face in slumber was irresistibly boyish, the dark hair tousled from their loveplay. She bent and kissed a dark lock.

Tiptoeing stealthily from the room, she gathered up and donned the scattered garments in the hall. The wimple was hopelessly rent, so she left it where it lay crumpled and merely clutched the veil closely around her face.

I could wait until he wakes and tell him of our son, she thought, but Ranulf must be very hungry by now, and I could easily feed him and bring him here before Guy wakes. How I will rejoice to see his eyes light up with the knowledge that that bonny babe was created by our love, his and mine.

As he had reached his climax, Guy had moaned repeatedly, "I love you, Lianne, I love you, *bien-aimée!*" Though he had called her his "love" before, he had never before said those words—that exact formula necessary to lovers down the ages, the words for which she had thirsted. It was the knowledge of his feelings for her—he had surmounted incredible difficulties to clear his path to her, that they might love honorably before English and Norman alike—that made her very confident and assured as she stepped out into the street, which still echoed with the shouts of conquerors.

On the outside step she found Gilbert fast asleep but still clutching Nuage's reins, who started as he saw the dark-robed figure emerge, and bowed reverently.

"Nay, Gilbert, it is I, Lianne. Your lord sleeps within. Never fear, I shall be back, with a wonderful surprise for him!"

"My lady Lianne," he beamed with joy. "But—a nun?"

She had no time to give her story again —his lord could explain, or she, later.

"Until later, Gilbert." She began to walk down the street.

"Should I not escort you, my lady? It may be dangerous for a woman on the streets!" he called, torn between his duty to her and his master.

"Your soldiers will not bother a religious woman. I will be safe, do not fear."

But he could not be convinced, and, leaving the horses tied to a tree branch, he hurried after her.

Eighteen

Judhäel allowed a smirk to escape his vulpine features as he spied de Bayeux's dapple-gray charger still tethered outside the townhouse at the end of the narrow street. *Aha, now I have William's favorite in a trap of his own careless making! William will not forgive even Guy the sacrilege of defiling a holy woman. Damn his arrogance—he was always too sure of himself with a woman, had only to crook a slender finger to have a serving girl offer him—anything.* He had heard rumors that Guy had lost his heart irretrievably to one Englishwoman since the conquest, but his seething jealousy demanded revenge for being passed over by William and overlooked by women who could see only Guy's magnetic dark eyes, sensual lips, and perfectly formed body. I hope I can catch him in the act, he thought with a lewd chuckle, sticking it to the poor woman. Accompanied by half a dozen eyewitnesses, it would make a further damning impression in the Bastard's mind as he watched the earl's execution, so that he would never think to blame the Breton who had accused his favorite noble of the gravest sin.

Minutes before, Guy had awakened, conscious of a deep contentment welling up within him. He had found Lianne, and they would be wed as soon as possible. Surely in William's train there was a priest who would do it, or should they wait and be married by Father Thomas at Hawkingham? Nay, he could not wait so long, by the Splendor of God!

"Lianne?" Perhaps she had gone out of the chamber to find some wine to slake their thirst?

"Lianne?" He padded to the door leading into the hall while pulling on his undertunic.

Gone. She was gone.

"Gilbert!" he bellowed in the oppressing silence. Peering through a half-open shutter, he saw the two destriers standing outside and figured Gilbert was not far away. His mind returned to his woman as he began to dress again in the small chamber that had lately echoed with their cries of passion.

She was gone, again, forever. She had

not wanted his love, had submitted while she must, feigned an ardor to match his own until she could steal away. False, just as so many women! He had conquered such odds to love her honorably, yet given the opportunity she had fled like a thief. Better check if your sword and mail are still there, fool, she's likely stolen them, his mind went on bitterly, totally forgetting that their combined weight would make a difficult if not impossible burden for any woman to leave quietly with, never mind his squire guarding the door.

Fully clad now (done with some difficulty, for his squire usually helped him with the lacings on his gambeson and in donning his hauberk), he stood at the door, scanning the street for any sign of the Norman lad.

He saw the Breton noble ride up with the men-at-arms, and was puzzled when Judhäel dismounted and drew his sword. He had not yet belted on his own, and his eyes narrowed and his frown deepened as the soldiers leveled their spears on him.

"Guy de Bayeux, Earl of Hawkingham, Lord of Winslade, Chawton, and Lingfield, I am authorized to arrest you by King William and am charged to hie you hence to his presence, there to pay for your heinous crime, and that with your life!"

Guy stood more erect, his gaze burning into the Breton's. "On what charge, upstart Breton?" he drawled. He might have been asking what Duke William's cook planned for the midday meal.

One of the soldiers had entered the hall behind him and now returned, triumphantly bearing the ripped wimple between thumb and forefinger as if it bore the plague.

"There is none within, my lord," he said, bowing obsequiously. "But there's your proof." He thrust it forward, and Judhäel twirled it negligently on his little finger under the earl's pale but impassive features.

"Raping a nun," he sneered. "William has promised a speedy end for any who violate his decree, as well you knew, Bayeux! But you thought the rules did not apply to you, didn't you, William's favorite! He awaits you in the town hall, aghast at my accusation. I wonder whether he will stretch your neck, so that your noble career ends choking and dancing in the air—a most *unknightly* end for an unknightly deed!—or merely allow you a swift beheading with your own sword, more befitting your status? Ah, I doubt that—he is too horrified by that particular crime to grant you such a merciful death!"

It was absurd. It could not be happening.

Judhael had no proof beyond the flimsy evidence of Lianne's wimple, but William, a devoutly religious man whose entire venture had had papal blessing, could never allow such a crime to go unpunished, especially when the earl, marched into the king's presence at sword's point and with the halter already around his proud neck, would utter no word in his own defense.

Lianne's desertion had already killed his soul; how could William's lack of faith in him—the baron who had counted as a foster son—matter now? William's pronouncement of sentence barely penetrated his black despair.

Perhaps Lianne had betrayed him—told the scheming Breton exactly where to find him, for several English pounds, probably! Thirty, mayhap, like Judas Iscariot? But he could not find the heart to damn her—he had sinned too greatly against her to have expected her to return his love, and he would accept his fate without a whimper. Mayhap it was justice for his long-ago transgressions against Lianne, not for William's reasons.

Lianne's voice echoed through the empty dwelling. "Guy! My lord! Where are you? I have brought . . ." She turned to Gilbert, puzzled. The baby she held against her cooed happily, pleased at the adventure now that his stomach was full. "Where could he have gone, Gilbert? I left him sound asleep! There is no trace of his clothes or his armor . . ." Her voice trailed off and she blushed, thinking of the helter-skelter pattern their shed clothes had formed.

But Gilbert had no answers. "I know not, my lady, unless . . ." Of a sudden he remembered the scheming Breton and his nasty insinuations, and a horrible foreboding seized him. For a moment he did not understand Lianne's next small, cold words.

"Perhaps he did decide, after all, that it would not be well—was not worth the rich prize he had lost."

He looked up and was startled to see the radiance that had lit her features vanish as if it had never been there. Her mouth—how full and luscious were those lips—drooped, and the sparkle that had lilt those blue orbs turned dull with despair.

"N-no, my lady! I'm sure it is not that. He loves you, I'm sure of it. He wouldn't have searched everywhere for you only to abandon you now!" What could he say? He did not want to voice his fears and alarm her without cause. But they must move swiftly—for William's justice was swift. "He . . . probably was summoned to attend the king. Yes, that must be it. Perhaps we should seek him at the town's meeting hall, where King William will have set up his quarters."

"Nay . . . I think I should await his coming here. He would not like for me to appear like this—" she indicated the swaddled infant—"as if I were some angry serf girl demanding support for his bastard."

"My lady . . . I don't know . . . But I feel we must find him, and soon. Even my lord has enemies—men jealous of all he has, and is. My mind misgives."

She didn't understand fully, but she felt a *frisson* of fear touch her spine. Then she dismissed it as ridiculous. Even she could see that Guy was part of King William's trusted inner circle. No one could harm him, she decided. "I will wait here. Perhaps he had duties to attend to. He will return."

Nineteen

"Lord Judhäel, the Breton is here, Your Grace," announced the guard. "The Earl of Hawkingham is with him . . . in chains?" Confusion was evident on the man-at-arms' face at the sight of William's well-known favorite as he shuffled into the hall in shackles, escorted by half a dozen mailed soldiers. Bringing up the rear was the smugly triumphant Breton.

"Ah, at last!" William remarked with irritation. "I'm sure we can clear up this misunderstanding now with a few words from Lord Guy. Judhael," he said with an obvious grimace of distaste, "surely chains were an excessive touch for a noble of my kingdom, an *earl*," he finished, pointedly referring to the difference in Guy's and Judhael's ranks. "And that rope around his neck is presumptuously premature. Dismiss your men, Breton. I will be interested to know where my young *friend* has been without so much as a 'by your leave, sire,' but you may be sure I will not condemn a Norman, be he the commonest bastard in my army, without evidence, merely on the word of a mercenary."

The Breton flushed with embarrassment at this cool speech, but spoke with oily confidence as his retainers clanked from the room, and waited until the Norman and Exeter nobility who crowded the hall quieted expectantly.

"I have served Your Grace loyally, hoping for but a word of praise here and there," he began with spurious humility. "Though you have not deigned to notice my humble faithfulness, that being no more than a lord has the right to expect . . ."

"Get on with it, fellow!" Bishop Odo spoke up with impatience. Seated at the king's right, he was robed in the splendor of the Church, now that the battle was over. His purple chasuble—for he had just come from celebrating a triumphal Mass at the minster—was studded with pearls and bordered in gold thread. He looked almost more regal than William did in his fur-trimmed royal robes. That his half-brother would even *consider* hearing charges against Guy—some silly tale about a nun!—was a subject of disbelief to the bishop when there were so many matters of great importance to settle, such as the amount of the fine to be paid into the royal coffers by this conquered town! He winked at Guy, who stood rubbing his wrists after being freed from the heavy, chafing manacles in which he'd been marched through the streets. The earl, however, looked at no one, glancing disinterestedly at the rich tapestries on the walls of the long, narrow room and the beamed ceiling, as if the charges did not even involve him.

Judhäel began again. "Your Grace, I myself would *never* dare to violate your most casual wish, so when you made your royal command that the women of this town were not to be molested, especially the religious, I was *appalled* to see the Earl of Hawkingham *shamelessly* pursuing a nun who fled before his charger, screaming in innocent terror!" he said with a self-righteous smirk. "He pursued this virtuous woman into a house, in which they stayed all night, for I took it upon myself to have the place watched, being conscious that you would want to know of this *heinous* transgression," he continued. "Early this morning, the same women fled the house, her very being a picture of shame and degradation, a part of her habit missing, torn off, no doubt, in his savage lust as he despoiled this innocent Bride of Christ."

"The evidence, Breton. . . ." ground out the king, tired of his endless embellishments of the tale.

"Is this, Your Grace." From beneath his worn cloak Judhäel gloatingly pulled out the torn wimple.

King William gazed at it stolidly, while the bishop rolled his eyes in disgust.

"Is that *all* you have? Pretty flimsy evidence, I'd say. Where were *you* all night while this poor woman was being raped, if you were so concerned?"

"One does not lightly interfere with the doings of such as de Bayeux, even when he is in the wrong," whined Judhäel. "Besides, I had been given duties by my king, so leaving one man to guard the place, I sent a messenger to the king immediately . . ."

"I spoke to no man regarding this," said William with a frown.

Hoping there was no way his lie could be revealed, the Breton went on, "Perhaps my man has been assassinated in this nest of rebels, for I have not seen him since, either. It was cockcrow before I finished the tasks assigned me and could turn my attention once again to this awful crime against the Church."

"Indeed." William turned to Guy, his visage stern and implacable. He had been surprised at the earl's disinterested demeanor, as if it were the weather being discussed. He hoped that indicated a clear conscience. He waited, but the earl was mute and gave him back stare for stare. William felt a flicker of irritation. Like Odo, he felt the pressure of matters of state that needed to be dealt with firmly and quickly. He had little time to spare for a vengeful mercenary trying to puff up his own importance at the expense of one of his finest men. Therefore, he wished Guy would bestir himself to put this ridiculous matter to rest, if it lay in his power to do so!

"My lord of Hawkingham, have you nothing to say in this matter?"

"I chased a woman clad in religious garments into the empty house, Your Grace," he admitted impassively. "Inside, I lay with her—carnally," he added baldly, while his mind screamed with pain at the thought of Lianne's abandonment after such lovemaking. His bitter thoughts continued, mayhap she's in league with the Breton. Giving my heart to a woman has caused me to be placed in a pretty position!

"Were you not aware of my command regarding women, especially those of the convent, Guy?"

"I was, Your Grace. The woman was known to me—and to you, sire: Lianne of Fairlight. As you know, I had searched everywhere for her after she disappeared. She is mine, and when I found her in Benedictine robes, I felt entitled to know why."

"If she fled your protection for the sanctuary of a convent and religious work, my lord, she is no longer yours," William shot back.

"She is not a nun, Your Grace," Guy

said simply.

William sighed. "Then surely you can bring her forth to explain why she fled you, and was dressed so."

"No, Your Grace." His bitterness rose strangling in his throat. His words fell like a stone in the still pond of the hall, and the ripples were the growing whispers of the witnesses to this trial.

"Where is the woman, Guy? Let her prove she is no nun."

"I don't know, Your Grace." His bleak dark eyes said, And I don't care. What are you going to do about that?

"Surely the woman's lay status is but a minor point," inserted the local bishop pompously. "Did you not promise all females who observed the curfew protection?"

"You have nothing more to say, Guy, Earl of Hawkingham?"

"Non, mon seigneur."

At that moment William wished he had had forethought enough to clear the hall of all the important officials, Norman and English, who now hung on the outcome. He had been placed in an uncomfortable position, for he truly loved this young man, but his word had been given to his newly conquered vassals, and a show of outright favoritism would weaken future relations with Exeter. Word of his leniency would spread, and his barons and even common soldiers would feel free to wreak havoc. He hardened his resolve.

"You are aware that raping a nun is a capital crime, my son?"

"I am, my liege. I have not done so."

"Make him furnish proof, William of Normandy!" cried one of Exeter's prominent thegns. "The Breton has witnesses, and the nun's wimple! What does this *rapist* have but his *words?*"

William's eyes locked with Guy's, and Guy could feel the icy withdrawal emanating from them; already overwhelmed by Lianne's desertion and the Breton's treachery, Guy was powerless to do anything but gaze back defiantly. If he could not have Lianne, and William would take the word of a foreign mercenary, let come what may!

"Hang him! Behead him!" shouted voices in the crowd.

William's fist connected solidly with the nearby table, causing parchment documents piled high to flutter briefly and then settle back. "Damn it, de Bayeux! You leave me no choice! I therefore condemn you to death—"

"God's Blood, brother! If he won't defend himself I will! I can't believe you're serious!" Odo hissed in a whisper audible to nearly all.

"*I—have—no—choice,*" the king growled stiffly.

"You've forgiven men who've done worse than this—Guy's own father led an *insurrection* against you, remember? He's served you well, *and* saved *my* life! *Eh bien*—some royal clemency, when it is

457

called for?"

There was a long pause as William considered. Englishman and Norman alike hardly dared breathe.

"I suppose, *if* he indicates true contrition . . ." William said at last.

But the earl, reckless with resentment, merely repeated, "I have nothing to repent, save perhaps being absent from my duties. I have forced no woman against her will, now or ever."

There were murmurs from the onlookers at Guy's recalcitrance, which turned to a collective gasp as his next words rang out proudly in the hall: "I have said the woman was no nun—but let all know the woman is *mine*—and I would keep her if she were the veriest abbess!"

Odo groaned and hid his face in his hands.

The English bishop, livid and trembling, pointed his finger at the proud dark head, saying, "Need you hear more, Your Grace? A complete lack of shame, placing his fleshly lusts above all else—"

"Enough of this!" William rose, clapping his hands, weary of the yelping pack of hounds, hot on the scent of Norman blood. "Take him away, guards, till a block for his beheading can be erected—"

"Hold, William! Don't be so hasty! You have but to seek for the woman, and surely she will confirm whether she is a nun or not, and willing or not!"

"All right, all right, Odo! But I will not have this matter dragged out! All must know the king's justice to be swift and sure! You have until sunset to bring her here to tell her side. Find her by then, or I'll wait no longer!"

"Your Grace, be sensible—all is total confusion out there! She could be anywhere, even outside the city by now!" Odo protested, plump beringed hands waving.

"I suspect, my lord bishop, you will find her at the convent!" thundered William, and the subject was closed.

Twenty

But Odo and his men-at-arms found no golden-haired beauties concealed in nun's robes at the convent, and merely succeeded in terrifying the good sisters as they wrenched open doors to cells and searched the cellar, the kitchen, and the infirmary, even peering into the shadowy recesses of the candlelit chapel. Before leaving, they lined all the nuns up against the convent wall and ordered them to remove their veils.

Mother Mary Algifu bristled with indignation.

"My lord bishop, surely it is not necessary to shame these good women! Who is it you seek?"

AH, I should have known, she thought when she was told it was Lianne. "My lords, she was here, living with us, but after being absent last night she returned at dawn this morning and left with her infant son—something about showing him to his father?"

Infant? thought Odo, puzzled, and then forgot about it as the abbess admitted she didn't know where Lianne had gone.

It was past midday, and Gilbert was so restless he could not stop pacing.

"I'm certain something is amiss, my lady! He would have returned by now!"

Even Lianne had to admit to a growing forboding as she dandled an increasingly fretful Ranulf on her knee and waited for the sight of the Norman earl. When Gilbert said decisively at last, "I'm going to find him, my lady, and bring him here," she let him go with a wave of a slender hand.

But Gilbert did not find his lord in the Norman camp just inside Exeter's gates. No one had seen the Earl of Hawkingham, answered the men questioned, men-at-arms mostly, who would have had no business inside William's headquarters. Feeling he was losing valuable time, Gilbert impudently snatched a chicken leg from the cook's pot, dodging a hastily aimed kick.

Pounding at the convent gate brought forth only an angry old nun who described at great length the indignities suffered when "that Norman bishop's monsters ransacked the convent" in search of Lianne, but she knew not if Guy de Bayeux was among them, nor did she care. She would wear out her knees with thanks to the Saints, she declared, that she had lived through the terror! Some man of God that Bishop Odo was!

Gilbert left her still fuming at the gate, now intent on finding Odo.

He headed now for the town hall, thinking the bishop had returned there, but he stopped outside the half-timbered hall, mesmerized by the sight of two burly men-at-arms lifting a boulder onto a rudely constructed small platform, while nearby another ostentatiously sharpened an axe. Obviously, an execution was to take place—but whose?

"Why, you're de Bayeux's squire, *n'est-ce pas?* Where have you been? It is your very own master who will lose his head—unless the woman is found, and can prove she was not raped and is not a *religieuse.* It is but an hour or two till sundown, and then he is to die."

Gilbert, wasting no time in further inquiries, turned and raced back through the gathering crowd toward the house where Lianne waited. Holy St. Martin! What if she had left?

Odo, meanwhile, had arrived back at the hall with his retinue, their search fruitless. There simply wasn't time to search each and every dwelling, and the possibility that the young woman might have already left the city made him frantic in his entreaties for more time.

The king, however, was adamant, and Odo, defeated, went to perform his last service for Guy de Bayeux.

As the sun began its westward descent below the horizon, Odo reappeared before William. "I have shriven him, brother." He did not trouble to hide his disgust. "If one can shrive a stone, for he seemed that aware of me. His neck is free for your most royal 'justice,' though why you'd punish a man for acting a man I'll never understand."

William, facing the open window that looked out on the execution site, did not turn to face the bishop so that Odo could not see the tears welling up in his troubled eyes.

"Odo, do you not think I wish it was any one of my nobles but Guy? It grieves me sorely to do this—"

"Probably not as sorely as it will de Bayeux," Odo interrupted drily. "Nay, I but jest poorly. He seems not aware of anything in this world. Those deep brown eyes look right through one."

"He is weighed down with guilt," William opined sententiously.

No one else could have said that with a straight face, thought Odo. Sometimes I wonder why God made me a priest and him the duke. "Poppycock, brother. He's one of the best fighting men you have, and you'd execute him for a *woman*?"

William was spared further argument by the arrival of the men-at-arms escorting the condemned man to the block.

William, avoiding Guy's eyes, made a gesture of resignation to Odo. "It's time. Will you witness the deed with me, Odo?"

"Certainly, Your Grace. Nothing would give me greater pleasure," murmured the bishop with heavy irony.

At that moment, Lianne and Orm were pushing their way to the front of the crowd. Lianne, burdened with the baby, was finding it difficult to persuade any to let her through. Word had spread about the execution of the young noble, and no one wanted to make way for the young pair.

"The nerve of her, coming late and expecting the best view."

"Shameless!"

"Watch who ye're pushin' aside, Norman cur!"—that to Gilbert, uttered by a stolid, red-faced yeoman who stubbornly refused to let him by. But his wife, turning from the sad sight of the Norman noble looking up one last time at the amethyst-and-crimon glow of the sunset, noted Lianne's nun's robe and the absence of a wimple.

She spoke sharply to her mate: "See thee, Sigurd, it's a nun! Let her through, she might be the very one yon demon wronged!"

Others in the crowd took up the chant, and Lianne suddenly found herself being pushed eagerly to the front as the crowd took up her cause. "It's the nun herself! Let her see justice done!"

A moment later, she was screaming over the rumble of the drum and the voices of the crowd, "King William! Stop! He is *innocent!*"

The procession toward the block stopped in its tracks. Guy stared at the apparition in nun's robes who, carrying a wee babe whose dark head peeped from his blanket, shrieked at the king alternately in Norman French and English.

Odo, startled, put a restraining hand on his brother's shoulder. "Isn't that the woman he spoke of, brother? Hear her out!"

The crowd had fallen silent at the sight of the woman, kneeling now in front of the Norman king, though hampered by her small burden. She was intensely aware of all eyes being upon her, including the unreadable ones of her love, who kept shifting his gaze from her to Ranulf.

"Your Grace! I beg of you to hear me! I am Lianne of Fairlight, the Earl of Hawkingham's leman. Do you remember meeting at Barking, at the Christmas court? I am no Benedictine! I only took shelter in the convent while I bore my babe, Guy de Bayeux's son! Please, Your Grace! Do not deprive my child of his father before he has had a chance to ever know him!"

Lianne would have liked to watch Guy's face as he heard the news of his son, but dared not turn her pleading, tear-streaked eyes from the monarch who held the power of life and death over Guy, and whose features still gave no hint of whether he believed her.

"How do I know you are in fact a lay-woman and not a professed religious? You English would swear to anything and never feel the stain of perjury on your souls!"

She thought he was refusing to spare Guy, and began to sob afresh. But at that moment a black-robed figure reached her side, and her flooded eyes recognized the commanding personage of Mother Mary Algifu, flanked by two elderly nuns, who had finally succeeded in making her way through the mob from the convent.

To William the abbess looked as diminutive in stature and just as regal as his own Matilda.

"Thank God I am in time. One of my nuns brought me word of this horrible mistake about to take place. King William, I am abbess of the Convent of the Benedictines. Lianne of Fairlight speaks the truth. She has never taken the vows of a nun. She wished to do so, but I refused her, sensing her heart was already given, irrevocably, to an earthly man. Proof of my words is on her head. Child, remove your veil."

As the full golden beauty of Lianne's thick hair was revealed, the abbess went on. "Before a woman becomes a Bride of Christ, she is shorn of her hair, a source of worldly pride. Lianne is free of the

Benedictine order, Your Grace, having taken no such step."

William still appeared unsatisfied.

"But did he take you against your will last night, Lianne of Fairlight?"

Lianne, face aflame, nevertheless managed to smile radiantly as she said, "Oh *no*, Your Grace," so warmly that the crowd roared with laughter.

The king began to smile, relieved that he would not have to execute the young noble he held in such esteem. Lianne visibly relaxed. Guy stood still as the guards backed away; he watched his sovereign warily, as yet not trusting himself to look at Lianne.

"Yet I think there is sin to be atoned for," King William said conversationally to Bishop Odo, but in a voice that carried to Lianne, Guy, and most of the crowd.

"Ah, *oui, mon frère le roi*," murmured Odo, openly grinning. "The matter of fornication, a sin as St. Paul writes, for which penance must be paid."

"What penance would you require, my lord bishop?" returned the king with mock humility.

"I think marriage would be a just punishment for these two sinners," answered Odo, enjoying himself now, "the one, to atone for wronging his lovely young maid; the other, to punish this *damoiselle* for tempting our formerly *chaste, sinless* young earl to sin with this lusty beauty!" He roared at his joke, but Lianne blushed scarlet again and would not lift her gaze from the ground.

Guy, having already made his confession, needed only to be led away to be clad in more suitable raiment for a wedding, since it seemed he was not to be a corpse. The Benedictines took charge of a pale Lianne, who trembled as the realization took hold that she could have been moments too late to save him. They bore her away, one of them carrying baby Ranulf as well, who would have to be nursed and soothed while they found something suitable for his mother to wear for her marriage!

Twenty-one

William, partly to atone for his hasty judgment of Guy, presented the bridegroom with one of his own gowns, a dark green velvet robe of ankle length, trimmed at its square neck and hem with silver scroll embroidery, plus a mantle edged in the softest squirrel.

The abbess, for her part, performed a near-miracle in producing from somewhere in the convent's vast, dark storeroom, a lovely gown of cream silk, which fell loosely from the shoulders and had wide sleeves that ended just below the elbows. The garment had been discarded by a world-weary Danish woman years before when she entered the notiviate, but it had been kept covered and looked none the worse for its long storage. Several nuns helped with the bridal bath, giggling all the while, for all the world like frivolous court ladies-in-waiting. Now they placed a sheer veil of ivory sarcenet with a gold fillet to hold it in place over the burnished gold of Lianne's hair, worn unbound beneath.

"You're lovely, my dear Lianne," the old abbess beamed. "I know there must have been a reason Our Lord kept telling me to refuse you entrance to our community."

"Thank you, Mother," Lianne said meekly, smiling radiantly but full of tears.

"What is it, child? Something still troubles you."

"Oh, Mother," the words tumbled forth in a rush, "what if he doesn't want to marry me? He's being coerced! He dare not refuse his suzerain's command, or the bishop's. He will hate me, and our babe, who he hasn't even seen yet . . ." She would have dithered on, but Mother Mary Algifu stayed her with a gentle gesture.

"I saw how the man looked at you when you did not see, once the execution was canceled. He looked like a man who, while at the gates of Hell, sees another entrance, to Heaven, with a beautiful angel bidding him enter. You are that angel to him, my dear. Be happy, and any small misunderstandings will clear up in their own way." She laid her hand on Lianne's shoulder and blessed her.

"Thank you, Reverend Mother, but you must tell me: How did you know I—we—needed you there to vouch that I was not a nun?"

"Why, God told me, while I was at my prayers, of course," the older woman answered, as if surprised Lianne could wonder. "God, in the form of Sister Osburga, who cannot resist a crowd and saw you plunging for the center of it," she added wryly, "and ran back shrieking all the way to the convent."

Lianne stood by the side of her tall bridegroom as the altar boys swung their censers and Bishop Odo pronounced the words of the Sacrament. The shade of Edwin hovered near in her consciousness, flanked by Robert, her tutor, and Rolf Rolfsson, her father. A part of her silently asked them a question, but they said nothing. Yet she did not feel a spirit of condemnation emanating from them.

She was reminded that this was not the first time she had stood thus before God, promising to love, honor, and obey her lord. How different had been that first time! She had been a girl then, innocent of men and harsh reality. Now she was becoming Lady Lianne of Hawkingham, a countess, wed to the man she had once counted as the deadly enemy she was sworn to kill. Now she loved him with all the fire and passion and, yes—adoration—of which a woman was capable. A woman—*his* woman. That first night had branded her forever his, or possibly that first kiss, high in a tree! She smiled up at him, thinking of the first time he had made her unwillingly glow with passion. Solemnly he returned her gaze. It was not a hostile look, nor an unhappy one. It was as if he were trying to read her soul without revealing his. Uncertainty flashed across her smooth brow. Then Odo was asking for her response, and she left the question in her eyes until later, when they could be alone.

The rest of the ceremony passed in a blur, until it came time for Guy to slip his heavy unicorn signet ring over her finger. She relaxed somewhat to feel the firm, warm pressure of his fingers.

The hovering spirits sighed, and were content, and faded from her awareness, until she could summon them again as happy memories.

The wedding feast was endless, and after that they had to endure the bawdy bedding ceremony, even though Lianne was a widow and was not expected to display any virgin blushes or bloodied sheets the next morning.

Odo, much flown with the effects of a potent mead, repeatedly blessed the couple until even Guy's polite smile turned to annoyance and an apologetic King William urged him to depart with the rest. Odo stumbled from the room, still muttering lewd suggestions for their wedded bliss.

Now they were alone in the chamber, the curtains having been pulled about the bed, creating a silent, tension-filled island for the two. The house was one owned by a prosperous thegn of Exeter who had been "persuaded" to loan it for the use of the newlywed pair.

"Where is . . . the babe?" Guy said at last. The raw uncertainty in his voice vibrated in her ears. This, then, had occupied his thoughts during the ceremony.

"He . . . is out there . . . in a room off the hall. He . . . Ranulf . . . sleeps through the night . . ." She found herself wanting to giggle nervously—for she had been trying to hint that the baby would not interrupt their wedding night by wanting to suckle. "One of the nuns is sleeping by him, lest he need anything before morning . . ." Her voice trailed off, then she plunged ahead, wanting to rid them of any barrier to their joy.

"Guy, my love, I have not been able to tell you privately about the baby before this. . . . He . . ." She was not doing well. She stammered, and was not able to read his eyes in the dimness.

He plunged in gallantly to rescue her, taking hold of her shoulders gently.

"Lianne, *ma bien-aimée* . . . I can imagine that in your dreadful journey here you must have encountered great hardship and misery, and were perhaps taken advantage of by some huge Saxon oaf you could not fight off, even with your courage, *ma chere.*"

"The babe was born in February," Lianne pointed out flatly, as if that were an explanation. To any *woman* it would have been a stimulus, at least, to set one counting backward on their fingers.

Guy, however, was thick-headed as men can be at such a time. "*Ma chère* Lianne, it is of no import, even if you did —*whatever* you had to in order to keep from starving! The important thing is that we are together again, man and wife forever, and . . ."

He was being so lovingly forgiving, so needlessly generous, and wouldn't even listen as she tried to tell him Ranulf was his!

"You great Norman lout," she shrieked exasperatedly at last, interrupting his flow of soothing words. "I know you cannot read, but can you not figure either? Count back, by the Saints! Ranulf is your son! Wulfnoth threatened to force me, but became ill before he could ever do so. But even before I left Hawkingham I already knew I carried *your* child."

"And yet you fled . . ." he whispered, cupping her face in his strong hands, studying her face. She was unable to meet his eyes, sensing his hurt.

"I thought you were returning with a bride," she reminded him honestly. "It would have been no better a life for the child, as the earl's bastard son, than I imagined for myself, as your cast-off—"

He interrupted her with a slender

index finger placed on her lips. "Yes, I can see what a dreadful fate you thought awaited you. But it will never happen, my lady. Have I not told you that you are mine, *pour jamais?* Forever," he repeated in English. "I love you, my beautiful Saxon. And now, my dear wife, I would meet my son."

She stared up at him, noting the great joy that suffused him, like a boy in his eagerness. She did not know that the emotion was mirrored on her own face, that he at last knew and accepted the truth.

"But he sleeps, Guy . . . it will be dark . . ." she protested, laughing at his impatience.

"I *will* behold my son," he insisted with mock severity, and, placing an arm beneath her legs, lifted her off the bed as he arose.

Just then a far-off wail reached them through the thick oaken door as Ranulf voiced his reaction to the unfamiliar surroundings.

"Come, *ma dame,*" Guy said gaily as he handed her a furred robe and wrapped himself up in the bedclothes, and they hastened toward the sound. "My son would know his sire. He has better things to do than sleep."

Encouraging the drowsy Benedictine who was rocking the swaddled baby to return to her slumber, they took Ranulf out into the great hall. There Guy lit a candle from the smoldering fire and sat down close to mother and child to watch, enraptured, as Lianne nursed their son back to sleep. Occasionally his hand would steal out and stroke the baby's downy hair, as black as his own, and the candlelight danced on the gleaming ebony of his eyes.

When Ranulf had suckled his fill and was sleepily stroking his mother's breast, Guy took him from her and holding him gently against his powerfully muscled chest, leaned his cheek against the soft head in a gesture so poignant that Lianne felt the pricking of tears.

"He's beautiful, *ma dame*," he whispered, "my son—our son. You have done well, my darling."

"I would give him a sister, my dear lord," she laughed tremulously.

"*Tonight?*" he laughed and the gleam in his eyes set her blood ablaze.

"Why not, my lord?"

Epilogue

Lianne waved a smiling farewell to the nuns of St. Benedict's Convent who stood by the gate to watch as Earl Guy, Lady Lianne, and their retinue rode out of Exeter. Without the kind, wise care of these women, she might not now be safe, carrying her son toward Hawkingham on the back of a gentle mare who could be reined with one hand while she held the babe in the other.

"How does Elfgift, my lord?" she inquired. Her guilt at leaving her sister had been an ever-hanging burden though there had been no choice. His reply, which described Elfgift as whole in mind and body, and growing more beautiful every day, was immensely reassuring.

"She shows one wonderful virtue in

particular," he informed her with a meaningful smile, and inclined his head toward Gilbert, who rode just behind them.

"My lord?" she questioned, puzzled.

"She loves a Norman lad, following the good example of her sister." Lianne, turning, observed Gilbert's fiery blush, and smiled.

"Should you mind if the two became betrothed, when they were of an age? He would be knighted by then, of course," he added hastily.

"Nothing would please me more, my love."

He went on to tell her of Mold and Tofig, who were expecting a baby too, very soon, and of Orm, who, he told her with a modest pride, had become a model squire in her absence.

A thrush burst from cover then, almost under their horses' hooves, and Lianne felt he soared no higher than her heart.

Guy had been given leave to return with his lady to Hawkingham until his suzerain should summon him again to his side. He was again secure in William's favor (and Judhäel of Totnes was keeping decidedly quiet in Exeter). The Norman king was in a generous mood, having taken the city without great loss—and, most importantly, with the aid of English soldiers.

England was changing, beginning to accept the inevitability of William's rule, her citizens knowing they would enjoy its benefits if they did.

There would be difficult years ahead, Guy knew, for William had won only the southern portion of England, and the rest of the island had ever been wild and freedom-loving, never really accepting the rule of the "southrons" of Wessex, an entirely different breed. English had fought alongside Normans at Exeter, true, and William had thus far dealt fairly with those who accepted his sovereignty. The taking of the North, however, would be a different situation, and both sides might well struggle to their own destruction.

Guy hoped not, though he knew that he and others of the Norman nobility would stand to gain in lands and possessions the more the North rebelled. He did not want to spend his years killing the English, but rather in loving the beautiful English-woman who by some miracle loved him also, and had given him a son, his heir. He would have to confer with Odo about seeing him legitimized.

"What are you thinking, Guy?" She touched him gently on his mailed sleeve as she noticed his thoughtful smile.

"I? Well, beyond my thoughts of the joy of at *last* having a properly submissive wife," he could not resist teasing, "I wondered if you could teach me to write, as I would write my *chère Maman* to invite her to Hawkingham to see her grandson. Gervais could escort her and Mabile could come with him, that is, if you do not . . ." Suddenly his suggestion seemed awkward.

"Feel strange about Mabile? No, of course not. How could I help but love her? She gave you back to me. But as for the invitation, I had best go ahead and write it. If I wait for *you* to master the art, my lord, your son will be ready for knighthood first!" she said tartly.

He grinned, and his gaze swept her hotly. She found herself wishing they were already home at Hawkingham, safe in the great bed.

"God's Blood, I will learn faster than you learned to love me, Saxon rebel!"

"Then it will be a matter of days only, Norman."